Praise for *The Lost Civilization of Suolucidir*

"Daitch's fantastically fun novel has shades of Umberto Eco and Paul Auster and is brainy, escapist fiction at its best. Structured like a Russian nesting doll, the book conceals several overlapping tales centered on the search for the mythical lost city of Suolucidir. The novel begins with grad student Ariel Bokser's present-day search for the city, located somewhere in modern day Iran. The book then shifts to the heart of its story, the so-called Nieumacher papers, an inheritance from Ariel's father (a consulting mineralogist for a mining company) that relates the narrative of Sidonie and Bruno Nieumacher's quest for Suolucidir, beginning in 1936. The Nieumachers are a husband and wife; he's a rare book forger and she's a law student, and they are fleeing the West as much as they are searching in the East for Suolucidir. Setting off under the guidance of Bruno's former Berlin professor, now a black market profiteer, the duo brave adversity to find the lost city, dodging British agents and Russian spies. The book then shifts further back in time to the story of Hilliard and Congreaves, two mismatched British explorers who met at the Possum Club, an explorer society, and who set off in 1914 in search of fabled fortune and instead encounter their fate. Daitch has constructed an intricate, absorbing narrative. The novel is like a Scheherazade tale, never quite giving the reader time or reason to pause. What exactly is Suolucidir? Lost city of the Hebrew tribes? A stand-in for colonialism's heart of darkness? Wisely, the MacGuffin remains elusive. As one character says, 'Invisible cities sometimes leave no trace of themselves. Who knows what cities lay under our feet?' Perhaps Suolucidir is real, and still out there, awaiting discovery." — *Publishers Weekly*, starred review

"Susan Daitch has written a literary barnburner of epic proportions. The question buried at the core of *The Lost Civilization of Suolucidir* is one of empirical—or is the imperial?—knowledge itself. Her labyrinthine tale of archeological derring-do calls to mind both *1984* and *2666*, and does so by looking backward in time as well as forward. It is also utterly original, the work of a visionary writer with an artistic sensibility all her own."—Andrew Ervin, author of *Burning Down George Orwell's House*

"Susan Daitch's *The Lost Civilization of Suolucidir* is a daring undertaking, the creation of an ancient land of fantastic proportions, its borders touching other countries we think we know while still remaining elusive and mysterious. This is a novel of archeology and history, of mythology and empire, powered by an undeniable call to adventure and a deep yearning for understanding, written by a novelist who manages to surprise on nearly every page."
—Matt Bell, author of *Scrapper*

"In *The Lost Civilization of Suolucidir*, history is revealed as ghost and prankster, archaeological remnant, information feed. This search for a vanished city takes in rare book rooms and obituaries, travel records, borders drawn and redrawn by war, boxes of records from a sanatorium where Kafka stayed, a statuette of Disney's Aladdin, and quotes from Ignatz Mouse and Samuel Johnson. Where is the city? Where are we? We are lost, and will one day be someone else's Suolucidir, at best. In the meantime, Daitch's latest is a beguiling and virtuoso companion to our inevitable end: a novel that wrenches, sentence by fine sentence, some order from the chaos, while never shortchanging the chaos itself."—Mark Doten, author of *The Infernal*

"Daitch's novel is Indiana Jones for the introspective crowd—a continual, thrilling, and harrowing search for historical treasures."
—*Foreword Magazine*

Praise for Susan Daitch

"One of the most intelligent and attentive writers at work in the U.S. today."—David Foster Wallace

"It's always a delight to discover a voice as original as Susan Daitch's."
—Salman Rushdie

THE LOST CIVILIZATION

OF SUOLUCIDIR

Susan Daitch

City Lights Books | San Francisco

Library of Congress Cataloging-in-Publication Data
Names: Daitch, Susan, author.
Title: The lost civilization of Suolucidir / Susan Daitch.
Description: San Francisco : City Lights Publishers, 2016.
Identifiers: LCCN 2015049535 (print) | LCCN 2016003408 (ebook) | ISBN
  9780872867000 (softcover) | ISBN 9780872867017 ()
Subjects: LCSH: Archaeological expeditions—Fiction. | Extinct
  cities—Fiction. | BISAC: FICTION / Literary. | FICTION / Historical. |
  FICTION / Action & Adventure. | FICTION / Jewish. | GSAFD: Adventure
  fiction. | Satire.
Classification: LCC PS3554.A33 L67 2016 (print) | LCC PS3554.A33 (ebook) |
  DDC 813/.54—dc23
LC record available at http://lccn.loc.gov/2015049535

City Lights books are published at the City Lights Bookstore,
261 Columbus Avenue, San Francisco, CA 94133.
Visit our website: www.citylights.com

CONTENTS

FIRST COLLAPSE

A soldier looked over the parapet and thought no army could even begin to crack open the towers that marked the corners of the city. A mason, though his spine ached from being torqued and twisted as he worked, wiped his nose on the back of his hand and was confident few foreigners could navigate the labyrinth he'd helped to construct. It ringed the metropolis like a moat, although no one in the city knew the word. Both the soldier with a view of the desert to the east and mountains to the west and the mason down below on the street felt safe; both looked out on landscape and urban geography from opposing perches, convinced there was no threat that would change the pattern of one day to the next. In the center of the city a cook watched her pots dance on hooks and knew that even if she ran out of her house, odds were good she wouldn't make it out of the city before everything she took for granted would collapse around her ears.

Elsewhere in town at that moment:

A child was about to apologize for tormenting a cat. He twisted his hands behind his back, nervous, expecting blows, not sure what form punishment would take.

A woman was about to drink a glass of wine when she thought her overseer wasn't looking. She leaned against a broken mosaic of a winged lion, tiles making a cool grid pattern on her back. She thought she was hidden by a column and intended to swallow the glass in one gulp.

A man was about to kiss his neighbor's wife. He pulled her into an alley as she was leaving what passed as her house. The street was so busy, he thought, they both thought, no one was looking.

An executioner was about to cut off the head of a runaway slave. The slave shook, so the executioner was unsure what the blade would actually sever when it fell, though he didn't care much either way. Whatever body part was lopped off was all in a day's work.

A hungry traveler, having seen Hamoon Lake evaporate into a shiny crust that crumbled into sand underfoot was relieved to see the city rise before him like an oasis. He knew it was real, and it was also home. He quickly ran through the maze, reached his house, a square two-story building the color of melon rind. In his long absence he'd so often dreamed of its two rooms, one on top of the other. Ravenous, when food was placed in front of him, he scooped up sticky pieces of rice and lamb with his hands without stopping for any ritual washing. Before he could show his family the silk and spices in his bags, just as he was about to swallow a mouthful of lamb, a sandstorm swept over the city like a tidal wave so high even the square lookout towers were buried without a trace. If this wasn't what reduced the city to a basin of sand, the catastrophe might have taken the form of an earthquake. In a few minutes all that poked out above the surface of the rubble was the jagged edge of a wall, the blade of an axe, a human arm, maybe. And if the city survived the irritated shoulder shrug of tectonic plates there was Taftan, four thousand forty-two meters in height, a volcano that rose abruptly from the midst of the flat landscape. One big burst of lava and groves of olive, almond, and cherry trees would be reduced to cinders, the child offering milk to the cat, the lips about to touch, blade suspended mid-air, all frozen, turned to stone. For whatever reason, the city was destroyed.

SILENT, DESERTED,

FALLEN CITIES

The tradition of all the dead generations weighs like a nightmare on the brain of the living. And just when they seem engaged in revolutionizing themselves and things, in creating something that has never yet existed, precisely in such periods of revolutionary crisis they anxiously conjure up the spirits of the past to their service and borrow from them names, battle cries and costumes in order to present the new scene of world history in this time-honored disguise and this borrowed language.

Karl Marx
The Eighteenth Brumaire of Louis Bonaparte

BARELY HAD THE FEET OF the last Shah of Iran left the ground in Tehran when hundreds of miles away I was sitting on a ledge in the mountainous region of southeast Sistan-va-Baluchistan watching a herd of goats make their way though a wadi in search of grass or water. I'd been exploring the caves in the area, even though my visa was about to expire, and it was becoming clearer by the hour that I was as likely to find the object of my search as to find hidden shahi missiles or the demon Zahhak himself, snakes growing out of his shoulders. Evidence that hinted at earlier cultures hidden in the foothills of the Black Mountains was just out of reach. European digs in this province once yielded slight clues of an ancient civilization, but even with little to go on, archaeologists were able to speculate that a city-state that had resisted both Alexander and Mongol invaders may have flourished here. Others claimed it was all hoax. There had never been such a city, only the feverish dreams of Victorian adventurers who had become lost en route to Khandahar or Lahore. Speculations persisted, but the arguments surrounding this controversial lost city with its rumored splendor, mechanical inventiveness and imperial culture grew so contentious (threatening to reach a pitch not unlike the arguments of Darwinian evolutionist pitted against devout creationist) that the discussions died down to whispers and then finally nothing at all was audible in any language.

Nineteenth-century and early twentieth-century digging parties exploring this segment of what is now the beak-shaped area bordering Afghanistan, Iran, and West Pakistan generally came up empty-handed. During the Victorian era there were rumors about relics glimpsed by a few, and these tales fueled the dying embers of the debate. Prior to the Second World War a few parchment scrolls were alleged to have been found by a pair of Soviet émigrés, Sidonie and Bruno Nieumacher. Mishandled, as some of the Dead Sea Scrolls would be years later, most of these priceless records were said to have been reduced to lumps of glue, unredeemable, and therefore rendered utterly mute. Those fragments that did survive lay in an archive in Tehran, rarely visited.

Others may have been eager to follow in the footsteps of these earlier archaeologists, but intervening wars, earthquakes, sandstorms, and landslides made the area particularly inaccessible. Pahlavi had come to power in 1925, changing the name of Persia to Iran. The Pahlavi shahs and the theocratic regimes that followed discouraged excavations, and indeed, the translators of what were known as the Zahedan fragments were arrested and most likely executed in the prisons of Shah Reza Pahlavi during the era of Iran's alliance with the Axis powers of World War II. After the war no one picked up the thread of the Nieumachers' work. It was as if the couple had never existed, either one of them. Even today, when one arrives at the foothills of the Sistan-va-Baluchistan mountains, local legends are so rife with stories of djinn-haunted caves that it remains difficult to hire a guide who will take you into the area where the lost city is likely to be located.

I knew of the Nieumachers from my father, who traveled to Iran after the war as a consulting mineralogist. He worked for a mining company and made many trips abroad. Usually the gifts he brought home were in the rock department: agate ashtrays from lava beds around Lake Superior, feldspar bookends from Colorado, carnelian and turquoise from Tibet, sheets of mica which gave the room a kaleidoscopic appearance when held up to the eye, bits of fools' gold I brought into a second grade class claiming the chunks were real, a jagged piece of smoky quartz that when tilted a certain way looked like Groucho Marx in profile, smoking a cigar. A trip to Iran in June 1967 yielded no souvenirs apart from Sidonie Nieumacher's field notes, which he told none of us about. The Nieumacher documents had been given to him by an Iranian mineralogist who had found them during the course of renovating a house he'd bought in Zahedan. The pages were confusing because Sidonie Nieumacher's identity documents tucked into an inside cover indicated she was a Christian, born in Alsace, but she wrote in Yiddish. Because of the Hebrew script my father's Iranian colleague had not wanted her field notes in his house, fearing it would be incriminating should his home be searched for whatever random reason, as was often the case. People informed or misinformed, but the result was the same: those reported on disappeared. This was how my father acquired the Suolucidir papers. I'd never seen him so relieved to be home as when he returned from that trip.

He worked from a room in the attic, a mess full of papers, books and journals, some stalagmite-like piles weighted by a lump of jasper or a slice of blue slate sprinkled with the impressions of fingernail-size fossils. Here, at night, he translated the field notes, writing the English into a separate notebook, tapping a Chesterfield into the agate ashtray. Though Sidonie Nieumacher's notes revealed that she had actually been born Eliana Katzir of Grodno Gibernia, she was not, as far as my father could tell, an agent of the Zionist state (as his Iranian host feared), which had not yet been officially declared at that time anyway. The two notebooks, Sidonie's original and my father's translation, were bound together by a thick rubber band that cracked and broke but stuck to the covers of the books long after it lost its elasticity. What my father thought of the contents I'll never know. He returned to his work surveying volcanic outcroppings that dotted the western plains, compared the sediment of Jurassic and Mississippian layers of rock, sending back model airplane kits, fluorescent rocks, postcards of geysers, the kinds of things he thought I would like. I remember him holding a metamorphic piece of quartzite up to the light. The veins switchbacked on its surface like frozen billabongs. You could, as a very small child, think big was as big as stretching your arms wide as far as possible, but at the same time I knew that for my father big was measured by unimaginably vast units. The universe for him was the pre-lapsarian universe: billions of small or enormous planetary rocks hurtling around, sometimes under fantastic pressure and thereby transforming parts of themselves from magma to marble, from anthracite to diamonds. Animals and humans have yet to evolve, and when they do, their tantrums and triumphs appear too minuscule to bother with. It was just as well he lived, to a degree, so armored from human activity. Sidonie's field notes are terrifying.

As I said, my father never mentioned the notebook to me, so I didn't know what he thought about its contents. His second wife was cleaning out some drawers after his death, and it was only by chance that I stopped by her bungalow and rescued it from a Miami incinerator. That night, on the flight back to New York I avidly read his translation of Sidonie's field notes as if they were a window into a hidden part of my father's life as well.

Somewhere in the southeastern edge of the Pacific a shark is spawned who will, in a few years, eat a surfer, a boy still in middle school in a suburb of Sydney and, though a strong swimmer, not yet a surfer dude. The shark DNA and RNA are doing a dance of acceptance and elimination of various traits. The shark's incisors are still years away from completion and, though the odds of the surfer and the encounter with the shark are, at this point, infinitesimally small, the two are hurtling toward each other. The papers Eliana Katzir wrote under the name Sidonie Nieumacher sparked the end of my marriage. Perhaps I'd been swimming with sharks for a while without paying much attention to the dorsal fins breaking the surface, circling ever closer. It's a long way to Tipperary, but eventually you get there. Tipperary, in my case, was Iran.

Ethnology, n: The science of different human races, such as knaves, swindlers, imbeciles, clots, and ethnologists.

Ambrose Bierce
The Devil's Dictionary

I MET RUTH KOPPEK IN Chichén Itzá, Mexico, on *Ix*, the day of the Jaguar. We'd climbed different sides of a Mayan calendar pyramid, one with four sets of stairs of ninety-one steps each, and ran into each other only when we'd arrived at the top. She got there before I did and had her back to me as she looked out over the trees and plain. She had a long stiff braid down her back. It was never undone. You could imagine it dipped in tar as pirates did who found this procedure easier than washing. She pointed to Eb, a figure with an angular face, a long hard jawline, associated with rainstorms. Nearby was Oc, thirteen, a lucky number, the dog who acted as a beacon, guiding the night sun through the underworld.

According to Mayan creation myth, Ruth said, the gods discovered yellow and white corn, the ideal essence from which men could be made. Four corn men were created, and they turned out better than expected, flawless creations with perfect vision and comprehension of the world. The gods felt uneasy about the corn people's close resemblance to themselves, so in order to make men more fallible, their gifts were deliberately diminished. After their powers were adjusted, the corn men were given four corn women, one each.

Leaning against a huge limestone serpent with a human face staring out of its mouth she told me that she had once stolen something from a site. It was at a tomb in a border state few people visited. Looters had dug a tunnel into it and so had gone about their work undetected. Bones were strewn around, bits and pieces of pottery were scattered into random corners and heaps. Nearly everything had been taken from the site, but she found a nose ring which depicted a little man wearing an identical nose ring in a piece of a *mise en abyme* puzzle of which only a living human nose was absent. Pieces of frieze that had been chiseled off walls lay on the ground, and when she put the pieces together the result was images of men and

17

women intertwined, ancient pornography, maybe. The images themselves, rendered in burnt limestone rubble and marl, might have been a joke planted by the looters who were hungry and wouldn't have bothered with things that couldn't be sold, but she also imagined the middlemen, the dealers with residences in New York, London, Tokyo who wanted to leave a message, as if to say: dusty digging knuckleheads with your brains full of clan relationships and calendars, it all comes down to this: screwing. She pocketed the nose ring and a little figure of a man with an enormous dick and then walked away from the site, never to return.

"Look," she opened her hand, and the little figure lay nestled in her palm.

Later Ruth marched ahead of me, map folded into back pocket humming *My World Is Empty Without You, Babe* combined with the Perry Mason theme song, as performed by the Del Byzanteens, but nodding her head back and forth in a way Phil Kline probably never did. The rhythm of walking while hacking your way through the jungle, heavy deliberate steps, kind of lends itself to the Perry Mason theme song, if you think about it. The advocate of the concrete and knowable kept an amulet, a small silver fish, round her neck. Ruth's grandmother had given it to her to ward off the evil eye, and she believed in it completely. The two inches of silver scales and blue beady eyes was never removed. (I tried once and was pushed away.) Sometimes I let her get ahead of me and completely out of sight just to get a break from her sureness and confidence. I was somebody's graduate assistant. What did I know?

One evening when we were still out and darkness was falling fast, not leaving us much time to get back to town, in a effort to talk to her, I tried to make the following point. Even the edifice of provable facts is within lasso reach of any itinerant fantasist. The chacmools she studied, for example, with their languid reclining bodies and sphinx-like faces, bearing stone trays to support human sacrifice, were named by an eccentric nineteenth-century Frenchman, Augustus Le Plongeon, who christened the things he found according to his own random system as he traveled with an assortment of the concertina-shaped cameras of the era, and a monkey who carried his own private embossed–leather satchel. Ruth shrugged her narrow shoulders, spades and compass jangling from her backpack. How long does a human heart keep beating after it's pulled out of a chest cavity? How long does the person whose aortas and ventricles dangle above their face remain in sentient terror?

"Plongeon spoke to the monkey as if it were a co-antiquarian, trained in a *lycée*. The little fellow had its own monogrammed trowel and ate with him in the dining car, " I said.

Ruth scratched an ankle where she'd been bitten by a mosquito. One of Ruth's eyes was slightly bigger than the other so that I sometimes wondered if two different personalities lodged behind them: one who had no argument with a monkey in the dining car, and the other who called the conductor to complain and spoke to him in his own southern Mexican Spanish. The *it's really no big deal* eye shared the cranium space with *this is entirely unacceptable*. So, I think part of her would have traveled through swarms of locusts with me while the other half never imagined she inflicted a thousand cuts with one snicker.

"He retired to Brooklyn where he died in 1908 with a view of the East River," Ruth countered.

It was true. Laughed at, his theories in disgrace, Le Plongeon and his wife retreated to Brooklyn. Even in retirement Le Plongeon still claimed a dethroned Mayan queen fled to Egypt on a winged boat, and that the city of Palenque sent ambassadors to Polynesia.

Like Le Plongeon I found something compelling in the idea of going full steam ahead and building an entire universe out of flotsam and jetsam: grab a barque known to the Nile delta region, a Mayan nose ring, a Berlin U-bahn ticket with faces drawn on one side, a giant sandstone ashtray that could also serve as a vessel for containing a human heart rendered in sacrifice, tie all the pontoons together and walk across the Mississippi. Why not? I asked Ruth, which was mostly like asking the air. We were traveling with a few others, but at this point our team was far ahead and not visible. There's a feeling you get when walking in remote places that someone is watching you, someone you can't see who travels on a ridge to your right, over your shoulder, who hides behind thick palms or blends with a screen of vines. We were in the jungle to find what we could, while all the while some person or group of people was watching us, even if it was a tribe without written language, someone was noting how this man and woman talked loudly, gestured, didn't seem to get along or agree about anything and sprayed the air from time to time with some kind of mist that came out of a metal cylinder. How had the Le Plongeons plunged on, perhaps along this exact route, and remained adoring of one another's schemes and inventions?

"Alice Le Plongeon, though twenty-three years younger and devoted to Augustus," Ruth reminded me, "was herself a formidable photographer of the concrete and knowable, risking her life to photograph precipitously placed sculpture located in the territory of hostile tribes and vicious white looters eager to turn chacmools into cash. She left a vast archive, pictorial records of what she called 'the departed grandeur; silent, deserted, fallen cities.'"

Together Le Plongeon and his wife created a box made up of compartments that could be reassembled to form a portable dark-room complete with sink and black curtain, impervious to sunlight. Two people could set it up in less than five minutes. Something carried in a bag you could snap open almost with little more than a flick of the wrist, the anonymous black box, was converted into a complicated functional structure. The same imagination that gave life to chacmools and studied monkey chatter invented some very practical things as well. Couldn't you be a crackpot, your ideas held up to ridicule, and still be happy? I fished in my pocket for a jack-knife and traced the outline of a glyph in stone until Ruth told me to stop, the noise of the blade against rock was irritating.

Ruth shook the bottle of Rambug she'd bought at a camping store and sprayed the chemical infusion not just on herself but into the air. As far as she was concerned the discussion was over. She had the world on a string. Walking far ahead of me she relegated nineteenth-century antiquarians and their cabinets of curiosities to useless storage. An emerald-green snake hung knotted from a branch overhead. Ruth eyed it with a raised eyebrow before walking underneath. I'd seen her lop the head off a rattler that came too close and do so in a blink, then move on as if she'd done nothing more than swat a mosquito. Members of the reptile family didn't occupy her nightmares. These were inhabited by other phantoms, as I would eventually learn. She was afraid of the interiors of local churches, hollowed out, they contained no pews or benches of any kind. Incense burned and people came and went, lighting candles and chanting before saints, offering Coke or Fanta, eggs, or a dead chicken. The saints were lined up along the walls, and each had a mirror hung around his or her neck to keep evil away, and no, Ruth wasn't some kind of reincarnated demon. She just felt creeped out by churches.

Imagine being interviewed on a television show and when asked how you met the person you married, you have to say you collided at the top of a Mayan calendar pyramid. The audience is cued for laughter, the interviewer raises his eyebrows. He thinks you're making this up. We stayed in Mexico for a year, then moved back to New York.

I never spoke of Suolucidir to Ruth until I arrived home after the flight back from Miami. She hadn't met me at the airport, but stayed at home, working, and barely acknowledged the difficulty of my trip, visiting my stepmother, going through my father's things. The emotional register was often out of reach for Ruth. Dead was dead. Get over it. I left my bags by the door, sat opposite her, and told her that I was going to find Suolucidir.

Ruth barely looked up. She considered the study of the Maya to be constructed of concrete and knowable building blocks of evidence. This wasn't strictly true, even she would admit that, but the project I wanted to undertake was, she felt, built on a foundation of complete absurdity, hearsay, and postwar quicksand. Chasing a whisper of a myth, the ghosts of Victorian explorers and shadows of Soviet refugees down a desert rabbit hole made her shudder. Jacob's Ladder looks real, but you touch it at your peril as it crackles into nothingness.

She wasn't alone in her derision; my academic advisers also threw cold water on the idea of the lost city. If the subject of Suolucidir was raised, I was reminded about the paucity of evidence and told that the Nieumacher relics were now, after the intervening years of turmoil in the region, unlocatable, and perhaps had been fraudulently manufactured in the first place. I was warned that the artifacts the Victorians, Hilliard and Congraves, had sent back to the British Museum were in all probability just negligible offshoots of the Burnt City civilization, a city-state that had flourished to the north of the reputed site of Suolucidir. Even if I traveled to London to examine them, I would find the bits and pieces were merely evidence of far-flung provincial villages, not worthy of serious study. It was all deeply discouraging.

We were on the F train, and it had stalled above ground. It was late at night, and the car was empty except for a couple of snoozing subway workers in orange vests, tool boxes at their feet, and a man sitting directly opposite us who was immersed in a Russian newspaper. Light reflected off the oily surface of the Gowanus Canal and the huge Kentile Flooring sign while searchlights scoped the sky signaling the opening of a store somewhere to the west of the tracks. Ruth was staring glassy-eyed at the furry skunkweed that managed to grow between the rails of the train when it was above ground. Maybe it wasn't the best moment to have a discussion of this kind, but whether the canal inspired me or the searchlights it's hard to say. I just plunged right in. I tried, one more time, to interest Ruth in Suolucidir.

"Imagine it's four thousand years from now and you're wasting your time excavating Yuba City instead of Los Angeles," she said. "Suolucidir isn't even a speck on a page. It's like those display cases of sparrows and field mice in remote corridors of the Museum of Natural History, lines of tiny carcasses you barely notice on your way to the Hall of Bio-Diversity or the planetarium. Why stand in front of the dead fur commas and question marks when you can go a couple of floors down to the Imax, and watch sharks circling a cageless diver or a special effects re-creation of the eruption of Krakatau, fatal vibrations spreading across the Indian Ocean? If you go too far afield, you'll end up chasing little nothings and their shadows."

I argued the comparison to a row of Truman-era stuffed stoats was unfair.

She reminded me of the controversy surrounding Margaret Mead's *Coming of Age in Samoa*. Had Mead, and consequently her readers, been snookered for years by prankster Samoans? And then there was the scandal surrounding the Tasaday people of the Philippines. The same swamp of uncertainty surrounded the subject of Suolucidir.

"Were they real? Had they existed in isolation in the jungle for millennia? Were they actors playing Stone Age tribesmen with Bic pens, Swiss Army knives, and transistor radios hidden under a rock in a cave? Even if you're right," Ruth insisted, "and they're not actors, and there are no hidden plastic buckets and metal spoons, the charge hangs in the air. Once the seeds of doubt have been planted, you can never get rid of them."

I wished she would spare the plant metaphors; they seemed like a set of straw men.

"Most people who seriously tried to find Suolucidir disappeared into the Shah's prisons. There were no artifacts, and they were never heard from again." Ruth was right, but this was a risk I was willing to take.

The New World with its lost tribes and waves of immigrants was terra firma for her. She was afraid to fly over large bodies of water, which she hated in their endlessness. The deserts and mountains of Sistan-va-Baluchistan were, for her, a sandstorm you could never claw your way out of, a gale of locusts that blinded you, their dry little corpses filled your shoes, piled outside your tent like hail, crunching under foot. She felt ill at ease in places where she didn't know the language, as if all noise around her was reduced to a series of sequential sounds, and her perception of meaning was no better than a two-year-old's.

Ruth despaired of imagining upward from a rubble-strewn landscape, or to be more precise, from certain kinds of incomprehensible rubble-strewn landscapes. If she walked through a bombed city, a city of which no building survived, no brick lay squarely on top of another, and she found a shattered shell of a tin can, could make out only the letters . . .*oup* on a shred of paper clinging to it, she would know how to re-animate a kitchen or a grocery store.

There were readily available mental pictures for cupboard and shelf, walls, windows, doors, a radio playing in the background, a ticking clock reminding one of dinnertime. The street bustle, the arguments, the traffic crossings, these she could project in all their particularity, she could reconstruct scenes from the ground up, but for a city like Suolucidir, this would be impossible, she knew it. It was even more forbidding than a city of chacmools. It was a heap of stones resistant to that kind of personal holography. Aerial photos of ancient rubble looked to her like teeming, interlocking bacteria seen under a microscope. Helter skelter, job lot of primitive life forms, impossible to extract any meaning.

Though Bruno and Sidonie Nieumacher disappeared sometime in 1939, fragments of Suolucidiri writing from pieces of the scrolls and parchments they discovered found their way to Tehran. While bombs began to fall on London, experts in Old Persian, Farsi, and Baluchi at Tehran University began the work of translating the fragments. It was a daunting task, and at first the lines of symbols appeared to the untrained eye to have no or little relationship to any known linguistic system. Two linguists, Farouk Rashidian and Ali bin Dost, spent years studying the shreds of parchment, and determined the writer or writers were not Suolucidiri, but citizens of a city established by a group related to the Seleucids whose Persian king was Seleucus, satrap of Babylonia. Though his reign was brief, he was one of the most powerful satraps to succeed Alexander the Great. However, there were differences between the writing in the Nieumacher scroll and the alphabet used by the Seleucids. One theory connected their language to Aramaic and ancient Farsi with some Urdu inflection, but so few written fragments of it have survived that its linguistic relatives in the region can only be the subject of conjecture. Rashidian and bin Dost declared the Zahedan Parchments were written in a combination of Elamite and Akkadian cuneiform.

There was a partial copy of the Rashidian bin Dost grammar and lexicon in Columbia's Butler Library, which I was able to access. Though it wasn't supposed to leave the rare book room, and couldn't be photocopied, the grammar had already been vandalized. Despite missing bits and pieces, I needed it. Lessons in deviousness acquired years ago from a college roommate expert in shoplifting (among other things), those remembered conversations came in handy. Over a period of several days when alone in the library examining room I cut the pages of the book with the blade of an X-acto knife and replaced them with pieces of ordinary paper; in this way the theft might not be detected for years, perhaps never. No one was interested in the analysis of this long dead language by two linguists tortured by Reza Shah. Presto: the only section of the Rashidian bin Dost grammar and lexicon known in the United States found its way to Brooklyn. What I studied on my kitchen table wasn't even the entire work. Others with an unknown agenda had desecrated the book, though why they would bother with something so arcane and, for most people so inconsequential, is unknown. Perhaps it was a lark while high, perhaps they were agents of Savak masquerading as Columbia students. I can only hope somewhere in the world the book remains intact. If Ruth didn't want to go with me, I'd travel on my own.

Two days after the letter arrived announcing my small research grant from the Zafar Institute, Ruth was on her way to the airport back to the land of Quetzalcoatl, and I now think she had her ticket from the moment our conversation turned to shrews that had visited the taxidermist. In four thousand years the sun explodes, and we're not here anymore anyway. There's no human life remaining to dig up the intersection of Sunset Boulevard and Camden or the Yuba City 7-11. Ruth left with Larry Saltzman, an anthropologist who called at all hours and whose speech was sprinkled with what he claimed were Mayan truisms like *your festivals fill me with terror*. Ruth thought he was hilarious. When she took his calls behind closed doors I could hear her laughing. Ruth, wedging the phone between her ear and her shoulder as she doodled chacmools dancing the fandango, playing drums, fucking their stone brains out, was the kind of person who never needed to say I'll get back to you on that, she always had the answers at hand. You would be glad she was on your side of a debate until one day it turned out she wasn't anymore.

Sometimes I did have the sense that every square meter of the earth and sea had been excavated, and there were no unknown clusters of people who'd built cities, created systems of government, mythologies, established rituals of birth, marriage, death, harvesting and eating, still to be found. All past human habitations have been mapped and inventoried. To go any deeper was to hit magma or deep ocean volcanoes inhabited by translucent shrimp and hairy white crabs. What remained? Had I hit a brick wall? I would find out.

I packed my topographical maps, compass, measuring tape, bundle of flag pins, trowels, short hoes, and camera and flew out to Tehran, stopping only to change planes in Istanbul. Ruth would be sorry. She might be lounging poolside in Cuernavaca with the king of Aztec one-liners, but I was confident that treasure lay under my feet if only I could find the right map. Once it was located and verified, she'd read, entirely by accident, about my triumph and would leap up, kicking sand in the king's face. Why are you wasting time on that beach? I said to the chair next to me. She'd dash off a letter from the nearest hotel desk, begging to help me catalogue relics and translate the surviving scrolls and tablets of Suolucidir. It will take years, but I'll agree, yes, she can return and act as my assistant, my Alice Le Plongeon, camera in hand, ready to chase Mayan queens to Cairo and beyond.

"History my foot, it's money!"

Shirley Pemberton
Passport to Pimlico, 1949

A MAN ON A MOTORBIKE, rolls of carpeting stacked behind him, cut off another biker who toppled over, hitting the curb. Cylinders wrapped in brown paper spilled from the back of the bike rolling into traffic, some, tied with twine, came undone and streamed red, gray, and blue into the road. The injured cyclist managed to stand, and a fight ensued. I watched along with a group of men leaning against the glass window of a kebab joint, listening to them argue in Farsi with a smattering of Arabic words. Whose fault was it really? The carpet man has a knife. Look out. Was that other fellow in the proper lane? Perhaps he turned a bit to the right when he shouldn't have. I could have been anywhere, maybe, but I had arrived in Tehran. Shouting insults, one of the two combatants, limping, managed to get back on his bike and drive off. The other sat on the curb and waited for help. Fight over, the men discussed a public hanging that was to take place later in the day. A convicted murderer would be suspended via crane. I listened to their conversation a bit longer, then made my way back to the hotel.

The university archive was on the outskirts, some distance from my hotel. Flattening the letter I'd received on archive stationery I memorized the number and made my first call in order to make an appointment to view the scroll the Nieumachers had found on the site on the outskirts of Zahedan, the document that, according to Sidonie's field notes, was the remains of detailed records of daily life in the city of Suolucidir. I'd written to the director of the archive, and our correspondence was part of the basis on which I was able to obtain funding for the trip. In his letter Dr. Haronian assured me the Zahedan scroll was accessible and available for inspection.

I hoped my Farsi didn't betray an American accent. It was something I'd worked very hard on, and though I was often told my accent was undetectable, you never know how you really sound with any consistency or when in a difficult situation. I practiced a few lines before I picked up the telephone, then dialed. It was with a great deal of anticipation I listened to the clicks of the Tehrani dial tone. Soon I would finally be able to see the only physical proof I knew of that confirmed the existence of Suolucidir. After many rings a man picked up, saying only hello, not stating the name of the archive as businesses usually do in the west. For an instant I wondered if I had the wrong number.

"I'd like to speak to Dr. Haronian."

Some shuffling that sounded like boxes being moved came through the line, the scratching sound of cardboard pushed across a gritty, unswept floor. I looked out at the street while I waited, half expecting to see a person leaning against a wall looking up at me, but the street was empty except for a woman carrying a bag with branches of dates poking out the top of it. Across the narrow street I could make out a room filled with blue TV light. A man came to the window, looked up, noticed me, and pulled the curtains shut. Finally a man got on the line.

"This is Mr. Bastani, at your service. I'm sorry to tell you Dr. Haronian is no longer at the institute. He's retired." As far as I knew, Haronian was not very old, so I was surprised to hear he was no longer at the archive.

"I have letters from him." I immediately regretted blurting this out. If Haronian was gone, there was nothing I could do about it, and so I tried to take a more conciliatory tone. "Are you his replacement?"

"No. I'm just answering the telephone in the interim." Bastiani didn't know where the former archivist had gone, so it was impossible for him to give me a forwarding address.

"Can I speak to Dr. Haronian's replacement?"

"No one has yet been appointed."

Pacing the carpet, one foot after the next, I tried to pull something out of my brain to prolong the interrogation before the line was cut off. One foot covered the border pattern of linked diamond shapes, the other was planted solidly in the middle of a quatrefoil design. I asked Bastani if he could help me, then, in viewing the Suolucidir Scroll. Dr. Haronian, with whom I'd been corresponding for nearly a year had assured me it would be possible to spend some time studying them, as much time as I wanted, in fact. This accessibility was critical to my funding from the Zafar Institute. Without access to the Suolucidir relics, I felt like a fraud.

"The Suolucidir Scroll? We have no such documents. I'm familiar with our entire collection." He paused, and I heard the sounds of a match striking, then Bastani inhaling. He was smoking a cigarette. In an archive? The idea that I had misdialed again occurred to me. It was the wrong number, and some knucklehead was playing along as a kind of impromptu prank. I hung up and carefully redialed the number, but the same affectless voice of Mr. Bastani answered. I mumbled about a lost connection, sorry.

"The Zahedan Scroll. It could be archived under the name of the site where they were found."

"Zahedan? There's nothing here Zahedani. Zahedan is a city of dust."

"They could be filed under the city's former name, Duzdab." Duzdab meant the Watering Place of Thieves. When Reza Shah came to power he changed the name to Zahedan, which means place of noble people.

"If you like, arrangements might be made for you to view some scrolls from Susa. This I could fix for you. Susa, the town where the Hammurabi Stele was kept until it was removed to Paris, as you know. These items are very old and can be viewed for only two hours on Monday afternoons."

I explained that as interesting as these might be, they were of no use to me for my current project. The Nieumacher Parchments, I asked again. Could they be filed as the Nieumacher Parchments? I could hear Bastani laughing.

"Why would we call anything here by such a name? Our archive goes back to the time of Darius and beyond, but includes nothing Germanic. You haven't told me why you want to see our archives. We aren't a museum. We don't ordinarily open to random passersby, even if they have a letter from the late Dr. Haronian."

"He's dead?"

"No, I meant the former Dr. Haronian is no longer working here, as I told you."

I explained my research, what I was looking for, but Bastani then asked me if I had a girlfriend or sisters? This he would like to know about, and had they accompanied me to Tehran? Even if I had sisters, why would I bring them with me?

"You have girlfriends then?" He repeated. "Maybe several." This was a statement, not a question.

"No."

"That's unfortunate." He paused, inhaling and exhaling smoke. "You can't just walk into the archives," he said. "I don't care who you think wrote to you saying this is possible."

I mentioned a sum of money. It wasn't much, but it was all I could offer him. For a moment neither of us spoke. I walked over to the window of my hotel room and twirled the cord around my index finger. Finally the man on the other end of the phone told me that until such time as Dr. Haronian's successor was chosen, it would be impossible to view any of the archives. To do so, for whatever stated urgency, would be considered a grave security risk. People, even foreigners, have disappeared for less. When I asked when the next director would be at his desk, Bastani had no idea, nor would he tell me if he did.

The door to a shop across the street was locked. The shopkeeper vaguely looked up at the array of windows presented by my hotel, but he didn't appear to be watching anyone in particular. I heard more shuffling noises from the phone receiver, then the line went dead. I dialed one more time. No one picked up.

That was to be my last conversation with Mr. Bastani. In the morning I packed my bags. I was anxious to press on to Zahedan and the site of Suolucidir itself, if I could find it, leaving the study of the scroll for my return trip, despite the knowledge that reversing the order of reading, then excavating would be far less useful. During the excavation of Esther's Tomb in Hamadan in 1971, in the hurry to build a new temple that would attract visitors, all kinds of ancient significant objects were tossed out. On the one hand I understand at a certain point the bathtub is full and overflowing, you can't hold on to and read everything; on the other hand the lost museum is something to be mourned, no? It was possible I'd never see the Nieumacher relics. There was nothing I could do about it.

"I yama sad dictapator. Me sheeps ain't got no sense. I yam king of 10,000 fatheads."

E.C. Segar
Popeye August 21, 1935

JAHANSHAH ROSTAMI, SON OF THE mineralogist who gave my father the Nieumacher field notes, was very eager to help with the search. He had already collected old survey maps and interviewed tribal leaders and shepherds who traversed the area from the Burnt City in the north to Zahedan and farther south as well. On my way to his house I stopped to watch a man with an orange-hennaed beard sit on the floor of his shop hammering copper bowls into shallow lakes; other smaller vessels like jazvahs for making coffee were strung from the roof over his head. I walked on, the sound of hammer against copper following me down the lane. At a fruit stand a bare bulb swung above a pile of cherries and baskets full of branches of green dates. A pile of garnet-streaked pomegranates spilled into the road. Filling a bag with them, I bought some to bring to Rostami and his family. I knew they were well off and lived in a wealthier quarter of Zahedan. Like his father, Jahanshah worked for an oil company, determining the structure of oil fields hidden as deep below rocks and sand as a Suolucidir courtyard.

Expecting me to call on the very evening of my arrival in Zahedan, he opened the door almost before I knocked. Jahanshah remembered my father's visits from when he was a child and claimed he could see the resemblance, but since he was only a few years older than I, more likely his memory was helped by a photograph of a group of geologists taken at a meeting in Tehran at which our fathers were both present. I had a copy of the same picture at home. Rostami had curly black hair receding in a V shape, '70s-era sideburns and a moustache. Actually it was he and I who looked similar, though people who look alike rarely recognize the similarity themselves; others usually point it out.

I was not to spend much time in Rostami's house, but in some ways it resembled the house I grew up in. Apart from turquoise tiles decorated with Kufic script, the Rostamis had the same feldspar bookends, probably from the same conference in Pikes Peak attended decades earlier, a relic, for both of us, of another age. Next to the bookends was a picture of Jahanshah's brother, who had died in a car accident. Also on the shelf was a rocket-shaped mug from NASA and a statuette of Aladdin from Disneyworld as well as a small rubber Mickey Mouse. I was told that Rostami no longer studied rocks, now he taught math at a local school. Mrs. Rostami stood in an arched doorway tapping red fingernails against the jamb, waiting to be introduced. Her eyebrows met like a black tiara that had slipped down her crown, and she smiled in my direction, but also looked at me as if I were a large, new piece of furniture whose use was unclear, the kind of thing that would cause as many unforeseen problems as provide dubious entertainment, like a record player that arrives with no needles. Nice in theory but presenting complications before it can fulfill its promises.

Rostami had two very young sons, one who pushed himself in a sitting position from one stair to the next, making a thumping sound as his butt hit one step after the next, accompanied by a humming at the back of his throat, while the other one hid, reluctant to meet me at all. I presented them with a box of Batman figures, which they swooped down upon. I had opted for several varieties of Batman (Batman the color of blue Jell-O, Batman with armaments, Batman with a long voluminous cape) but forgot the batteries that would make the superheroes light up at knee and elbow joints. Near the bookcase, displayed on a pedestal was a silver hookah, the red snake wound around its engraved body, ending in a silver nozzle. One of the blue plastic Batmans quickly made it his lair, riding the snake like a fiend.

That first night we ate jeweled rice and chicken with pomegranate, and drank cardamom-scented tea. Rostami was gregarious. Holding the small glass of tea up to his eye he swirled the leaves and cardamom shells as if it was going to explain something to him. Finding Suolucidir would be like driving a stake into the ground, making a claim for a story that would be definitive and unalterable. His wife went to look for batteries for the Batmen. She didn't like me very much; that was clear. It was as if she feared I was some kind of thief.

Like many Zahedanis, Rostami had visited the Burnt City site to the north, the way Americans would tour an Iroquois village, but he confessed he'd had an odd feeling at the site, as if he were looking at the severed half of a Siamese twin. In the 1970s Maurizzio Tosi, an Italian archaeologist working in the Burnt City, had found the oldest known dice, caraway seeds, a backgammon set made of turquoise and agate, skulls that exhibited signs of brain surgery, and an artificial eye made of gold and bitumen paste, the iris engraved with sun-like rays. Rostami felt the Burnt City couldn't have been an isolated prodigy city-state. There had to be others. Something was missing.

"You must understand there have been major earthquakes in the region since the Nieumachers were here. Whole villages were flattened in one spasm like so many houses made of cards." Jahanshah picked up the rubber Mickey Mouse and referred to him in English as the Hebraic mouse who pops everywhere. He was skeptical about the Nieumachers, I could tell. The shape-shifting Nieumachers were far more troublesome to him than the English who had come before them. The British had just wanted loot. It wasn't clear to him what the Nieumachers, who had come to Persia under the auspices of something called the "Franco-Soviet Friendship Dig," had wanted. They were protean, ambiguous, claiming land, maybe, more meddling and more dangerous, he thought, though in this he was mistaken, not recognizing the true fox that had had every intention of biting Persia on the ass.

He, too, knew about Hilliard and Congreaves, the pair of Englishmen who had come looking for Suolucidir maybe fifteen or twenty years before the Nieumachers arrived. Of the English not much was known, but he was acquainted with a man, Javad Eyvani, who claimed his father had worked for the Nieumachers, and he might have some clue as to the exact location of the site.

The next day we drove to a block of low, anonymous apartment flats that looked as though they had been built recently. A child peered at us from a doorway; a woman in black passed us on the stairway, her chador making a swishing sound against the tile. We made our way up a staircase that smelled of garlic fried by the fistful and the sourness of dried limes left too long on a windowsill.

Jahanshah knocked on door number nine, which was guarded by a blue glass orb intended to ward off the evil eye. He zipped and unzipped the pockets of his leather jacket as we waited. Somewhere in the building, or just outside it, dogs barked. After a few minutes an older man in billowing sherwal trousers, obviously annoyed at the sound, opened the door and yelled down the hall, but when he recognized Jahanshah he smiled in a 'what do you want?' sort of way, glad to see Rostami, but suspicious of the cause of the visit. Rostami introduced me to Javad, a retired oil rig worker he knew from years ago when they had both worked in the western part of the country in Khuzistan. When living on the gulf, both men had reminisced about Zahedan, the city of their childhood, and both had since re-turned to it, although for different reasons. Javad now lived with his daughter and her family who were rarely home, either out at work or school, so he spent much of his days alone in the apartment or at cafés. Javad wore a long white shirt like an Indian kurta, a brown coat, and had a piece of cloth wound around his head like Marat in the bath. He had very dark circles under his eyes and, though finally smiling when he showed us in, he didn't really look very happy. Muttering something about the Sikhs down the hall he motioned us in with the wave of a cigarette. We walked through the kitchen to a small room lined with pillows and sat cross-legged on the floor while Javad poured tea. A news anchor was visible on the television, but the sound was turned down. Bollywood music played softly from a cassette on top of the television. Javad and Rostami asked about one another's families, then got down to business.

"Do you remember the city you used to talk about when we were out in the oil fields in Khuzistan? Do you remember those stories? Was it your father or your grandfather who worked for those what were they, Russian? Long time ago."

"It was my father," Javad said, offering us a bowl of green pistachios.

"Do you think you know where the site was located? Did your father ever say?"

Javad laid his hands out palms up to indicate they were, by and large, empty, but there were possibilities. His father had taken him to the site once.

"A road lined with cypress, a grove of almond trees. It was over forty years ago, but perhaps not a great deal has changed since then."

He grabbed a fistful of pistachios, cracked them open, then popped them into his mouth. If it were possible to do so, the city would be an interesting thing to find, he said, licking salt and green dust from his fingers. The search would get him out of the apartment building and away from the Sikhs who irritated him on a daily basis. He would make some money from us and a lot more if any Suo-lucidiri treasure remained to be unearthed. I found myself grinning and humming along with the music, tapping fingers on knees. This was turning out to be easier than I thought.

The next morning we picked up Javad and headed out of the city, driving south by southwest. It had been a wild desolate place where people hunted, Javad remembered. The almond grove and line of cypress trees perhaps marked a tamer part of the route closer to Zahedan, before you got to the real wilderness. Not as much hunting now, Javad, said, but then it was more common.

We looked for groves and tree-lined roads, backtracking, trying other ways out of the city. I turned the dial up and down on the car radio, but all we got was crackling buzz. Forget it, Javad said. I slumped down in the front seat. Was he giving up already? You'll find no music was all he meant. Rostami nodded and switched the radio off.

In the forty years since Javad was a child, the trees could well have been cut down, if not for McDonalds, oil pipelines, poppy fields or interstate highways, then for something. We spent days driving around with the retired oil rig worker, but as we turned off a particularly bad road, he jumped up in his seat. We stopped the jeep and continued on foot as he instructed. An outcropping of red rocks shaped like a pod of whales looked familiar to him. Javad was sure the cave had been close by. The rocky cliffs, the stunted trees marked the entrance to a cave.

"This is where the camels were loaded. There were no roads,

but they traveled east of Zahedan, then followed a trail up to these hills and this cave."

"How do we know this is the one?" Jahanshah asked, but he was grinning slightly.

"I remember exactly," Javad answered, squinting into the sun.

We spent days exploring the cave, looking for some remnant, some fragment the Nieumachers might have left behind. After about a quarter of a mile slowly sloping underground, passages branched in many directions, some with precipitous drops. The channels, Jahanshah had warned, were not safe, prone to pockets of toxic gas, cave-ins, and not well explored. In 1939 with equipment not as good as ours they had no chance of going far into the cave, even allowing for seismic activity that could have altered some passages and sealed others completely.

One afternoon I went a little ahead of Javad and Jahanshah and down a passage that inclined steeply while becoming so narrow I had to duck, nearly doubling over. A ledge containing what could have been fragments of pottery jutted into the space, but the pieces were so small I couldn't positively identify them as anything. Pottery or crap? Bits of bone no bigger than a fingernail were scattered nearby. Even Le Plongeon had his glyphs and chacmools to misinterpret. Here was only dust. Though the three of us explored the area with high hopes, there was nothing more in the cave, and we never found any further evidence of human habitation. Leonardo Da Vinci designed a kind of lethal chariot, a plan that expanded on the Roman Scythian chariot. He added four large scythes which would rotate and cut down everything in their path, but the problem was that the horses themselves were vulnerable, too, and if they bolted, they could themselves be sliced. I felt as if, like this faulty vehicle, I was taking a few steps forward, but I ended up shooting myself in the foot and going nowhere. What once seemed like a brilliant plan turned out to be a dangerous waste of time. I paid Javad for his time out of the Zafar money, but finally all we had were dead ends.

Why young Englishmen wear top hats, which were prevented from engulfing their entire countenances only by their ears puzzled me for some time afterwards. I subsequently learned that the supply of these social weapons is limited in Tehran and as they are hard to transport over the Elburz Mountains, they are treated by the junior diplomats as official heirlooms. From which I take it, megalocephalia was prevalent among their predecessors in office.

W. Morgan Shuster
Strangling of Persia, 1912

I BEGAN TO NOTICE THAT we were followed whenever we went anywhere; even if we were in the desolate area near the caves, someone would appear with a goatherd who could have passed as a villager, but somehow the glasses were too new and modern looking, or shoes were an odd color, something wasn't entirely convincing. In the city an unmarked car trailed Jahanshah's beat-up Paykan, and when we walked on the streets of Zahedan or stopped in cafés there seemed to be a pair of men or one man not far behind. The tails were simultaneously identifiable and anonymous; they looked like any number of other men on the street wearing sunglasses. Sometimes they wore western clothes, sometimes traditional dress or a combination: baggy dark pants and long jackets, buttoned-up shirts. Renting rooms a few blocks from the Rostamis, it was easy for us to meet without necessarily having conversations via telephone to make arrangements. Apart from one day when I did ask him about these shadows, we never acknowledged the peculiarities of the situations we avoided, commonplaces like using a phone or lowering our voices in a crowd. If I was by myself, no one dogged my steps that I was aware of, so it seemed the tails weren't interested in me, the American, but there was no way of knowing this for certain. Jahanshah was evasive in his answers so I didn't ask again. It was a time of transition in Iran. The men could have been agents of anyone or no one, freelancers of a sort. My father who traveled all over the world looking at rocks, appeared to know little about what he saw as the less permanent forces fighting it out above the topsoil, and somehow, for the most part, he always came home as if he'd only been taking a nap on a fishing boat on a peaceful river. The last time I saw him alive he'd just returned from Argentina where prisoners rounded up from their homes were dropped out of planes, and I argued with him, how can you not know? Unlike my father, I couldn't concentrate on exploring caves to the exclusion of the men lurking in the shadows. Needing to know what they wanted, what they were looking at, was more than a continual distraction; it was a survival mechanism my father ignored.

During my months in Zahedan, Jahanshah did disappear for periods of time without warning, and if I asked his wife where he was, she grew nervous, and only said she didn't know where he was. She removed the photographs of the dead brother, the group of international rock hounds, the statuette of Aladdin, and Mickey Mouse. A crooked blue-black arm still stuck out of the coils of the hookah snake, Batman's hiding place. Each time Rostami returned without warning, it was as if by magic. Mineralogists, like Rostami and his father before him, could read rocks like books and could be seen as gatekeepers or interpreters: what kind of oil might be found where, what rocks were signs of the presence of bauxite, gypsum, chromite, glass sand, iron ore, gold. What began as a child's fascination with the crystals hidden within a geode or the phosphorescent rocks that glow in the dark turned into a useful profession and then into a job with risks. Rostami's post had involved making detailed studies of field structures, overseeing drilling, maintaining a history of oil production, and most important, estimating the size of the oil reserves that remained. One day when we were on one of our hikes, looking for evidence — a cornice sticking out from the ground, a pottery shard etched with an unknown script, the tops of long-buried capitals, the gateway to a lost city, an old shoe, anything — he told me the story about his job and how he had lost it. We were looking for ancient footprints, but we talked about the present.

"I'm not organized and left papers lying around, but in any case nothing was under lock and key. A few days later the file reappeared with my signature on it, but it wasn't the same file. I remembered enough of the original findings to know that the replaced file exaggerated the size of untapped fields under my purview. The director of my division was a man who was rumored to have dined on gilt quail eggs and the most rare golden Caspian caviar with the Shah and Queen Farah, but it's also possible he never in his life was anywhere near them. It's possible he only glimpsed them inspecting an installation or new facility. In any case, I had stumbled across a dangerous piece of information that linked me to him. Had this man deliberately overestimated the size of the reserves? Maybe, maybe not, but by coming across these adjusted numbers, by being aware of them, I was the man who knew too much."

"So what did you do?"

"The question was: did the adjuster of numbers know that I was aware of the altered figures? I think he did."

"How could he, whoever he was, have suspected?" I stopped, my shoes filled with sand.

"At first I made no secret of the discrepancy. I talked about it, calculating that if I did talk about it, I couldn't be blamed for a deliberate miscalculation I knew was wrong. Talking outright about the inconsistency, dumping the scorpion from my shoe so everyone could see it, seemed the safest thing to do. This was naive optimism on my part. I was told ink doesn't change its position once laid on paper. The molecules don't realign themselves overnight. How did my signature get on the file? It did look just like mine. I was set up to take the fall if the incongruity was discovered. The file had my signature, while the file with the accurate numbers was nowhere to be found. To save my life, I resigned and moved back here."

Being the supposed author of a doctored file wasn't the only reason he was a sitting target. His work was seen by those who watched neighborhoods as a symbol of the west and its appetite for oil. No matter who he said he worked for, Rostami was considered to be leaning towards traitorous by nothing more complicated than blind association. Like his father before him he went into semi-retirement in Zahedan, but the remote province wasn't a foolproof escape hatch.

I often wondered what would happen if I was mistaken for him, and I was picked up off the street and questioned? Two men grab my arms as I'm about to pay for a spare set of batteries in an outdoor market. Coins, water bottles, sunglasses all go flying. No one says anything or appears to notice. I'm led out of the market and shoved into the back seat of the car. My passport is pulled from a pocket, and one of the men yells it's a fake, and that I should shut up, even though I haven't said a word. The taller of the two, maybe he's wearing an eye patch, maybe he accepts I'm not Jahanshah Rostami, but he demands to know if I'm not Rostami then where's the spy hiding? The other one, a man with a low, calm voice tells me he knows this Suolucidir business is a ruse to infiltrate, destabilize, steal reserves, sabotage pipelines. It was the same with the English, French, Russians, and Americans. I pretend not to understand their Farsi. Shrugging holding my palms out, they punch me again as the car careens down the Zahedan road. A hood is placed over my head. I don't know where we are. One of the men hums a Bollywood film song. Finally the car comes to a halt, and I'm ordered out of the car, but I still pretend I don't know what the man's talking about. *Out*, he says in English. I obey because what choice do I have? My feet touch something soft: sand. It's not easy to walk on but I'm told to walk, and I listen for the sound of a gun going off, the last thing I'll hear. I imagined many such *Spy vs. Spy* scenarios: the beak-nosed spies pop up from beneath blocks of pavement that fan apart and hit the sidewalk with a resonant clunk, they emerge from panels in a ceiling, invisible joists sliding apart with loud creaking noises, they spring from spandrel-shaped doors and bungee cord from lofty arches to bop me from behind. Despite the loud noises, I'm oblivious, my head is in the clouds. In a year or so the spies will be sent west to Khorramshar when Iraq will invade with an eye on the oil fields of Khuzistan. Once, in the street, someone really did address me as Jahanshah Rostami.

Not only that, but the unveiled women of Zahedan looked uncannily like Ruth, as if some branch of the Koppek family had wandered from Tehran to Baghdad to Lvov, retaining their black hair, mad dash of a single eyebrow, yet benefiting from a strain of aggressiveness, grabbing the last place on the last boat or caravan west, grabbing the last bag of rice or couple of potatoes, and so they survive. Ruth's grandmother, Ada, would personally sew tumans into her headscarf and bribe her way over the border while humming Ladino songs she no longer remembered the words to.

A few miles outside of the city I set up camp in an abandoned hut with an awning made of woven palm fronds that looked like it would blow away with the first strong breeze but never did. From here I made my day trips to outlying areas. I didn't have an infinite amount of funding and consequently not much time. Also, since the revolution had ousted the Shah, there was growing anti-American sentiment in the country, though more so in the cities than in outlying areas. Every day brought word of more violence in the capital. The Shah's people met with firing squads, and though many thought this day couldn't have come too soon, at the same time there were protests and shootings; newspapers, radio stations, and movie theaters were closed. Even in isolated Zahedan of white stone buildings and nightingales, there was a sense of foreboding. It had become a major gateway for drug smugglers sending product in from Afghanistan and Pakistan. While pretending to look for oleaginous rocks, Jahanshah had told me, some apparent geographers were really posting couriers, so the dangers of poking around outside the city were many and unpredictable.

Rostami returned for a few days. One night when I was back at my hotel he called uncharacteristically late and asked me to meet him at his house as soon as possible. I got dressed, ran out, and was at his door within an hour of receiving the call. The house was dark. His wife and children were asleep. He gestured that we shouldn't stay in the house. Words, even those that hang in the air, can never be made completely invisible.

"Just keep walking," Rostami said. A few cars still prowled the streets, and overhead lights glowed intermittently. We passed a large dress shop, windows empty except for decorative plastic columns, fluted with winged lions for capitals, intentionally broken to look like Sassanid ruins. Behind folding screens you could make out dresses and mannequins peeking out from purdah. They were posed for women customers only. Rostami told me he needed to leave the country. Dust had settled in the curved flutes of the plastic columns. In the depths of the shop a dummy winked, frozen, perched on high heels, mini-skirt a slash of red. Her wig was askew as if she, too, needed to depart in a hurry.

Leaning against a stone wall I took out my passport, opened it to the page with the photograph and ran my thumb around the edge of my picture as if to remove it.

"Put your picture here. Jahanshah Hossein Rostami becomes Ariel Bokser, born in Flatbush, educated at the University of Chicago, briefly married to Ruth Koppek, present whereabouts unknown. As soon as you're safely in New York I'll report my passport missing or stolen."

Rostami shut his eyes and repeated the bare facts: address, phone number, date of birth, social security number. His English was actually very good, but the pronunciation couldn't fool even the most stoned customs official at JFK.

"Say you lived in Jerusalem for years, that's why you have an accent. They won't know the difference. Look, you have the stamps on your passport to prove it."

I flipped to the Israeli stamps. Rostami took the passport from my hand, snapped it shut, and put it in his pocket. He was vague about how and exactly when he would depart, but I assumed the urgency of his situation meant it would be as soon as possible.

"We'll give Javad's caves one more attempt," he said. "One last try before I leave."

We walked a few blocks together, reviewing the dead ends of our search. I was uneasy discussing the Nieumacher notebook with my Iranian host. It had exited his household ten years ago like a hot potato.

"Your father had the opportunity to destroy the notebook, why didn't he?"

"My brother was much older than me. Just before your father's visit he was already attending university, and he was interested in Sidonie's papers. He'd found an old Persianist from Berlin who had sat out the war in Tehran and remained until the 1960s. This man was willing to translate the notebook."

"What happened?"

"My brother was killed in a car accident, though his injuries didn't resemble the kind you would receive in a head-on collision, or so I was told."

The Persianist, too, disappeared, but it was rumored he landed in Tel Aviv, though this could be neither confirmed nor denied.

"I have here a dish of 'mud' which represents an oleaginous amplitudes of pellets."

George Herriman's *Krazy Kat*
Ignatz to Offissa Pup. March 3, 1940

I STOPPED BY HIS HOUSE the next morning as planned, intending to pack Rostami's equipment into my rented car, then we would drive out to the foothills together. The house was dark, shutters drawn. His wife let me in, closed the door, but made it clear I was not to sit down or step far into the house. The children were watching television, what sounded like Tweetie Bird in Farsi, in another room. Somewhere between our parting on Fazl Street last night and this morning, he had vanished. Mrs. Rostami put on a headscarf though she wasn't going anywhere, just opening the door enough, so she could be seen showing me out. She asked me to leave, not in an unkind way, but she was afraid my presence put them all at risk, and I should understand that. Fedeyroon Rostami dismissed Suolucidir as a phantom city, a hoax. She saw me as an American adventurer who had gotten her husband involved in something that should have been left alone. There was little I could do to persuade her otherwise. I had nothing to do with Jahanshah's disappearance, but my voice sounded feeble and unconvincing, even to myself. She gently pushed me out the door, then slammed it shut.

I drove out to the foothills alone, as I had already done on numerous occasions since I'd arrived. It was blistering hot. Usually I brought adequate supplies with me, but that day, in my despair at certain failure, I'd only packed a small bottle. Jahanshah had had the maps and other equipment for caving in his car. Even after more than a month spent in Iran, no new proof that Suolucidir ever existed had been unearthed. I sat on a rock and stared at the horizon, swatting flies. Soon my water bottle was empty. Though sheep and goats dotted the landscape, no shepherds were visible, but I assumed someone must be watching in the vicinity of the flock. It was a habit of mine to converse with people I met in the region, always hoping, naïvely, that someone would know of a cave somewhere that held untold archaeological riches. I'd gotten to know a few of the inhabitants, since I had some knowledge of the local dialect. They were friendly and eager to talk, share meals, and they tolerated my presence with my jangling tool belt and backpack full of inscrutable objects, even if they secretly believed me to be a crackpot, referred to among themselves as Shovel Man.

One group of goats and sheep clustered around a clump of bushes. That wasn't unusual in this kind of heat, but there was something desperate about this tight huddle. I went to take a closer look. The reason the animals wouldn't budge soon became obvious, but the cause was like nothing I'd ever seen before. They were crowded near a crack in the ground from which cold air blew out as if someone had left an enormous underground air conditioner on high, facing straight up into the desert. It was like when you walk past an abandoned building and cold air blasts out onto the sidewalk. I went closer to the edge of the crevice, feeling the cool breeze on my face, when the ground suddenly gave way. I fell maybe fifteen feet, landing on a pile of sand.

How I survived the fall with no broken bones remains a mystery to me to this day. I'd fallen through what must have been the roof of some kind of structure, and just missed crashing into a dozen massive clay jars. There were instances in the past of archaeologists stumbling, falling into sites entirely by accident, like cartoon characters, legs bicycling in air, but instead of turning into a peelable pancake upon landing, they find treasures of Incans or Chaldeans and live to be photographed with their arms around totem and taboo. Standing with difficulty, I gasped as I looked around. Friezes like sandstone filmstrips and very life-like statuary ran the length of the room. Areas where the sand hadn't drifted over revealed a checkerboard marble floor littered with bits and pieces: small oil lamps, silver coins, flint tools, pieces of colored glass. Had Romans been here? There were even a couple of glazed vessels. Did Crusaders make it this far?

I took a brush from my backpack and whisked millennia of dust from an oil flask. Because of erosion and recent earthquake activity the earth had, after keeping its secrets for thousands of years, kindly shifted, and in the hours that followed, I dusted layers of dirt and sand from a variety of objects, writing notes, quickly cataloging while the sun was high and light fell into the chamber. But eventually the shadows grew longer and a problem presented itself. It would soon be night, the temperature would drop, and I would be stuck on an underground island with no way out, destined to die of hypothermia in the desert. If I couldn't get back to the twentieth century, the waters would close over my tracks, as if I'd never existed. My flashlight hadn't been smashed in the fall. I flipped it on and turned its beam down one corridor selected at random. There were passages leading every which way. How was I to get out? No one would survive long in this hole. There were hazards associated with staying in one place and dangers of getting lost in what might be miles of underground corridors that had once been streets.

A phantom Ruth, eager to be photographed with me when news crews arrived on site, who stood by my side at awards dinners, vanished, laughing in a haze of Rambug and snake parts. No, my remains would lie in a heap beside an ashlar to be found, if I was lucky, before the earth collides with the sun. I decided to keep moving.

Down a short stairway, around a corner: mosaics of rams, red calves, fish with golden scales, gilt frescoes worthy of Nero's palace. High above me the beam of my flashlight illuminated a second bestiary, and among the winged serpents and central sphinx was a creature with the body of a bird, head of a lion, something in its talons that had been worn away.

I scraped dirt from a fresco with the edge of a small spade and then leaned against a lever or pipe of some kind that was flush against a wall. A low gurgling sound could be heard coming from somewhere behind the tile, and suddenly I was drenched by a rush of water, water that hadn't been turned on in over two thousand years. It was fresh and cold and poured over my head, soaking my shirt and all my equipment. A shock at first, where had the water come from? I was in the middle of a desert. Then the ancient spigot made sense. Mesopotamians developed irrigation, using a series of underground quanat channels and kariz, a network of smaller canals that relied on gravity to transport water, the sources being higher than the water's destination. The citizens of this place took it one step further by inventing plumbing.

The next hall I entered appeared to have been part of an arsenal. The implements resembled an armory of the comic book heroes my younger Flatbush Avenue self had collected and could have spent an eternity with these objects, making connections, inventing territories, superpowers, and battles. One object resembled the golden trident from Batman's Blue Devil, a demonic-looking set of mace clubs rivaled those of Hawkman from Justice League, a set of large, formidable hammers reminiscent of Steel's (from Superman) weapon of choice, and laid against a mottled wall were dozens of notched shields, similar to those used by the Mystery Man, Guardian of Metropolis.

Another series of open passageways led out from the armory, and eventually I came to what must have been a bath house. A mosaic of a bull balanced on the back of a giant fish glittered at the bottom of a pool. The earth was balanced on the horns of the bull, a reference to the Persian myth that explained earthquakes. When the bull grows tired, or in another version when humans overburden the earth with atrocities, the bull shifts the earth from one horn to the other. You would think the result of this action would be that, pierced by the horn, some kind a giant sink hole would dimple the Pacific or Sahara, but the answer is no. Not only did the movement of the bull produce seismic activity, but there were augurers who were called on to predict tremors and seemed to know when the bull had had enough of man's stupidity.

I passed through the nymphaeum, colonnaded porticos, elaborately carved stone structures, square water storage tanks, stucco houses, all populated by skeletons. While imperial powers engaged in skullduggery and building massive weapons, inconsequential citizens left behind readable footprints, just before they were trapped by some kind of Pompeian catastrophe, or a current of naturally occurring nerve gas floated over the city long before Archduke Franz Ferdinand was shot in Sarajevo. Those who stayed behind succumbed: inhale and you sleep forever. This inner part of the metropolis seemed pretty much intact.

The path began to slant downhill, and I had a sense I was approaching the walls of the city, or at least one part of the outer battlements.

At the edge of the city guards posted in towers see the horizon blur and unravel: horsemen, not traders, they decide, traveling in hordes, not caravans. Those on the edge have time to flee. There are no skeletons here. With catastrophe looming, sentries who'd been captured from as far away as Baghdad and Amman escape through the maze and return to their native countries. A nervous jeweler puts emerald chips in his shoes, packs only his chisels and flees in the middle of the night. His neighbor, a perfumer, fills his pockets with vials of attar, saffron, lotus powder, bitter almond oil, and chunks of resin. These scents will always remind him of the city. Along with a mapmaker and his five children, an oil merchant carrying a sack of olive stones, a coppersmith who walks out empty handed, the residents of the outer ring of the city who see and hear more, all depart taking whatever they imagine they'll need for their new lives. Even if the new lives are empty promises, sketchy at best, and the relics are only to be found scattered around the landscapes after their deaths, no one knows this yet. Those in the center go about their business as if the exodus from the periphery was carried out by delusionals only. They drink their coffee and believe the age of cataclysm is blissfully over. They had no language to fear a Pearl Harbor–like event, so they stayed.

Another path led me in a C-curve from the periphery to the center of the city. Increasingly narrow streets led to an airy piazza, water spewing from the mouths of marble lions and serpents, men and winged sphinxes. Running water, whether dripping from a cornice or gurgling from a fountain, was the only sound in the city; even my footfalls were muffled. I entered one house to find ancient bags of rice, spices, lumps of gum resin, a small ivory camel, and more human bones. As I walked deeper into the phantom city the semi-paved streets began to go uphill, turning into terraces. What would Ruth have done here? Hum the hip bone's connected to the thigh bone, the thigh bone's connected to the knee bone, and not worry about what couldn't be known for certain.

Climbing up narrow earthen steps to rooftops, I found storage jars used for wine and oil, a long silver ewer with a spout in the shape of a cheetah. Though not really tamable and now practically extinct, Asiatic cheetahs were used like hunting dogs for chasing wild sheep. People ate on their rooftops, a practice continued by Iranians during Passover. I picked up a thin, battered, wheel-shaped object that crumbled in my hands. Hopping from roof to roof humming the old Mickey Katz song *Pesach in Portugal*, which turned into *Pesach in Peshawar*, I must have passed out in some kind of delirium. When I came to under the remains of an archway, I looked ahead to see the city growing more illuminated, as if someone had flipped a giant switch.

A coruscating light seemed to be coming from somewhere, and according to my watch it was now morning on the surface. Walking in the direction of what might have been the source of the sunlight, I turned a corner to find a gap in the earth overhead. The opening was similar to the one I'd fallen through, but it was too far overhead to reach. I was now in an oblong yard, perhaps what might have been some kind of zoo. Elephant, camel, peacock skeletons lay scattered around. I leaned against a small tree that received enough light to grow underground. An elephant rib cage arched overhead a few feet from the tree. If I could climb the bones I might be able to reach a series of roots that threaded the opening and, swinging from those like a subterranean Tarzan, pull myself back out to the earth's surface.

The elephant's bones snapped under me. He was old and brittle, not a ladder. I moved some stones to buttress the remaining ribs and tried again. This time I was able to jump from the topmost rib to one of the dangling roots but my hands slipped off it, and once again I landed on my butt. I shouted. Nothing. A beady-eyed goat peered over the edge of the hole, then looked away. I lay on the floor and balanced hunger versus thirst, which should I give in to? I had a handful of salty pistachio nuts in a pocket, but the fountains were nowhere near my present location. Sunlight cast shadows of ancient animal skeletons on the walls. Turning my head I saw the remains of a human body that had not been reduced to a skeleton. Anyone could have fallen into the hidden city. I took a closer look at him. The man was wearing the long shirt, narrow trousers, shawl and turban of a Baluchi tribesman, and glasses still remained hooked to shriveled slices of ear. Due to the dry underground air he hadn't been reduced to bone, but it was difficult to say what color his skin had been. I took off his glasses and looked at the frames. The engraving on the ear piece was barely legible, but the lettering read Gunst-Optiker, Rosenthalerstrasse, Berlin. Clutched in his hand was what at first looked like a phoenix trampling an antelope. Its human-like head sprouted big ears and horns, sign of its divinity. The creature's wings were tipped with human heads, mouths frozen mid-roar. I rummaged through his pockets and found, among other things, a visa for Ramin Kosari and a leather-covered metal cylinder, about the shape of a child's kaleidoscope but larger. I put it in my bag, then pried the phoenix out of his fingers and took that, too. I had read the name Ramin Kosari before. He was the Nieumachers' guide. His remains were well preserved. He had no broken bones and must have become trapped in the city. I had found Suolucidir.

Twilight approaching, I had about thirty minutes of sunlight left, and then I would be spending the night, if not all the nights that were left to me on earth, with the body and the remains of an unknown number of animals. I leaned against the wall, took a deep breath, then turned so my nose faced the cliff, and tried again. The rocky surface was cracked here and there, enough for tenuous footholds, but I was climbing blind. I felt with my feet as if they were hands and the face of the wall were Braille. Halfway up, I fell again, so I shifted to a section of the cliff I could still see, where more plants grew out of the stone. If desert plants had taken root, then there were cracks in the façade, enough for foot and hand holds — possibly. A stem or stalk meant a root system had been slowly working to crumble stone. As I made my way up I felt for green bits and pieces I could no longer see. Finally, breathing hard, mouth full of dust and pistachios, I managed to shimmy and haul myself out of the city. More than forty-eight hours after my initial fall, I found myself lying on the surface of the earth back in the twentieth century somewhere in the middle of another small herd of goats. They were huddled near another crack in the earth enjoying the cool air that blasted from it, oblivious to the city and its secrets that slept just under their hooves.

In Persia, as in Egypt, the distribution of water was precisely regulated; hour-glasses were used to measure the length of time the farmers utilized the water and a system of sluices made it possible to gauge the volume of the water. Leo Africanus speaks of the measuring clocks that operated by water: "When they are empty the watering period is over." Mention is also made of skilled personnel and even teams of divers.

A History of Technology and Invention, Islam and Byzantium
Gaston Wiet, 1962

THE ZAFAR INSTITUTE WIRED MORE money. Working fever-ishly with the help of a local crew, the excavation began. For months I'd walked this territory, shovel clanging, while only a few inches under my footsteps rested the capitals, two bulls set back to back, of slender Persian columns, thinner and more fluted than Greek, of the great city of Suolucidir. I was sure this was it. The supports of this vast honey-combed metropolis were buried all over the land-scape, their bell-shaped bases hidden intact deep within the earth. The palace at its center with its colonnaded porticos was set on a high terrace approached by a double flight of stairs. The rest of the city spiraled out from this locus. During the excavation we learned my hypothesis was right: the Suolucidiris defended their city by con-structing a series of labyrinths, switchbacks, and elbow turns more circuitous than even those imagined to exist in the Burnt City to the north. I tried to get my crew to map out as much of it as possible and as quickly as possible. I attempted to find the thread of the path that led me to the underground zoo and the body of Ramin Kosari, but in the time left to me, the route was never successfully retraced, and no twentieth-century remains were discovered.

The English traveler Laurence Oliphant measured what he claimed were the ruins of an ancient synagogue at Deir Aziz in Go-lan in 1885. Oliphant was said to have been an unstable mystic, and his claim was all but forgotten. Nearly one hundred years later a con-temporary archaeologist found the site again, and his measurements were identical within a few inches. Mad Oliphant was right all along. Some people anticipate what they'll find, and so are blind to certain kinds of discoveries that contradict their expectations, but I believed the Nieumachers, and I was only following the measurements they'd laid out when no one had believed them either.

The city proved to be enormous. Around every turn lay some other spectacle; the friezes and statuary I saw before me the day I fell through the earth were only the beginning. Unfortunately, it was also the end.

Only the pen of a Macauley or the brush of a Vereschagin could adequately portray the rapidly shifting scenes attending the downfall of this ancient nation — scenes in which two powerful and presumably enlightened Christian countries played fast and loose with truth, honor, decency and law, one at least, hesitating not even the most barbarous cruelties to accomplish its political designs and to put Persia beyond hope of self-regeneration.

W. Morgan Shuster, *The Strangling of Persia*
Washington, D.C., April 30, 1912

ON NOVEMBER 4, 1979, HOSTAGES were taken in the American embassy in Tehran. They demanded that the Shah, who was in Egypt receiving treatment for cancer, be returned to Iran to stand trial. American flags and effigies of Mohammed Reza Pahlavi (though the exact physical template used by his Savile Row tailors remained untouched) were set on fire, and since the United States had supported the Shah, this shouldn't have really come as a surprise to anyone. Why were my co-nationalists so shocked and so angry? Even children wrote anti-American messages on the embassy walls and elsewhere. By July 1980 diplomatic relations between Iran and the United States had deteriorated. The Ayatollah Khomeini, who returned from exile in Paris to take over once the Shah was deposed, turned out to be, in his own way, just as brutal as his predecessor. Even in my remote corner of the country, individuals weren't invisible to the long arm of whoever was in power in the capital, and further excavation was becoming increasingly difficult, as people lived in fear of the army, the Revolutionary Guard, Khomeini's Basiji, and others I couldn't identify. Just as the door to Suolucidir creaked open after being locked and bolted for thousands of years, it was swinging shut again.

In Zahedan, where every market stall had had to post a picture of Mohammed Reza Shah Pahlavi, suddenly all those portraits, big and small, were reduced to ashes and smoke. Late at night, during an insomniac's ramble, I saw a lone orange fire, a solitary kebab man at the end of my street, enveloped by the smell of grilled lamb and advieh, a spice mixture of cumin, cardamom, ginger, and rose petals.

A Kurd, perhaps, he wore a black-and-white-checkered jamdani around his head. Leaning against a high wall of sun-dried brick, a second man laid out branches of dates, oranges, and bundles of henna leaves, and beside him another merchant polished his array of samovars, fluted and pinch-waisted; elongated passersby were reflected many times over in the silver and brass surfaces. Another man set up a line of narghile, coppery, engraved, silver and glass-bowled. The kebabwala threw a scrap to a dog.

I was working deep in the Suolucidir site when I heard someone yelling for me to hurry back to the entrance. We had to leave quickly. Soldiers were coming. The yelling got louder, more frantic. No militia of any kind had visited the city before, or at least not for thousands of years, and it was safe to assume these men weren't here for a friendly field trip. The shouting grew louder, I heard the sound of jeeps pulling up to the edge of the site, and running through the labyrinth as best I remembered it, I emerged to see soldiers herding some of the excavators into trucks while others were being questioned. I was the only American, but I no longer had my passport.

A soldier pointed his Kalashnikov at me and yelled I should stand in line with others on the edge of the pit. One by one each man was asked his name and to surrender his identity papers. I had thirty seconds to decide whether to say Ariel Bokser. Ariel Bokser, I'm American. I lost my passport, and no I haven't yet reported it missing.

It just came out instinctively with no premeditation. Ariel Bokser was back in the United States explaining that his accent had been acquired during years spent in Jerusalem living in an apartment above a falafel stand named Shushan. Ramin Kosari's papers had been lost or stolen. I groped my pockets like a cartoon character who's just been pickpocketed. The last thing I heard was an explosion near my head, and I felt a searing pain as I fell backward.

I passed out for the second time in Suolucidir. It was as if something in the underground city could snatch your consciousness if you weren't vigilant. When I came to, it was night. I'd been thrown over the side of the pit, landing on a mess of straw and sand. Around me were the bodies of six of my fellow diggers. They had been shot and then toppled over the edge.

A jumble of limbs lay under me. If I knelt to get up, my hands and knees pressed into someone's spine and shoulder blades. Finally standing, I backed away, retreating into the site. The passages were dark, but I made my way to the arsenal, where I picked six weapons and wrapped them carefully. They were among the most valuable objects we'd found. In the early morning hours I made my way back to Zahedan and left the tridents, hammers, and notched shields at the doorsteps of the six men who had been shot.

Arriving in Tehran from Zahedan without a passport, and with the American embassy under siege, I was trapped. My hotel was full of journalists hoping to outlast the hostage crisis, enjoying martinis poolside, comparing the backgrounds of their drivers and their skills at navigating parts of Tehran where you could get into trouble. They listened to tapes of Duke Ellington, Mahler, Sting, and Abba. They had photographs of Khomeini's family, of tortured corpses dumped in a street behind a half-burned-down movie theater, they had addresses of apartment towers where secret parties were held and where alcohol could be found and people danced like crazy until their drivers came for them early in the morning. I was in limbo, had the language to clink glasses with my compatriots as if I were in any random office celebration, but also stuck, unable to go forward or backward. The Zafar money was nearly depleted, and the person at the institute who was supposed to get back to me never did. I'd written about the killings at the site, but wasn't sure whether my letter had yet reached them or whether it ever would. One night I heard a story about an American woman in Isfahan whose passport was stolen along with all her clothes. She borrowed a chador and made her way to the British Embassy in Tehran, even traveling part of the way on foot, but she was able to get her documents and finally depart. Waking at sunrise the next day, I tried the British Embassy and was able to secure emergency temporary papers from the skeletal staff still going to work. I could now leave. But did I want to go? No, I didn't.

With just one day before my flight I called the university archive for the last time. Stating that my name was Kosari, I asked for Mr. Bastani as if I'd never had any conversations with the man before. I mentioned a payment that would accompany my access to the documents. He murmured a sound I interpreted to mean the sum I named could open certain doors.

"I'm afraid they aren't available for public viewing. In any case they're out on a temporary loan. Call back next week, and I'll see what I can do."

"But if they're loaned out then somebody must be allowed access." I asked him who'd borrowed the scroll, though I didn't expect an answer.

"They're being restored in a lab in another part of the city."

Restorers, as opposed to conservators, were notorious for destroying as they attempted to preserve. Christian monks used scotch tape on the Dead Sea Scrolls, doing so much damage, it was commented the parchments had survived more successfully underground for thousands of years. I was worried.

"It can be a slow process, as I'm sure you're aware, Mr. Kosari. Call back in a few weeks, just to be sure. I'm optimistic we can accommodate you sometime next month."

At night I could hear the sound of gunfire, and soldiers patrolled the streets. Tehran was motionless, as if someone put a spell on the city at nightfall, and almost no one went out on the street at all. On television people held pictures of the missing, hoping for information about friends and family members who had disappeared. On their way home from school, children dipped notebook paper in blood found on the street. They waved these small flags as they went on their way to let others know a demonstration a few blocks away had turned violent.

The next day I got a cab to the airport, sharing the backseat of the rattling old Paykan with all kinds of interesting stuff: an electric mixer, a radio, a small TV, a shoebox of GI Joe dolls, objects found on the street after the Americans left.

"If you know where they lived you can find strange and astonishing things: photographs of Jimmy Carter, hair dryers, an Elvis lamp with a beard painted on, furniture of all kinds, a Madras porkpie hat, which you shouldn't wear outside, since it will arouse the suspicion of those who watch the neighborhoods," explained my driver, a lean man with a long moustache. Many of his fares, in the past, had been American, and so though he spoke in Farsi, he said porkpie hat in English. "I wouldn't want to look like one of the fun-loving *Shahi* who ate gilded oysters filled with real pearls while Israeli soldiers fired on Iranian citizens."

He talked non-stop about the Zionist Iraqis at the border, the use he might have put the Elvis lamp to, but he hadn't, in the end, taken it. "What to do with such a thing?" We negotiated the price of the ride, and he threw in a couple of miles gratis, even if I was going back to my paymasters in Washington or Tel Aviv, he said. I hadn't fooled him. I wished the driver well and faced the crowds and security checkpoints.

At the airport it looked as if all the hotel rooms in the city had emptied out. Reels of Super 8 film, video and tape cassettes lay in piles, confiscated. My photos taken at Suolucidir were confiscated. Perhaps for the customs agent I was the kind of American who was so spacy that, while intending to travel to Kathmandu or Dharamsala, I had wandered into Zahedan by mistake, and so I deserved to have my things taken from me. Or maybe the confiscation was executed on nothing more than a whim. I'm not sure what value or significance the pictures would have had, but for whatever reason all my photographs and negatives were seized. I felt no remorse or regret because I was certain I'd be back.

I boarded one of the last flights out of Tehran having had what seemed like only a glimpse of the treasures of Suolucidir.

Somehow I got through Customs. I won't divulge here the manner in which the valuables taken from Suolucidir were hidden in my bags. Though nervous when I reached Kennedy Airport, it wasn't for nothing that my previously mentioned college roommate had also been a small time drug dealer whose contacts were ingenious in smuggling and devising hiding places — useful knowledge he had freely passed on to me, but I'd no reason to draw on until now.

But for sorrow there is no remedy provided by nature; it is often occasioned by accidents irreparable, and dwells upon objects that have lost or changed their existence; it requires what it cannot hope, that the laws of the universe should be repealed; that the dead should return, or the past should be recalled.

Sorrow, Samuel Johnson
Tuesday, August 28, 1750

SONGBIRDS HAVE ACCENTS. THE SONG of a Montreal robin sounds slightly different from the song of a Nova Scotia robin. With each generation there are slight changes. A robin raised in isolation invents his own song, and it doesn't sound very melodic, but over time, with each generation raised in isolation, slight improvements are made, and the song gradually begins to sound more pleasant to the human ear. Each bird knows how to imitate and improve. Experiments have also been done with the zebra finch and other birds. Finally each bird's trill converges to a species standard. Where, in each DNA strand, is the code for this song?

I was back, but I wasn't back.

Joe Lewis died in Las Vegas, subway workers threatened a strike, it was already freezing cold, and Ada Koppek kept calling, looking for Ruth, not remembering that she'd just rung and confusing me with her grandson, Adam, who was working as a pothead eighth-grade science teacher in Los Angeles. Ada complained that her vision was failing her. Ruth's grandmother was my only caller, and that was only because she didn't know who I was.

"Adam, Adam, why don't you know where your sister is?"

"It's Ariel, Mrs. Koppek."

"Ariel? I don't know any Ariel. What are you doing in my granddaughter's apartment?"

I explained to her.

"I don't remember Ruthie getting married. That I would have remembered. Why wasn't I invited?"

"You were there, Ada, really you were. You must have photographs somewhere in your apartment."

Ada was fantastically disorganized. Pictures were stashed in desk pigeonholes in between bills and receipts going back to the Nixon era. She used to know where everything was, but now it sounded like she was defeated by her own stacks of memories she didn't have the strength to sort through, so all were equally reduced to irritating detritus she couldn't get rid of.

"You danced with your cousin's husband, whom you hadn't seen in years. He spilled wine on your dress when someone knocked into him. It was an accident, but it really pissed you off."

"No," Ada said. "I'm a drowned rat."

I was on my way out to see Marcello Pagliero's *Roma città libera* at Bleecker Street Cinema, a 1946 movie about four characters wandering around Rome at night. For two dollars, you could sit in an air-conditioned room and see two movies, and wandering around an ancient city at night was an activity I was familiar with. Anxious to be on my way, while Ada spoke I punched my fingernails into the collection of Styrofoam cups collected on my desk. Crescents outlined eyes, nose, and mouth, teeth punched out. Kufic script written in fingernail impressions decorated another, random parabolas a third. On a fourth cup I'd engraved the Hebrew letters *lamed*, followed by *vov*, spelling *lamed vovnik*. The lightning-shaped *lamed* zigzagged down the side of the cup. Following the *lamed* I engraved a *vov*, the sixth letter of the alphabet, the Hebrew prefix that acts as a conjunction, the letter responsible for joining two halves of a sentence, sometimes linking two recalcitrant clauses that shudder when joined. At any given moment there are supposed to be 36 (twice 18, a number for miracles) *lamed vovniks* or holy men in the world. They may not know they're *lamed vovniks*, and they could be almost anyone: an ambulance driver cursing at the traffic, a drunk who runs into a burning building to save a stranger he only half heard cry out, the woman who puts children on a train out of the country and remains behind to an uncertain fate. Personally, I like to think *lamed vovniks* aren't perfect, each is flawed in some way. Andalusian Sephardim believed that if you found a rock shaped like a teardrop it was the petrified soul of a *lamed vovnik* who had suffered a great deal. So I sat punching *lameds* and *vovs* into a Styrofoam cup, as if doing so would will one to appear at my door. I missed the movie.

Hope dwindled for the fate of people I'd befriended in Tehran, Zahedan, and other parts of the country. In September 1980 Iraq began bombing Iran, and I followed the path of the explosions on the news and in the papers as best I could. Once again Suolucidir might have been saved by its isolation. Mines went off, chemical weapons full of nerve and mustard gas, agents whose formulas went back to the Battles of Ypres. The gas is heavy. It settles to the bottom of geographical depressions, poisoning low-lying towns, villages, train stations, cities only partially buried. The reporter described how you didn't smell the gas immediately, then it did its corrosive work. By the time you smelled the vapor, a process that took a few minutes, the damage to your lungs had begun. The screen blinked to footage of people coughing violently, unable to speak. The camera backed off. Outside the hospital, palms were split or sheared off to half their former height. Buildings of stone, steel, and clay were equally reduced to clouds of smoke in an instant.

I put on white gloves and unrolled the smuggled parchment that could so easily crumble to nothing. I'd barely looked at it until I returned to the States. I'd been afraid to open the cylindrical case while still in Zahedan, afraid once exposed to the atmosphere it would completely disintegrate unless examined in a controlled environment. Now I was confronted by the problem that, because the thing was stolen, I couldn't take it to the Metropolitan or any other institution that would ask questions about the object's provenance. With the images of gassed, inert bodies lying in village streets came the gradual sense that there would be no going back; those people and things I had assumed were in some way retrievable, were no more. I unscrewed the lid of the black enameled cylinder, its top and bottom rims rusty and corroded, marking my hands with stains and red rings that remained for days. As Alfred Döblin said of photographer August Sander, he created an atlas of instruction, and this, with unreasonable optimism, is what I hoped to find in the Suolucidir scroll, at atlas of everything Suolucidiri.

The first inches were as Sidonie Nieumacher had described them in her notebook: intertwined hands made of Hebrew letters giving way to blocks of text. What surprised me was that beyond a few inches the text was written in a Hebrew I was able to read. Like many Judeo-Persian manuscripts it would jumpcut from medical advice to Talmudic commentary to interpretations of dreams to a form of local gossip in verse, all in a range of styles from formal literary to colloquial. I sat at my table with a view of the clock atop the Williamsburg Savings Bank and began to translate the document before me, which at first explained a social system organized around a strict set of laws.

Suolucidir, a lost world extinct several times over, seemed reasonable and orderly with its judges, scribes, legal system with no intentional death penalty. These laws tied language to act to punishment. Capital punishment, when it occurred, was accidental, almost comic. Unlike the images of the war flickering on the television screen, the concept of retribution, to the isolationist Suolucidiris was an embarrassment, something you didn't talk about very much in public. If you ignore something long enough, their legal system seemed to say, it will depart.

According to their legal code, the Suolucidiris took literally the concept of eating your words, although their language didn't include that idiomatic expression. Neither could a Suolucidiri talk about eating his hat, or crow, or swallowing his or her pride. A burglar had to eat a clay tablet bearing the words for *thief* as well as a description of his crime; a killer was compelled to consume the word for *murder* and a narration of the circumstances leading to the crime; an embezzler, and apparently the crime existed even then, had to chew the phraseology for *cheat*, and so on. Depending on the chemical composition of the clay and the length of the crime's description, which could be extensive, the felon might be lucky enough to get off with just a stomach ache, but fatality was also a common outcome. Swallowing your words could kill you. Those falsely accused and convicted might protest, declaring the tablet before them represented neither their words nor deeds, but the luminaries who ruled Suolucidir enjoyed absolute power within the city, and their inedible words were final. There was one advantage to the Suolucidiri penal code. This wasn't even the age of incunabula, and obviously since there were no presses or means to reproduce copies, each piece of parchment or tablet remained essentially unique. Once consumed the record of the crime disappeared as well, so if the perpetrator lived, he was more or less granted a clean slate. Forgiveness was an important moral concept in Suolucidiri life, but the scribe who made the words that were to be eaten was enormously powerful. Since few could read, he could write whatever he felt like.

Specific examples followed the legal code, and here I began to wonder if the scribes did, from time to time, make things up. For example, and I translate loosely, Citizen Q is accused of making unwanted overtures towards Citizen L. Q makes suggestions. They should meet in the alley around the corner from the baths. L states she finds Q repellent: his vanity, self-absorption, lack of control. (He exposes himself in the middle of a crowd, he deliberately makes loud sucking noises when women walk by.) On one occasion he suggested what he claimed was a primo location for trysts, promoting its virtues by saying: the noise of running water covers all sound, it's a part of the city no one ever goes to, and so on. Q now says L is imagining things. He never uttered a remark more suggestive to her than have a nice day. Maybe a wink once in a while, but that's it. No law against that as far as he knows. Although Q annoys her no end, the commentator reports L has the cynical composure of someone who's sure she's facing a liar who will only choke himself given enough time. L accuses Q of stalking her, of lying in wait outside her house to the point where she felt she was a prisoner in her own home. Liar! Prostitute! Q shouts. Why would I do such a thing? You're not worth that kind of effort, that kind of desire and scrutiny — you're not worth it by half. The city is full of women just like you. What makes you think I would give you a second glance? Q continues to deny the charge, shouting: You can't make me eat words I never uttered. There were no witnesses who could say L was in the prostitution business. There were no witnesses to Q's alleged stalking her, although he had often been seen in the vicinity of her house. L seems at Q's mercy, overpowered by the accelerating rock slide of his accusations, but Scribe X notes that Q does seem obsessed with L. She isn't just anyone. She has something Q covets, something he wants to possess. Scribe X chuckles behind his glass of wine. With the bat of an eye he can have white clay fed to both of them. He writes, don't vomit on my feet and tell me it's a divine sign. Scribe X, they may not realize, is a god, at least for the moment. I remember the clay tablets found in Suolucidir still smelled 3,000 years later. Eating them must have been a frightening and nauseating experience. Perhaps so few of the clay tablets survived because everyone was a criminal, and so everyone had to eat his or her words. Maybe that was the true apocalypse for a city in which every citizen was guilty of something.

Citizen Q declares it's L who has a history of lying. Nobody takes her seriously. She, in effect, fucks everyone and anyone like crazy. Q is told enough already, you've made your point. This command could not have boded well for Q. L asks for it, he barges on. Look at her! Look at the way she dresses and stands. Q imitates L swishing down the street, his sandals flapping. He's a complete clown. Unfairly, I imagine him acting like Mel Brooks' very confident Thousand Year Old Man, and L's laughter, like a sucker punch, stops Q in his tracks, baffled. L's laughter at his mimicry disarms him, leaves his defense in ruins, makes him look like a liar or a fool, a role that doesn't advance his case at all.

Fools were the first to be fed white clay, choking on their words, their comic routines reduced to bile. On the other hand, suppose the accused, framed and convicted, survives the ordeal, but someone needed the ingested text to be destroyed. The ancient murderer, who knew nothing of digestion or anatomy, could not be sure the body would do this work for him, and therefore would personally resort to the blade to finish the job.

Out my window I could see a plane skywriting a series of letters that finally spelled out: *Luna Park*. I turned back to reading the scroll in my narrow rooms, as if it were no more rare or unusual than Sunday morning funny papers. The apartment next door had been broken into twice in the middle of the day. I'd been home during one incident and hadn't heard a thing. The safety of the scroll wasn't a major concern; rare would be the thief who knew or cared what the hell this thing was. In case of fire the scroll was kept in the freezer, which was usually empty anyway. On one occasion, my neighbor who lives on the floor below me nearly burned the place down when one of her candles fell over and ignited a dishrag. There's a fire house a couple of blocks away, and with little traffic in the middle of the night, they managed to get here instantly. My downstairs neighbor writes a syndicated astrology column, and even though she writes under a pseudonym and makes no bones (to me at any rate) about the fact that all her predictions are stabs in the dark, she's not the kind of person who will ever give up candles scented like vanilla, gardenia, and a chemically produced lemon that smells like floor cleaner. We all ran out into the street. While others worried about clothes, photographs, valuables and jewelry left upstairs, and how lucky we all were to get out in time, all I could think about was the contents of my freezer. The astrologist babbled, in black pants and pink shoes ready to go clubbing, to go see Stiv Bators at Darinka or 8BC, high as a kite: Virgo this, Capricorn that. No wonder she hadn't been able to predict the fire in advance. No flames licked the windows. The fire department contained the blaze to her place, and red-eyed, we all trooped back in. The phone rang. Ada Koppek, who else?

"Ada, we just had a fire here. I have a headache from the smoke. Call back another time." The building smelled of burnt astrology books.

"Darling," I could hear her playing with the silver links on her watch, "why don't you just swallow a tablet? Adam, my one and only grandson, a headache isn't the end of the world."

The fire was too large and potentially catastrophic an event for her to assimilate. She would skip it altogether. I agreed with her, yes, most definitely I'd made a mistake. I'll eat my words. The Williamsburg clock tower was shrouded in black netting, as it was being repaired, but I was aware of the time. I wanted to get back to work, to find out what would happen to Q and L.

"So do you know where your sister, Ruthie, is? I heard she's getting married."

"Yes, I know, I'm her husband. She's already married." I didn't tell Ada we were in the process of getting divorced. There was no point. It was more information than she could handle.

"Not you. To someone else. A Choiman. Listen, a Choiman from France. I told you. His uncles read Gerta from Nancy to Drancy. Who was Gerta?"

Translation: someone read Goethe from Nancy to the transit camp at Drancy. Ada was baffled. No one told her anything. She sat in the dark. But maybe she was right, and in a moment of lucidity she realized that she wasn't talking to her grandson, but to me, and Ruthie was, in fact, planning to marry Saltzman.

"Ada, I'm watching the news. Call me later." I hung up knowing Ada would forget the conversation we just had and call me again within the week. More pictures flickered across the screen: desert explosions, oil refineries on fire, a glimmer of an interview with an Iraqi soldier who hoped the war with Iran would end soon.

"Why don't you get out and walk?" Southern Gentleman Gambler
"You can't put me off a public conveyance!" Gatewood, banker

Stagecoach
John Ford, 1939

THE PHONE RANG AGAIN.

"Hello. Ariel Bokser?"

"Yes."

"This is Ariel."

"Who?"

"It took me a while to find you, but I'm at the corner of Neptune and Coney Island Avenue, at Mezzenotte Pizza. This is near you, no? I'm waiting. Come as soon as you can. We shouldn't be seen together, but we need to meet."

I recognized the voice and unmistakable accent before I had a chance to speak. The intersection of Neptune and Coney Island isn't near where I live, but I rushed out the door to the subway. A train was just leaving as I ran down the stairs to the platform. The platform, the subwayness of the subway made it difficult to retrieve images of the city almost halfway around the world. Every detail of my present city bombarded.

While I waited, leaning against a blue column, I noticed someone had made an origami swan out of a white gum wrapper. The tiny bird was stuck to the column with bits of gum, so it looked like it had stopped mid-downward-swoop. It occurred to me that I spent a lot of my life underground, and I was reminded of a song on a science record I had when I was a child. *The earth is like a great big grapefruit. Twenty-five thousand miles around. You could dig from here to China, if you could dig through the ground.* The lyrics were followed by tinkling music that was meant to sound Chinese, then the voice resumed by saying in a minatory tone: *But you can't.*

Ten minutes later the next train arrived, crowded because of the delay. A deaf mute entered the car honking a series of horns in a rendition of *Oh What a Beautiful Morning!* He moved his head back and forth in time, and he lurched when the train swerved. He must have suffered a stroke at some point in the past, because half of his face had fallen. "Yo, Harpo, c'mere," a man standing next to me shouted in futility as the deaf mute approached our part of the car, then we staggered toward him to put some coins in the paper cup, our change falling to the floor, quarters, nickels swallowed up, disappearing. It's rare to see subway performers this far out on the line, but then the deaf mute got off at the next stop, crossed over to the opposite platform, honking out his songs up the stairs in order to reverse his trip.

The train stalled between Kings Highway and Avenue U, but forty minutes later I was at Mezzanotte Pizza. The walls were covered with drawings of local people and celebrities who ate there: Tony Bennett, Abe Beam, Barbara Stanwyck, if you could believe it. Teenagers sat conspiratorially in one booth, an old man sat in another, but that was about it. No Rostami. I ordered a slice at the counter and asked if anyone fitting his description had come into the restaurant in the past hour.

"A guy who looks kind of like you?" the fellow at the cash register asked. He drew with a pencil whose silver finial was chewed down to a molar-shaped nugget.

I nodded.

"Yes, he was here for a while, then he left." He held up his sketch. On the back of a receipt he had drawn a picture of Javanshah Rostami. He was here.

I expected to hear from Jahanshah Bokser again, but in the days that followed not even Ada Koppek had any interest in talking to me. Rostami wasn't listed in the phone book under my name, his own, or some hybrid combination of the two, unless he'd devised an unknown anagram. The shells of Bokserness can easily be shrugged off like a snake's old skin, passport tossed out, lying in a landfill upriver. There are always those pieces of home under your fingernails that you don't want to clean, and leave as they are for as long as possible. Or you gather around you all the rags of your past life that you can muster until they become a kind of shelter. Rostami had left his children, his family, a longing greater than any I could imagine. Followed by now unemployed Savak agents, I imagined him as me reunited with Ruthie, teaching at a university with office hours and assistants to look up details about the Anglo-Russian Agreement of 1907 that divvied up Persia.

Sometimes I sensed a man or woman was following me, but it may only be that I was anticipating Jahanshah to overtake me, tap me on the shoulder. Once in midtown a woman in a leather jacket with very wide lapels and sharp-toed boots seemed to be only a few yards behind me. Every time I turned around, there she was. This went on for blocks. I watched out of the corner of my eye as if I were a garment district tourist looking in windows as I slowly made my way across 36th Street, taking in windows full of mannequin parts, felt hats, feathers and buttons, small plastic toys from Japan. There was a Pronto Photo at one corner that guaranteed one-hour processing time. A dusty cardboard blow-up of Cybill Shepherd on a bicycle occupied most of the shop's small plate glass window. She turned and held an instamatic camera, her expression hopeful, the edges of her blonde head frayed; she was larger than life. A man in a stained shirt and thick glasses entered the window to remove a projector from the display. He put his hand in Cybill Shepherd's crotch in order move her to the left. He saw me watching and winked as he wiggled his fingers in the cardboard shorts, but I wasn't watching him; I wanted to see if the leather woman was still following me. I turned around slowly, and there she was, but when I waved at her like a bobble-head with hands, she disappeared into an office building.

One night coming home late I was mugged, but it was a random mugging, the kind of thing that happens at two in the morning in the entrance to my building. The mugger was incoherent, but he had a knife, and took my wallet. He didn't threaten more than that, or force his way upstairs to ransack my apartment, looking for a Suolucidiri relic that provided an uncanny model for the construction and contestation of competing notions of the truth and crime.

Wearing surgical gloves I continued to unroll the scroll, but the Q and L story was left unfinished. What remained were just clumps of letters that didn't seem to form words anymore, at least not any I could find a translation for. Unless the remainder was written in another language, though the alphabet was the same, the writing no longer made any syntactical sense. I held the cylindrical case up to my eye as if it were a pirate's spyglass, then tossed it on the table. My neighbor's cat, who came in via the fire escape, played with the cylinder, found interesting smells in the decades-old leather. She sniffed it from end to end, batted it off the table, reached a long paw into the case, but it rolled under the couch. She was desperate for this new toy, so I moved the couch to retrieve it. Under the couch were dust bunnies the size of Mars, loose change, chewed pencils, subway tokens.

[Money] only made its way into certain sectors and certain regions, and continued to disturb others. It was a novelty more because of what it brought with it than what it was itself. What did it actually bring? Sharp variations in prices of essential foodstuffs; incomprehensible relationships in which man no longer recognized either himself, his customs, or his ancient values. His work became a commodity, himself a "thing."

Fernand Braudel
The Structures of Everyday Life, 1979

MONEY WAS RUNNING OUT. THERE was no institution or foundation that would fund work translating a stolen artifact. Necessities had to be balanced: rent, food, electricity, telephone, how long could each remain unpaid? Subway ads that ran headlines like *Need Cash?* or *Is Debt Your Middle Name?* beckoned. I wrote 1-800 numbers in the margins of papers but didn't make the calls.

I began to construct imaginary Suolucidiri relics, made from all kinds of junk salvaged from dump sites near the Gowanus Canal: a god made of bathroom tile (though the Suolocidiris weren't idol worshippers), a weapon made of orange insulating wire and rusted box-cutter blades, a funerary ornament from soles of Nikes hot-glued to a diamond-shaped piece of sheetrock. More exact might be a simurgh, the phoenix-like bird, made of gaskets, dead batteries stripped of their plastic coating, horns and claws made of dental picks and bent nails. My neighbor Alyssa, the astrologist, who had a habit of knocking on my door from time to time to borrow things, asked if she could photograph this ersatz simurgh. The idea of re-cycled, reinvented deities made of yogurt containers and electrical wire intrigued her. She didn't actually ask, but just appeared, camera in hand. I saw no reason to object, sure Alyssa, go right ahead.

There was a story Ruth had told me about a wealthy Mexico City doctor, a Dr. Saenz, who, one afternoon in 1966 received a phone call suggesting that if he flew to the town of Villahermosa in Tabasco, good news lay in store for him. He was interested, and he was fearless, no reservations tugged at his sleeves, no thoughts that anonymous calls directing you here or there might not be in his best interest. He followed the anonymous caller's instructions to the letter. When he reached Villahermosa, he was met by two men who marched him to a small private plane, and off he flew once again. Although the plane's navigational equipment was deliberately concealed from him, Dr. Saenz sensed they were flying farther south toward the Guatemala border, and he was correct. Landing on what could only have been a makeshift jungle airstrip, they were met by a group of local men who immediately offered Saenz a series of objects they claimed had been dug up recently. A man holding a rough wooden box was particularly persuasive, and Saenz opened it to discover a codex the man explained he had unearthed in a nearby cave. Most Mayan books, all but three, had been burned by the conquistators, so this was a spectacular find. Saenz snapped it up, but serious questions remained. When had the codex been hidden in the cave? 1532? 1962? The location of the cave was and remained unknown, so the authenticity of the Saenz Codex is still questionable.

You are free to imagine the contents of the last codex, the pages of symbols and drawings, the last evidence, like the last phone book, encyclopedia, catalogue of science, philosophy, religion, and pornography. A whole forbidden world in one book that may or may not be decipherable. Possible secrets: how to heal, cure, travel to other planets, etc. How to do everything that we aren't.

Once removed from its context in the site, whether a grave or a temple, it's impossible to know the meaning or use of the stolen object, Ruth had explained, as if I didn't know. She stole from sites, too, at least once. The thing's history is then erased, broken off, too much time between death and the present to follow any story, it could have been a doorstop or a cigarette case. Suppose you're offered a jade mask that you know was probably made to replace the head of a ruler who had lost his own in battles. When his body was discovered, his subjects buried him with jade replacement parts and five or six adolescent boy sacrifices, sealed alive in the tomb, that was the practice, and when dug up hundreds of years later, their skeletons were just by him, along with incised bones, obsidian flake blades, jade beads and stingray spines used for ritual bloodletting, or so you're told. Without actually traveling to the site and comparing chisel marks, footprints, depressions left in the dirt, you can't prove these things came from that particular place. Match between site and object can't be declared beyond a shadow of a doubt.

The object scuttles around the boundaries of its meaning: had it been used in ritual sacrifice or was it a can opener with a face? The mundane and the sacred jumbled together with no way out of the maze of connotation, no way to organize them into hierarchies, and the divine was often tied to the treacherous. I was busy constructing my own personal version of the Saenz Codex. Ruth would be the first one to taunt me, to ridicule the hot-glue gun and imaginary gods. I pushed my artifacts aside.

Sitting at my kitchen table circling jobs I had no qualifications for, finally led to an interview for a position writing voice-over scripts for a series of science programs: this is what happens when you mix thermite with liquid nitrogen, this is how the hip bone is connected to the thigh bone, these are the invertebrates that live in a range of underwater volcanoes in a section of the Pacific as big as New York State. I'd been late to the interview at a small company run by a woman whose desk and Steenbeck editing machine were one and the same L-shaped surface overflowing with reels and coffee cups. She, herself, was a flowering plant with jagged petals of rusty blonde hair and black-framed glasses, a perennial producer of projects, perhaps only a fraction of which ever got off the ground. In describing them to me, one sentence, half finished, led to the next, and so on. The principle behind the series was that any naturally occurring phenomenon, could be taken apart and explained in terms of its smallest parts: molecules, atoms, quarks. Protons, photons, futons, electrons, neutrons, wontons. Her partner, who handled the technical side of the company, produced special effects for commercials: the glow on Eveready batteries, the twinkle on Mr. Clean's earring. He was fed up with television ads and wanted to do something other than enhance or propel animated objects to make them more enticing to prospective consumers. Can you blame him? she asked me, though she didn't expect an answer. She inquired about my work in eastern Iran. In the words eastern Iran, she confessed, she heard only American hostages. It was an impossible jump cut. I told her the truth. I had been nowhere near the embassy where the hostages had been taken.

But what about meteors and fossil beds, my potential employer asked? Have you written about cloud formations, extreme weather (tidal waves, typhoons, hurricanes), evolutionary theory, the possibility of life on Mars? She played with Boris and Natasha Pez dispensers, explaining that she was trying to quit smoking, and the Pez candy gave her something harmless to suck on.

We need someone whose expertise is varied, she said, but nice to meet you, and we'll be in touch. It was over in an instant. I shook her hand and left to wait for the elevator in an empty hall paved with the kind of composite stone that looks like black vomit with white chips. If the city, just before it collides with the sun, becomes someone else's Suolucidir, then these crappy office towers are the nymphaneums, arsenals, temples, and coliseums of the future. Good luck, dude, trying to figure out what went on in these cubicles.

I decided to walk east to grab the F train. The fruit man, a big, bearded Dominican with a square face, long hair in a ponytail, stood on the corner of Houston and Broadway stacking bags of plantains and avocadoes. Paintings of pineapples and bananas still floated on the side of his stall, but there were far more people walking through this intersection than there had been before I'd left the city. A bank had replaced an old man who repaired sewing machines. A hardware store had become what looked like a showroom for shoes that resembled small sculptures you could hold in your hand. I still wasn't acclimated to large crowds. Then I saw her: Ruth, across the street, laughing, arm and arm with someone, another ponytailed man, though his was short and looked like a shaving brush. I took him to be Saltzman, but it could have been anyone. I didn't know Ruth was back in the city, but why would I? I started to cross the street to talk to her, then stopped, because I didn't know what I would say. Ruth, I found the lost city, I was left for dead in a pit, Ruth, call your grandmother? I turned on my heel and ducked into a bar that catered to tourists. It was dark and loud, but the swinging double doors were right there, so I stood at the zinc or zinc-ish counter and ordered a beer. A man in a sweatshirt that read, *If there's no gambling in heaven, I'm not going*, pored over a guidebook, and I was about to ask him if he needed directions when I heard a voice calling my name. My first impulse was to be happy to hear the cheery *Ash-shor*, but this reaction was quickly followed by a different instinct: oh fuck. It was Ruth, smiling as if glad to see me. She had cut off her hair and was wearing big silver Frida Kahlo–like jewelry. Her voice had a new slightly Mexican accent when she said words with r in them. If only I'd chosen another bar, or gone deeper into this one. Larry hung back a few feet away, holding a rolled-up newspaper in one hand while he put change in a telephone near the entrance, and looked up briefly to give me a smile that would only tax his face for a second until he got back to more pressing matters. Phone wedged between ear and shoulder, he had a concerned expression on his face, so I hoped the call would last a good half hour at least.

"I saw you from across the street. Didn't you hear me? How have you been?"

I ping-ponged the question back to her, though I didn't really want a response, and knew I'd get one whether I wanted one or not. She and Larry were only in the city for a week, then they would return to Mexico where they were now working, making a film about Augustus Le Plongeon and his photographs of Chichén Itzá. There was no monkey with a monogrammed case, but she was interested in the story about the platform of the Eagles and Jaguars high on the calendar pyramids, the spot Le Plongeon said was the burial place of Chacmool, prince consort to a dethroned Maya queen who had escaped to Egypt. From the Chiapas to Ghiza, they planned to follow a footpath of memes. They had gotten enormous amounts of grant money from Kodak. When she asked me what I was doing I told her I had a job producing films for NASA on interplanetary travel. I was so preoccupied figuring out how to illustrate jumping from Jupiter to Mars, in other words, that I hadn't heard her call my name.

"I saw you last week on the Q train platform at Union Square, and yelled your name, but you didn't turn around then either. Your train came, and you disappeared." While pronouncing this sentence she became annoyed, accusing me of avoiding her, of making our

75

split more of a cataclysm than it needed to be. Insisting that the un-paid delinquent taxes and late fees that still dogged her, all of it was my fault, I'd disappeared into what was it called? Soul Disappear? Sole Sidur? No, Suolucidir. Okay, yeah, where should she send all the letters from the IRS? The gust that began sort of friendly turned into a tornado: your enthusiasm is like a firehose, you don't take anyone else into account, she shouted over the man in the gambling sweat-shirt who was asking the barmaid how to get to Grand Central. He wanted to take a train, not a shuttle, and didn't seem to understand that the shuttle was a train. Why are you telling me all this now? I shouted. Ruth kept raising her voice. She remembered when she wanted our apartment to be a meat-free zone, and I brought home smoked shoulder of something, some animal, just to spite her, and the apartment was filled with the smell of meat, spicy and salty, the air made you hungry every time you inhaled. The time I left her waiting at the airstrip because in my experience, arriving flights to central Chichén Itzá were always late, and I assumed her plane would be, too. I'd landed a few weeks earlier in order to set up camp, so I knew the odds of an on-time arrival were small. How was I to know that one time the plane would be on time? Ruth was alone, pacing the airstrip in front of a small one-room structure that served as a station, you couldn't really call it an airport. Even the woman who sometimes sold polenta and chilies wrapped in banana leaves to pas-sengers, even she was gone. Ruth had steam coming out of her ears. It was not an image I wanted to remember. I began to wish Larry would get off the phone already and tell her they needed to leave immediately in order to make a bus to Susquehanna to see a man about a hat company.

"I didn't take a Q train last week. I never take the Q and less than never from Union Square. It must have been someone who looks like me."

"No one looks like you."

"Thanks."

"Don't thank me, I didn't have anything to do with it."

"I figured." It was familiar joking banter, and though she smiled almost sweetly, full typhoon averted, when she spoke, I glanced casually at my watch, calculated that if I didn't leave soon the conversation would spiral and include the new boyfriend, so I left Ruth with my half-finished beer, tipped my hat at Larry, still on the pay phone as I passed him on my way out.

When I got to my building the astrologer was leaving her apartment, taking out a stack of old newspapers, archival evidence of her columns giving love and money advice for a future that will never happen.

"Are you having work done in your apartment?'

I shook my head.

"Someone was making a racket up there."

"When?" I shouted at her as I leaped up the stairs two at a time, looking down at her hair dyed in olive and grape-colored feathers. She shrugged.

The door was ajar. I only had to look in at the stuff thrown all over the place in my apartment to know the refrigerator door would also be open, swinging in the breeze, orange juice concentrate melting and pooling into a small lake. The scroll and the simurgh were gone, as was Sidonie Nieumacher's notebook, and Rostami had left no forwarding address.

"Ariel? Thank God it's you. I'm still looking for Ruthie, and now I'm getting very worried. Did you see the paper this morning?"

"No, Ada, no, I haven't read anything yet."

"There's an obituary for Ariel Bokser, a thirty-six-year-old man who lives in Brooklyn, left an ex-wife and a stepmother behind, but no other relatives."

"It must be someone else because you're talking to me."

"Well, I don't think so. It sounds just like you. How's your stepmother?"

"I don't know I haven't talked to her in a while."

"A strange woman. She argues with everyone, and she can't stop talking. It's like there's a button on her butt, and when she sits down you can't shut her up. I don't know what your father saw in her. You can't trust Tchoimans."

Ada, who often appeared to be easily steamrollered, but in fact was no pushover, said this about a lot of people. The truth was I didn't know my stepmother very well and needed to get the paper to see if I'd died overnight, but Ada diverted from the subject of my demise, carried on about my stepmother, a woman she'd only met at my wedding — an event she otherwise claimed to have no knowledge of.

"If she told me once, she told me a hundred times that Bokser means carob, a tree that doesn't bear fruit for seventy years, so you plant knowing that even though it will offer you nothing, the tree will benefit someone in the future. Like by telling this story she proved that she, a Bokser by second marriage, was providing for her grandchildren while the rest of us were deadbeats. What she was really doing was stealing from you and Ruthie."

"Ada, are you at home?"

"I'm not going anywhere." She sighed, remembering our conversations were often short. "Call me if you hear from Ruthie."

I borrowed a paper from my neighbor's doorstep and quickly turned to the obituaries. It was true. Ariel Bokser had died, no memorial service, no dearly missed stepson, etc. Just a short notice:

Deceased: Ariel Bokser, Aged 32. Born May 19, 1950 Brooklyn, New York. Died suddenly of unknown causes, March 18. Graduated from the University of Chicago. Did field work in Iran. Survived by former wife, Ruth Koppek Bokser of Mexico City and stepmother, Miriam Raub Bokser. Contributions can be sent to the Zafar Institute.

I didn't know whose body was found in the Gowanus Canal. It couldn't have been Rostami, because Ruth had seen him (mistaking him for me) waiting for a Q train at Union Square. Assuming Rostami wanted to shed Bokser, but didn't want to kill me, perhaps he'd found some anonymous shmuck on whom to plant my passport, fake tax returns, whatever, and put an end to him, so Rostami could become Jahanshah again. Well, it's a theory. Now I, too, was going to have trouble being Ariel Bokser. I could no longer apply to the Zafar Institute in order to return to Suolucidir, for one thing. I was floating, like a man walking on a wire between tall buildings, or only navigating the possibility of a short drop between sawhorses weighted down by sandbags, not sure whether the risks of reinventing myself were life-shattering or more inconsequential than one might think.

Pin Trays (first half of the nineteenth century), although they are authentically of the seventeenth century; nonetheless, this description leads one to believe they were in fact used as pin trays in the period indicated by the antiquaries of Pittsburgh, Pennsylvania.

Apollinaire's version of *Cinderella*,
cataloging the fate of her renamed squirrel-fur slippers

"MY TELEVISION ISN'T WORKING, AND I need to watch the Iran Contra hearings." Alyssa, who lived downstairs, was at my door holding her cat, Catullus. This seemed out of character for an astrologist; perhaps it was just an excuse. Alyssa was wearing a striped man's shirt over black tights, not something she would wear on the street, I'm guessing, possibly something one would sleep in, so it did occur to me that watching the hearings wasn't the only reason she'd knocked on my door.

"Sure, Alyssa. I was just about to turn them on." This wasn't exactly true, but my apartment was small, and if one person was watching television, everyone else present was as well. I flipped on the set, fiddled with the channel until Oliver North's gap-toothed hound dog expression filled the screen. His voice trembled, he pointed to the ceiling and talked about his willingness to meet Abu Nidal anywhere at any time.

Alyssa flopped into a chair and put her feet up on the table, littered with my artifacts constructed from found junk. I looked at her feet, but she was oblivious. Among the pieces of tile, bottle caps and the hot-glue gun was a letter from the Red Cross office in Zurich that still handled queries about possible World War II refugees. She picked it up and looked at the envelope.

"A registered letter? Ariel? Do you owe someone a lot of money?" She flicked the envelope making a snapping noise as fingers hit the return address. "Are you studying to be a doctor? We'll be sorry to see you leave, but Zurich is a cool place. You can hang out at the Dada café, Apollinaire's, around the corner from where Lenin plotted the revolution."

"It's Café Voltaire, not Apollinaire." Who was the royal *we* who was going to miss me when I left to work for the Red Cross in Swit-zerland? Alyssa and the spirits?

The letter confirmed that a Bruno and Sidonie Nieumacher had been students in Berlin, moved to Marseilles, and a year later were listed as passengers on *Le Faroan*. The dates of the International Red Cross records and the dates in the Nieumacher documents coincided.

"If you can predict the future, why do you need to watch? I mean don't you already know the outcome?"

"That's not what I do. I just write an astrology column."

"But it's related."

"Not really. I've told you before, my horoscope predictions are all pretty much made up, and listen Ariel, that's just between you and me. Give it a rest, hey, I want to listen to this." But she got up from the chair, walked into my kitchen, looked through my fridge, found some orange juice and vodka, and made herself a drink.

"Make yourself at home," I said.

"Well, I wasn't sure you would offer. I'll make you one, too. Actually, you may find this hard to believe, but I've found watch-ing the hearings helps me with my work. My column's not all love and romance and money, money, money, mo-ney." She sang the last words to the tune of the O'Jays song. "You've seen Fawn Hall," she said. "If I looked like Mrs. Oliver North, and my husband had a sec-retary who looked like that, fuck Iran, I'd be worried about some-thing else."

The astrologist walked back, paused to swallow, then handed me my drink.

"So I write: Taurus, watch out for a threat to you that is present in a loved one's life. Perhaps you never thought about this person. He or she could be someone you overlooked or took for granted, but they might very well spell trouble."

So that was how it was done. I was impressed.

"Did you watch any of North's testimony?" she asked.

I nodded. I had seen Oliver North testify that he met Iranian arms merchant Manuchar Ghorbanifar in a men's room, and it was here, leaning against a wall graffitied with initials, penises and jokes about bodily fluids, that Ghorbanifar had given him the idea to divert profits from Iranian arms deals to the Contras.

"A men's room. I ask you," Alyssa commented, though she didn't say what exactly she was asking. "Reagan uses an astrologer to make decisions. I'd bet my life on it." She didn't have a very high opinion of her colleagues. I began to realize this was just a day job for Alyssa, though I never found out what she did when she wasn't writing her column.

"Sometimes you have to go above written law," Fawn Hall squeaked into her microphone. "You have to heed a higher law."

"What fucking higher law?" Alyssa shouted at the screen. She sounded like my grandfather, a cranky *alte kahker*, yelling at the radio during the McCarthy hearings, the Rosenberg trial, when election returns were announced. "Dumb shite. Look at that hair! She looks like she's got a Pekingese puppy sitting on her head."

Hall had shredded a stack of documents relating to the illegal war against Nicaragua, a war effort funded by the sale of arms to Iran. The known dimensions of the stack measured a foot and a half high, but it was probably bigger, and included memos, codes, telephone logs, notes of all kinds. This speaks of spectacular patience and stamina in the face of a boring, time-consuming, repetitive task. Fawn Hall, patriot and former Playboy Bunny, had the strength of her convictions. Sometimes pouty and biting her lip, yet Hall voiced no doubts that she had done the right thing. Confident of the body she inhabited underneath the loose shirt and tight skirt, she invited anyone who watched her to imagine her standing over the shredder, long fingers slipping one document after another into the moving blades, long strips of confetti coming out the other end.

"These are like the people who advertise on late night TV or in the margins of magazines, promising miraculous vegetable peelers, extra sharp knives and certified gold dust for sale." Alyssa insisted on the banality of the players on the screen that night, they were too fundamentally bland to be perverse, too empty to house dark secrets, no gargoylish imps scampering around in their brains. "Believe me, I'm an astrologist," she said, "though not a committed one," and I laughed with her, though I wasn't convinced the parade of the indicted and subpoenaed were just any old anybodies for whom the sale of missiles (huge profits skimmed off the top) to Iran was just a day at the office.

We argued back and forth for a while. The masterminds were very ordinary people who wiped inky fingers from reading newsprint off on their pants and then took out the trash, or, no, they were devils of ingenuity and originality, architects of secret second governments, coups, the man or men behind the curtain. Alyssa made herself another drink, then fell asleep on the couch. I touched her shoulder, close enough to smell her orangey breath, but she didn't move. The big shirt wasn't big enough to cover her butt when she snoozed on her side. It hiked up to reveal a band of sunburnt skin. When she woke Alyssa would be embarrassed to find she had conked out on my couch. My neighbor liked to present herself as the kind of person who could eat nails for breakfast, but I turned off the television and let her sleep. Her olive feathered hair was brown at the roots, and her ink-stained hands were partially hidden under her head. Catullus was nowhere to be found.

Alyssa stopped me in the hall. She had signed for a flat package, a ten-by-fourteen-inch envelope, but she admitted she'd been sitting on it for awhile.

"How long have you had this?"

"A couple of weeks. I hadn't seen you, so I held onto it. I could have shoved it under your door, but the envelope is thick, as you can see, and might have torn if I really pushed it, and you never know. What if you got broken into again?"

"What if you knock into one of your candles, a rug catches fire, and you burn the place down?"

Alyssa ignored me. She worked from home, everyone in the building knew this, so it was assumed she would sign for deliveries. I wonder how much mail traffic found a home in her column. *Virgo: You will get something important in the post, possibly bad news. Ignore it.* She followed me up the stairs chattering about the Chernobyl disaster. In her column she had written: *Capricorns: Beware of explosive and poisonous workplace situations. This could be time to consider a new form of employment.* It looked like she was going to follow me inside.

"So who's writing to you from Iran? Are you an arms smuggler? There's no return address, but I looked at the stamps."

"Yes, bombs are mailed to me in packages just like this one."

"It's too small."

"These are only bomb-making instructions. I run a Do It Yourself operation. The bigger operators have warehouses out in Queens and live on Park Avenue. I'll tell you about it later."

"When later?"

"Maybe tonight. Thanks for signing for the package." She lingered in the doorway as if she expected me to invite her in, so I would open the package in her presence. I didn't want to be rude to Alyssa, but was compelled to practically shut the door in her face.

"I'll bring the vodka this time," I heard her say in a singsong voice from the stairs. I opened the package. Inside was a long letter in Farsi.

Dear Ariel,

I'm very sorry we weren't able to meet while I was Ariel Bokser. Your country was generous to me personally and for that and to you, of course, I'm grateful. By giving me your passport, I'm certain you saved my life. However on a snowy Monday evening evidence of your return made the urgency of my repatriation more acute. I learned quite by accident that you had come back to your city of origin. Walking past a storefront gallery on Avenue B I saw a large black-and-white photograph of a creature, a kind of totem made of dead battery innards, wing nuts, bent nails, horns and claws bristling with shreds of steel wool. It had a half human, half canine face, wings and talons, more leonine than bird-like. Was it meant to be a simurgh? At first I didn't think this obscure symbol displayed in a narrow window could possibly be such a thing, but then I stepped closer to the glass. A small card posted below said the object in the photograph had been made by Ariel Bokser, and then I knew that it was signal, random and coincidental, odds against the indicator reaching its intended target were small, but nonetheless, the sign told me you were back. If I'd taken a different walk, I'd never have known. Why you would make such a cartoonish object, a parody of what you had searched for years ago, I didn't know. As walnut-size clusters of snow fell to the sidewalk I felt very far from home, and knew it was time for me to return no matter what the consequences. Perhaps there is room enough in the world for more than one Ariel Bokser, but despite all you sacrificed for me, the Bokser suit with its wide lapels and baggy pants was beginning to feel like a style I could no longer inhabit. It was time to turn it in.

But first let me tell you a little bit about my life as Ariel Bokser, to explain something of what I did in the five or so years that I was you. You have a right to know what I did and how I lived under the umbrella of your identity, so I will give you a short account of my travels.

Upon arriving, nearly penniless with no place to live, I fell in with a couple of cab drivers who knew about a squat on

Avenue C. A few other drivers, illegal Punjabis, lived in this place. They kindly informed me there was space on the fifth floor, knock on door C, and so I made my way up stairs worn to the point where because of an aggregation of dirt and garbage, the stairs were more of an incline with footholds rather than clear steps that met sharp ninety-degree risers. The hallways on the lower floors will one day be an archaeologist's dream: layer upon layer of paint seen through banana peels, sprayed names, obscenities strangely absent, a mural of Che Guevara shaking hands with what might have been a local notable whose wing feathers shone silver and white. Boughs of wires that led through cracked windows to streetlights from which electricity was pirated, these festooned the ceilings. When I reached the fifth floor the decoration changed. Here walls were plastered with black and white posters for someone called Eek a Mouse, Durutti Column, Scritti Politi, Cocteau Twins, the Del Byzanteens. (I corrected spelling with marker. Even I know this word in English.) Later I asked the Punjabis if this was some kind of dialect, but they shook their heads. They knew little of what went on in the heights of the upper floors.

A very tall man dressed in a gorilla suit opened the door to 5C, and yes, they had room. He introduced himself as Phoenix, and told me the only other person living there at the moment, was his girlfriend, Daisy. His accent was hard to place. South Effrica? I asked. He sounded like an engineer I'd met from Johannesburg while working in the west of my country. (The Shah imported experts from all over the world.) No, he answered, he and Daisy were from Australia. They had an extra mattress on a floor in one of the rooms, and this I was welcome to as long as I needed it. Phoenix had a job that required him to wear this suit for one day only. He had to stand on a corner and pass out small pieces of paper, notices of a sale on something called deluxe sound systems; discounts, the paper stated, that would make you go ape, though why you would want to enact this evolutionary regression to sell objects, I never discovered. I didn't understand, and he had neither the time nor the patience to explain, he simply told me, "Samir, buddy, it's National Gorilla Suit Day." Where he got the idea my name was Samir, I don't know. I had introduced myself as Ariel. Phoenix left for work, but his girlfriend, Daisy, was just getting up. The apartment had many rooms, wires everywhere, as I mentioned, to convey stolen electricity; water came like magic from who knows where, since no one was supposed to be living in the crumbling warren of flats. I didn't know Americans domiciled in piles of old bricks and cardboard, more or less.

I sat on the floor until Daisy came out of the bathroom wearing almost nothing. Before he left, Phoenix had yelled through the door that Samir was here from India. She was of the conviction that in India people are more open, she later explained to me, so it was okay to walk around this way. I tried to think of nakedness the way Ariel Bokser, a man who grew up with bikinis and short skirts, would think of it. No big deal, right? But this was blonde nakedness. Maybe it was nice that she could walk around like that, feel the breeze all over her skin. I tried not to think of nakedness in terms of my reaction to it, but rather as a matter-of-fact thing for her. Well, I tried. Obliviousness, was one of Daisy's great talents, but may also be her downfall. She was the kind of girl with the heart of a rabbit who might enjoy the midnight party scene in Tehran, but wouldn't ever notice the police tailing her. In fairness, not everyone did, but you know what I mean. It turned out that Daisy had the day off and did not need to put on a costume of any kind. She made fried eggs with chili peppers and curry, hoping it would remind me of home, and that home was something I would want to be reminded of. This was a charming, if misguided, act of kindness.

I insisted my name was Ariel. Okay, whatever you say. That was the end of it. Clearly Daisy and Phoenix didn't believe me but were going to accept whatever I told them.

Phoenix and Daisy were acquainted with a few things about Iran. Savak, agency of torture, they knew, just as they knew about the Ton Ton Macoute in Haiti, the Somocistas in Nicaragua, death squads in a variety of countries I was ignorant of.

They complained of the short memories of their compatriots regarding the hostage crisis at the American embassy in Tehran. What did one expect, they said, when, via the CIA, the United States supported the Shah? At night Phoenix worked at a place called the Pyramid Club setting up musical equipment or something to that effect, and Daisy wrote a zine that she photocopied at her temp job. Life for Phoenix and Daisy was always summer, at least that was the impression they gave.

They were fanatic about something called health food that they bought from Prana on First Avenue, and though it would have been easy to shoplift there, this was not something they would do. They would steal from power companies, but never small shops. Not a bad credo when you think about it. Here among cardboard cartons of root vegetables and bottles of vitamins worked students of massage and acupuncture, and former Hare Krishnas. The owner has a big heart, Phoenix said, and gives work if you need it. I once asked Daisy what is food that is not health? The talk she gave was illuminating in its far-reaching implications. Corporate chemically manufactured food substances, made mainly of sugar and corn have tentacles in every aspect of American life, apparently. The way these substances were described to me I had images of astronauts on feeding tubes, and yet when I traveled, large supermarkets with bright lights and taped music made on instruments, if they were instruments, I couldn't identify, were sources of great confusion for me. So even if Daisy was spinning one of her conspiracy theories, maybe she was right — or I was hopelessly depressed when I would later visit these big concrete emporiums where large people pushed carts full of Coke bombs, ground meat sold on plastic containers the size of trash can lids, liquid cheese that would emerge from squeezable bottles similar to the way you package glue. Not knowing how to decide, I would leave without buying anything, not being able to choose between each slick and shiny surface. In Zahedan bread, olives, dates all bore the fingerprints of whoever kneaded, picked, or soaked them in brine. Here food appears as if extruded from a nozzle of some kind.

The months on Avenue C, however, were relatively easy going, though not happy, how could they possibly be? But it began to feel like a kind of home. The lower floors smelled of Punjabi cooking. Phoenix and Daisy were friendly with the various inhabitants: the Korean war veteran who had what he called a recycling business in the basement, runaways from Seattle who worked off the books as bicycle messengers, an elderly Neapolitan who never migrated to the boroughs or suburbs decades ago, he was the last one left of that generation. He was so old he'd abandoned all his English and had lapsed into a dialect no one understood. The bicycle messengers brought him food from Mulberry Street where some *latticini freschi* owner still remembered him. A Guatemalan man and his brother spent a few days before a van took them to Vermont to work at a ski lodge at the top of a mountain cleaning the restaurant, running the ski lift, and making hot chocolate and coffee drinks, or so they had been told. They had never seen snow before. Many languages were spoken in the building, but none of them Farsi. I was surrounded by friendliness, but everything was unspeakably foreign, and to be honest, there were moments when daily life was a translation from nonsense into nonsense. I had no ability, as Phoenix would say, to just go with it. My isolation eluded definition in any language.

Eventually, still maintaining I was Ariel Bokser, I did tell them something that revealed my past as a geologist. It was the occasion of the Mexico City quake. Their television had been retrieved from the street, from a tonier neighborhood where on Thursday nights Phoenix and some of his friends would rove from block to block and find amazing trash left out for the Friday morning garbage pickup: perfectly good appliances, clothing, books and records of all kinds, some even quite valuable. I still have a copy of *Brave New World* gleaned from one of these outings, though I suspect the signature, *Love Forever Aldous*, was some high school student's idea of a prank. The Sony Trinitron was a big boxy thing, and we could never get it to work in color, but we did watch its jumpy, grainy pictures once in a while.

Daisy had been to Mexico City, and she was both terrified and intrigued by this idea: what if her current city suffered an earthquake of the same magnitude? What mountains of broken buildings and rubble would be formed into what the Punjabis called Himalayan proportions! I allayed her fears, though I didn't really know what I was talking about entirely, but told her some mishmash about shifting tectonic plates, underwater volcanoes, Ice Age glacial deposits, and that she sat on an unmoving bedrock of gneiss and schist. Okay, Daisy said, I can fix you up. Let me fix you up. I can get you a job related to your field, sort of.

It amazed me in your city how one thing led to the next. This was not, in my limited universe, a system of patronage, bribes, jobs attained or deals made via a spider's web of social connections, or reliance on family ties. I'm sure this impression is quite false, but that was my experience. It was through Daisy that I began working street fairs selling rocks and semi-precious stones, and from here on Daisy and Phoenix exit my story.

I shared a table with a woman named Cindi, a friend of Daisy's, though they were very different and rarely spent time together. Such is the nature of friendship when you're constantly, as Cindi said, on the go. Daisy did not entirely approve of her friend, who took things at face value, a bull in the china shop of more nuanced, subtler ideas, who was blind to the conspiracies around her, but Daisy wanted to help me out. Cindi was an old pro at this business and had been working the fairs for many years. She was a big girl whose jeans split from the strain, and she smelled of the bleach she painted on them. When one pair disintegrated she would cut off the rhinestone patches and sew them on the next pair. You can interpret this as attention to detail, interest in recycling, or parsimoniousness, but it was one of my first images of her, a large woman bent over a wrinkled lump of blue material, needle held high above her head, electric light glinting off those tiny glass chips. She looked up and said, you must be Arielovich. When she smiled I noticed she also had a rhinestone chip embedded in one of her front teeth.

On her own since she left high school, Cindi (i's dotted with circles) called herself a businesswoman, too busy for romance, but in truth she was always in one's face, is the American expression. We managed the table together, but she was a harsh piece of work. I kept my distance from her, as did most men, I would guess.

We sold cheap birthstones, geodes, polished lumps of jasper, turquoise, carnelian, tiger-eye, and moonstones. We also sold some bigger items: malachite bookends that looked like chunks of green swamp, small electric fountains, fake jade Buddhas, lamp bases made of agate soaked in sugar and sulfuric acid to bring out the black rings. 17,000 bands per inch, Cindi would tell a customer, a piece of petrified Jurassic history right in your living room. A certain kind of guy really went for this approach. Crystals were very popular with women. Regardless of what they picked up, Cindi would say, That's a very special stone you've found there — or maybe it found you. This is a piece that radiates positive light. Or, if the customer looked perturbed, uncertain, she would say, With that stone you'll find the nature of your burdens released: it absorbs negative energy. Don't ask me how, but it does. Most people seemed to buy this. Once I began to tell a customer that Greeks called quartz *krystallos*, clear ice. They believed the rocks weren't rocks at all, but a form of ice, so hard, melting was not one of their features. Cindi became very quiet, but as soon as the girl put the stone back in the bin and left without buying, Cindi, snapped at me: Ariel, Arielof, Arielofsky, Ariel El Habibi, Bin Ariel! In the future let me do all the talking! You say all the wrong things! You blow it all the time! I lose business because of the stupid bits and pieces you think people want to hear! I didn't tell her that saying the wrong things in some parts of the world isn't about whether or not someone buys a thirty-five-cent bit of mineral, but can cost you your life.

We would only accept cash payment. Cindi bought the rocks from a supplier in the Bronx whom I never met, and she kept track of where and when the fairs took place. These street fairs are the American souks, stuffed bears and inflatable rabbits replacing the jazvahs and hookahs of my childhood, but if this sounds satiric and unfair, making fun of cheap thrills and toys, that isn't my intention. Comfort can be found in an inflatable rabbit, and comfort can be a very rare commodity. From time to time a plane would write the name of the fair in the sky overhead: *Meadowslands Circus, Willow Creek Fairgrounds, Mermaid Avenue: Noon to Midnight.*

So this Cindi, friend of Daisy, who lived off caramel corn, hot dogs, and Sprite, and listened to something called Gang of Four, which I believed was a group of Chinese officials, but was actually a group of musicians, knew all kinds of places to hide cash, so we wouldn't get robbed. Robbery, when you have a cash business, was always a problem. She was also expert at catching the sticky-fingered who would pocket stones from our array of bins. Cindi liked to say she knew a dickhead from a dickwad, but I never asked her to explain, please, the niceties of difference. I worked with her for a little over a year, learning to make do with tea that tasted like metal filings and the odd halal shwarma stand. The Pakistani operators gave me food gratis. I insisted they take from me a handful of beryls, citrines, tourmalines, whatever I had from our sorry inventory that was genuine and worth a little something.

I'm sure you can understand I was very homesick. Cindi had no family, a mother killed by a drunk driver many years ago, a sister who had disappeared, no idea where she was and didn't care. This was something very hard for me to understand, how can you function without a network of aunts, uncles, cousins, grandparents? When I heard this story I felt very sorry for her, especially for a woman, this state of unmooredness is dangerous, but she seemed to feel the idea that "there was no reason for existing like the tip of a lone iceberg" to be what she called a sore point. What's the big deal? I heard this tip of iceberg expression all the time.

While working fairs, Cindi also taught me the art of picking locks. She had learned this on her own by studying locks, taking them apart, examining the internal mechanisms, then putting them together again. It was like a science for her. She carried an assortment of basic keys, lock picks, and other tools either in her pocket or in a plastic bag that said, *Thank You Come Again* on it. Don't worry, I was never caught. There is no rap sheet for Ariel Bokser. My main concern was to make enough money to return home. No one gets rich working street fairs. Cindi took the lion's share anyway, handing me some small percentage that was eaten up by motel rooms, food, and so on. Sometimes I was so desperate to save something, I slept in fields. So I began to do small break-ins, sometimes with Cindi, sometimes solo, though she always knew the fences in whatever town we were in. The riches of America lay before me: stereos, televisions, jewelry, mementos of surprising value. It was dangerous, of course, there were a few times when I heard the key in the lock, someone was home early. Our rule was: always have an exit plan. If possible, more than one. You must understand how desperately I wanted to see my family. Cindi was a fantastic mimic, from Presidents and movie stars to the fences she did business with, men dressed in powder-blue double knits, but her mirth wasn't a laughter that could cure. Also, my goal in these thefts was to repay you a debt that I fear is too great to repay.

Eventually Cindi and I got on each other's nerves. She was taking too much, giving me too little percentage, and we argued without resolution. When I packed my things and quit, she shrugged, said whatever, no big deal, and went back to sewing rhinestones — just as the time I first caught sight of her.

So I returned to the squat on Avenue C. The Neapolitan had died, and everyone I'd known had moved elsewhere, apart from the Korean War veteran, who was not very interested in talking to me. He referred to me as Mr. Arab or that Arab here. So many people I met here, from junkies to Daisy, said, I can fix you up. Let me fix you up. But all these good intentions hardly amounted to anything.

A few days after my return I saw the photographs of your ersatz simurgh, a copy of a Persian phoenix made of gaskets and diced circuit boards, in the gallery. You were the only person who could have constructed such an object; you must have returned.

I found your number (I have no phone and you are, as you may know, the only Ariel Bokser in the phone book), and called to arrange a meeting, finally, at Mezzanotte Pizza. When I arrived I was very nervous and, to make matters worse, while I waited I noticed the man behind the counter started drawing me, or so I thought. It must have been a slow afternoon, few customers, he had all the time in the world — that was one explanation — but I was still afraid of informants, those shadows that dog some emigres, not all, but a few. I heard rumors of Iranian exiles disappearing in London, Paris, Washington, under the bright sun of Los Angeles with a view of the Pacific Ocean and the Beach Boys on somebody's boombox. How much farther from Tehran could you get? But still they could find you. So I left Mezzanotte's, walking out on you, and I'm sorry, but I expected you would understand. Of course, I was followed from the restaurant. The sound of footsteps grew closer, sped up when mine did, and so on. I lost the man when I ducked into the subway. A train had just pulled in, I jumped the turnstile and left him, a man in an oversize baseball jacket, standing on the Q platform at Kings Highway.

Afraid to telephone you again, even from a phone booth, some time later I just knocked on your door. When no one answered I broke in. What did I see when I entered? I discovered you had found the city of Suolucidir.

The creature you modeled out of grommets, tie pins, and deadbolts lay next to its ancient twin, and that, of course, was the crown jewel. Without hesitation I wrapped the original in newspapers and put it in my backpack, along with some other things, a couple of books, a watch. A farewell drink seemed in order, a bottle of scotch beckoned, and when I looked in your freezer for ice I found the last treasure, the scroll, in a clear plastic snap-lid container nestled between a hoary frost-covered bottle of Stolichnaya and orange juice concentrate. If you had put the scroll in an opaque container, I would have assumed it was food, and never had seen it. You must understand this was a great opportunity for me. By claiming these objects and repatriating them, I could return home a hero. I also wanted the

Nieumacher notebook, which would tell me more about Suolucidir than you were willing or able to. I would find someone to translate it.

I ran from your apartment until I was breathless, and at this point I made a critical mistake. Running to the edge of the city along East Tenth Street until I got to the river, I wanted to be alone with the things I'd taken, and the apartment on Avenue C was full of strangers. I should have known — standing still, alone at night in a deserted part of the city is a bad idea. Someone came up from behind like Iron Man, no attempt to mask footfalls, and hit me on the head. When I awoke, the most valuable things I'd ever seen were still in my possession, but my wallet, your watch, and papers that identified me as Ariel Bokser, such as a driver's license, library card, fairground permit and ID, all those were gone along with about sixty dollars cash. The mugger or muggers probably believed the funny statue and old papers were worthless. You might look at this as retribution for breaking and entering, thieving, in some abstract form. I suspect the body in the Gowanus Canal belonged to the gangbanger who mugged me, than got fatally assaulted himself.

Enmeshed in one urbanography, you blink, and you're somewhere else entirely. I didn't return to Zahedan immediately, but felt Tehran would offer the cloak of a big city, where few knew me. My wife and sons visited, and in that first moment when they walked in the door, all the strange visions of my American sojourn seemed to have happened to someone else. The boys had grown up, almost, and knowing the war with Iraq was being expanded, one of my first wishes upon seeing them was to get them out of the country as quickly as possible, and indeed they now reside elsewhere. The moments between hugging them hello and goodbye seemed a slice of time no bigger than a sneeze.

Upon returning I needed to find a person who could tell me something about the Suolucidiri relics I took from you. Such a person would most likely be found in certain cities like the capital, though the search would not be easy. Blocks of half-burnt build-ings were barely recognizable. Movie theaters, markets, banks, all were reduced to shells identified by the bits and pieces that survived: a teller's station, a shattered projector, a movie screen turned to flags, the shell and metal ribs of a refrigerator case.

I looked for the remains of neighborhoods called sar-el-chal, edge of a pit, because shops, businesses, houses were centered around a trench into which garbage was both thrown and re-moved from time to time. There is a reason, you see, occupants of these ghetto-like neighborhoods have long been considered impure and to be avoided. By rule of law residents of the sar-el-chals had to stay indoors when it rained, for example, so they wouldn't pollute others. (Please note, this concept came to Iran via the Spanish Inquisition, which considered even conversos or chuetas to be pollutants, if you know what I mean.) It's possible sar-el-chals no longer exist, but I had to start with what I knew, as little as that might have been. In the mahellahs, down streets so narrow they're called forgive-and-forget streets because if two estranged friends should happen down one of them from opposite ends, they couldn't pass one another without touching, I might come to a series of brick arches ending in plain doors, easy to miss. Frankly, these people didn't want to be found, but occasionally I found something, a temple, a ritual bathhouse, a butcher shop; however no one within would talk to me. Some of these places smelled of ground metal, like what you inhale when a dentist drills away old fillings, others looked as if they hadn't been swept in centuries, a path through dust and debris led from the door to other rooms or sanctuaries. In one temple I was told to wait in a genizah, a kind of final resting place for books so old and brittle, it was if they lay in a quarantine of meaning before totally disintegrating. From this place, I got no further, and after waiting nearly an hour, was ejected the way I'd come. My interlocutors were old men, distracted and suspicious teen-agers, women veiled just like their Muslim counterparts, but the answer was always the same. As soon as I gave my name or said anything about Suolucidir, the door was essentially shut in my face. The scene was more or less repeated at maybe a half dozen locations. But at one point someone to whom I gave my name must have passed my number on to someone else, because after about a month of searching, I got a call from a man named Dr. Haronian. Dr. Haronian agreed to meet me, but not in the city, rather, at a house in the hills on the outskirts.

I drove out the next day, objects safely stowed in the back of my car, in the same backpack from which they were conveyed from your apartment. (Think of what that faded green knapsack has seen, from New Jersey street fairs to the aftermath of riots in Tehran.) Dr. Haronian lived in a neighborhood that was unknown to me. His house, like many of its neighbors, lay behind a high-gated wall. After waiting maybe fifteen or twenty minutes, I was about to turn around and leave, when I was buzzed into a garden that looked as if it hadn't been tended for years. A small tiled pool surrounded by a tangle of untended grape vines, pomegranate and fig trees lay to one side of the path as I made my way to the house that, too, must have been kept up better in the past. I pushed the door open, and a man's voice instructed me to walk down a hall to the back of the house, and there I found Haronian sitting in a wheelchair.

He was old, maybe older than he looked, not exactly crumpled into the chair, the lower half of his body hadn't yet atrophied in it. His hair was at one time colored black, but had grown out of the dye job. The white parts surrounded his head like a halo. A cat was curled up in his lap, and he spoke to it in a language I didn't understand, though it sounded something like Farsi, and maybe a bit like Arabic, too. Scratching behind the cat's ears, he introduced himself, and the cat, whose name was Ra'ashan. A large cluttered desk almost filled the room. I could see access to the desk was important to him; he never wheeled himself far from it. In terms of navigation Haronian was unable to sit on the floor, because he would be unable to rise by himself, and for this, as he pointed to a chair, he apologized. His housekeeper, who looked after him, was visiting her daughter so he was alone in the house.

An Oum Kalthoum record was playing; he wheeled himself to the record player and carefully lifted the needle. Not a simple task — his hands suffered from tremors — but he waved away my offer of assistance. Since we were strangers, he told me a bit about himself, going off into all kinds of side alleys as he did so. As a result of some of his injuries, it was very difficult for him to stay focused on one subject, he explained, and once again asked my indulgence. When Haronian smiled I noticed he had a gold tooth glinting in the recesses of his mouth. In repeating his story to you, if he comes off like a meek, shuffling behind the bookcase kind of person, this is a mistake. Haronian grew up on Eslambol Street and never left Tehran as far as he knew. He had always believed in minding his own business, but his father, who owned a small dried fruit and nut shop, had not. He changed the color of the displays on the sidewalk in front of his shop according to a complicated set of signals: sacks of green pistachios, red sumac, fresh yellow dates all meant that riots or violent incursions into the mahellah were imminent, and in this code he gave others in the warren of streets a rough idea of the location of the storm about to befall them. If things were really bad, nothing was put out, and the shop was closed. How his father knew or was informed of such things, Haronian never found out. Like many of his generation, his family was able to provide the means for advanced education, and he had no intention of staying behind to run the store with its complicated obligations and warning systems. Talented in linguistics, especially interested in Aramaic and languages from the Safavid era, after university, Haronian got a job in a state archive.

It was while employed here that he became curious about the Nieumachers, whose names were attached to a pair of boxes he came across accidentally in one of the archive's basement annexes. As if someone had forgotten them, they had been left on top of a stack of folding chairs. A label read Nieumacher in Latinate letters, which Haronian could read. The name, he assumed, was German, and the date, though the ink had bled and faded, looked like 1930-something. He knew Persia had been full of Germans building railroad lines, and after 1936 agents of all kinds had turned up, in cities mostly. Germans, even then, weren't new to the region. Haronian mentioned a Berliner, Robert Koldewey, who while digging in Iraq had discovered the ancient city of Babylon and invented a way to excavate and preserve mud bricks. He packed up the Gate of Ishtar, blue and crenellated, fourteen by thirty meters, it all went off to Berlin where it resides to this day. But who were these new Germans, the Nieumachers? He assumed they were German, but then it wasn't clear. Maybe they weren't. He looked things up, made inquiries, unaware his work was becoming troublesome, as if the parchments and papers he handled were actually growing hotter in his hands. He found a reference to the Franco-Soviet Friendship Dig. So maybe these Nieumachers were Russian. (His father had encountered Hebrew-speaking Russian soldiers decades earlier and had hoped to arrange marriages between them and Haronian's sisters. Hands trembling, my host removed a brittle old photograph from a stack on the desk. Seated in a row were six Russian soldiers participating in some kind of ritual meal eaten in a hut made of palm leaves. After they returned to the Soviet Union the Haronians corresponded with the Russians for many years, but then at some point, all replies ceased.) At any rate, were the Nieumachers Russian? Haronian was unable to determine their exact country of origin. There were gaps in what he could learn about them, but then he came into possession of a surprising document: a copy of the police account sent from Zahedan when Bruno Nieumacher was reported missing. Yes, such a document existed, it had been stored in Zahedan, located and obtained by a lawyer of his acquaintance. Its acquisition was the source of Haronian's undoing.

Or perhaps the Nieumacher business had nothing to do with his arrest. Haronian's shoulders lifted to his ears, he held his palms outward as if to indicate he no longer was asking these kinds of questions or expecting answers. It was in 1974, the occasion of the 200-rial-note scandal. You remember, he said, it had a six-pointed star printed on its reverse side, and of course

I did remember. Haronian recounted this was the currency that launched a thousand conspiracy theories, or you might say some people have an uncanny ability to see the figure in the carpet, even if there was nothing there at all. Though a six-pointed star will be formed when hexagonal tiles are placed in a ring, a common pattern all over the country, the rumors about the star-studded money gained momentum. According to one rumor, the notes had been printed in Ashdod, underneath a nuclear facility. Everyone who handled them would become radioactive. Some claimed the notes did, in fact, glow in the dark. The Shah was selling cheap oil to Israel, he was being bankrolled by Jerusalem. The 200-rial notes only existed for a few hours, then they were burnt, but Haronian reached over, pulled open a drawer and reached in the back for a crumpled wad. Pale green and blue, with the Shah looking out from under a dangerous, unscrupulous watermark in a vague and unfocused way.

Haronian's arrest happened in a way that many did. Two armed men soundlessly descended the steps to the archive base-ment where he pored over documents, hands sweating inside disposable plastic gloves, one of the few luxuries the archive in-dulged in. They always seemed to have an inexhaustible supply, to be found one day, Haronian smiled, lining some 36th-century archaeological dig. Without saying a word of protest, knowing there was no point in doing so, he let them lead him into a small white van. What could he do? Neither he nor his co-work-ers made eye contact with one another as he left the building. The van, though undersize, was divided into cubicles. Haronian sensed there were other people in it also, but no one spoke. They were driven somewhere, he didn't know where, or what he had done, nor did he have any sense of how long he was held in a solitary cell. He had seen this before. Many people he knew went about their business in their homes and workplaces; there one day, gone the next. Sometimes they returned, sometimes not. Unlike his father, who took great risks, but died at home, Haro-nian had thought he lived outside the boundaries of arrestable offenses, even though that perimeter didn't really exist. You could get arrested for using the word oppressive when talking about the summer heat, you could get picked up for using the same pay phone more than once. He described himself as an ordinary man with no attachments. (His wife had run off with the owner of a carpet company years previously. It sounded, he admitted, like the beginning of a joke, but this is true, she left him for a man whose main topic of conversation seemed to be questions of whether it was halachically okay to mix cotton, silk, and wool threads.) In his day-to-day life Haronian had been careful to voice no criticism, offer no speculations about what might or might not happen in the vague future. He informed on no one; he knew no one to inform on. He made no comment about the inventory of disposable gloves. Until he himself was picked up, he shrugged, he would say, that's the soup we swim in, but it was impossible to interpret your own imprisonment with that kind of matter-of-fact fatalism. I don't know if he was the simple dried fruit and nut heir he presented himself to be, but of what happened to him during this period I could only ascertain that previous to his arrest he had not been in a wheelchair.

First I showed him Sidonie's notebook and asked if he could translate it for me. He knew the alphabet, but not the language, so he returned it to me. Since it's useless to me, I'm returning it to you. I do know that she titled her notes "The Book of Smoke." I'm guessing she was referencing the ephemeral nature of writing, its ability to disintegrate physically, or to be written in a language that will eventually become extinct. That her notebook set so much in motion, events she could have no knowledge of, is a testament to the poisonous nature of smoke, even if it's short-lived.

Next, I took the scroll out of the bag and slid it across the table to him. Haronian slipped on a pair of white cotton gloves and carefully unspooled the parchment. He moved his lips as if reading out loud, though no sound came out of his mouth. Reading rapidly, which surprised me, he stopped, unspooled and read more, but then began to laugh until tears ran from his eyes.

What did I learn? Your artifact was a worthless invention, something about a man and woman, L and Q. It made no sense. He wiped his eyes with gloved hands, and pushed the thing aside. I was incredulous. Had I unwittingly taken one of your fakes?

What else do you have there? You mentioned something else. His voice was soft and gentle, not impatient that I'd wasted his time, but eager and still curious. I took the simurgh out of the bag, handed it to him, and then his demeanor changed. I'd like to think that if he could have risen from the chair, he would have. The creature, you will be surprised to learn, though unusual, has nothing to do with the Lost Tribes. Some uninformed, or marginally informed amateurs in the far-flung corners of Europe had made that mistake. Nor was it unique to Suolucidir, though it was nevertheless an interesting find. Interesting, that was the word he used.

Unlike your fake, the Nieumacher scroll that had been in the Tehran archive was genuine, as far as he knew. Sometime during the period of his arrest, that part of the archive, the annex, had been burned. The location of that scroll, if it had survived at all, was unknown, at least that's what he'd been told. The Nieumacher scroll now exists only in his memory. Ra'ashan stretched and clawed at the carpet.

As he rolled his gloves into a ball, the buzzer that activated the front gate sounded. Haronian shifted uneasily in his chair. It was by now close to midnight, but Haronian, who had little family and few friends, seemed to know what this call was about. Uninvited guests, he said, have come for my teeth. He told me in the kitchen was a closet, and if I pushed carefully behind the brooms leaning against its back wall, I would gain access to a tiny room, nearly another closet, and I should make myself at home in it until whatever voices I might hear ceased. I asked if I could wheel him into it, but he shook his head; there was no point. Even as I left Haronian, the noise of almost, but not quite, soundless footsteps echoed in the corridor, coming from the entrance into the rest of the house.

The kitchen was in disarray but smelled of warm roasted

walnuts; garlands of dried chili peppers had fallen on the carpet and crunched under my feet. I froze for a moment, then found the closet, just as he had described it, and pushed the panel aside. I guess you could call it a room. There would have been space for a wheelchair, but not much else. It was empty except for an electric light whose base had been a small hookah. I sat on a rug that covered an earthen floor, listened and waited, perhaps fell asleep.

When I woke the house was completely silent, no, not quite. Somewhere was the sound of Oum Kalthoum, but the record was scratched and the same words were repeated over and over, no one was lifting the needle. I ventured out of Haronian's hiding place. The house was empty. Even the cat was gone. The room where I'd been received had been ransacked. I lifted the needle from the broken record; its album cover, a picture of Oum Kalthoum wearing sunglasses and a turban, lay on the floor. The simurgh was gone. No wings or talons poking out from under a pile of clothes or books. The scroll lay in shreds. What I did find however, among the papers scattered over the floor, was a copy of a police report, an interrogation of Ramin Kosari, the Nieumacher guide in Zahedan, which I have enclosed with this letter. There were also a few typed pages in English, written by an Alicia Congreaves-Sutcliffe about an earlier expedition to Suolucidir by a pair of British explorers, one of whom must have been a relative of hers. I am sending all of this to you, in appreciation for having saved my life. As far as the lost city is concerned, it has cost me too much, from the moment my father acquired Sidonie Nieumacher's field notes, if that's what they were, to the present, and I'm done with it. The pages are radioactive, I'm convinced.

Wishing you all the best and hope we meet again with our feet on the ground, not under it.

Jahanshah Rostami

THE BOOK OF SMOKE

Sidonie Nieumacher

Marseilles, Autumn 1936

September 18, 1936

You could feel the sun on your face, the warmth of Turkish coffee through thin yellow cups, and even inhaling the decaying salty smell of the pier, you felt as stable as a tripod on flat ground, utterly still. The waiters who asked to be paid straightaway melted into the walls. Men tapping spoons against glasses of absinthe managed to arrest their jitters, spoons frozen in mid-air. Bruno stopped reading his paper for a moment and stared out to sea, as if with telescopic sight he could clear the Balearic Islands and watch a man in a café in Algiers drink the same cup of thick coffee with the same amount of sugar and curl of lemon peel floating on the foam. If the camera had frozen us at that moment in that sea of calm, if all other fitted gears stopped turning the world at that moment, September 9, 1936 wouldn't have been such a bad place to come to a halt, but soon enough the ground tips. Waiters re-appeared, Bruno resumed his scrutiny of a speech by the populist mayor of Vienna who used the word mongrel oftener and oftener, unknown cargo was unloaded on the docks while women with nervous frowns, brows like plucked ledges, wheeled prams on walks that skirted the piers. Seagulls snatched and scattered rinds, fruit cores, broken clams, whatever they could scavenge along the edge of the sea. Algerian and Senegalese seamen didn't even look up at the city, sprawling gate to what? Bruno read on, falling deeper into the bottom of his paper. I couldn't concentrate on anything. Coming down the street toward us a man pushed a wheelbarrow full of junk: old clocks, bundles of cloths, dusty books and magazines. As he got closer I could hear his singsong croak, *alte zabken, alte zabken!* His jacket was expensive and badly mended, big stitches sewn in the wrong color thread said some unskilled person had used whatever was at hand. After sizing one another up, we each instinctively turned away from each other. A woman on the dock pleaded with a tall man who listed to one side as if he might tilt into the sea. Her suitcase was tied with string, and a child picked at the stickers that covered the case: Odessa, Bremen, Trieste, Rimini. I can't actually see that far. I'm just imagining. Bruno yawned. He noticed nothing. A man to my left complained about someone named Mirabelle, she was too expensive, he tapped his glass as if doubly communicating the statement in Morse code. To my right a woman said, no one could have feet that large. I looked at mine just to be sure she wasn't talking about me. Then out of nowhere, maybe sprung from a trapdoor in the pavement, a voice crackled, directed at myself and Bruno and no one else.

"Excuse me so much for interrupting, but I've got something to sell. Perhaps I could interest you. A treasure you'll know as soon as you see it."

The outdoor part of the café was full of people whose clothes were made to order, whose shoes were polished with something other than black ink. Why did the old woman hook her talons onto our table and perch there so tenaciously, so absolutely sure we, alone, would be interested in what she had to offer? The woman spoke to us in broken German. Bruno, his crinkly brown hair oiled back, arched one eyebrow above his glasses and told her in perfect French to go away, please, then descended back into his paper.

The woman tottered, mildly rebuffed, but she was nothing if not persistent.

"Look, really. I think you'll find what I've got to show you quite interesting."

Her French was slow, with long pauses as if the right word was adrift at sea, and she was trying to retrieve it without a net. I couldn't place her accent. She warrents close description: rail thin, bent, nervous as a starling, wrapped in a cocoon of tattered silk shawls leaving a trail of fringes and tassels. No dress underneath, no shirt either. As she re-wrapped herself when these coverings slipped, the upper part of her body was a frightening stark white and entirely visible. Legs encased in dirty silk pantaloons worn out at the seat – no underwear discernible. Her face was powdery white, heavy black lines rimmed her rheumy eyes and false eyelashes like whiskbrooms weighted down her lids. A net veil hung from a small, black felt hat, and it was tied behind her head. She lifted the veil to speak more clearly, but that didn't really help. The words tumbled out in a blizzard of sound, some English and Arabic poking through the storm. When she calmed down, I took a closer look at her face. She wasn't as old as I first thought, but disease and sleeping on the streets, I'm guessing, had taken their toll.

"Let me show you. Please. I'm not asking much. A few thousand francs for something that's worth millions." She drew up a chair. "My name is Esme Canonbury," she slurred the syllables of her name so it sounded as if she were saying K'onburee. "I've come upon hard times as you can see, and I need to sell my last treasure. It was given to me by a man who made the pyramids speak, who danced like a hooligan on skates." Her eyes rolled upwards in ecstasy. I wondered what a hooligan on skates was or what such a dance

108

might look like but didn't interrupt. An English music hall performer in a plaid suit, bowler in hand, flailing his arms and hopping around?

"What makes you think we've got a spare few thousand francs?" Bruno looked over his paper again. I could see he was annoyed. When we lived in Berlin he'd acquired that air, that manner of dismissing someone in such a way, so that they ought to take the hint that he was done with them and had no interest in giving second audiences.

"I can tell. I can spot you people."

Bruno stood up. Did other café patrons turn from their drinks, pause from organizing their baggage and tickets, their last farewells? Perhaps I only imagined he drew attention to us. I pulled on his jacket to indicate he should sit down.

"Do you want me to call the police?"

"You're not going to call the police." She waved at the waiter, a little girl wave, waggling fingers as if playing a clarinet made of air. "Gin and tonic, if you please." She smiled a big, how-delightful smile.

I knew she'd tilt her head toward Bruno when the bill came. One hand released its grip from the table's edge and rummaged around in her morocco leather bag. She placed an object wrapped in newspaper on the table. The dry old *La Provence* (the paper was the local one and gave no clues as to the woman's origins or peregrinations) crackled as she unwrapped the package about the size of a hammer. There were so many layers to be unfurled until she got to the thing itself, and the noise was so loud, once again I imagined everyone was staring at us, though Bruno later observed one is rarely under scrutiny when one feels most raucous, guilty, or red-faced. It was a heavy bronze creature, sort of like a phoenix but not entirely, half-human, half-bird maybe? Some other creature was clasped in its talons.

Bruno picked it up in a desultory manner, then handed the monster to me. My hand nearly dropped to the table with the weight of it, yet sinewy Madame Canonbury lifted and carried the object as if it were a bundle of feathers.

"Sorry, I can't help you," he said, "I don't know what this thing is."

"This is all I've left, and it costs me to part with the creature. He has been my only comfort, though princes and archdukes have offered kingdoms for him."

Bruno picked it up and turned the thing over and over. I could tell he was a bit curious about the odd hybrid animal that landed on our table and wasn't surprised when he announced he was going to make a phone call. It wouldn't take long. I fingered the gold cross around my neck. It was small and unobtrusive, so sometimes I held it out a bit, especially when introducing myself.

"So your name is Sidonie," the woman's gluey eyes grew even more glazed, and she took a gulp of gin. She pronounced the name as if it made her tongue stick to her palate, and the *nee* at the end gave her trouble. "What's your brother's name?"

I explained Bruno wasn't my brother.

"Sidonie and Bruno what?"

I would not have been a very good lawyer. I always let other people grill me, and even strangers, from the moment they laid eyes on me, sense here is an easy mark, a complete pushover.

"Nieumacher." I pronounced our name: New-ma-shay in a quick sprint.

"Noy-mach-heir," she said, giving the *ch* a guttural shove and underscoring the *r*. "Sounds German to me."

"We're from Alsace."

"That might explain it."

I didn't ask what *it* was. The *alte zahken* man appeared again in the distance, coming toward us. No, don't stop, I secretly pleaded, hoping to telegraph to him, to this stranger. No *alte zahken* here. The first gin had disappeared, and Madame Canonbury ordered another. I looked around for Bruno. He was still at the bar speaking into the telephone.

"Where did you get your crucifix?" She pointed at the centime-size sliver of gold I still pinched between thumb and forefinger. The little silver man, nailed on, imprinted on my fingers.

"It belonged to my grandmother."

"I suppose she was from Alsace, too."

"Why wouldn't she be?" Bruno had returned.

Madame Canonbury smirked into her glass and mumbled about the man who sent the phoenix, how they used to meet in Cairo hotels, how he would disappear into the night smelling of rancid cooking oil, smoke, a number of things, but she didn't mind the odor, even grew to find that it reduced her to feeling like a wind-up toy, a mechanical drummer who'd hit a wall and could only drum frantically in bursts of nervous energy. I think that's the analogy she was making. She attenuated the syllables of every word as if each one were wet clay. It was not easy to understand Madame Canonbury. She looked at me, then at Bruno, as if drawing an invisible line, and raised her eyebrows as if to ask, could you say the same about him? No, Bruno never made me feel like a wind-up toy that had hit a wall.

In a low voice Bruno stated the news I'd been expecting. He'd telephoned a colleague, a former professor of ancient history from Berlin in retirement here in Marseilles. Doctor Feigen would be happy to look at the ornament.

"It's not an ornament," Madame Canonbury grumbled, restoring her veil. "It's a *simurgh*, a figure from Persian mythology, winged with a dog's face and lion's talons. It was supposed to be copper-colored, large enough to carry an elephant. Sometimes a *simurgh* would have a human face, but as you can see, this one doesn't."

A car standing in front of a shipping office a few doors down suddenly backfired. I jumped as if a bomb had gone off and crossed myself.

"Interesting you Alsatians cross yourselves right to left. I believe it's usually done the other way round; hand touches your heart first."

I looked over her head as if I hadn't heard, but Bruno glared at me, a stage glower that telegraphed: Don't be jumpy. Calm down. Let's get the old goat to Feigen as quickly as possible before she scurries off weighted by treasure that could be ours, leaving only a trail of tatters.

~

Shuki Fingers Feigen, formerly Dr. Frederick F. Feigen, had traveled a long way from our first meeting at his apartment in Oranienburgerstrasse. During our first year in the city, Bruno had been one of his students, and their relationship opened a new and entirely unfamiliar world to me. Feigen had worked with the archaeologists in Mesopotamia who brought the Gate of Ishtar to Berlin's Royal Museum. It was a massive structure of pure blue stone. How did they do it? An inventory number had been given to each fragment, the pieces were desalinated, then the whole edifice put back together again. All of Europe marveled at their achievement. The directors of Royal Prussian Expeditions declared the monument had been saved from certain destruction and now had a home in Berlin. Feigen had been very young when he traveled to Iraq, and felt as if he'd been transported to Babylon as an exile. Though the expedition had made everyone connected to it famous, years later he confided to Bruno that he was happy to return to Berlin, to take up teaching. He never again wanted to leave the comforts of rapid trams, reliable newspapers, butter and sugar. He presented himself as a native of the city of clocks and statuary where stone wings on a Schlossbrucke angel never lose a feather, and no one paints an obscene word or a pornographic image on the pilings under the bridge, and then blows the whole thing up. Over the years many students became his devoted followers, though not everyone was chosen or invited to bask in his illuminating light. To be chosen by Dr. Feigen, singled out for praise about one's work on demons and monsters, drought and flooding in Mesopotamia, made Bruno feel as if he'd been knighted. It was an honor the person Bruno left behind in his parents' house could not have dreamed of. That person was in the final stages of evaporation anyway, and his replacement grabbed the trophy with such joy I can't in any way cast discredit on him.

Invitations for dinner at the Feigen household were met, on my part, with a mixture of excitement and dread. I still wore long sleeves and long skirts, as dark as the bottom of the ocean, that first year, and you couldn't travel in Feigenische circles dressed like a small-town hermit who only emerged on Friday mornings to beg for bread. Shops in Berlin I entered as if blindfolded and bought whatever my hands touched first. These box-like shops, smelling of primroses, walls covered in feathery silk, were rosy Venus fly traps, and I wanted to flee as soon as I entered, yet felt hopelessly stuck in these sites of ridicule, making small talk with smart shop girls. I didn't want them to look at my body, or size me up in any way, to tell me what color I should wear or how to arrange straps so they fell or stayed in place. I learned to change my accent, say as little as possible, and eventually talk down to them as if I knew or cared what dress was a knockout and which looked completely ridiculous.

The Feigen apartment — or was it a house? I couldn't be sure which. You entered through a series of courtyards to end up at a narrow building at the very end. Their apartment occupied several floors, so it was as if I was swallowed in the dark by an animal I hadn't really seen, I was only judging its size by the dimensions of its stomach. Such a place I'd never seen before. Flowers spilling over balconies, there was a telephone in almost every room, tall radios, wooden replicas of cathedrals purred and buzzed with concertos, arias, news in several languages, and not only that, but the Feigens had an actual music room, domed and enclosed in long narrow panes of tinted glass. The dining room was painted with murals of allegories (warriors in ridged helmets dropped out of a wooden horse, a man with the head of a bull squatted, cornered and snarling, four children hatched from a blue egg). I couldn't identify these characters and hoped I'd never be asked my opinion of the trials they represented. I always attempted to mirror the accents of the other students, young professors and their wives, but had no clue as to how well I succeeded. When Bruno commented that I used my hands too much when speaking, I took up smoking as a way of doing something with them that wouldn't draw attention. You flap around like a Russian crow, he said.

The conversations at these dinners were like walking into a library rearranged by a tornado. Feigen's wife, Trude, talked about recent elections then abruptly described a doctor in Vienna who interpreted people's dreams, transformed hysterics into docile house pets, metamorphosed monstrous Hydes into merely inquisitive Jekylls, though who these English Hydes and Jekylls might be and what they were doing visiting a doctor in Vienna I don't know. One of the wives was a real rocket scientist who had studied Chinese explosives and was interested in the possibility of traveling by submarine through the Adriatic and across the Aegean, dodging small islands and coral reefs to eventually reach the shores of Palestine. I suspect her bags were already packed: oxygen tanks, underwater suit, globe-like helmet with grill. I would have been happy to excuse myself and listen to music on one of those radios, but there was no way to politely leave the table for any length of time. The menu, too, was astonishing in its own way. There was often some kind of fried sausage I didn't want to eat, but Bruno nudged me, and I took a salty forkful. Once there were smoked mussels scattered on a plate inlaid with mother of pearl. Fragrant steam, I only inhaled. Later, silver plates laden with sacher tortes and desserts of cream and crystalline sugar flavored with chocolate and almonds arrived like small palaces placed up and down the table, glowing as if lit from within. After such a meal even these seemed forbidden.

As the year drew on Mrs. Feigen's smile grew more fixed as she spoke to some of the other women present: wives, students. When a glass fell or even when the telephone rang, she jumped. I didn't like being seated next to her, watching her knot her napkin into nervous shapes, and always hoped that honor would go to the submarinist or someone else. She asked me too many questions. *Where do your parents live? I was in Strasbourg once before I was married, a charming town. I remember the way the houses were so perfectly mirrored in the canals like a reverse city set just under your feet. What do your parents do? How do they feel about your being so far from home? How did you and Bruno meet? Frederik has never had such a dazzling student.* I evaded her questions by telling her my parents died a long time ago. The truth is: 1., all of my family is, as far as I know, very much alive and 2., my marriage to Bruno was arranged, an aunt acting as go-between for the two families. We never met first in a café or a park or even in a classroom as people in Berlin do.

Much to my surprise, when the racial laws were enacted Frederik F. Feigen lost his position. Bruno teased me for my naïveté, of course Feigen would be dismissed. What did you think? Then things got worse. How could a man as smart as FFF, a man who knew so many people, not have foreseen how much worse it would get?

～

Bruno rounded the corner right after the crowds dispersed, at the intersection of Joachim Strasse and Gips Strasse; those streets meet at such an acute angle, you know that corner, he said. I did know that corner in Scheunenviertel. It was here where I found shops, dark little boxes, hidden in courtyards or upstairs where I didn't have to change my accent or could speak a different language altogether. Here you could find furriers with Siberian connections, silk merchants with family ties to Samarkand, used junk washed up on these shores via Austro-Hungarian channels. Through big double doors lay winding alleys where balconies hung with washing, children ran and screamed, and unemployed men argued and waited, tried to catch your eye, thieves and shysters plotted. How was his day different from mine? I'd stayed inside studying for exams I'd never take, and knew nothing of what was happening outside. Bruno was returning from scouring a flea market in Kreuzberg, looking for old books he could buy and sell. Walking back through Mitte Scheunenviertel he passed the crumbling Schablonen building, gold-colored, lintels decorated with shells, but nothing he went by predicted what he was about to see. The street was littered with broken glass. If the day had been sunny, you would be blinded by thousands of splinters, he said. Bricks had been thrown through shop windows. Wounded by the flying shards, a woman and the owner of one shop, a jeweler, had been yanked bleeding into the street where they were beaten and left by the curb. The woman had been wearing a fur jacket with a collar made of fox heads, but her face was smashed, so damaged, that the animal heads, though stained with human blood were more intact. The man she'd been visiting was stripped naked and hung from a lamppost. Bruno, wafer thin, some of his hair unglued, falling in ribbon-like bands, spoke like a hysteric but brittle and affectless at the same time. Bruno never told anyone about what he saw, no one but me, and I didn't one hundred percent believe him, even when he described the bare, stained legs of the jeweler and Trude's eyeless face. What she had been doing on streets her husband would have avoided, no one knew.

About Feigen's fate there were rumors: he was arrested, or he sold everything he owned, but though he himself may have been allowed to leave, he wouldn't have been permitted to take anything out of the country. Whether he was in prison or exile, all we knew for certain was that he disappeared. Other people soon moved into the flat in Oranienburgerstrasse. You could tell if you ventured into the courtyard, as we did, and happened to look up into the window. The music room, you could even see from the street, was completely empty. By now Bruno had abandoned his studies and soon, I too, could no longer continue at the university. Another former student of Feigen's claimed to have seen him enter a shabby building behind the Hackescher Market, but Bruno wanted to believe the man who had helped unearth the Gate of Ishtar (even if he'd only apprenticed as little more than a lowly German-speaking digger) had made his way to Palestine in a submarine with the rocket scientist. People had begun to disappear, and you could hope they parachuted whole into Buenos Aires, Shanghai, Trenton, New Jersey, somewhere, and began transforming themselves to suit new streets, new accents, new clothing, new street maps.

Bruno struck up a friendship with a small-time leonardo who lived in our building. The leonardo made good money, and soon Bruno, always in need of cash, began working for him on the side, forging pages of rare old German books, incunabula, which he undertook with the accuracy of a Talmudic scribe. Our two-room apartment was littered with black-and-white or tinted photographs of the originals and drying pages that he had bent over with quill and colored inks, copying Latin and 14th-century German to the exclusion of everything and everyone, so dense was his concentration. There wasn't a big market for these things by the time they joined forces, so the leonardo soon branched out into forging marcs. The actual printing was done somewhere else, but plates that were off on one detail or another were brought home from time to time, used as paper weights, then disappeared. Bruno Nieumacher, quiet scholar, learned to be direct, abrasive, a man who took no detours between hunger and putting food in his mouth. No prevaricating, no what ifs, or maybe we shouldn'ts.

I could no longer study law, but pretended not to notice the shingles of drying paper creating rooftops around our kitchen, and then the bedroom was taken over by jars of ink, as he experimented with potential materials. Just when there was no room to move without ducking, the leonardo got put out of business, in other words, he was put in jail. Bruno gathered armloads of fake bank notes and stuffed them into an incinerator. We left in the middle of the night, taking a train from Berlin to Marseilles, abandoning our books and the few possessions we had accumulated as indigent students, packing only a few clothes. I left the winter coat my grandfather had made for me years ago, because he believed we were going to New York, city of palm trees and coconuts, not Berlin which was only more of the same kind of city on almost the same latitude, only much bigger. Why would you go there? But we did, and now we were leaving again. We're traveling south, Bruno said, you won't need a winter coat. We locked the door as if we would one day return, though we each knew this would never be. Bruno was more resolute than I was, or seemed to be so, with each muffled footfall down those five flights past the sound of the Ellenbogens' quintet of violin-playing children, past the police photographer, Baum, who worked all hours and when I ran into him in the courtyard would describe crimes in lurid detail, past the lonely Lydya Moskcowisc who lost her sons in the last war. She used to ask us to dinner on Friday night, but we always refused. Finally she gave up. Bruno didn't want anyone to get to know us, it was too dangerous, and he was not, under any circumstances, looking back. His university studies of ancient history— Mesopotamia, Alexander the Great, the sexagesimal numerical system, and Sumerian maps—all evaporated into thin air. He wouldn't need those books again and shed no tears over their loss. As the last night train pulled out of the Hauptbahnhof, I thought I would always miss snow and frosty nights, hands buried deep into linty pockets. Then, with our identity papers burning holes in our pockets, we were gone.

～

Once in Marseilles, Bruno began poking around in used bookshops for the odd rarity that might have tumbled into a bin. We were broke. So what else could possibly be new? Bruno had few contacts in France, and he felt we needed anonymity, even more than in our days in Berlin. Picking up his old trade provided a less public channel of employment than applying for a teaching post. He didn't want to meet new people who would ask him where he came from, invite him to dinner, or say if you came from Berlin you must know Herr X who trains lorikeets to recite Virgil. He needed to work alone. We'd been in the city about a year when poking around a used book shop he spied a short man, black hat perched on the back of his head, prayer fringes visible under his jacket. Never thinking the customer could be his old professor, a fellow who bought his tree well in advance of December 24, Bruno was shocked when the man tapped him on the shoulder, and greeted him by name in whispered, raspy, Berlin-accented German. Yes, it was Feigen, such purple bags under his eyes, face grown so narrow, he was hardly recognizable.

Once across the border it had taken Feigen a long time to recover from enforced penury. He'd changed his name back to the Shuki that had disappeared decades earlier, leaving the Frederik at the German frontier, expanding the F to Fingers, and it was by this middle name he came to be known. Feigen believed war was imminent; people were already racing to sell paintings and other possessions. He put a wet digit in the air, sensed the direction the wind was blowing, and set himself up as a first-rate appraiser of antiquities, also becoming an exceptionally talented black marketeer putting his expertise to good use. Shuki Fingers Feigen became known just as Fingers. It didn't bother him in the least.

When I met him again it had been several years since our last dinner invitation. Feigen was still the avuncular professor of ancient history, though the sausage and ham dinners were long gone, nor were they replaced by mussel-laden bouillabaisse. Fingers did no business from sundown Friday until sundown Saturday, and he went to synagogue with a bunch of local

Sephardim for whom he was the picture of an inscrutable easterner, rather than a lost eminence from Berlin. Of the transformation Feigen said, "I'm no longer sending all this mail Return To Sender, but accepting that yes, indeed, I do live at this address. I go to the *Maariv* service in the evening with displaced Tunisians who hum ancient *cancioneros*, pop olives into their mouths like *pfeiffernusse*. I can't understand a word they're saying half the time, but so what?" Later, Bruno explained, Doctor FFF with his lecture notes, monogrammed silver, crystal chandeliers made in the Kaiser's glassworks, and radios beaming broadcasts from the BBC, all that was murdered with Trude.

"Sidonie, Sidonie, my dear." As Dr. Feigen, he had barely paid any attention to me, but for Fingers, I had my uses. I was enlisted in the service of their schemes.

"Why study law? Soon there will be no laws; there hardly are anymore as it is. Married to Bruno, you're complicit in his 'creations' anyway, so join us, Sidonie. We can use you. Your French is, naturally, better than your German."

Feigen had lost something of his gold-plated smoothness, his manner, though he could still draw on a wealth of facts about the calendar system of the people who dwelled between the Tigris and Euphrates rivers or the importance of decoration in the story of Ishtar and Tamuz. But, even more so than Bruno, he didn't want to meet anyone, not really, and he didn't want to kiss the hands of women who reminded him of his wife or men whose foresight was so much keener than his had been, men who got their francs and family on boats and trains well in advance of mobs, their ropes and stones.

So I became their front. My job was to find future refugees and immigrants who didn't yet realize how foreign they were to become. We helped them liquidate their assets: their Degas, their Cézannes, their whatever, and took, besides our commission, various secret cuts along the way. Fast and cheap. With this in mind I might have found Madame Canonbury before she found us, although my clientele generally lived in houses and possessed leases, titles, deeds, and passports ready to go, but this apparently stateless apparition provided the most priceless thing any of us had ever seen.

Feigen set up his shop in rooms he occupied in a western part of the city, though also not far from the port. We all had our eye on the exit door. His rooms were dark and chaotic, as different as possible from the elegance of the Oranienburgerstrasse flat his wife had ruled. Artifacts, sculptures and statues were scattered everywhere, paintings leaned against walls. Some art books lay stacked around haphazardly. It was into this complex half-warehouse, half-shop that we led the gin soaker, not to fleece her so much as to enlighten ourselves. For all Bruno knew, she was out to rook us, passing an odd twist of bronze off as something ancient and rare. For Feigen it didn't matter who Madame Canonbury was or had been. She was just a customer, an old woman, come this way, sit down, let's see what you have. He never took his hat off, this slight fingernail clipping of a man. It was already evening, but he only turned on one floor lamp and unwrapped the phoenix as soon as it was handed to him. Newspapers fell to the floor.

"Do you know what this is?"

Madame Canonbury once again stared up towards the tin ceiling and began to mutter something about a man who promised to send for her. He'd found a vast Persian treasure: bath houses of solid gold, fountains of wine still running, streets paved with diamonds and emeralds. It had all disappeared into the Gulf of Oman when he tried to return to England but there was more, surely, where that came from. She would never live to make the trip, but more artifacts lay in those caves or under the desert just waiting to be found. Fingers left us to consult some book or other and returned wiping the dust from his hands on the sides of his already fairly dirty jacket.

"I'll offer you ten thousand francs."

"Come, my friend," Madame C said in a low nasal voice. She collected her bits and pieces as if to leave, but hers was the kind of violent resentment some people feel when they hit their head against a table edge, enraged at an inanimate object. Anger at Fingers was just as pointless. "Let's not joke here. The creature's worth ten million francs. It's a god, not a jar opener."

"Then you must find someone who will pay that amount. It's a copy of the ancient Persian phoenix. Not original, not by any means. Many copies of these were made in Tehran to sell to European visitors during the end of the last century. It has some interest as a curio, but not as an antiquity, no, I'm sorry to say. See this seam here."

It was hardly a seam, more like a haphazard ridge along the sides of the figure. Feigen was speaking to senses dulled by glasses raised and glasses quickly downed.

"It was a primitive sort of casting, but this isn't an original piece, no, Madame, sorry to disappoint, but I will pay something for it, just to take the thing off your hands. Victorian travelers brought these phoenixes back from Persia, and they were used as door stoppers or paperweights." The emerald city swayed, then crumbled into a cloud of green dust. If it really didn't exist then Feigen was giving accurate information about the value of the thing, but I had no way of knowing which assessment was the true one. Ever the dupe, I believed him. Esme Canonbury looked stunned, as if she'd been socked in the jaw. I felt deeply sorry for her and despised Feigen, though I'd often felt sorry for him as well. Her eyes watered, and she pulled her wraps, her binding tighter around herself. Fingers had a stern, yet placid expression on his face.

"In Cairo, before the war, I was attached to the British embassy, but I lost everything. My husband threw me out," she stuttered. "I was seduced by a story of a lost city and wanted to follow others in its quest. The gangplank had long been drawn up, and *HMS Dorchester* was disappearing over the horizon. It had a rendezvous with a German submarine that had wandered into the Gulf of Oman, having reversed direction in the Strait of Hormuz. And while torpedoes pierced its hull, I was left marooned on the desert coast with no money, only my camera, and not a soul of my acquaintance within three thousand miles."

She pulled her veil back over her face, and leaving the phoenix on the table, wandered out the door, heading toward the elevator. I felt miserable for her, and whispered to Bruno, can't he just pay her whatever she needs? If Fingers was telling the truth, and the creature was only a cheap copy sold to nineteenth-century tourists traveling in Persia, he could still pay her a bit more. If the simurgh was real, then he was playing a cruel trick. I twisted a loose button on the cuff of my jacket until it came off in my palm. Bruno wouldn't look at me. He cleaned under his fingernails with a matchstick. It was a habit he'd abandoned in Berlin but it had now returned.

Fingers followed her out of the room, but without taking the phoenix with him. Bruno walked over to a window and played with the dial of an old bakelite radio balanced on a pile of newspapers. After what seemed like hours, his former teacher returned. Feigen swept the crumpled paper from the table, wadding it in his hand. He didn't look like a satisfied person who had just eaten a good meal. On the contrary Feigen looked like he was on the verge of losing what little was keeping him moored.

"I know what you're thinking, but I paid her more than my initial offer, though not quite what she demanded. If Madame Canonbury wants a shylock I'm happy to fulfill the role, that's all." He said the words *alte goya* with a razor's edge that made me uneasy. It was not a phrase that would ever have been pronounced by the late FFF, but Fingers used the words as if they organized Berlin, Marseilles, all of it, so that its laws and boundaries made sense. "So this is what I think," he continued. "Part of what she was rambling about is true, the question is: what part? Most of my former colleagues in Berlin believed there is no lost city once known as Suolucidir, and if you were to go looking in the foothills of the Black Mountains, all you'll find are bones of mirage-obsessed pilgrims. However, if some amateur Rawlinson found evidence of the lost city then we've stumbled across something very valuable indeed."

I assumed by Rawlinson he meant any Englishman explorer, the kind you saw in newsreels about India, a man who looked like the father of Tarzan, maybe. Church bells rang five o'clock. The subject of the lost city nudged Fingers out of the way, just a speck. I expected he would once again hide his prayer shawl fringes, just as he had when Madame Canonbury appeared (which he untucked at her departure) and with the subject at hand, Frederik would return, rhino horn cigarette holder and the gold cufflinks of FFF restored. The university professor took off his gold-rimmed glasses, polished them on his *tallis* and led us to a part of his apartment I'd never seen before. It was a room with no windows, lined with creaky bookcases, lamps without shades, assorted clutter. He pulled a string to turn on a bare bulb overhead.

He moved a bookcase to reveal a door that led to another room. It wasn't large, maybe it was no bigger than a closet you could walk into, lie down, not much more than that. Feigen snapped open a slat-backed folding chair and table, dusted them off with his hands and gestured for me to sit down while he and Bruno stood. The room smelled of dust and mold.

"In my father's house he always made sure we had such rooms," Feigen explained. "Not to hide valuables, but to hide yourselves."

The chamber was bare except for a mattress on the floor, a crate of dusty tinned food, and a locked cabinet. Feigen unlocked this to reveal more small drawers, glass-faced panels, and other smaller locked doors.

"A cabinet of curiosities." Bruno said, and Feigen nodded, but it wasn't just any hodgepodge of strange things.

"Some of these objects have Kabalistic significance of which I'm ignorant. You have a thing," he patted one of the drawers, "that in some parts of the world might be considered holy, can't be touched by human hands, yet somewhere else, these same bits and pieces are considered capable of casting spells, deadly, or they're considered by others to be nothing more than garbage. The cabinet is the only object I took from Berlin. It was old and damaged, as you can see, and no one at the border bothered with it or knew how to open its doors anyway. There are some compartments even I don't know how to open. There are other sections which, even if you took an axe to the main body of the cabinet with the intention of reducing the wood to kindling, let me assure you, some of these smaller segments would remain intact, indestructible. In the pile of wood you would find these boxes, turtle-like, head and limbs tucked in."

Trude's picture peered out from behind a glass panel, perhaps safe-guarded in one of the unbreakable compartments.

Feigen unlocked a curved drawer and removed a silver-plated fish that fit in the palm of his hand. He held the object up by the tail as if it were alive and struggling for air.

"This was said to ward off the evil eye," he explained, "but the fish also represented a warning, a suggestion that if you swim in the lower parts of a river or sea you will go unnoticed by predators. Even given the proscription against graven images from mosaics in pre-Roman Tunisian temples to nineteenth-century silversmiths working in the ghettos of Venice and Prague you will find these fish, and this is what they symbolized."

How like Feigen to miss the fact that predators lie on the bottom of the sea just as they do near the surface. Under the fish was a leather-bound portfolio. He untied the folder and pulled out a piece of paper that, when unfolded and laid on the table, was a fragment of a map, about 18-by-18 centimeters, edges torn.

As soon as Fingers' hands touched the map, the last traces of Berlin departed. His voice and his accent changed completely.

"Before I came to the city as a student I lived in Vilna with my family."

Bruno, who'd been eying the cabinet, looked startled. We'd always believed Feigen, despite his newly found religiosity, was a tenth-generation Berliner, or something like that, a man who could trace his family back to Leibnitz.

~

"We were Russian speakers but moved west to Vilnius a few years after the revolution. Even then I had my eye on the door, and wanted to travel even further west, but one day a man came to town who called himself Yanek Motke, and this Yanek, whether he knew it or not, was to provide me with a road map for my departure. He appeared in the spring a few days before Passover and said he had come to perform *bedikat chametz*, the search for leavened bread that must be completed before noon on the 14th day of Nisan. I was thirteen years old and home alone. It was my sisters' job to clean the house before Pesach, not really my concern. We'd already heard of this Yanek Motke. My sisters were more interested in accidentally bumping into this bicycle mechanic or that printer's apprentice than looking for crumbs of bread, so if the man came, they said, let him work his magic. It's one less chore for us. It was evening when he knocked. I opened the door to a man who didn't look like any itinerant *tzaddic* I'd ever seen before. Instead of a fur or felt hat, he wore a rag tied around his head in a haphazard fashion, a black coat that buttoned on the side in the Chinese style, and his baggy black pants were tucked into his boots. He looked beyond me at our brass samovar and candlesticks. I agreed to his price, which was only a few coins for his services, and he brushed past me into our small house.

"Yanek performed entirely as was customary. He lit a candle, pulled a long bent feather from within his coat and began the search, chanting as he brushed behind stove tiles and even in between pages of books. Yanek left no surface uninvestigated for renegade crumbs, scouring even *chametz k'zait*, pieces of bread less than three centimeters, and those you don't even have to bother with, halachically speaking. All of it he swept into pieces of newspaper that were rolled into a paper bag later to be sold to a non-Jew. When he was finished he began boiling water, and I began to hope my sisters would come home soon to put a stop to this cleaning frenzy.

"Finally he sat down, and I offered him a glass of tea, putting a sugar

123

cube between his front teeth. He made me nervous. I was only thirteen and didn't know how to say to him, well, you're finished now, I paid you, thanks, now you can leave. His reflection in the brass samovar looked like a long column of copper with a fringe of gray hair poking out from under the turban, small eyes, nose, and mouth stretched in the middle.

"Yanek looked at my stack of books on the kitchen table as if they amounted to nothing much, as if to say, smart guy, what do you know? 'The Egyptians,' he leaned in close, 'believed that they had been awarded nine of the ten measures of magic dispensed to the world. The tenth flew further east, landing in my country, in a city now buried but just waiting to re-emerge. The right party need only travel to Persia, tap the ground in the right place and the city that slept for so long will, in effect, come back to life.'

"I didn't know what he was talking about. Then he asked me if I knew about *die Roite Yiddelech*, the red Jews?

"'What,' I asked, 'like in America?' 'No,' he answered, he wasn't talking about Jewish Apaches, please. The lost tribes of Israel, that's what he was talking about. Do they still exist? Did they ever exist?"

"What Lost Tribes?" Bruno asked. What a fantastic faker. Even now I admire his sleight of hand as an actor.

Feigen continued: "The Israelites who disappeared in the 8th Century B.C., forced into exile by invading Assyrians. These ten tribes were dispersed, vanished, but in the intervening centuries a few travelers here and there have tried to find out where this mass of people might have landed and what their fate might have been. Pragmatists waved their hands, dismissing the tribes as a chimera as if to say, get on with it, if you're fleeing Cartagena or Venice or Prague, what difference could these ghosts possibly make? Dreamers like Yanek, on the other hand, stirred up the dirt, outlining the footprints of the departed tribes; even if in doing so, they tampered with those footprints, that evidence, saying, wait, not so fast, they're among us still. Well, not us exactly, but in other parts of the earth: down the Nile, across the mountains of Dagestan and Kipling's Kafirastan. They turned up in many places, only, often enough, they turned out to be either just like the rest of us or complete frauds. They were soldiers, sailors, farmers, all-night partygoers (according to the Midrash), whatever mirror you wanted to hold up, whatever you imagined, that's what the lost tribes would be. They were supposed to dwell in unmapped and unmappable parts of the world. In the

Babylonian Talmud the lost tribes of northern Israel were located in Kurdistan. According to the Jerusalem Talmud they were 'across the Sambatyon River, enshrouded in cloud beyond the mountains of Darkness' and 'under Daphne of Antioch.' Rabbinical documents stated that the tribes, concealed by an earthquake, were permanently entombed in an underground city. If one found this city you would see streets and houses populated by our ancestors, each and every citizen frozen in suspended animation. The Book of Elijah predicted the tribes would return in 614, and with them 'a new Jerusalem and a new temple would descend from the skies.' We're still waiting.

"So I stared at Motke while he looked around the room carefully, though he'd just cleaned it, as if scanning the kitchen for eavesdroppers. He pulled his chair closer, shook his hands and cuffs, dispersing the crumbs he's just cleaned back into the atmosphere. His attitude was one of collusion, as if to say, you and I understand these things that most people going about their workaday lives are, as they put one tired foot in front of the other, completely oblivious to. Then he began to tell me the fantastic adventure story of one of the first recorded seekers of the lost tribes: Mar Eldad Ha-Dani.

"Sidonie, Bruno, please, you must try to understand, to a thirteen-year-old boy growing up with no movies and few secular books, the story of Eldad was the greatest comic book, the greatest radio play, I'd ever heard. Who was Mar Eldad? A dark man with long braids from Ethiopia, maybe, or Yemen, he appeared in Quirawan, Tunisia, in 883 making spectacular claims. Speaking in Hebrew, a language no one in the ninth century used for everyday discourse, Eldad claimed to be a member of the lost tribe of Dan himself. Ha-Dani, you see, of the tribe of Dan. Even his first name, an ancient Hebrew calling, long out of use, was a clue as to who he was. No one had heard of such a name. Crowds were held spellbound by his descriptions. His words were said to be sweeter than honey and honeycomb: the Lost Tribes lived in peace in a land where each man owned only one knife used for slaughtering animals, and no person outlived their children. Why did he leave this paradise? No one knows. Eldad described how he was captured by cannibals who kept him alive as long as he was entertaining. When interest in him began to flag, and let's face it, the cannibals were probably not a very sophisticated audience, just as they were about to roast Ha-Dani, a ship appeared out of the mists of the Straits of Hormuz. Eldad was rescued by pirates who worshipped fire, and whose vessel was accompanied by a ring of sharks trained to eat the men frequently thrown overboard. Living among the brigands for several years, he sailed to Cochin, Bandar, and parts unknown. Eldad was finally ransomed from the Asiatic buccaneers by a merchant from the tribe of Issachar who paid for his freedom in ruby-colored glass that really wasn't worth all that much, but how were they to know? Traveling by camel and boat he encountered other tribes east of the Persian Gulf and beyond the Caucasus. Finally Ha-Dani was shipwrecked on the coast of Tunisia. He became the authority on the lost ones, though he was often lost himself. According to Eldad, the tribe of Issachar 'dwelled in the high mountains near to the land of Medes and Persia. Simeon and half the tribe of Manasseh were in the land of the Khozars.' That is to say, the plains to the north of the Caspian Sea," Fingers pointed to the map.

"Though dead for over one thousand years Eldad spoke to Yanek Motke in his dreams. Ha-Dani's work was unfinished, and Motke could, in his travels, do a great deal to hasten the return of these lost peoples. Motke took up the quest, and he sensed in me," Fingers pointed to himself, "an intelligent, willing accomplice. You might ask what did Yanek Motke, an itinerant who-knows-what, want with a thirteen-year-old boy who'd never been anywhere? I've no answers. In any case, in the dream Eldad told Motke where to go and what he would find when he got there. In a genizah in the Crimea, itself rumored to house members of the Lost Tribes, Motke found this map," Feigen pointed to the paper on the table, "which confirmed Mar Eldad's claims. I don't know where the map really did come from, maybe where he claimed, maybe he drew it himself to pass the time on a train to Moscow. Those were the last words I remember hearing from Motke, though I've often since repeated them to myself. I fell asleep, and when I awoke our candlesticks were gone, but the map was lying on the table.

"After his visit I became more intrigued, obsessed with that margin of time before the common era, but to find it you had to first enter a modern age of radios, automobiles, elections, doctors in Vienna. In four years I was gone, too, never to return.

"When I began my studies in Berlin I learned that even if Motke had been a charlatan, Eldad was a real person, and his story had caused so much excitement that several versions of it appeared soon after his arrival in Tunisia. If you lived at a time when beliefs in unknown lands populated by unknown people were strongly held, even with little or no concrete evidence to support every Camelot and Atlantis, Eldad gave the lost tribes gravity and residence in a specific topography. His tale was much in demand, so much so that his so-called diary was one of the first books ever printed. The first edition was printed in Mantua, Italy in 1480, only twenty years after the Gutenberg Bible. He wrote, *no worldly yoke is upon them, but only that of heaven, they are not at war with anybody, but their energy is devoted to the discussion of the Law; they are at peace with all, and have no enemies. The only weapon they possess is a knife for slaughtering animals. They speak Persian, Hebrew, and Tatar,*" Feigen quoted

"Over the centuries others followed in Eldad Ha-Dani's footsteps, or tried to. In 1160 Benjamin of Tudela traveled as far as the western reaches of the Qing Empire and far into India and Ceylon. He, too, claimed to have located four of the tribes in northeastern Persia. Next of note, Manasseh ben Israel, a contemporary of Spinoza and Rembrandt, tried to find the tribes. So maybe there was something to the stories of Yanek Motke, the thief. Then in 1840 Lost Tribe studies suffered a terrible blow. A man named Abraham Firkowitsch, a fellow with both one of the largest collection of Hebrew manuscripts and a record as a con artist, concocted a fraudulent document, which he claimed had a message from the Lost Tribes. Many were duped, and those who contributed both large and small sums of money became seriously and very publicly disillusioned when he was unmasked. You see, the document also declared Firkowitsch himself to be a descendant from the tribe of Naphtali. Firkowitsch was not a name that was in common usage in biblical times. Newspapers in all the languages of Europe blasted the faker, and for years afterwards the smear of Firkowitsch tainted the whole subject. To speak of the lost tribes was to have your name associated with fraud, and eventually in Berlin, I gave up talking about the search to anyone. Even my wife knew nothing of my quest, its origins, and how it had propelled me to Berlin in the first place. It became clear that no one would take me seriously if I continued along those lines of inquiry, and unwilling to risk being known as that knucklehead embarrassment Feigen from the east, and finally unwilling to be associated with subjects that smacked of quakery, I soon devoted myself to other things. The tribes are fixers, instigators, promoters of a longing for something perhaps never experienced; I turned my back on them and in exchange was rewarded with a professorship and a house on Oranienburgerstrasse. There were stories about two Englishmen who found a Babylonian

Talmud in a Persian cave, but no confirmation of this came from London or anywhere else. From Motke's visit I've never seen concrete evidence of the city until now."

Feigen translated the lettering in the margins of the map, which described the lands, mountains, rivers and deserts represented by a variety of pictures and symbols. This is Persia, he pointed, and then his finger landed on a black creature, a simurgh similar to the one Madame Canonbury had valued so highly. This symbol, Fingers said, marks the spot where the city of the Lost Tribes will be found. Salomon Reinach, Dreyfusard, archaeologist, believed civilization began in the east. Some thought he was a crackpot, too.

One of Feigen's radio's cackled in the background. The voice reported the Belgian Fascist Party, the Rexists, had won twenty-one seats in their parliament, Britain warned Italy not to meddle in Palestine or Egypt, Mussolini declared total victory in Ethiopia. It would take more than a golem descending over the Quai de Rive Neuve to save Fingers, to save any of us.

He held up the bronze object, the simurgh. "It laughs at me, the Persian bird; my colleagues in Berlin called this a phoenix, evidence that Chinese travelers had passed through what I called Suolucidir, but they were wrong."

October 1, 1936

The phoenix re-emerges after perhaps thousands of years underground. Feigen had been looking for it without really remembering what he searched for, getting lost in Berlin, which turned out to be a long detour, he said, and now an old woman wandering randomly down Rue de la Canebière produced bronze proof and patches of a story to go with it. The ghost of Yanek Motke, breadcrumb cleaner, had returned. But Fingers was no longer thirteen years old and aching to travel. Someone else would have to follow the map and make the trip to Suolucidir, but how were his nominees to get out of France?

"I have a cousin in Kaliningrad," Feigen said. "He's a printer with no academic credentials whatsoever, but like myself, he has needed, in recent years, to develop a sideline. He's a very good printer; he once engraved for the tsar, but of this we don't speak. A small shop, just two people besides himself, and both of them are relatives by marriage. In this sideline they have developed, the business is very discreet. We need papers whose provenance is in part Soviet, part French, whose description and *raison d'être* I will draw up. I'm about to launch the Franco-Soviet Friendship Dig. We will obtain patrons, funding sources. The Friendship Dig will be based on my scholarly investigations and fronted by you: Bruno and Sidonie Nieumacher. With grants provided by investors you will pack your bags, book passage to Beirut, and from there travel either overland directly to Zahedan, or by sea through Port Said, and then on to Bandar Abbas."

Feigen unrolled maps. They covered the surface of a dining room table —not his, this one, designed for large dinner parties was for sale, and it was the only surface large and clear enough of debris for his purposes. From all these names, my head was whirling. On top of the maps of the Mediterranean, Arabia, Persia, he laid a list of designations, contacts in Tehran, an old catalogue from the British Museum, lists of supplies we should purchase before we left, lists of supplies we should collect when we arrive. On top of the layers of contemporary maps he laid the fragment left behind by Yanek Motke.

Bruno, however, wasn't convinced. He leaned against the doorjamb, cool as a cucumber, yet I knew Bruno wanted nothing so much as to bolt from those suffocating rooms. Despite the years spent on his own, he was still a student whose shoes were too tight, and he couldn't quite come right out and say to his teacher that the whole thing sounded like a lot of hooey. It was, as far as Bruno was concerned, not a time to be launching out to sea in a boat full of holes when there were enough problems and promises on dry land.

Fingers raised an eyebrow. Suddenly he was Feigen of the pearl tiepin having to put up with a moron. "This," he pointed to the simurgh on the map, "is an amalgam of several symbols of the lost tribes. The eagle is the symbol of Dan, the lion of Judah. It stands for the city, itself a symbol of Simeon, and just by it is an olive tree, symbol of Ariel, and a goat, symbol of Naphtali."

I bent over to look closely at the Motke map. The faded ink drawings were just as he described them.

"I'm not getting run out town on a wild goose chase. We have a business here. What do I care about your lost tribes? Why chase djinns in a desert?" As he backed away he knocked over a Chinese umbrella stand filled with canes, and horn bills, silver tops, and carved ivory clattered to the floor.

Feigen stopped short of saying, You may soon wish you had a choice; I knew he did. He turned the pages of the old catalogue, pointed a dry, blunt finger at a plate, a frieze, a column. His narrative sounded like a well-rehearsed one, something he'd stored and had only just now revived.

"This is a golden opportunity. A woman who barely speaks any language at all sees you on the street, and picks you of all people to sell her last treasure. Bruno, listen to me. Yes, you could have become an old snob of Oranienburgerstrasse with students and sycophants and hangers-on scratching at your door, just as I did, but you got washed up here. Just when you feel your accounts are in order, and the black columns outdistance the red, there's an earthquake, and the dirt under your feet breaks into unstable clods. The wharf turns into a prisonhouse, and the hospital that was once down the street is now an abattoir. You feel the way to fight back against all this running from place to place is to say no to me, to drive a stake in the ground, and refuse to go anywhere."

I have to admit he had me a bit puzzled. Bruno looked annoyed, but he nodded and went along with Feigen's tirade.

"Of all the people in the city, and with very limited means, a woman who is half blind, without even a cane or a dog, finds you, and gives you a creature that I, who once studied these things, have only seen one other time." Fingers reduced his voice to a whisper, as if he'd given up arguing or pretended to give up. "Until I saw this phantom, Yanek Motke's map was buried, dismissed by Berlin Persianists as the illusion of a primitive people beneath consideration. I showed it only once to one of my teachers, and he barely glanced at the chart that had sent me west to his city where I got stuck for what looked like the rest of my life. To him, it was the chimera of an uneducated wanderer, mad and completely fraudulent. You're more fortunate than I was. You can follow the map to its source. If the map is right, then what you trusted to be an empty desert, won't be empty at all; you'll find the lost city and the remains of the people who lived in it. Should you look in the right place you'll discover its minarets poking above the surface, and from there you dig. You come back a rich man, if you want to come back at all. Maybe you won't be interested in returning here. Please Nieumacher, don't raise your eyebrows at me. If you find the city of the lost tribes no one can touch you. I'm too old or I would be on the next boat to push off from the Vieux Port." He referred to himself as an *alte kabker*, and in the accents of those four syllables were the footprints of a young man who traveled west, far from the printing business, and re-invented himself in Berlin, rarely writing back to those cousins and relatives by marriage, and only when he absolutely needed them.

"Why Franco-Soviet?"

"Some time at the end of the last century Shah Nasr-el-Din granted France extensive archaeological rights in order to settle his debt to a brothel in Paris. These rights were the envy of Germany. Since you're from Alsace, you already have French documents, but you need exit visas, letters of transit. My cousins should be able to provide these. Soviet, because the Soviet Union already has a foothold in the region; it's a marriage of mutual interests."

Feigen wasn't asking me what I thought of leaving for Persia; it was assumed Bruno would make this decision. Had Feigen thought to enlist my help I would gladly have become his representative and ally. You know how cloth feels against skin when you have the flu or the beginning of an illness and the sense of touch seems hyper-aware, hyper-sensitive? As soon as the possibility was raised about traveling to the desert, that's how I felt. Berlin and Marseilles had each seemed as solid as paper umbrellas, temporary shade from the sun, soon to dissolve in the oncoming storm. Like thirteen-year-old Feigen, I was ready to leave whatever ersatz makeshift nest I found myself in, and toss it all in order to engage in a venture that at best could be described as highly risky. The sinkholes didn't seem to register for me as they did for Bruno. If the phoenix was an agent of transmission for a virus, a contagion that induced the desire to search for the home from which it had been snatched, then I'd caught the bug. My bags were packed. Swindling the old woman was unpleasant to witness, but that was part of the price out of Marseilles.

From the balcony the sun could be seen setting, and Feigen braided and unbraided the fringes of his prayer shawl as he looked out the window. "The word for travelers and emissaries searching for the lost tribes is *shelihim*. Think about it," he said, and he left to join his Tunisians for the *mincha* service.

December 1, 1936
We continued to do business with him for many weeks, over a month. Nothing more was said directly about the lost city, but he gave us short lessons

in archaeology and the Lost Tribes. Feigen's lectures took the form of non-sequiturs, fragments of information, seemingly unrelated to moving merchandise from one part of Marseilles to another.

"It took Benjamin of Tudela eighteen days to cross Arabia to reach the City of the Lost. Eighteen," Feigen said, "is the number that signifies good luck and life itself. According to Dr. Gustave Solomon Oppert, orientalist, who held the chair in Sanskrit at a university in Madras for twenty years before taking up a post in Berlin in 1894, the Lost Tribes could be found in India. Rumors of kingdoms in the east were blank pieces of paper on which any metropolis could be drafted, and these whispers have only increased when a mass murder, deportation, or exodus is about to occur, as if to say, by looking for lost peoples you'll be redeemed."

Trying to catch the lost tribes is like trying to pin down your shadow, it seems to me, or the memory of a shadow. The outline looks like you, but will always be elusive, can't ever be captured, questioned, no dialogue can be engaged with it, but the nostalgia for this lost version can't ever be gotten over.

The simurgh became a source of anxiety for Fingers, and handling it, making sure it was still there, was like a nervous tic. The object was rarely out of his sight, and he could be caught obsessively tracing its markings as he shifted the creature from hand to hand. Dark circles under his eyes turned into bags, and he grew more anxious with each hour, unable to concentrate on selling the violins, sets of encyclopedias, empty picture frames and various things we'd collected. We arrived early one morning to find him in an uncharacteristically jolly mood as he inventoried some glass animals ready to board an ark, itself carved from a discarded carousel horse, or so he said. The Kaliningrad ghosts had completed the job. The package Feigen received from his cousins contained every document we could have wished for.

"If you wanted to go to America, this would have been beyond their skill," Fingers assured us, "but for where you'll be traveling, less precision is required. It's fortunate that even from Berlin I still wrote to this cousin from time to time."

To my untrained eye all the papers spread before us looked completely authentic, and the Franco-Soviet Friendship Dig was inaugurated. Feigen whispered the Russian words aloud, a language I'd never heard him speak before.

"The Russian archaeologists are to join you later." He pronounced their names, these bogus characters, Gennady Pavlovich Antonov, and Ivan Sergeevich Bezymensky. "It's a shame you and Bruno don't speak Russian. Try repeating some of these lines after me."

"*The Franco-Soviet Friendship Society was set up to promote mutual. . . .*" He began, then stopped and looked up at me. "Come on, Sidonie, let me hear you say a few lines."

Bruno and I were careful never to speak Russian in front of Feigen. Had this happened, the former Berlin professor would have recognized our accents immediately.

"*The Franco-Soviet Friendship Society was set up to promote mutual. . . .*" I tried to sound like a French person speaking Russian.

"That's very well done," Feigen smiled. He was so drunk with the illusion he set up, he turned a deaf ear to what was actually fairly confident and competent Russian.

"What's the good of this act? This is no time to learn a new language." Bruno entered the room carrying several violin cases under his arms. They were old and moldy, probably not worth much. Soon, I hoped, I would no longer have to be concerned with how much someone's beloved cello or viola would fetch. Sidonie Nieumacher, a Berliner, was an identity that fit like a coat whose sleeves are too short and tight, so it clings, and is hard to take off, however Sidonie the archaeologist, sun-burned, shovel in hand, that was a daring and exciting image. Maybe from a flickering newsreel it really comes, but who cares? I threw the crumpled coat in a corner. You can plan for heat, dust, for scorpions in the desert, while here there are rumors of people who fire guns, and you don't know in which corner they're lurking.

Bruno picked the papers off a table and looked over the signed and decorated letters authenticating our dummy organization. The red and black Soviet stamps with their angles and intertwined calligraphy were works of genius if you asked me, though no one did. Most important of all were entrance visas for Persia, issued in Paris. Feigen's cousins were grand viziers of illusion, yet Bruno stood in the doorway, half in one room, half in the hall, still unconvinced.

Feigen explained each document to him, translating from the Russian, slowly putting one sheet of paper on top of the next, in a very orderly fashion. Some were on onionskin, others on thicker paper, and the leaves floated one on top of the next as he argued the case for Suolucidir. Here was the charter establishing the Franco-Soviet Friendship Society, accompanied by letters from its Soviet and French board members stating its exploration agenda and goals to foster friendly scientific explorations that would in turn engender good will between nations and expand the horizons of all the peoples of the world, etc. etc. The Society was launching a dig in Sistan-va-Baluchistan, looking for Seulucid artifacts. Nothing was said about nearby Suolucidir and evidence of the Lost Tribes. Feigen didn't want to raise any red flags as to our true project. As far as the Friendship Society was concerned we were looking for relics from an ancient city, nothing more. Here were our exit visas based on documents Feigen's cousins had obtained at great risk on the black market in Vilna. They were based on a French visa, stolen from an Alsatienne Communist fleeing Stalin's midnight knock on the door. She'd had her fling in Leningrad and was lucky to get out when she could, even if she'd lost this along the way. Apparently they'd made an exact replica, changing only the USSR to the Kingdom of Shah Reza Pahlavi. Poor Mademoiselle X. If she made it as far as Vilnius she could get into Finland or Poland and eventually travel back home to Strasbourg. The Soviet Union was full of French, German, and Italian communists who'd had to flee Hitler or Mussolini, but now had to go elsewhere, often traveling through the Baltic states. Perhaps Mademoiselle X didn't exist and never had. The provenance of the visas could have been entirely invented by the slaphappy printers. I hoped not. Feigen was beaming as he shuffled the papers, replacing them in their box. With these forgeries the dreams of an itinerant *lamed vovnik* and the lost child version of Shuki Fingers Feigen would be realized.

We left soon after, walking home in silence, stopping momentarily to light cigarettes, leaning against a door whose keystone gargoyle spat an arc of rainwater into a gutter. If we didn't accept the passage and identities produced for us, I felt like these were the equivalent of our last cigarettes, the ones we'd smoke on the way to the gallows. Bruno scoffed and walked ahead of me. He didn't see it that way at all.

The concierge handed us our keys and tried to engage in small talk about the price of bread and the scarcity of eggs, yet I couldn't bring myself to make conversation with her, however fleeting. She wanted to tell me something else, to prolong the conversation, but Bruno continued to walk on ahead, through the courtyard, and I hurried to catch up to him.

"The papers look real to you, but what if we're turned back at the docks?"

He turned to me as he unlocked our door. "What if we're not allowed to disembark at Bandar Abbas, and we're left afloat without a country to return to? This is a letter of transit to a city that lives only in Feigen's imagination."

"What makes you think customs officials can read Russian? French, maybe, but not thorny academic Russian." I began to make dinner while Bruno walked up and down the length of the apartment.

"People at borders aren't idiots. They can certainly read the Persian. How do we know Feigen's relatives didn't make up their own Farsi documents and seals based on what they imagine they might look like? Oh, let's draw an imperial winged lion here, yes, that seems about right. For all we know these are visas to Chelm, City of Fools. We have nothing to compare any of them to. The whole stack smelled of herring oil."

"Feigen said his cousins were professional, very good at what they do."

"He hasn't seen them in over thirty years." Bruno gave a you-know-nothing shrug. "These people could be working out of a stable with machinery powered by a lame horse made to trudge in circles, led round and round by a deaf mute."

"I thought they looked like they'd been issued on the Rue de Lille and signed by Molotov himself. It doesn't matter if the signatures from French and Russian archaeologists who have joined together for mutual advancement of scholarship are forged. These people don't exist. You can't forge something that wasn't real in the first place." He plopped himself down on the bed, opened up an old copy of *Arbeiter Illustrierten Zeitung*, picked up who knows where, and thumbed through its satirical cartoons and photomontages. We knew these by heart. I found the *AIZ* magazines depressing and tried to hide them, but Bruno always sniffed them out.

"This whole thing stinks, Sido. I have appointments set up for months from now, and there'll be others following those. The Rothschilds are leaving for Switzerland, the Weils are leaving for Spain. They all have valuables to dispose of. No one, neither you nor Fingers, has explained to me why I should give all this up to look for evidence of an ancient utopia."

"We'll be rich. You won't need the Rothschilds' cast-offs. You'll get credit for discovering the lost city." None of the families he mentioned would ever deal with him, a Nieumacher, a nobody, who lived in cheap rooms close to the port. Didn't he think I knew that?

He shrugged and went back to writing in a pocket calendar.

"What if the door swings shut, and no one is allowed to leave? Immigration stops at the border. Even fake passports will have no more currency, and there will be no more sellers or buyers, what then?"

"Traffic never comes to a complete standstill, whether human or material, molecules are always in motion." He bent down to tie a shoelace. "I need to know the café around the corner where they know what I smoke and drink, and I'm on familiar terms with the topography of the zinc countertop. On the intersection of Avenue Zola and Rue Clemenceau there's a kiosk that's also a drop-off for a numbers game where a former sailor with one arm shortened by half, a Corsican milliner, and a man in a cassock with heavily pomaded hair who may or may not actually be a priest can be seen depositing little pieces of paper from time to time. I recognize which fishmonger rests his thumb on the scale just behind the head so you can't see it unless you know what to watch for, and which one will give away the stuff he can't sell just before closing time because he suffers anxiety, having recently witnessed a murder a few blocks away, and he wants to get home before dark. If you know all these things you have some idea of who you can trust when the wolf is at the door, and also who will hold the light for the wolf and, for two pfennigs finders' fee, point out exactly where you live. In Sistan-va-Baluchistan you won't know a camel's ass from its eyeballs."

"I'll go on my own if I have to."

"Fine, go ahead. I'll leave you to your preparations. Your services aren't keeping my operations afloat. Be sure to leave your keys with the concierge."

With that Bruno walked out, not slamming the door, but still very much gone. Departure was quick and simple, but I thought he'd be back. He'd had these tantrums before. I couldn't say, even to myself, Bruno is a coward, or Bruno is a pragmatist, but I was charmed by the idea of the lost city this mystic Motke described. Bruno, who read stolen physics books as a boy, was immune, inoculated at an early age against *lamed vovniks* who sucked you in with promises of lost cities, but my bags were packed, well, not really, not yet. I looked around the tiny flat. If I had to scram at a moment's notice what would I jam into a case? I was methodical. From the closet I took a small bag fitted with a piece of cardboard that could be removed from the bottom. I placed the Franco-Soviet Friendship papers under it, packed the suitcase, locked it, placed it in the middle of the bed, then sat on its edge, not sure what to do next. I could see the light from the concierge's post.

The woman was a problem. Why was she so solicitous to me instead of, for example, the sunny Corsican widow or the retired silk salesman who was still always offering "good deals for the ladies?" If she saw Bruno leave so late at night she might draw conclusions, might want to confide a little; she was a foreigner like us, like so many of our neighbors in the apartment building in Berlin. We find these kinds of immigrant honeycombs, or they find us.

When Bruno returned later in the evening I was asleep with the bag at my feet, but I heard him come in and sat up in bed. His profile was visible from the streetlight spilling through the unshuttered window. A chill wind blew in off the sea, he said, as if nothing had happened and I'd asked for a weather report. He'd walked around close to the piers, stopping in a bar, but finally he had nowhere else to go, and no one to talk to. He wandered the streets alone, not for the first time. We keep to ourselves here, and rely on one another, a closed universe of two, there is no one else. Feigen survives, even thrives, living in a half-dream world. His feet weren't quite on the ground anymore. Could you trust him, really? Yes, I said, I still thought so. Why? Why are you so sure of him? Bruno wanted to know. It's as if he'd been knighted somewhere, and once the sword touched his shoulder, everything he said had the stamp of authority. He'd unearthed the Gate of Ishtar and been part of the expedition that spirited it thousands of miles away from its place of origin. Feigen of Oranienburgerstrasse I would never have questioned, but even in his Fingers incarnation, I was ready to follow him into the desert. He made everything sound reasonable and possible, even though the journey was sparked by a chance encounter with a nut job clutching something I'd never seen before, even though he wasn't actually going into the desert with us, only giving us the most general idea of what lay where. Bruno sat on the edge of the bed, head in his hands.

"Feigen is good at business, better than I would have thought possible, but not capable of throwing out a lifeline if you fall overboard."

"Let's talk about it in the morning. I can't argue in my sleep." I was very tired, sleep claimed me along with a small imp of glee that I could become Feigen's favorite for a moment, his devoted, unquestioning acolyte, while Bruno slipped into an of abyss of skepticism.

Bruno is wrong about Feigen. Even as he lives increasingly in the world of his childhood, this time around with the Tunisians rather than with the ghost of the Gaon of Vilna, he is, in fact, throwing us a rope. Bruno just doesn't know the extent to which we're losing sight of the shore. I'm sure of it. He got into bed fully dressed without saying a word. It was a kind of reconciliation, though nothing was resolved, nor would it ever be, truly.

The next day Bruno left to meet with a wealthy family who were selling what property they had that could be liquidated quickly. Not the Rothschilds or the Weils, but whoever they were, the family was leaving for Cuba that very night. Bruno was to do a quick appraisal, give them cash, and arrange for whatever he bought to be transported to Feigen's apartment warehouse. Sometimes I went with him. My French was a bit better, but that day there was no need. The family, like us, were recent arrivals from Germany, and all parties concerned wanted to finish business as quickly as possible and walk away.

I wandered back toward the café where we'd met the old woman who sold Feigen the simurgh. There was a lot of activity on the piers: shipments loaded and unloaded, but I found myself looking, more than usual, not at the transport of things, but at the people leaving. Some were very public about their departure, hand clamped on fur collar, hats pulled low, issuing orders at ships' porters, sometimes at captains, even. Others left more quietly, secretly, barely visible as they slipped cash to first mates or cooks, whoever might secret them away in steerage or hidden in freighters bound to unnamed ports. I wondered if she would reappear, and scanned the street for some sign of her tattered costume, but she was nowhere in evidence. A peddler scurried away when he saw me. Was it the same one as the other day? I'm not sure. I wandered around a market, and finally after buying olives, lemons, and artichokes, I made my way home. Late afternoon turned to evening. I went out, came back again, but Bruno, who should have long ago completed business, did not appear. He didn't like carrying a lot of Feigen's cash around Marseilles. It made him uneasy, so he would have wanted to return to Fingers as quickly as possible. Bruno was not one who could effortlessly have fought off even a lame thug, and with his dapper clothes and small build, he was a walking target. Feigen trusted him, and despite our fears, he was often right. Bruno was only robbed one time, and that was before we'd even become reacquainted with Feigen. It was past six in the evening. I decided to go to Fingers' to find out what had happened. As I walked through the courtyard Lev, the concierge's sixteen-year-old son, called out to me.

"Madame Nieumacher, stop, please, for a minute."

Unlike his mother, Lev rarely spoke to us at all. I don't think he talked much to anyone. His speech was often difficult to follow, as if the road from thought to expression was full of doubt and marked by stuttering. His left eye drifted to one side, while the other was able to focus.

"What is it, Lev?"

"I saw Monsieur Bruno this morning. I said hello to him, twice I said hello, but then some men put him in a car."

"You mean he was arrested?" If someone had reached out from the mop cupboard and strangled me, that's how I felt. One minute your shoes click on the flagstones as you put one foot in front of the other, the next you have trouble finding oxygen. Why did he wait until now to find me to tell me this?

"I don't know for certain if it was the police, you know? Don't go to the station to ask about him," Lev warned. "Even if it wasn't the police who took him, they'll arrest you, too." He abruptly covered his tracks. "It was an un-marked car. No one would arrest M. Nieumacher. He isn't a thief is he? Has he killed someone?" These were the questions of a boy who knew the streets well, and who countered mysteries with the worst possible outcome. His mother poked her head out to yell at him, he should come back in already, dinner was on the table.

I leapt upstairs, grabbed my bag and ran back through the courtyard, hoping the concierge, busy with her cooking, hadn't noticed me. Lev wasn't quite right in the head. He could have seen many things that hadn't neces-sarily happened. Still, as I made my way to Fingers' apartment, I avoided the Rue de la Republique, a more direct route, and walked instead down narrow streets, zigzagging, and back-tracking as the sun dropped lower and lower in the sky. I picked streets that were as empty as possible, using the reflections in shop windows to determine if anyone was following me. Business streets gave way to residential blocks whose buildings or houses were fronted by porticos carved with lion heads, phoenixes, pineapples and intertwined fish, symbols of the merchants who had once lived within. A woman pulling laun-dry in from a balcony stared at me, at least I thought she did. A man in a fez appeared behind me on Rue des Saltimbanques, so I abruptly switched to the elbow-shaped Rue le Chatelier. It was probably just chance that explained his walk on exactly the same route as mine, but with his repeated presence in the glass I walked faster, yet at the same time tried to appear unhurried, just out for an evening stroll, as if that were possible. Finally I reached Feigen's street in a neighborhood genteel enough to just pass (our clientele was picky, but nervous, and in a hurry) but also near the railroad. Ringing the doorbell over and over until his concierge opened the door, I fell into the entrance of his building just as the man in the fez rounded the corner. Had he seen me? Had he even been following me? The woman was silent and only gestured with her head that yes, Monsieur Fingers was upstairs. I could take the lift.

Feigen came to the door with a prayer shawl over his head, swaying, mumbling in Hebrew, refusing to speak French or German.

"Dr. Feigen, I need you to speak a language I understand." He turned away from me, but continued to mutter prayers in a low sing-song voice. I asked him again, and he only walked further into the cluttered apartment. Who was he trying to resurrect with this endless loop of chanting? Thirteen-year-old Shuki dreaming of Nevski Prospekt, Potsdammer Platz, the Eiffel Tower? Mar Eldad Ha-Dani back from the dead ready to explain everything?

"Bruno was picked up."

He paused for a moment, still swaying a bit while clutching the top of a chair. Finally, in German, he asked if I had the Franco-Soviet Friendship papers with me. I nodded. Feigen led me deeper into the apartment to the room with the sliding panel, and once again pushed the bookcase away, dusted off the chair with a handkerchief and opened the cabinet of curiosities. I noticed more cans and bags of food had been stacked against one of the walls.

"What the police were looking for could be any number of things. They may have found something amiss in his papers. At worst he'll be deported back to Berlin."

"Or he could be shot."

Feigen looked at me as if I were an idiot in need of being lied to. He let the shawl slide, catching it just before it hit the floor. Of course he could be done away with, what do you think, we're watching *Dr. Caligari*, only waiting to be told all participants are hearing voices while strolling the asylum grounds?

"The papers took too long to arrive from Kaliningrad. You should have left long before this. Also, the French police won't believe he was from Alsace, gone to study in Berlin." He raised his eyebrows the way Bruno often did, as if to say some secret, you schmendricks, I was on to you all along, but I ignored him. "They'll probably come for you next, as early as the morning, perhaps even tonight. There's a ship leaving for Alexandria in a few hours. I've booked passages for two."

"When did you meet with this captain?"

"Two days ago."

"You were going to leave without telling us?"

He nodded. At first, yes, that had been his plan.

"Who was the second passage for?"

He extended an arm, hand open in my direction. I looked down at his saucer palm, fingers splayed, ready to catch any fish that swam too close, but kept my arms clasped behind my back. What did this mean? I'd never imagined either FFF or Shuki Fingers thought of me as anything other than Nieumacher's wife and mostly silent accomplice. His conversation was always directed at Bruno, and he rarely looked in my direction. I was the hat check girl, the waitress, tray in hand, the tailor's assistant whose measuring tape never touched an inseam, and I was perfectly happy being that person. Feigen hadn't ever really impressed me as a human with corporeal needs. At those dinners in Berlin, he didn't touch his food. He smoked and talked, pushed plates away so he could hold court, perhaps to eat alone in the kitchen late at night. Whether Dr. Feigen or Shuki Fingers, he was a thought machine, a brain on stilts, stuck in a pale, melting, fallible body I tried not to notice. I didn't know what to say. Once, at a dinner in Berlin he described an English Egyptologist, Flinders Petrie, who sometimes worked completely naked. Was he looking at me as he spoke? That's how I remember it, and I looked at his wife who had turned red, though I would have expected she was used to his stories. Someone else diffused the awkwardness at the table by going on to describe how in 1917 when the British captured Palestine from the Turks, Petrie proposed the entire population of Jerusalem be moved elsewhere so excavation would be facilitated. I still couldn't get the image of Feigen himself working naked out of my head.

"I could become the Bruno Nieumacher named in the Franco-Soviet organization. I thought, well, there is always a possibility, and maybe this plan would appeal to you. When Bruno failed to appear this afternoon I was alarmed, but also a little hopeful. We could leave together as the Nieumachers. I can change the date of birth on the Franco-Soviet Friendship Dig documents. It's not a difficult operation. And look what I have here."

From his pocket he removed a flat maroon object, held it toward me, and slowly turned the pages. It was a passport for Bruno Nieumacher, born in Alsace, but where his picture should have been, was a photograph of an old man, Frederik Feigen. It was very well made. Better than the one Bruno carried.

"I had it made just in case, you never know, just in case, you see . . . for a rainy day, should one arrive, and I think it has. In my opinion."

He reached for my hand, then let it go as if he knew every cell in it was racing in the other direction, sorry, back against the wall and through the plaster, down the street, across the city.

"You know there are worse things that could happen to you." (Looking down from his post in an imaginary classroom would he tell me a story of Russian rapists, arsonists, murderers, as if I didn't already know all about these? Just around the corner there are always phantoms, everyone has them, and often they have sharp knives, x-ray vision, and the power of surprise on their side.)

I pulled my hand away.

"So that's how it is. I see." Feigen looked deflated.

"Bruno wasn't picked up by accident?' My voice went up slightly at the end of the sentence. I couldn't help it. I didn't know if I was asking a question or stating a fact. Feigen shook his head ambiguously. Was he denying he'd tipped off the police exactly, or was the movement of his head meant to indicate avoidance, refusal to answer in so many words, walking in a different direction now. It was growing darker. I was uncomfortable in the small room with Feigen and reached for a light switch, flicked it. Nothing happened. Feigen took the perfect passport, held it under a faucet, drenching the pages, so laboriously constructed, which much have cost him a fortune. He exhaled deeply.

"Last night, later and later it got. I looked around, I found myself completely unable to pack, to put anything in a container or a suitcase. I no longer knew how to decide what to hold on to, what to leave behind. I'm finished with moving from place to place. The comforts of a small enclosed room are sometimes greater than you might imagine." He pointed to the room concealed by the bookcase. He gave up the image of traveling east with a student wife and would retreat into his room when the time came. If I had agreed to his plan, well, that would have been a different story, but I hadn't.

Without saying another word Feigen handed me the more current maps, and though it clearly pained him, he also gave me Yanek Motke's map, the most valuable thing, perhaps the only thing, to survive from his childhood. We said our goodbyes, and when he turned to the east to continue praying, I grabbed the simurgh from the cabinet, snapped open my bag, and dropped it inside. I needed the creature to prove I had a destination, to put a seal on the idea that I was going somewhere, and wasn't to be left *aladrerden*, adrift in a sea of shit.

~

Running in the rain to the piers, I looked down at the pavement cracks, not wanting to take a last glimpse at the city. Lights from the ship, *Le Faroan*, twinkled from the harbor, and I boarded without looking back.

An Egyptian boy who spoke a little French showed me to my cabin. He told me I had arrived just in time. They would be setting off in only a few minutes. When I unlocked the door Bruno was lying on my narrow bunk smoking a cigarette as if he had all the time in the world, and it was I who was late. He rubbed his wrist then rolled up his cuff as if showing me a bracelet he'd lifted from some unsuspecting patron.

"I hope you brought papers for two."

~

Despite the story we floated as students in Berlin, we weren't French citizens and never had been. We had German passports, but when we entered France we needed visas, as well. Having left in a hurry, like many others, we didn't have them, and if caught, we could be expelled, sent back to Berlin. It was a well-known fact that the French bureaucracy and immigration moved like a sleepy, overfed sloth, and its filing system was an inefficient, disorganized mess. In other words, the odds were good you could stay on indefinitely, never caught, but sometimes one was caught. Then Leon Blum was elected, and things got a little easier, but one couldn't breathe entirely freely, not at all. Bruno's visa-less German passport, his identity card, all of it, were no more real than the papers sent to us by the printers in Kaliningrad.

"I was picked up on the Rue de Forbin and locked up in St. Pierre prison. I thought it was a random sweep."

He described being thrown into a cell with a group of skeletal lice-ridden people he described as Judeo-Boches. They're particularly at risk because they need special police permits to move from place to place, which they rarely have. Bruno was sure his arrest was a mistake.

"There were a few depleted, *vahntz*-ridden straw mattresses on the floor percolating with bugs, and a small barred window overhead. I was the only one whose suit was intact; the other inmates wore tattered clothing, cuffs so frayed they looked fringed, buttonless jackets held together with pins or with their hands. Some had been interned for months or even years, but the majority of them arrived at St. Pierre prison already in bad shape. Some spoke neither French nor German. One man wouldn't leave his post from the furthest wall where he rocked, hitting his back against the stone. He feared flood, waters rising, no way out, everyone struggling hopelessly to keep their noses above the surface, but then when someone managed to light a cigarette he grew afraid of fire and tried to climb near the window. Though the men paced and shifted like a mass of fish all swimming in the same circle, I tried to stay away from him. It was because of this choreography that I struck up a conversation with one inmate in particular. Pinza, sitting on the floor, cleared some space beside himself with one hand and extended a hairy, dirty paw. It felt like a limp wharf rat. I told him my name."

"'Nieumacher is a funny name for a yid. What were you picked up for?'

"I shrugged, not sure why myself, really, so I said, *papiers*. Pinza pretended not to understand this simple word, as if he were egging me on for a different language choice, so I finally said, *papiren*.

"'Yeah, we all have no *papiren*,' Pinza said with a tell-me-another-one shrug. 'What we got here,' he made a sweeping gesture to include the whole cell block, 'are all slaughterers but no chickens.'

"Who was this Pinza? Pinza was a *ganef*, a thief, he admitted it himself, and he was a fountain of slang.

"Each word I thought I knew was, from the mouth of Pinza, twisted into a different meaning." So they used a language he knew and didn't know at the same time. It was as if every word were turned on its ear and had to be interpreted according to some kind of core meaning, the meaning one ordinarily took for granted.

"'I shouldn't be here at all. I'm here because of my worthless *shutaf*. It's all his fault and no one else's. We'd been on a job, and the shithead hadn't alerted me to the fact that the handful of gold necklaces I was about to lift was *treyf*.'"

"*Treyf?* You mean he had ham in his pocket?" I was confused. Bruno leaned against the wall with a bit of a smirk on his face.

"No, not ham. At first I didn't understand either, what he was talking about, then he explained, in the language of thieves *treyf* means there are police around, and the things about to be lifted turn into *treyf*, that which shouldn't be touched," Bruno explained. Even after what was really only a few hours in this cell Bruno sounded peculiar. How seamlessly he hop-scotched between student, leonardo, black marketeer, and jailbird.

"Even in the prison Pinza had managed to keep his black felt hat pulled down to his ears, and he spoke with confidence, tapping the hat to the back of his head with a flick of his forefinger. His coat with a ratty fur collar had once been snazzy and may have had another owner or two before it fell into his hands. That we weren't wearing uniforms, that our clothes hadn't been taken from us, hinted to me we wouldn't be in the cell for long, but Pinza said, 'Hey, Sherlock, I wouldn't be so sure.'"

"How long had Pinza been in the cell?"

"A few months, he guessed, but it could have been weeks just as easily.

"Pinza pointed out members of the Waks, Feintuch, and Lipsker gangs, all stuck together in the lockup. 'Ha, ha, those three mobs, they hate each other and now look what they got. The Russians who have split into two factions have the north and northeast side of the city, the Moldovans have the northwest slice, and they all have to deal with the Sicilians. Now look at them with no turf and nowhere to go in the middle of a *machlokets*.' A *machlokets* means a rabbinical dispute, but in their slang the word referred to a shady business deal or a gang-style fight on the street."

Just underneath the surface of Bruno the student, the careful artisan, dealer in black market reichsmarks, was the deal maker who, within the span of maybe a couple of hours, felt at home with gangsters, as if they were his family, and truly, for all I knew about Bruno before I met him, this was entirely possible.

"Could you follow what he was saying to you?"

"Most of it. A *meline*, Pinza explained, a hideout full of stolen things had been raided, and both groups were arrested, though each blamed the other for the tip-off. Pinza was the calmest crook I've ever seen. He just leaned against a wall, watched the turmoil around him, and explained things to me."

How did he recognize Bruno as an ally? Who knows, but his intuition would turn out to be right. A few oddball Yids, as Pinza called them, had, like Bruno, been picked up off the street for no reason anyone could figure out. Though he looked down his nose at them, a pretty much undifferentiated mass, this was the soup he was going to have to swim in.

"One of the prisoners, Rudnicki the Stutterer from the Waks gang, had fashioned a screwdriver out of a spoon handle and was working at the door hinges. No escape was possible. Even if we could get out of the chamber, there were guards everywhere, and how would we get out of the St. Pierre unnoticed? No one in the cell had the power of invisibility. But the three men who worked at the hinges in turns were obsessive about it. They had nothing else to do, and Pinza kept assuring me you didn't have to be Houdini to get out of a Marseilles hellhole. It wasn't so hard. He'd done it before, though there was a shift in the air lately. There was some conjecture among the prisoners as to what would happen to them. Once in a while one or two would be hauled out seemingly at random. They were never spotted again, whether freed, deported, or shot, no one knew. Being let go seemed an extremely unlikely outcome to me. Clank, the doors open, and out you stroll, it's over.

"After twelve hours, two gendarmes and a couple of men who wore no recognizable uniform looked into the cell, pointed at me and Pinza, handcuffed us together, and yanked us into the corridor. One of men nodded, affirming that I was the one. Pinza, it appeared, was going along for the ride. We were marched into the prison courtyard and pushed into the back seat of a large black Fiat. Two other men were already sitting in the front seat. Prison gates opened, the car was driven out into the city, and then to its outskirts.

"The men in front spoke between themselves and paid little attention to us, only squinting back once in a while. Pinza inched to the right, pulling me with him, trying the car door, slowly, quietly, just trying the handle, and figuring with the satisfying way the handle met with no resistance when he pressed down on it, that it was unlocked. Our guards were very sure that even unlocked doors offered no promise of escape because we were traveling through a landscape where no one could or would help us, so why bother? I shook my head, no, don't do it. I imagined falling under the wheels of the car, chained to Pinza, the thief whose pockets had briefly contained tangles of golden *treyf*. If we were being deported back to Germany, I could live by my wits again if I had to, but dead in the road because I jumped from a moving car — that's a stupid choice. Pinza whispered, 'You don't get it; we're going to be shot.' How did Pinza know what he knew? Pinza's body was tight against the door. The men in front talked between themselves and never turned their heads to look in the back seat.

"Rounding a curve in the road, Pinza suddenly lurched out of the car, yanking me with him. We rolled down a steep embankment, over and over each other until we came to a stop near the bottom of a ravine. The Fiat veered sharply and screeched as the driver hit the brakes. However, the momentum of curves and brakes was too much to keep the car on the road. As if its occupants all leaned to one side with the swerving, it tipped over the edge and fell off the road, somersaulting downwards almost in slow motion before exploding into flame when it crashed into the bottom of the ravine. The shock of hitting the ground fast, nose smashed against weeds and grass, the momentum of the fall, was like a film run super fast, then the projector suddenly lost power. I was able to sit up and I stared at the burning car, stunned. One of our captors burst out of the wreckage, completely on fire, running toward me, his uniform glowing orange and black, before he collapsed into a heap of burnt flesh, bones, and cinders."

Bruno, small-time fixer, pushed into it by circumstances, a fellow whose crimes were all non-violent and based only on the need to survive when he couldn't be a gentleman scholar, lost his footing and was unable to stand.

"I lay back in the spiky stalks of lavender and rosemary. Pinza lay a few feet away, the chain had come apart in the fall where it was joined to the handcuff. Only his nose was bloody, but his head was snapped at an odd angle. A few centimeters in either direction and it might have been me who smashed his head open on a rock." He rubbed his wrist still encased by the band of metal. "The good fortune of being shackled by lousy equipment, a weakened, rusty solder, saved me, but not Pinza — still grinning — so at least you know his death came fast. Which was a shame really, because had Pinza been a magician he couldn't have caused a better outcome, apart from his own demise, of course."

Bruno, alchemical genius though he was, turning thin paper into identifiable cash, would never call himself a hero or someone with large stores of nerve to draw on, most of the time. For a man who lacked such qualities, he was so lucky that night, and when I told him this, he answered that any croupier in Deauville or Monte Carlo or a barely identified back room will tell you sometimes a poor joe comes along who's just plain lucky. It sounded like an explanation someone else would give. Since when did he know anything about the odds at the tables in cities we'd never been to?

"The road was deserted, nothing but scrappy pine and olive trees as far as I could see, but a small-town train station lay close by. I caught a night train, largely empty, no one asked for papers, and I was able to arrive at Feigen's shortly after you had left.

"Feigen wouldn't open the door, and only barked at me that if I caught a cab I would make it to the pier on time. He said a doctor was due to arrive any minute, and I shouldn't be seen by anyone, leave immediately, a flat bundle of franc notes slid into the gap just above the threshold. Not so much, but it all helps. So we said our goodbyes through wooden panels. He said he hoped to hear of our travels and to see us again as ambassadors from Suolucidir."

He didn't care if the cab driver could later identify him. He would never set foot in Europe again. We had no choice now but to become the Franco-Soviet Friendship Dig. Just as the ship pulled out of port he declared he felt like the Count of Monte Cristo. I replied, this is no time to imagine you're royalty. We have a long way to travel and not much money to our names. The Franco-Soviet Friendship Dig is poor indeed and will have to rely on the generosity of strangers in lands that are entirely unknown to us.

December 10, 1936

Le Faroan isn't exactly a pleasure cruise or even much of a passenger ship at all. It's more like a freighter with some odd rooms fixed up so the captain could take on a few passengers who paid him in cash with no guarantees they'll be welcomed at destined ports, and then they'll have to pay for the return trip, as well. As Fingers promised, *Le Faroan* is bound for Alexandria, but it's not a sure thing that all will be able to disembark there. Though we go on deck and wander around the ship, we feel like stowaways. Almost as soon as Marseilles disappeared from view, a Mr. and Mrs. Spektor from Vienna approached us like two skaters looping from one side of the pond to the other until they finally reached us, temporarily putting aside suspicion and reluctance. Then it was as if Mrs. Spektor, at least, was magnetized. She spoke to me familiarly and stood very close, assuming we were both on the ship for the same reasons. Her children were put on trains bound for Dieppe—she gestured open-palmed at the ocean as if to indicate they're out there some-where—and from Holland were supposed to go to England, but they've had no letters from them. Mrs. Spektor is tall, smells of a grapefruit-like perfume, and peers through perfectly round tortoise-shell glasses like a hawk, looking around the deck as if a gunman might suddenly appear from behind a coil of heavy chains or pop out of a hatch. The agency that organized the transport assured her the boy and girl had been placed with a family in a town called Jarmouth, pronounced Yarmouth, but Mrs. Spektor imagines they should have received letters by now. She doesn't know if they ever reached England. No longer in Vienna and not at all certain where they are going, Mr. and Mrs. Spektor have no address that can be written to. Sometimes we pass tiny islands with little more than a couple of trees on them.

"If we're not allowed into Egypt perhaps the captain could let us off on one of those small islands that don't belong to anyone," she said.

I've actually considered the same thing myself. To be planted on an empty principality ruled by ants and gulls would be bleak, but safe from armies and unmarked cars. Though if we were on the same island as the Spektors, I suspect I would be called upon to wait on her, find shade trees, fetch water, invent soothing lies, and over time begin to feel protective of my mistress who had suffered so, eventually forgetting there had ever been law books in Berlin, a thriving, though risky, black market business in Mar-seilles, and a city-state somewhere in Persia waiting to be unearthed. Mrs. Spektor has that kind of hold on people. I snapped out of it when she asked how many days do I suspect it will be before we land in Alexandria? She doesn't like to approach the captain. She admits she's a little afraid of him, but says we are fortunate to have gotten on *Le Faroan*. There aren't to be many more such opportunities.

Mr. Spektor, a retired diamond cutter, never had his own business and always worked for others. Mrs. Spektor has repeated this several times al-ready. He had an offer to go to Argentina two years ago, but they stayed, and it was her fault that they did. Had they gone she wouldn't be here now star-ing into the water. All her family, aged mother, beloved aunts, uncles, cous-ins who were like siblings to her, were in Vienna. She hadn't wanted to leave them, and so now here they are stuck on this freighter in rooms little better than steerage. Mr. Spektor, a crown of spiky hair blowing in the breeze, pulls his jeweler's loupe from his pocket, spins it on the edge of the gunwale, always catching it before the little glass-eyed cylinder topples into the sea. He carries it with him, I assume, because it's one of the important tools of his trade, but it turns out they have no bags. Last night there was some kind of fried octopus and garlic for dinner, which they didn't eat, though Bruno dove into it with gusto, as if it were his last meal. Mr. Spektor referred to a movie called *Monkey Business* in which Groucho, Harpo, Chico, and I think he said Zeppo Marx hide in a ship, concealing themselves in barrels of kippered herring, in closets, under desks.

"Where on this tub could you hide if you absolutely had to?" Ernst Spektor asked. "In the water ballast tanks? Just for a few minutes, of course. The cargo hold, crouching between crates of car parts, spools of wiring, imported dogs in their cages, the only living things to keep you company? This is possible. You are like these Marx brothers playing pinochle and singing while everyone searches for you. Maybe, as you prowl around the hold, you find bottles of wine, olive oil, wheels of cheese, you can eat and drink, be happy, and then you find a box of 45 Mausers with clips, of course. If so, take one. You may soon need it. Now not only are you drunk, but you can defend yourself. The cargo hold is the obvious place they will look for you. Another choice: maybe in the engine room, dodging pistons and the engineer as he makes his rounds. Maybe this is a better place, though there will be no food. Or in the pilot's cabin. But can you be sure you can trust the pilot?"

Bruno, elbow propped on the table, a ring of octopus pierced on the end of his fork, dripping olive and garlic onto his cuff, looked at Spektor as if he'd just popped out of a barrel himself.

"We are like these brothers Marx," he said, trying to sound jovial. His smile faded, and his wife pushed her plate away, untouched, and told him to take a walk. I felt sorry for him.

Mrs. Spektor is very shrewd, so sure of her opinions there is no membrane between what she thinks and what she says. It's difficult not to accept her confidences and the intimacy they usher in, and then it's as if we're close friends, but only on her terms. She's suspicious, asks questions, but it's only to figure out how we might be useful to her at some unknown point in the future. It's difficult on the ship with few places for passengers to congregate to avoid her, to find a room or a few feet of deck she might not likely be. Today she found me on deck just as we passed Malta. The shore with its white city could have been another planet, it was so remote, and perhaps unfairly,

I imagined people going about their lives with no one chasing them and no fear of a knock at the door.

At first we stared out in silence, then she suddenly said, "You're not from Alsace. Like my husband you come from further east. I can hear it when you speak German. Only a native Austrian with good ears, like myself, could hear this in your accent."

Under a peel of gray paint, *Le Faroan* had been blue, and under that was a lighter gray. Scraping at a peel of paint with my fingernail, I told her she was mistaken, and she smirked. "You don't have to tell me anything. I know what I know. So your husband is a rare book dealer. Why did he leave Alsace for Marseilles? I would suppose business would be better there. Marseilles is a city of foreigners and thieves. Why do you speak German fairly well? Why does your husband have an iron bracelet around his wrist? How are you going to get into Alexandria?" Is it an exaggeration to say her questions came at me like bullets? Yes, but there was a note of anger behind her questions, as if she was saying, don't think you're so smart, missy, don't think you're so different from me. I fled as soon as I could, finding Bruno in our cabin. He stays there most of the time reading books on Persia that Feigen had given to us. When I told him about Mrs. Spektor's inquiries and assumptions he turned prickly, the old condescending Bruno was back.

"Just stay away from her." He lay in his bunk with his back to me as if I was an annoyance who couldn't figure out how to solve simple problems.

"How can I avoid her? What am I supposed to do? Follow the sailors around while they wind up rope and oil gears? There are hardly any other passengers on this ship." Bruno barely knows the layout of the boat, much less who the other voyagers might be. "She misses her children. She wants to talk to me."

You see her here, you see her there, that damned elusive Mrs. Spektor. Bruno quoted Leslie Howard in *The Scarlet Pimpernel*, a movie we saw long ago in Berlin. He used to repeat lines from it as we newcomers found ourselves going in circles in the city, but now he only shrugged, while his eyes roamed the page from left to right. Absorbed in reading about Suolucidir, he was no longer listening to me. Since we'd left Marseilles Bruno was more and more submerged in reading about the lost city. Sometimes trying to talk to him was like taking a crowbar to a manhole cover heavily rusted in place: almost unpryable. Whether I opened the subject of lost children or the fog blowing in from the east, he made me feel as if I spoke another language reserved only for articulating trivialities, and I was reminded of our early days in Berlin when he constantly corrected my accent, told me not to use my hands to carve the air, spoken words were enough, and to wear shorter skirts, we're in the west, please.

So my only company, and I took her on reluctantly, was Mrs. Spektor. A desperate conversationalist, she was stymied on *Le Faroan* for lack of an audience. I once saw her hesitate on the stairs to the bridge and again at the door to the officer's cabin. Captain Raffarin is half Algerian, speaks French to us, Arabic to his crew. He's remote and clearly concerned with running the ship, not to be bothered with us once he'd taken our money for passage. We are here at his sufferance, which could be rescinded at any moment. She's afraid Raffarin will ask for more money before he lets them off the ship, or threaten to turn them in, and they've nothing left to pay him. Even if they could meet on some imaginary neutral deck, no demands made either way, what would Mrs. Spektor say to him? I backtracked but later ran into her on the steep stairs that connected our cabins to the deck. Going in the opposite direction, she was impossible to evade. It was as if Mrs. Spektor could be in several places at once. Taking my arm she steered me to a corner of the deck near the bow light, and before she could pepper me with any more questions, I asked her about the doctor in Vienna I'd heard about so many years ago, the one who listened to your dreams.

"We were diamond cutters. It was a dangerous business, and we didn't talk to anyone about our dreams. My husband was hired based on a particular lot of stones that came from South Africa via London or Antwerp. He worked in a secret shop. The location was always changing, and he never had his own business, though this was something we both wanted. Now he's old with unsteady hands, and it will never happen. Who would pay a doctor to listen to their dreams? You really must be from some Russian backwater."

She put her hand on my sleeve and started to talk about what would happen if they were sent back. I so wanted to get away from her, and at the same time there was something that kept me listening to her, as if when I did so, I was outside myself, watching an old print of *Dr. Caligari* once again. These things would never happen to me, only a silent witness lost at sea. Her husband, I rarely saw after he compared us to the stowaways in the cargo hold of a movie-set ship. Perhaps he was researching hiding places, secret berths, filling his pockets with walnuts for the day when the food ran out. I noticed

Mrs. Spektor had no wedding ring and the holes in her ears were without stones or gold. The sea was black, then grey-blue. We're almost there.

December 13, 1936
The port with white domes and palm trees looked nothing like Marseilles or anyplace I've ever seen. In the crush of porters and crates being carried off *Le Faroan*, I lost sight of Mrs. Spektor and her husband who wanted to be a Marx brother, and never saw or heard from them again.

December 27, 1936
From Alexandria we traveled overland through Egypt, Palestine, stopping in Amman, and it was here that the Franco-Soviet Friendship Dig came under the most intensive scrutiny. We had no trouble entering the city, but leaving with the intention of traveling to Tehran and beyond alerted the attention of the British authorities. Until this point Bruno and I traveled more or less on our own, just as we had in Europe, sometimes joining a caravan, sometimes not, but the next leg of our trip couldn't possibly be made by ourselves alone. The iron band had disappeared from his wrist, but he wouldn't talk about how and when this happened. While in Amman we heard about a caravan of local merchants: Turks, Persians, Armenians, and Frenchmen who were traveling east for reasons unknown to us, but it seemed wise to join up with them. As we made our way through the last gate on the outskirts of Amman, the convoy of jeeps and camels was stopped. The Arabs grumbled. They had never needed papers to travel across the desert before. The Turks shrugged. The French and Armenians took the randomly established checkpoint as a nuisance, but matter of course, and indifferently handed over their papers for inspection. Especially the French, even a lowly merchant, was at pains to barely make eye contact as a way of letting the English know their soldiers would be tolerated but not aided and abetted. Some years the French were in charge, sometimes the Turks, sometimes the British. Finally they arrived down the caravan to us. Some sort of custom agent or army officer in charge of the crossing stuck out his hand for our papers.

"Friendship Dig," he said in English, translating aloud, and never once looking up. The skepticism and suspicion in his voice couldn't be misinterpreted even by optimistic shyster mystic Yanek Motke in his grave.

The man's khaki uniform was starched and without wrinkles, but he had a dusty moustache, as if he'd been at this post for so long he no longer bothered to tip the sand from his boots. Though young, the skin around his eyes was a web of fine craquelure from exposure to desert wind.

"Friendship Dig," he repeated, then took a pair of glasses out of a pocket in order to review our documents again, more closely, then called another officer over, pointed to the page allegedly from a government in Tehran. The glasses alarmed me. Could their magnification reveal blots of ink, inauthentic roundels in script, pens pressed too hard that would reveal us as no more Franco or Friendship or Dig than Winston Churchill? The two men spoke in English, an opaque language of hard k's, no lilt, a certain sibilance, and an excess of interrogative sounds. Bruno knows a little, but he insisted they speak in French, asking them what was the matter, everything was in order as far as every other border we'd crossed, could we please proceed? We needed to make a wadi, an oasis, before nightfall.

"We don't understand," said the one with the monocle, "how you came to have a paper from a Persian governor we've never heard of." His voice was as bland and crisp as dry toast.

Bruno countered. "These papers have been authorized in Moscow and Paris," as if to say he couldn't explain the ignorance of two English officials, delaying a whole caravan for no concrete reason.

The two whispered for a moment, then turned to Bruno. "We will need you to come with us. A few more questions, if you don't mind. Papers issued in other capitals don't automatically guarantee transit through third-party sovereignties."

Obviously, whether we minded or not was immaterial. There was no combination of phrases that would convince them to let us go, so we were put in a car with the one who seemed in charge and driven to a building in the interior of the city. Out the back window I watched the caravan pull itself together and move toward the gates of the city. We would have to pay for another to travel with, and in the meantime had no money to bribe these English, nor was I sure a handful of paper was what was needed at that moment. To pass them a bundle of francs or dinars would be to acknowledge we were frauds, and perhaps we weren't quite ready to lay bare the origins of the Franco-Soviet Friendship Dig.

Bruno and I were taken to a large white-domed building, led up a wide marble staircase into a hall that echoed a kind of controlled opulence I hadn't seen since we left Berlin, and even then it was only from a distance. We were ushered into a room with high ceilings, portraits of British generals and maybe a king or two, a fat queen stuffed into a diamond-studded dress. Her cousins, the tzaritzas, wore hidden diamonds that deflected bullets aimed at their hearts, but were killed anyway. You can't cover a whole body in diamonds. Englishman #1 put our papers on the desk of a large bald man, addressed as Major Blanckenship. Standing by a window, he looked, in profile, like the letter D. However, Blanckenship gave the impression that he was solid muscle, or close to it. Not happy to be disturbed (perhaps he'd been interrupted too many times already that day from nervous checkpoint officers who rarely turned up anything truly suspicious) Blanckenship walked toward us looking grim and annoyed. His uniform, looped with gold braid and covered with medals, looked like a costume from an opera. He nodded to a lean, sharp woman he called Rigg or Mrs. Rigg, who bent a goose-necked lamp over our documents. She looked as if she were about thirty and had narrow eyes that had migrated outward, cheekbones like a ledge, a pointed nose that led the way. Rigg said little, but the few phrases she spoke were uttered in a precise bone-china English I couldn't follow. In a navy blue suit, buttoned up but closely fitted and tight, she looked at me only once, briefly, registering my presence in the room, then never acknowledged me again. Her hair was waved, and she continuously ran her hands through the waves as she bent over our documents. Hair undone made her appear as if there were something hidden under her severity. Both of our interrogators were confident in their power and authority, their sense that all citizens in their dominion were like children, easily placated and manipulated. Blanckenship studied the Franco-Soviet papers through half-lidded eyes. Pages with black and red seals flew by, signatures like tangled threads, Russian diplomas, letters of transit in scalloped Arabic. I didn't look at Bruno. How much of a crime is it to be an imposter? Would we be sent back?

Rigg held a cigarette in clenched teeth. Really, she did, and I could see where some of her mannish confidence might seem seductive to a certain kind of officer who hadn't been home in a very long time. Blanckenship held a paper up to the light. His face was immobile. Then he spoke to us, not in English, but in Russian. His Russian wasn't very good, but he asked us who we really were. Did we face another Mrs. Spektor, another clairvoyant in the guise of a British major stationed in Amman? Bruno stumbled at first, giving him an opportunity to tap his cigarette into a china ashtray shaped like a turbaned head. Truly, when I leaned in to get a better look, in so far as I was able, I could make out the ceramic man's face, long curling moustache, and a scimitar in his teeth. Then Bruno collected himself and answered in French.

"My wife and I were born in Moscow. We studied archaeology at Moscow State University. In 1926 we were fortunate to also study in France, where we have remained since. When the offer came to set up an organization to encourage joint archaeological projects between our former and our adopted countries, we were eager to forge ahead with the possibility that the work of our organization would lead to the discovery of great antiquities."

Where this idea came from I had no idea; perhaps Feigen's books on Persia, or something Bruno cooked up while lying in his bunk in Raffarin's ship. A servant entered with a tray of tea in small gold-rimmed glasses. Bruno paused while tea was poured, sugar added, spoon hit the side of the glass while stirring. No tea was offered to us.

"We're looking for the lost city of Suolucidir, believed to be a kind of aquapolis, a utopian city-state, in the desert. The Suolucidiris were fiercely isolationist, the Switzerland of their era."

Within a moment Bruno turned into the Feigen he remembered lecturing in Berlin, addressing a room full of students. I barely recognized him. His voice and posture changed, and he spoke to the English as if they were Germanic tribesmen accidentally rounded up by Trajan's army – these two look half bright, let's toss them a few random ideas and see if they have any skills. The two of them leaned forward to follow his every word. He sensed this, and with a surge of confidence, continued.

"I've never heard of Suolucidir," Blanckenship admitted. The woman shook her head, no, she hadn't either. Though I never heard her speak a language other than English, she appeared to follow whatever Bruno and Blanckenship were saying.

"My theory is that in the seeds of Suolucidiri success lay their undoing. The inhabitants of the city were not particularly self-sufficient, and by turning their backs on their neighbors they stagnated and disappeared. Water was a valuable commodity, the oil of its time. The Suolucidiris would want to hoard water and keep it from other people. Suolucidir was a child prodigy of a city with an amazing water system, a city-state that leap-frogged over others, but despite their great talents, its citizenry perished. The moon, as with the ancient Babylonians, was a major figure in their cosmology, and over time their corner of the desert became like the moon, distant and inhospitable despite the city that once flourished within its narrow confines. In their isolation they were buried and vanished."

"And you plan to find this city?"

Bruno nodded. I believed, prematurely, that he'd convinced them.

"But you don't have Russian names, then do you? They sound French." Spoon clinked against the side of the glass. Monocle removed, polished, replaced.

Bruno paused. I could sense him pulling bits and pieces, unconfirmable and untraceable, from here and there. Switching briefly to Russian, he explained, the name was Germanic in origin, that his ancestors were among the Germans Catherine the Great had brought to Saint Petersburg to rebuild the Imperial Porcelain Works, but in the course of the two hundred years that followed his family had been completed Russified. Only the last name, Nieumacher (which he pronounced the way Madame Canonbury had, as opposed to the French sound we'd been using since arriving in Berlin), remained.

"Newmaker," said Mrs. Rigg with a smirk, though Blanckenship ignored her. "You know Iran is forming an alliance with Berlin. The Shah is an admirer of your Führer." She wasn't able to finish her sentence. In a clipped, impatient voice Bruno interrupted her.

"This is no concern of ours. Our first names, our Christian names," Bruno enlightened her, "had been Benyamin Mikhailovich and Eliana Zoyakovno, but because we became French citizens, these we changed to Bruno and Sidonie."

The Englishman looked at us over the tops of his thin glasses as if Bruno was a schoolboy reciting a well-known poem imperfectly committed to memory. He made up alternatives for the lines he didn't know, thinking no one would be the wiser. Blanckenship nodded, either with indulgence, or he was finally taken in, I wasn't sure.

"And when you reach Zahedan you expect," he looked down at the papers again, "Gennady Pavlovich Antonov and Ivan Sergeevich Bezymensky to join you?"

Bruno nodded, though one could wait the rest of one's life for Gennady Pavlovich Antonov and Ivan Sergeevich Bezymensky, old Tsarist-era pedants, inventions of Shuki Fingers Feigen.

"There are already many Russians in Persia. Did you know you would find some of your compatriots in the area you wish to travel to?"

"No." We shook our heads. And neither, apparently, had Feigen or his skillful cousins.

"So you don't know why they're in Persia?" Our D-shaped interrogator stood, and navigating the room's furniture, he walked over to a table, picked up a cut glass bottle, poured out two whiskeys, one for himself and one for the woman. I imagined his voice was the product of the green estates of Yarmouth or London or Dover – places on an island I'd pictured as populated by men who carried briefcases and women who rode horses. He swallowed the contents in one gulp, little finger arched over filigreed glass. He picked up his cigarette from the figurehead ashtray, inhaled long and hard, as if to imply, who's the barbarian now?

"Just before the Great War, Shah Muhammad Ali was in exile in Odessa, guarded by the Tsar's own offficers, eventually meant to travel on to Vienna and Carlsbad. We were informed that he had, indeed, left Odessa, but had arrived via Russian steamer, *The Christophoros*, at Gumesh-Teppeh, a small Iranian port on the Caspian Sea. Though his passport declared he was a Baghdadi merchant by the name of Khalil, and he sported a false beard, so that he matched his photograph, the Shah had, indeed, returned to his kingdom. His cargo, boxes labeled 'Mineral Water' were actually crates of rifles and cartridges. Only one box did not contain armaments. It contained the only sentimental possession the Shah had taken into exile: the tusk of a narwhal given to him on the occasion of his fourteenth birthday. It bore Perry's autograph, a souvenir from his last polar expedition. It was the only box that was opened, and so no one opened any of the other crates to check what was inside them. The Shah was back in Persia, as had been Russian intentions all along, you see, to re-install their useful puppet. What kind of fox was guarding the chicken coop? Let me assure you, there are no vegetarian foxes. The country was being sold to them, but what is the motive behind this Russian chicanery? I'll tell you: a naval base on the Persian Gulf, within striking distance of India, and most importantly, oil. The Tsar is now gone, but as far as Kremlin designs on Iran, nothing has changed. Just as your ancient Suolucidiris looked for water, we have Soviets looking for as yet

untapped oil fields. They have been sighted traveling in squads or individu-
ally, cavalierly exploring what we claim as our territory, territory they have
no right to. Sometimes they are secretive, other times quite open. You have
Russian connections, and it seems to us you could be very useful. We know
you're not really Russian, though you speak very well, but we'd like you to
keep an eye on your people. It would serve the interests of all concerned if
you would agree to do so." The *if* was inserted in his sentence as a formality.
The way *if you would be so kind . . .* really means, *the barrel is at your temple,
and the safety is off.*

"We can offer you a British escort as far as Baghdad. After that you're
on your own, but we would like you to agree to send us certain dispatches
during your time in the eastern provinces."

"How will we meet these people? If you can't give us names we're just
trudging through sand and haze."

"In 1912 when the Russian army uncurled its tentacles and laced them
around parts of Persia, it had soldiers of your tribe who, lo and behold, found
Persians of exactly the same tribe. The territory isn't called Yahudistan for
nothing, turns out. Here they were, from entirely different nations, but with
a language in common, making all kinds of nice alliances to the detriment of
their respective host countries. You people can always find one another, and
when you do," D-shaped officer said slowly, as if speaking to idiots, "you write
to us at this address." He passed a folded piece of paper to Bruno. "You describe your encounters. You don't have to think very much. Just send us your
observations, vis-á-vis your Soviet colleagues, your chance encounters, and so
on. It should be easy." He didn't say even for you, but that was the implication.

"It's up to us," Mrs. Rigg leaned into the cone of lamplight so her sharp
face was briefly illuminated, "to interpret your data." She poured more whiskey for the two of them, swirled the liquid in her glass, then held it close to
her chest, glass magnifying a comet trail of blue tweedy fibers, waiting for our
answer. She spoke in English. Blanckenship repeated in French.

"You don't understand our mission. We're not film cameras set into
place sweeping up, recording everything in our paths. We have urgent business and no grievance with our country of origin." Bruno eyed her glass
pressed against pearl buttons and collected a few shreds of fraying self-as-
surance. "If we don't find this lost city there are others, German and Greek
looters, who have already established camps in the province. We don't have

time to waste bumbling around, looking for some vague Ivanovich smelling of petrol, and as far as spying on Bezymensky and Antonov, I'm not in the business of ratting on those I work with."

"As far as your equanimity towards Moscow, I must say I am surprised. This attitude strains our credulity. Truly, it does. You are defectors, more or less, and defectors always have grudges, remorse, the things they long for and are angry about missing. We're looking for defectors. This is the reason you were stopped on your way out of Amman. Your ticking clock is of little interest to us, and as far as the parties right in your midst, Bezymensky," he picked up one of our papers before handing it back, "is of particular interest."

"Bezymensky is a recluse. He studies early forms of written language, with a special interest in questions of when the first laws were written. What determines when a crime has been committed and how it is punished? When are some acts considered crimes and when is the same act of theft or murder considered a legitimate solution to a problem? He's an old man and barely ever left Moscow; he has no interest in oil or where to find it."

Bruno could just as easily have agreed to spy on Bezymensky, a non-person. He didn't need to make all this up.

"I think you'll find it's in your interest to do what we ask. You seem like intelligent people, and I don't believe you'd really like to be sent back to France. Since you speak Russian with such competence, we want you to keep us informed of Bezymensky and Antonov's activities. Your wife looks like a native Persian, and so do you a bit, if you don't mind my saying so. You'll do just fine."

January 23, 1937
The further east we traveled, the less we fooled anyone anymore.

Once Amman was long out of sight we entered a territory of which there are no definitive maps, and boundaries are unclear. Bruno says he can make Bezymensky into whomever he wants, he can betray him with no qualms, no guilty conscience, send dispatches into the oblivion that the west will soon become. The English can chase shadows. Who will ever know?

Bruno writes long into the night, a labyrinth of field notes documenting the phantom Soviet half of the Friendship Dig, and in the morning he reads some of the pages to me before posting them to Amman:

We met Gennady Pavolich Antonov and Ivan Sergeevich Bezymensky in Baghdad as arranged, thus uniting the two arms of the Franco-Soviet Friendship Dig. Together we will travel to Tehran and from
there to the eastern part of the country to search for Suolucidir.

When they removed their hats and tucked them under their
arms, the Russians were considerably shorter in stature than they ini-
tially appeared, and both men look as if they've lived on burnt rice
scraped from the bottom of the pot. Bezymensky, dark circles under
his eyes like a raccoon, isn't as old as we'd been led to believe, though
I have some doubts about his physical ability to make the arduous
trip to Sistan-va-Baluchistan. Sidonie suggested they may be more spry
than they appear. It happens; some people who look like they're held
together by pins and rusty hinges turn out to have the ability to draw
on invisible reserves of strength and swim the Sea of Azov. Carrying
worn, leather suitcases that are never out of sight, they greeted us in a
rush of tortured, well-intentioned French, then we all switched to Russian. Bezymensky, excited to the point of agitation, grabbed my arm
and questioned me about Paris, a city I've never visited. He wanted to
know about the descendants of the giraffe that was given as a gift to
Napoleon by the Ottoman Viceroy of Egypt, the street where Balzac
dreamed of the Countess de Hansa, the Polynesian collections in the
Musée de l'Armée des Invalides. They had a difficult journey through
the Caucasus, beleaguered by bandirs brandishing curved scimitars
whose chests were bound by crossed bandoliers studded by dull green
bullets, as if they'd been cast during the last great war. Their supplies
ran out, and they had to live on berries and ferns since neither of them
could hunt so much as a squirrel or a starling. Both Bezymensky and
Antonov are tremendously relieved to be in Baghdad where it is quiet
and peaceful. Antonov, younger and taller, smells of stale tobacco and
stirs his drinks with one of his fingers. He also eats the local food with
his fingers, in the style of Punjabi. Why he does this I can't say. It
wasn't Napoleon who was given the giraffe but Charles X.

Bezymensky claims to have a map of the region, but it's a nineteenth-century map, allegedly employed by a Tatar division of Tsar
Nicholas' Imperial Army, and its accuracy is, in my opinion, highly debatable. Bezymensky claims the document is as precise as any

contemporary rendering, but the map looks crude and has obvious mistakes in terms of the position of foothills and bodies of water. Better than nothing, maybe, but a great deal is left out; you trip on a model electric train, your hand falls into something that feels like eyeballs, but it's a bowl of boiled eggs. Finally maybe you find a locked door.

Bezymensky believes Suolucidir was the first civilization to maintain written laws and is eager to find evidence to support his theories. Evidently he has never heard of Hammurabi, more hints that his academic scholarship has been restricted and parochial. According to his theory, the Suolucidiris believed every act leaves a mark of some kind. With laws and rules based on a concept of evidence, the trial system evolved, so the truth can be ferreted out, constructed and contested, if necessary, with the Suolucidir system. You now have procedures for how the thief, the adulterer, the murderer will tell their tales, and the procedure for how those tales may be argued for and against is based on a concept of hard evidence. When laws were written down they became less arbitrary, less liable to abuse by tyrants. Such faith in the power of certitude and written language is touching and when Antonov burps in response Bezymensky looks deeply wounded. He's convinced we'll find statutes, not statues, codes of ethics and codicils, not caryatids.

Antonov believes Suolucidir was a center for ancient pornography. He isn't joking. The two Russians glare at one another across the table. Bezymensky pounds one side of the table for law while Antonov gives a laconic shrug on the side of pleasure, and their arguments accelerate as if we're invisible.

"When crows fly backwards you'll find written laws, and they'll be pliable, subject to infection, gross misinterpretation, miscarriages of justice and bribery."

"You could write your own sex palace manual and try to pass it off as the genuine article."

Sex Palace Manual. I translate loosely.

"Mr. Archaeolosexologist," Bezymensky was disgusted. "These people have come all the way from Paris. They don't want to hear your disgusting repulsive theories."

Sidonie wanted to hear more and took Bezymensky's arm. No, no, let's hear what Antonov has to say.

162

Licking his fingers, Antonov posed the question: when is a piece of pottery not just a piece of dried mud? There exist plates, bowls, urns, you name it, painted as how-to sex manuals. All kinds of erotic scenes, like nothing you've ever seen before, he says. Our lost city specialized in this. Bezymensky accuses him of looking for a Suolucidiri Philaenis, a Sodom and Gomorrah franchise.

He pushes himself away from the table and indicates he has given up on Antonov, travesty artist. He only wants to find the city, then return home to his wife and family in the USSR as soon as possible. He misses them terribly, and his colleague's theories turn valuable artifacts into cheap toys. Sheer and utter C-R-A-P! He spells out. Antonov, on the other hand, makes it clear he is in no hurry to return. He leans over the table and goads Bezymensky, pointing to the ceiling with turmeric-stained fingers, and says your wife can't do anything for herself, not tighten a screw, not pay her bills such as they are, and will look elsewhere for service when her husband is away. This, apparently, is a well-known fact.

A look of anxiety crosses Bezymensky's face. Antonov has hit a nerve of some kind. Antonov, though he is intrigued by the idea that people who had very short life spans had sex in frequency and in ways modern people can't imagine, rolls a cigarette and launches a question into the air: could Suolucidir be a fraud? We have the only very flimsy evidence: a letter here, a footnote there, the story of two Englishmen currently residing on the bottom of the Gulf of Oman, yet we're happy to pack our bags. He shrugs; he himself leaves nothing behind but a communal apartment overlooking blighted horse chestnut and ash trees and rusty scaffolding downwind from a factory that leaves baseboards or even the slightest indentation in a wall coated with oily grime. Even your frown lines are filled in with black the next morning. Smell the sex lives of people who shook hands with the Sassanids? Find a lost city? Meet French people? Sure, why not? Who wouldn't jump at the chance?

Bezymensky is serious. Suolucidir is not a hoax. He believes in the possibility of the lost city, of early attempts at parsing truth-tellers and liars on opposite sides of a cave. If they find the lost city he can achieve a permanent post, respect, tribute and honors from university

chancellors and general poobahs. His wife grew up in the Crimea. She
had an uncle who told her stories of a lost tribe that found a foothold
in the east, in a place so isolated, these people so abandoned and scattered, set up their tents and prospered. The tribe delighted in every
aspect of this corner. They found a way to tap water from the desert
and jealously guarded their secrets and their laws. No one would ever
find them again, until they vanished.

His wife comes from Odessa, and you know what that means,
Antonov says, but we don't know. We're totally in the dark here as to
what he is referencing. She doesn't eat pork, he winks. Sidonie and I
look blank. Not shellfish either, though the city is known for its rich
Black Sea oyster beds. He keeps dropping hints until we finally understand what he's trying to tell us. This means, Antonov explains, that
my poor Bezymensky is under even greater scrutiny than the rest of us.
He really has to watch his step.

Bezymensky turns on Antonov and lists his companion's debts,
and the tailor, the bookshop, the doctor are only the ones he knows
about. Debt collectors dog his heels. Until they hopped a late train
traveling south Antonov was almost daily beaten by thugs sent by
those parasite lenders Stalin has yet to eradicate completely. They already took everything he owned and some things that weren't his, but
belonged to others in his communal apartment, and now those people
hate him, too. Bezymensky accuses him of wanting to find the lost city
because he needs cash. The sex part is optional, a sideline developed
as a distraction.

We let them bicker until it was late and they ran out of steam. We
pool what we know about Suolucidir. Their language is related to Farsi, Aramaic, and Samaritan but written in boxy, jagged letters. Nouns
have gender, Antonov winked. This is very important, many Suolucidiri jokes are based on these linguistic relationships and slippages.
Bezymensky speaks of human dictionaries: people tattooed and pictorial, guaranteed to disappear with the last speaker disintegrated. It
was a painful honor to become a walking reference, your body pricked
by bone and injected with cuttlefish ink. As the body goes, there goes
your pornography, he glares at Antonov. Antonov parries that tattoos
were taboo for the Lost Tribes and their descendants, so which is it?

Epidermus Bibliophilus or Day of Atonement mourners, make up your mind. Bezymensky wonders how Antonov knows so much about these beleaguered, secretive people. Maybe you're half one yourself? Was your mother's name Lydya Moscovitz? There is acid on Bezymensky's tongue, and this shuts Antonov up for a moment.

Bezymensky believes the city was full of gardens and fountains, an emerald in the middle of the desert. Dwellings were constructed around courtyards, life was internalized, centered around extended family and clan. The architecture, mirror of Suolucidiri society, reflects their secretive culture. Antonov, recovering from the stunner issued by his colleague impugning his ancestry, disagrees. He rolls his eyes. Though he had been slouching, he now sits up, no you're wrong. There is evidence their buildings were flimsy mud and reed affairs, and like the human dermal lexicons, none survive. Every aspect of life from government to market transactions, from eating, sleeping, and defecating was conducted out in the open. They had rooftops supported by columns, but the concept of walls did not exist. Everybody could see everything. The Russians call one another names: scoundrel, fraud, back stabber. The schisms in Soviet Suolucidiri scholarship seem unbridgeable.

On day three Sidonie encouraged them to explore Baghdad: visit the Abbasid Palace with its silent vaulted corridors and muqarnas arches, tessellated and shadowy, walk along the banks of the Tigris, look for the footprints of Kahramana as she went to the caves to pour oil on the heads of the forty thieves hidden in jars there. At first they were resistant, then wanted us to accompany them. No, we said, we've seen the sights, we need to arrange transport for the next leg of our journey. Finally we got rid of them for what we estimated would be a few hours.

With Sidonie as my lookout I gained access to their rooms. The locks were insubstantial and easily picked. In Antonov's chamber there was nothing of any interest except, as you might imagine, cheaply produced Soviet pornography of ridiculous characters doing predictable things, not so different from what you find in the West. Maybe the settings were slightly different, the battleship Pomtemkin in the background, say, or the Odessa steps. The magazines were worn, pictures blurred, ink smeared, and left out carelessly; anyone entering would have seen them. Perhaps, apart from the person who cleaned his rooms, he expected no visitors, at least none who would have minded his traveling collection. In Bezymensky's room I found photographs of his wife and letters to her, mostly complaining about Antonov and what a tragedy it was this dirty old man was selected to be one of the representatives the Soviet arm of the Friendship Dig, what a burden he is, how one must always explain this embarrassment of a human being to others. He also had a variety of Russian books on archaeology, which I paged through. Bezymensky is the owner of the usual array of the small tools one uses for digging. Among them was what looked like a small meter. This object is used to send electric current through sample rocks. Even the most dense rock contains microscopic pockets that may contain water or oil depending on the density of either material in the area from which the rock was removed. Rocks containing tiny droplets of oil are poorer conductors of electricity than those containing water, therefore the conductibility of an electrical current could be a sign of a hidden cache of either substance. The Suolucidiris found water, therefore this instrument would be useful for finding relics from an aquiferous city. Though it's not unusual for him to have such an instrument, it was located in a cavity hollowed out of a large out-of-date and irrelevant book on czarist-era expeditions to Siberia.

When I left Bezymensky's room, the corridor was empty. Sidonie was nowhere to be found. Bezymensky had returned prematurely due to a squabble with Antonov, who has no interest in Baghdad beyond finding the nearest Fun Palace. Bezymensky was intent on returning to his room, but Sidonie, who claimed she just happened to be walking down this hallway and had paused at the top of a flight of stairs, insisted he not cut his touring short. She would be delighted to take him to see the sights; they really should not be missed, having traveled so far. He was suspicious. There was no reason for Sidonie to be lurking near the stairs of his corridor. We will in future, have to be more careful around our Soviet colleagues.

Bruno folded the pages and posted them from a street that ran along the Tigris.

A collection of characters exploding like firecrackers, just as quickly absorbed by the night, poof they're gone. Where did all this come from? A man with an ourobouros tattooed on his ankle seen while he checked valves in the engine room of Raffarin's ship, he answers. He might just as well have answered: the moon.

What is oil? Highly compressed fossils. We'll all be oil some day. Oil is formed by organic matter under intensely high temperatures. Diatoms that once floated on the surface of ancient oceans are eventually converted to oil. They sometimes left the impressions of their bodies in shale.

February 3, 1937
My suitcase was stolen in Baghdad, and with it went all my European clothing, so I traded the gold cross for long dresses and a headscarf. We boarded a ship due to sail down the Persian Gulf and eventually came within sight of Bandar Abbas, Persia, the final test of the Franco-Soviet Friendship Dig papers. Officials appeared, chests garlanded by heavy cartridge belts, feet encased in high tight yellow boots. Bruno told me not to say anything about any lost tribes — not to anyone in customs, not even when we got to the city of Zahedan.

~◡

Since leaving Baghdad we no longer had an English escort, and once again we were on our own. We took a bus to the town of Alibad, and from there joined a caravan of silk and olive merchants making their way to Zahedan. On the first day I thought our group was comprised of only Persians, Armenians, and Arabs, but on the second day two real Russians, Darya Vasilisa Ulanovskaya and Maksim Petakhov, introduced themselves to us in Farsi. They looked shocked when Bruno returned the introduction in their native language, though he pronounced words with a fake French accent. Darya Vasilisa Ulanovskaya, sturdily built, sandy hair, round lined face, squints through perfectly circular black glasses and speaks softly. Maksim Petakhov, a former Olympic soccer player, now retired, is more garrulous, speaking in cynical interrogatives as if they were declaratives, a way of speech I haven't heard in a long time. They said they were surveyors, guests of the Shah's Royal Ministry of Cartography, on a mission to survey Sistan-va-Baluchistan in order to create maps of a previously unsurveyed region whose boundaries are contentious and unclear. They carried German arms, Glocks and Mausers, and told a story of an ambush near the border with Afghanistan that killed seven of their party during their last trip to the region. It was Maksim who told this story, patting his camel on its twitching nose as he described the quiet of the mountains and how their guides disappeared when the first bullets cracked a rock a few centimeters from his head, yet he smiled as he described their escape through ravines and mountains. Now they no longer travel in distinct easily identifiable groups but go in pairs to cover the provinces. Ulanovskaya and Petakhov were pleased to meet members of the Franco-Soviet Friendship Dig. It was not a meeting they had expected, and it's always a pleasure, they said, this kind of surprise. So we met two Russians while waiting for two others who will never appear.

"Antonov and Bezymensky, yes, we've heard of them, I knew a Bezymensky at university, an orientalist," said Darya Vasilisa. "Perhaps this is the same man. It would not surprise me."

"I hope they arrive while we're still in the province. We have other territories to cover, but it's always a pleasure to meet fellow Soviet travelers." Maksim Petakhov tucked his thumbs into his belt that jangled with a slide rule and other instruments.

"Bezymensky lived for awhile in the mountains with some of the tribal groups, recording their music. They have an instrument similar to the oud; he described in it some detail." Bruno played an oud made of the air. "He believed the sound of a group's native language influences the rhythm of its music."

Because I stood behind the Soviets I could slide my hand across my throat, silently telegraphing Bruno to shut up. Bezymensky is meant to be a digger, not an ethnomusicologist, enough already. Our comrades in the Soviet half of our enterprise are turning into an accordion that gets stretched to a ridiculous length, a giant slug of a thing. Who could be a master of all the trades he attributed to our Soviet Friends and still stand on two feet? Maksim asked me something about my studies in Moscow, and I wasn't sure whether to try to speak French-accented Russian with the pair, in a feat of linguistic gymnastics, or just speak normally, which would give me away as a native speaker. Fortunately Bruno answered for me in a rush of explanation. By the end of the evening I tried to say as little as possible in their presence, and since they didn't pay much attention to me, this wasn't difficult.

February 21, 1937

We arrived in Zahedan, a remote mountain town that Darya Vasilisa and Maksim knew well; they had visited it before. They helped us find lodgings, and on our second day in the town, introduced us to an excellent guide, Ramin Kosari, who spoke not perfect but reasonably good Russian. Kosari, a Kurd, is more fair than most of the natives of this region. He has light eyes and a long nose, trim brown beard, and a habit of making short bows in the middle of sentences, as if to emphasize a cluster of words that must surely be true. Reason he is in this part of the country: unknown. Kosari, like many residents, knew about two Englishmen, one dressed like a Pashtun sheikh, maybe, who found a cave full of ancient objects, but they took everything they could get their hands on. When they finished with that cave you were lucky there were any stones or scorpions left in it.

On our third night in Zahedan we took Kosari up to our rooms and showed him Feigen's map. So far we'd revealed it to no one, not the British sentries in Amman, not any of our fellow travelers, either. It had remained untouched, hidden between pieces of cardboard in Bruno's rucksack. As he looked over the map, his eyes lit up. He knew this region, the exact area marked by the simurgh, the symbol Fingers assured us indicated the entrance to a hidden city. Yes, this would be easier than any of us thought. We'd come so far, through deserts and seas, and what we sought was waiting for us as if it were no more extraordinary than a stowaway in a barrel of kippered herring, unusual, but easy to find. Bruno expressed guarded excitement, scratched the back of his head, raked his dry hair, and smiled a little. Kosari would hire diggers. Things would proceed rapidly. We would find the city of the Lost Tribes, bring Feigen whatever he desired that would put him at peace, make some money, and return to Marseilles as if the events of Bruno's last night in that city had never happened. That we can't go back the way we came is something he seems to have forgotten.

The next day I insisted on going with Kosari and the others to look at camels we'll need for the expedition. Kosari didn't want me to go. Bruno handed me a veil that flattened my corkscrew hair into a dense Cleopatra-like wedge, and this seemed to appease Kosari a little. Snub-nosed Darya always covered her head with a Ukrainian scarf printed with red cabbage roses. The two Russians, who were not part of our expedition but wanted to accompany Kosari and Bruno to watch the bargaining, were already loitering on the corner, and if they could go, I saw no reason why I had to stay behind. So, to Kosari's irritation, it was settled. I caught up with the others. How strange to hear Russian with its elaborate expletives and complicated diminutives spoken down dusty streets on the way to a market at the edge of Zahedan. Darya Vasilisa takes my arm and doesn't just say "that's a little house," but "that hovel is a wretched, little house with its stuffing coming out of the windows." Petakhov swears, probably under the impression that none of us understand him. But we all do, all the way to the camel market.

Darya has pale, unfocused eyes and when she asks me where I learned to speak such good Russian, a French woman who looked like a Pashtun, I inhale dust as deeply as possible, cough, and find it difficult to speak. What is Pashtun? I rasp out. She pointed somewhere to the east. Oh. Cough. Cough. My histrionic gagging cough probably fools no one, but what else could I do? The Pashtun, Darya Vasilisa said, are armed and militant, devout Muslims with Hebraic-sounding names, they light oil lamps on Friday nights and some claim they are descendants of the Lost Tribes. This time I really did cough, and the conversation ended.

We reached the camel market, which stank of animals standing around for hours with nothing to do but chew and shit, not so different from the Berlin Zoo, Bruno pointed out. I was thankful for the cloth that covered my nose. Do you remember the monkey house, he asked? Of all the animal houses, that one stank the worst, and even the monkeys seemed to know they were partially neglected by their cousins, who maybe felt uncomfortable with their resemblances, and so didn't attend to them as often as they should have. We visited the zoo in the western part of the city shortly after we arrived in Berlin. It seemed like the most foreign thing we could do, the thing most unlike what you would do of an afternoon in the town where we came from, a place where there were no zoos, where the concept didn't exist. A giant black U means, here you get on the U-Bahn. We got on at Alexanderplatz, though I lingered at the window of a photographer's studio, looking at the pictures of the families and portraits of men in uniforms. It was the first time I'd traveled underground. It was chilly and drizzling rain in fits, but we went to the Zoologischer Gartens anyway. The squirrel monkeys had hair on their heads that grew in such a way that they looked like Americanischer Mohawks. A bouncy female paused long enough to groom one of the males, starting with his head and moving toward his leg, which she stretched out, carefully straightening the knee and foot joints in order to work on his delicate limb. He sat passively, if not regally, until another monkey (male or female?), screeching in anger and hysteria, interrupted the procedure, and they all screamed at one another, a fuming triangle. The blue-faced mandrill next door paced back and forth, as if thinking who were these idiots in the apartment next door who had all-night parties, orgies, screaming fests, who didn't know how well off they were? No one groomed him. He sat alone in his shit-smeared cage. Bruno pulled me to another part of the primate house. Look at this one. The Hanuman monkey appeared like a wise old man, infinitely patient and sitting in forbearance of all the follies of all the silly fools who glanced his way, you would think, and you'd be wrong to read his impassivity that way. The sign on the side of his cage read that the Hanuman monkey kills his rival and his children, then takes his rival's wife as his own mate, and in this way achieves leadership of the clan and maintains his primacy. Bruno didn't remember the Hanuman monkey, but he recalled the lion had a deafening roar that brought visitors running, and a sign beside his cage warned that the lion shpritzed between the bars when he pissed, and he did, spraying a woman teetering on high heels very close to the cage, almost falling in. Someone said she was an opium addict, but no one stopped her or told her not to get so close — odd in itself for a city of laws like Berlin, but she did get sprayed by the lion. What did the lion think about the woman screaming at him, standing before his cage while other onlookers laughed? I don't know, Bruno, why are you telling me this? I have no memory of a woman in a filmy dress being showered by a lion. Homesick now for a place that was never really home? Nostalgic for wild animals living in the middle of a city?

At the camel market Bruno wandered off, and Maksim followed him. I stuck with Kosari who was doing the real bargaining, sizing up legs and looking at teeth. I stood close by, just to annoy him. Suddenly, thwack, I fell to the ground. A moody camel, coat clotted with dirt, had kicked me hard just under the knee. It didn't hurt all that much, but it was a shock, the knock coming out of nowhere. My veil slipped aside as I bent down to rub my shin. Kosari barked at the man trying to sell the animal. The man used the word *Jahoudi* looking in my direction, at least I think he did. Swift but short-lived arguing followed before we moved on.

March 10, 1937

A few days later all our equipment was loaded onto our three camels, who looked pained and bawled as they rose to their feet under the weight of shovels, coils of rope, buckets, baskets, containers of food and water. They reminded me of circus weightlifters who make a show of the effort they put into raising their dumbbells before suddenly and miraculously holding impossibly heavy iron bars aloft. We took turns with the binoculars, one of the few objects we still possessed that dated back to our years in Berlin. Its Zeiss lenses were remarkably sharp and clear, Feigen had said as he looked through them, the most precise lenses in the world. Formerly used for watching performances of *Die Zauberflote* or looking for scarlet tanagers in the Volkspark Friedrichshain, through them we now scanned desert and mountains, barren and deserted. How could a city have thrived in this landscape? When we stopped to rest, if I saw a single human being, a woman carrying a basket on her head or a child herding sheep or goats, I would sketch drawings of them, but this was rare. I developed a purple bruise in the shape of a camel hoof that didn't go away.

Kosari, as the Russians promised, knew the mountains and valleys well. Nonetheless, for two days we failed to find the site or anything that remotely resembled a ruin of any kind. The landscape is desolate, here and there a group of sandstone formations. The camels stop to munch scrub or the drivers give them *ajin*, balls of dough that they gobble up. Their ears look like skin shells, and in the sun they're translucent, like veined human ears. A fist would fit in one, and these are the kinds of absurd thoughts I had during the tedious journeys. Kosari explained that the distances may be greater than what was marked on the map, but he never questioned the reliability of the document, which any reasonable person might find to be more about a cartographer's dreams than an accurate rendering of the relationship between drawing and geography. He never asked us how old the map was or what the language or symbols written on it might mean.

Darya Vasilisa and Maksim haunt us, much like Bruno's version of our meeting with invented Soviets. Just as we dogged Bezymensky and Antonov, Darya seems to be just around every corner I turn. She's very curious about what we're doing in Iran, as if she knows everything I'm telling her leaves something out. She reveals very little about herself except that she has a daughter and grandson who were relocated somewhere farther east, and she doesn't know when she'll ever see them again. There is a point where even accurate cartographers must give up; space is so vast the phrase "to scale" loses its meaning. The last time she saw her grandson he wrote messages on paper airplanes and launched them out the window of their building when they all lived together. Do you think, she asked, children made paper airplanes before actual planes were invented? She asks me when did I become interested in digging up other people's petrified trash? There is an edge of cynicism in her tone that takes me off guard.

On the third day, about forty kilometers north by northeast from town, Kosari led us into a narrow gorge perhaps a few meters wide. The further we traveled, the higher and narrower the chasm grew, and it was like walking through a cave whose roof had slid off. Finally the rocky canyon ramparts rose to one hundred meters high, maybe more. Even with the swaying motion of the camel, I could touch both sides of the canyon walls with my arms extended. In fact, I couldn't straighten them if I wanted to. After an hour or so of riding, the rocks began to change. The cuts in the rock face started to look less like the natural cleaving of stone from cliff, but as if they'd been created by humans in an attempt to widen the channel. That was my impression; the marks were jagged and uneven. Maybe they weren't chisel or axe marks, just sharp clefts made when Ice Age temperatures caused microscopic crystals to be severed from granite, but I was cautiously hopeful. Then the sky darkened. If there was a sudden cloudburst a deluge would flood the gorge, and all of us would drown in an instant. Should I tell everyone, let's turn around? But what if I was wrong? Bruno and Kosari would say I was too nervous to travel, guilty of imagining horrors too extreme to be taken seriously. There was no space for the camels to turn around. The only possible direction was forward. Bruno looked up at the sky as if studying a flock of muddy storks and leaned forward to speak to Kosari, who shook his head. Was this an example of what

Bruno was afraid of, the blindness and paralysis he predicted we'd experience when we were up to our knees in sand? He made a sign to stop all the camels, and Kosari rode ahead. None of us spoke. The storms dump water in a matter of minutes. There was no time to ride back. Bruno got down and leaned against a rock for a moment, then calmly pulled out one of Feigen's books on the Seulucids, neighbors of Suolucidir. About thirty minutes later, Kosari returned on foot and motioned for us to follow him. .

We rode on single file but soon arrived at a clearing, a dead end like a small natural amphitheater caused by water or wind erosion. Rocks facing us did look slightly, ever so slightly, more cut than naturally fallen. We argued about whether it was worthwhile to try to move a few of them. Kosari insisted this was the exact spot identified by the simurgh symbol on the map. The entrance of the city was not immediately apparent. Large rocks had to be moved, and some scattered boulders, on closer examination, may have been ashlars, posts, and lintels from some fallen structure, yes, they were definitely man-made blocks. Ropes were tied to animals and men who pulled and pushed away obstructions until a decent-size opening was created, about big enough for two men and a camel to get through. By now most of the chasm was in shadow, it would be night in about an hour. A rock shifted to the left, crashed, another followed and then a distinctly man-made shape came into view, a column whose capital was carved with grape vines, and a dirt floor gave way to tile. Kosari broke off a flinty piece of stone and put it in his pocket. Bruno looked wary but pleased. Whatever the site was, we were surely the first live humans to cross the threshold in perhaps thousands of years.

Outlines of lintels, doorways led into partially collapsed rooms, some inhabited by skeletal remains, most not. The city was underground, just as Feigen had said it would be, concealed by an earthquake, the metropolis of our ancestors permanently entombed. Porters were assigned to make measurements and move more rocks. While there was still some light I took photographs of the site with and without half-smiling Bruno and Kosari.

By nightfall, back in town, we learned that Maksim and Darya Vasilisa had disappeared on one of their treks. Bruno paused in front of Darya Vasilisa's door, turned to me saying, should we take a look? Would we find a chronometer, a gizmo for running electric current through sandstone or Jurassic age crud, an astrolabe with Cyrillic markings? Or would Maksim's room, as a stand-in for that of the imaginary Antonov, reveal a stash of Trotsky-era porn? Bruno was anxious. That evening we should have been celebrating, cabling Feigen, drinking Georgian wine smuggled into the city by Chechen bootleggers. Bruno paused in front of their doors as if he had unfinished business, but didn't attempt to open them.

But was this actually Suolucidir? I went every day to the site, though my presence caused some of the workers to become disgruntled. I couldn't dig, or move heavy stones, but drew pictures of the place as they began to uncover walls, rooms, the remains of a fountain, pottery shards, and relics of weapons: knives and shields of some kind. Some skeletons still wore green stone necklaces, and loops of carnelian and agate around wrists and ankles, a sign no looters had ever found the site. The chambers were too dark for a camera to work properly, so my drawings were the only records. Maybe I got in the way, but that was my job. Kosari still didn't want me to wander around underground. It was dangerous. I assumed he was talking about cave-ins and shrugged him off, but no, he really did believe I had no business on the dig and should stay behind in town. I shook my head. That wasn't part of any deal. Berlin or Marseilles were, in their own way, also underground cities, and just as dangerous. We argued in Russian, and I completely abandoned the phony French accent.

"You're boiling my head like a teapot, Ramin." I used a language he'd never heard before, then translated my words into Russian.

"Your head was already a tea kettle." He offered me a cigarette. I didn't think he was supposed to do this, talk to me alone and make this kind of offer, but I accepted. Why not?

"Are you saying I'm steaming? Because what I mean is, you make me feel confused."

"I'd like to know what you're looking for here."

"A lost city. You know this."

"You have a map that looks like a very old joke put together by someone pretending not to know electricity has been harnessed and run though bits of wire and cord. Maybe it fell from the sky."

I pointed out that he had been able to follow it, and he shrugged. He had no answer as to why an old joke of a map turned out to actually lead to the right place. Inhaling deeply, tapping ash against what may have been someone's door, how could I answer this question? How could I explain the work of a visionary cartographer who probably also believed the world was flat? Kosari took out his knife and began scraping clay from the edge of a lintel, waiting for me to answer as he chipped closer to where my wrist dangled, cigarette in hand. He took it from me and put it out.

"All kinds of things find their way to Berlin. It's a big city."

He shrugged again and walked away. We never entirely understood one another, so when he got too frustrated he would cut off the discussion as soon as possible, leaving me to continue drawing or setting up a tripod, but then he would circle back and try to convince me I shouldn't be anywhere near the ruined metropolis, like it was some kind of poisonous quicksand. It's alright, I'd repeat in broken Farsi, I'll grab onto your sleeve so you can pull me out when the skeletons start to suck me down. I reached out and pulled on his white sleeve in order to demonstrate its saving qualities, and though I expected he'd snap his arm away, he said, alright then see if it works. See if *what* works? We fail to understand each other, all our languages fall into the rocks and vaporize as if someone were telling me, ha, morons, you should never have left this desert place to begin with, because if you return you will never entirely, or with ease, reclaim it. Too many armies have ridden over the city and now what was once yours belongs to others, and it's unrecognizable in daylight or at night. Why should it be?

April 4, 1937

For weeks neither Bruno nor I could identify any object or carving that could prove absolutely that the Lost Tribes had built and lived in the Suolucidir. The skeletons weren't talking. Though I was convinced from the outset, Bruno was deeply skeptical. It was the early Berlin version of Bruno, the one intrigued by scientific method, by empiricism, before he was jettisoned from the club. He was being cautious, but we both wanted to believe the Lost Tribes had left evidence of themselves, a way of tapping us on the shoulder and beckoning us, yes you'll be the ones to lead the way out of the desert that is the twentieth century for you people. I grabbed that idea with the

176

enthusiasm and obsession of a deluded missionary who's found a few huts in the middle of a jungle and is ready to start converting any lone souls who cross my path, I admit it. Bruno was more guarded.

Bruno's methodical way of working, marking off blocks of space with rope to be examined one by one like cubes in an ice tray, without jumping to preconceived assumptions, seems needlessly slow. This may not be the lost city, and interesting though our find is, this ruin isn't the one we're after, and we should move on. Bruno was sure we'd find a simurgh carved into a stone or some more transparent evidence, a series of block script letters, a sign of some kind. He knew ancient cities didn't announce their presence with obvious sentry gates, guard towers, refueling stations, immigration and customs, areas where your bags are searched and papers scrutinized, but he still wanted clear evidence: this was Suolucidir.

I was looking around a newly uncovered chamber near the entrance. Webs of dendrite crystals, delicate and fernlike, marked the surface of the rock face. Something caught my hair, and I swatted it away with the veil that had been bunched up in my bag. A small bat fell to the ground. I looked up to see a whole nest of them huddled into a corner. Water dripped overhead, a rivulet ran down the side of the room. I followed the trickle to the base of an ashlar like so many others I'd already come across. The layer of dirt that covered the top surface had accumulated in a pattern of depressions. I brushed off the fine grit and pebbles, and once dirt was swept from the sandstone ashlar, rough carvings were revealed: the eagle, the lion, the olive tree, and the goat, the symbols of Dan, Judah, Ariel, and Naphtali.

April 11, 1937

For the past week we've said nothing to the others about my discovery. Bruno asked me to explain the presence of the lion, symbol of Judah. Judah wasn't one of the lost tribes. But you know everyone gets lost sometimes, I said. We were having our boots mended by a man sitting cross-legged in the market, who spoke no language either of us could understand. Our immediate surroundings receded. We forgot about the Englishmen in Amman. We thought and spoke only of the site we'd found.

We bought pomegranates and figs, eating them in bed, biting the seeds, sometimes swallowing them, sometimes spitting them out, sucking our fingers and staining the blankets. The owner of the rooms we rented would bring us tea late at night if we asked for it, but one night when we hadn't asked, there was a knock on our door. I was half undressed and hurried to put on clothes. Bruno, sitting on the carpet looking at fragments of pottery, was startled, he swept them under a pillow, and gestured towards the door, it was up to me to answer it. The knock was repeated, and I opened the door mid rap. There was Petakhov with the usual big grin on his face. We thought he and Darya had disappeared into the mountains with their charts and surveying equipment, then suddenly here he was at our door unannounced. In Russia it's considered bad luck to shake hands over a threshold. We both knew this, so I was at a loss. I didn't want him to enter our rooms, but didn't know how to cordially block the door. While I stood, hand on door jamb, Maksim walked right past me, glanced at my dusty clothing that lay in a heap on the floor, and sat on the floor beside Bruno. He removed a bottle from one of his jacket pockets, Bruno nodded at me to find glasses.

"Where's Darya?" I asked, as if it mattered to me, as if the party wouldn't be complete without his partner.

"Darya's an early riser. She's been asleep for hours." Maksim took in our room. We'd left some other, earlier, pottery shards on a shelf near Feigen's books. I wished we'd put them away. Petakhov noticed everything.

"You've been busy, I see. Nice. When are your colleagues arriving from Moscow? Not arrived yet? Is there a problem?" His ear-splitting grin shifted to a look of concern. Ushering in a smell of fried onions, sweat stains on his socks, unappealing, perhaps, but Petakhov took over a room as if he were royalty. Ironic, but true. "We are most anxious to meet fellow explorers, you know. Perhaps they are delayed. I could send a telegram, make inquiries to resolve difficulties. Please, my friends. Is there anything I can do to help?"

Darya gave the appearance of being the kind of person who slept with her unfocused eyes open, but Maksim, so offhand and relaxed about everything, was actually more unpredictable and therefore more alarming.

"It would be no trouble for me to make inquiries, to cable parties I'm in contact with, offices in Grozny, the consulates in Tbilisi and Yerevan." He took a notebook and pen from a pocket, licked his finger to open a page and prepared to write. "Tell me their entire names." Raised eyebrows waiting to record full names of the dueling golems Bruno had created. He'd written *emes*, truth, on their foreheads and launched them from mud into the world to defend us, and now they were dissolving back into mud, just when we needed them.

"Please don't trouble yourselves. We expect Bezymensky and Antonov to appear any day. Meanwhile we needed to begin, of course, and so we haven't waited for them. They wouldn't expect this of us."

Maksim still held his pen, frozen. "Are you sure? There can be delays on the trans-Caucasus rails, especially traveling through Georgia as you approach Azerbaijan." He took a square piece of paper from his pocket, drew a rough wide-channeled hourglass-shaped map of the Caucasus, a line representing rail tracks, and x's marking spots of potential trouble, then folded the paper into a triangle. Not yet finished, he folded the triangle in half, and so on until he had a small nub of a triangle. "Okay, my friends, this is up to you." He chuckled as he tossed the nugget of paper high into the air and caught it in his teeth like a circus performer, then spat it across the room. "Darya and I have been speaking, and we would enjoy going to your camp, maybe tomorrow is good and alright for you."

How did he know about our camp? Who told him? Kosari, maybe?

"Doesn't your surveying take you further east? Our camp is to the north." I stood in front of Feigen's books, leaning my back against their spines. Bruno scratched the bridge of his nose over and over as if leisurely trying to reach bone. What he was thinking, I don't know. He saw no harm in conversing with the two Russians, in fact he enjoyed their company. For him they were charming and witty, joking about faraway Stalin and Bukharin, big deep laughs, very different from the secretive and desperate nature of life in Berlin and Marseilles. What did I see when I looked at them or heard their voices? Midnight arrests. Petakhov saying, fooled you with that joke about Lenin and a penguin walk into a bar. If you hadn't laughed you wouldn't be breathing your last now.

Petakhov nodded, yes, my Sido, that's true. He stretched out on the carpet like a lazy cat. They were, indeed, working in a different quadrant, but insisted they could afford to take a day off, and expand the purview of their researches, it all needed to be mapped eventually. He's curious about that area, north by northwest. He and Darya Vasilisa hadn't looked around there much, and that area has never been mapped. He sat up and, leaned towards Bruno who slouched against a wall.

"My work has taken me many places." Petakhov reached over and tapped Bruno's arm. Even if I held up a sign warning him not to laugh at Maksim Petakhov's penguin jokes he would wave me away. "Atlases give you instant histories with scarcely a printed word, imagine page after page indicating the shifting boundaries of our host country from the time of Darius to Reza Shah Pahlavi." He made a *bmm* noise as he exhaled deeply, eyes shut, miming serious thoughts. "My favorite atlas: the borders of Russia in 1900, 1917, and 1937. Governments need maps. Sovereignty is cemented by graphic models, no?" It was not a question that required an answer. He flipped the pages of an air book. "Maps don't only tell you where you are: 50 kilometers south of the source of the Nile or 10 kilometers from the center of Krakatoa, they also show you your past and possible future choices. An animated cartoon map would be best. Molten and evaporating lakes, mountain ranges folded up into escalating peaks, then wearing out into hillocks. One day you think your city is the center of the universe, and the next day it's vanished off the face of the earth."

Maksim pulled a small slide rule from a pocket and slid the bar up and down the scale while Bruno got up and poured more vodka. For a moment no one spoke.

"There are many precise depictions of the earth's surface. You can align the rhumbs, the Mercator points of any number of highly accurate two-dimensional maps, and each will contradict the next, and each will be true. I've examined the dream maps of the tattooed Siberian Chukchi, the charts of 16th-century Conquistadores who believed they knew the location of a city of gold guarded by a plumed serpent, though they never would see it, and maps of the soul drawn by monks who never left their island monastery. Here are the Straits of Redemption, here lies the Archipelago of Temptation and so on." He gestured into the air. "Or maybe it was the Straits of Temptation and the Archipelago of Redemption." He shrugged. "My favorite map, perhaps the most accurate of all, is the one Stevenson drew of Treasure Island. Who's to say any of them, even the fairy tales, are altogether wrong?"

"Where did you get a copy of *Treasure Island*?" Bruno asked.

"You find these things. It happens." Petakhov raised and lowered his eyebrows, a kind of facial shrug, as if to say, this is no big deal, what do you care?

"In Russian, you read this book?" Bruno could barely contain his skepticism.

"No, in English."

"What is *Treasure Island*?" I asked.

"A story about a voyage to the center of the earth," Bruno replied.

"Stick to what you know," Petakhov advised Bruno.

Bruno didn't appreciate advice from anyone, especially someone who, as far as he could tell, traveled with little more than a measuring tape and a bag of stakes. Maksim ignored him, and shifted around on the carpet, so he was positioned closer to me. He wasn't interested in humoring Bruno. I've often found myself on the receiving end of people's monologues. Tonight would be no exception.

"What is my personal map? Imagine your history in terms of a cartographic legend: red lines for willing travel, blue for other reasons, coercion, maybe or some form of relocation, not your personal choice. Broken green line stands for rail travel, violet for walking or automobile, whatever you choose. Here's mine: I, Maksim Petakhov, was born outside Moscow, served in the army near Turkey, played soccer in Berlin and all over Europe, before injury, went to university back in Moscow. Wait, let me tell you something interesting that will add to my map." He outlined these travels on the carpet, turning central diamond shapes into continents and border arabesques into rivers. "In the army I was trained in orienteering, that is, traveling by foot without a map or compass through the steppes, marshes, parts of Siberia. See, the map expands."

When did he learn English?

"Our maps, Sido's and mine, are practically contiguous, and not very interesting." Bruno leaned forward, elbows on the table. Bruno spun a tale of estates and dachas where none had existed before. I was the daughter of a circus performer taken in by his family. My mother was a trapeze artist who fell to her death, trail of feathers and sequins, a comet's tail behind her. That was all we knew. Too painful for Sido to talk about, but her map led her all over the Soviet Union from Ossetia to Uzbekistan until outside Moscow her father gave her to Bruno's family, wealthy porcelain makers. He wanted her to have a good education, so he left her, age nine, and here he exits the story. Bruno and Sido, therefore, met as children, fell in love, and so on. All this was news to me, though I nodded in agreement. Maksim leaned in close as if to examine the space behind my retinas with a tiny light. I panicked. Weren't we still supposed to be from Alsace? Or had we managed to leave Moscow to study in France?

"Yes, I can imagine you came from people who flew in the sky. You muttered to Kosari in a language you know he won't understand, a language one rarely hears in Moscow anymore. People who speak it disappear. Bruno, do you also speak this language?"

"She was speaking Esperanto, and no, I don't know any illegal languages."

"Esperanto isn't illegal."

"It is in some places," I said. "Esperanto is the most logical of all languages. I was just trying it out. His Russian isn't bad, but there are gaps in his understanding, you know. Nothing serious, but he needs to know what we're asking of him."

Maksim frowned and seemed to chew on this idea. He poured more vodka into the little glasses and said, "Let's get lost."

"Sure, Max, why not?" I said with false camaraderie, and I leaned closer into the chest of the former soccer player, closer but not touching. He closed his eyes for a moment as if again miming deep, hard to retrieve thoughts.

"My work already makes me lost. The more you find, the more you pin down, the less stable is the ground under your feet. The more likely someone is going to look at your work and say, go take a shit in the ocean, and you say what ocean?"

I'd heard that phrase in the language we weren't supposed to speak since I could remember, and now Maksim was using it, and winking as if to say you two know exactly what I'm talking about. He poured more vodka into his own glass.

"Who's to say the boundaries of Country X, the Disputed Territories of Discombobula, lie along this random crooked line, include this peninsula or that isthmus? Maybe the isthmus and the arbitrary line through the plains of Repetitia really all belong to the United Federation of Ironia and its far-flung colonies. What if we design countries based on languages rather than geography, whether posting our borders on man-made markings or those that occur naturally. Say, for example, if you speak Russian you reside in the Soviet state, but if a settlement of like-minded speakers resides in Berlin, maybe you lay claim to a bit of Soviet turf within a Rheinish protectorate, say. If you speak Russian, there you are. If you speak Chukchi, and there are no more Chukchi speakers, you are a nation of one until you die, and you take your language, songs, laws, holiday feast practices, everything about you goes down the hole along with your heap of interlocking bones."

I stood and walked across the room, so I blocked the front of the bookshelves again. He followed me, then reached around to my left, and picked up a pottery shard I'd brought from the site. He balanced it in his hand as if feeling the weight of it, then he held it up to the light.

"The body can also be looked at as a map, you know. Veins are highways, let's say, the heart is a metropolis, the brain is the control tower, eyes provide radar, but the map changes. The body map of a child isn't the same as that of a twenty-year-old or an old man, to say nothing of fossilized remains."

I didn't enjoy being looked at like an example of topography, not by Petakhov. When he entered a room, everything changed. He became the prime minister of all he surveyed. He appeared to be telling us a great deal about himself, yet I had the feeling he was learning more about Bruno and me than he revealed about Maksim P.

"What do you think this is?" he asked, holding up the shard.

"Part of an oil lamp, maybe," Bruno answered him.

Petakhov replaced it, then picked up my book of drawings and paged through them.

"I don't recognize any of these rocks."

Of course he didn't recognize any of them, they're paper. I'm not a geologist and didn't make detailed drawings. The angular shapes could have been shale, basalt, giant pieces of feldspar, mountains of diamonds and gold.

"You brought back rock samples from this site you've been visiting every day? No? Darya and I are very curious about this area. Rocks tell stories if you know how to read them. We could help you. We'd be delighted to be of assistance."

"It's dangerous. There is a constant risk of cave-ins. A loud sneeze could cause a roof to collapse."

Maksim shrugged. "We will need to travel to the western edge of the country in a few days time and will be leaving you. It's best if we go to your site tomorrow."

Much to my horror, Bruno gave in while I glared at him from behind Maksim's head. He was running out of ways to say no, sorry, comrade. The prime minister had spoken, but how did he become prime minister? Petakhov said something to the effect of delighted, he and Darya Vasilisa would meet us early in the morning.

After Maksim left, Bruno wouldn't speak to me about the ground he had just ceded and the problems that would come from Petakhov and Darya Vasilisa knowing what they knew. How could they or anyone else find us, here at the ends of the earth, pulling stones out of the ground that may or may not have been walked on by the Lost Tribes? His response was to sleep with his clothes on, or pretend to fall asleep, so he wouldn't have to answer my, now whats? Unable to sleep myself, I looked for my hairbrush but could find it nowhere.

The somnambulist only mumbled. Near our bed I kept one of Feigen's books on Benjamin of Tudela, one of the few associated with the search for the Lost Tribes who hadn't been considered a fraud. Hidden on page 118 was a fragment of a document I should have destroyed, but when I opened the book the bit of paper had been moved to the back, folded, tucked into the endpaper. Who had done this? Perhaps I had and didn't remember doing so. If Bruno had found these papers he would have burned them, and the fight we would have had over my keeping them would have been heard as far away as Baghdad. It was a scrap from our *katuba*, a marriage document, with our real names: Benyamin and Eliana Katzir of Grodno Gibernia. The rest of the *katuba* was lost, destroyed, left behind, but these two names, I saved.

April 12, 1937
True to Petakhov's promise, the next morning the Russians were waiting for us on the street. I was not happy to see the pair with their surveying tripods and private cook who accompanied them everywhere. Unfortunately the weather was good, and we made quick time through the chasm to the city's cave-like entrance.

Maksim and Darya marveled at its dimensions and the sophisticated design of its gates. They scrambled through the opening we'd made, and explored the caverns and chambers talking excitedly of underground topology and sources of water. Every few minutes Darya would hold up a fragment of rock, they whispered between themselves as if in a library, and put rock samples in leather pouches they each carried. When I asked him why he needed or wanted these small chunks of sandstone, he said they were only collecting souvenirs and would take nothing valuable, nothing man-made, from the site. The lintel with the symbols of the lost tribes, they didn't even look at. Petakhov tailed after me because Bruno, who'd abandoned the methodical sectioning off of the city into cubes, had become intent on finding its outer limits. Ignoring the Russians, he disappeared. No one would see him until the end of the day.

I knew nothing of what Bruno actually did in those remote regions, but in one of his explorations he found a cavern that he thought had been a prison cell. It was completely empty except for a skeleton whose head lay several yards away. There were a lot of tracks in and out of the space, and they looked almost like those of contemporary boots, though a landslide had blocked the way out of the cave. The footprints ended at a wall of rocks, but through a multitude of pinhole-sized dots, sunlight pricked the cell. A firmament, he said, lay before him, but the boulders couldn't be budged. On the ground near the sealed-off entrance Bruno had found a fragment of rough canvas, perhaps part of a bag, broken open and discarded. On it were stamped the initials, *H & C*, in block letters. Someone had been in this part of the city before us. Was the skeleton either H or C? Bruno thought it was much, much older than the scrap of cloth. Each day he explored deeper into the ruins, but he never found any other evidence of *H & C*. That was all Bruno told me about what lay in the remote parts of the city, though I asked several times. We were on our own in Suolucidir, and I was convinced that no others who had come before us knew what they had really found.

At night, exhausted, Bruno might barely speak to me but that morning, en route from Zahedan to the lost city, he talked his head off to Ulanovskaya and Petakhov. Bruno, who was usually so reserved and aloof, who didn't have much faith in the whole enterprise, became uncorked. The Lost Tribes meant little to him. *Have you ever been to Marseilles? The smell of the ocean, the sun setting over the Pyrenees, but what I miss most about Moscow is the way the snow sits on top of lampposts like a line of sugar cones down a street . . .* Blah, blah, blah. Did he think they were idiots? Of course the geographers knew you can't see the Pyrenees from Marseilles. Each scene, whether actually remembered or forgotten was part of a long branching story that got so complicated and layered, earlier circumstances, so vivid at the time, become fossilized and reduced to some compressed aggregate of memory. Grodno, Berlin, Marseilles, Amman, Baghdad. Childhood at the bottom, under the most pressure is compressed into coal, diamonds, oil.

April 15, 1937

Maksim's moral tales about cities that disappear as if they've never existed, continue to haunt. What did he actually know? Maksim and Darya Vasilisa didn't leave as they promised but came with us again for several more days. I asked Bruno why he allows them access to the site, but he claims he has no grounds for refusing them; they'll leave soon. I don't like the way they sniff at my steps. Petakhov, in particular, has no off switch. He talks incessantly.

Today, in order to get away from Petakhov and Ulanovskaya, I went into the north side of the dig, pausing as soon as I entered the city, stuffing my scarf into my backpack; it absorbed the anger and distrust I felt toward the two interlopers. I didn't go as far into the maze-like ruin as Bruno, but wandered instead into a large room he had recently mapped out. A small rockslide sounded like a waterfall hitting with enormous pressure. It startled me, and I had to make a quick decision: shout at everyone else to leave immediately, though the sound waves of shouting could cause a cave-in? But then it could be a small rockslide, nothing more. I was terrified of cave-ins, being buried alive in total darkness with the skeletons.

Kosari found me frozen in place. He grabbed my wrist and tried to get me to leave at once, I shouldn't go into remote parts of the labyrinth alone, the city swallowed people whole, it was easy to get lost here, and no one would hear you shout. But the rockslide was actually very small, and soon all was quiet. It was nothing really, as those things seem once the danger has passed. His Russian was mixed with Farsi, and sometimes his sentences were like loops of sound, lulling, compelling, but unclear to me. Was he communicating alarm or something else? Finally letting go of my wrist, he put his hand on my shoulder. What happened next? I put my hand on his arm. I looked over his shoulder. What had this room been used for? It was just an empty space with no history of its past use in evidence, little more than a cave. The cave of re-invention, of rebirth; I remembered Maksim's monastic maps. A room where you can do anything and nothing will remain of it, where you can re-invent yourself in a way that's totally unpredictable and will never be revisited. We could do anything we wanted to, but in an instant I glanced up to see Petakhov in a doorway, his grin disappearing around a corner like an afterimage that morphs into amoeba shapes inside your eyelids. I jumped backward, nearly knocking over a cluster of cracked, empty vessels. They were plain, ordinary pottery jars, examined days ago. The intact ones were empty, and my hand grazed their rough surfaces. What had he seen, the man with his bag full of rocks? His boots made no sound, nor did his equip-ment jangle, nor bag of stones click together. Petakhov, the orienteer, even underground, was sure-footed, as if he knew exactly where he was going. Kosari hadn't seen him and leaned against a wall, waiting for me. What did I want? To stay? To go? An ancient abandoned city was suddenly crowded. Maybe I did want to stay and listen to Kosari's strange Russian, just for a little while. It wouldn't have been so bad, no? A narrow stairway led down from this room to a curved space like an apse just below it. I hadn't looked into that room. No one yet had. He motioned to the stairwell, and I followed him down the steps so worn the passageway was like a child's slide.

Our footsteps tapped along the stone floor while our flashlight beams circled the lower room illuminating more plain clay jars. As with the ones upstairs, some lay in fragments. Others were intact. If Feigen was expecting golden oil lamps and silver *yadim*, silver hands used for reading sacred scrolls, he would be disappointed. We found no rare precious objects, everything was made of stone and clay and smelled like even the air had died. I held my light over the opening of one of the jars, and that's where I saw a black spiral curled inside. I touched the outer edge. It was parchment, fragile as smoke. Holding the flashlight in my left hand I carefully pulled the scroll out of the jar, held it out in front of me. The scroll was only about thirty centimeters wide, and so brittle it was risky to unfurl more than a little. It was impossible to know how long the parchment was. I uncurled a small edge, maybe a few centimeters. Even by flickering light I could make out boxy letters, a callig-raphy that was much older than the writing in the margins of Feigen's map. I felt as if I had stumbled across a dinosaur skeleton in a park, in a square thousands of city dwellers walked through every day, but no one ever noticed the edge of giant rib striations breaking through the dirt.

I unwrapped the scarf from around my neck, covered the scroll with it and quickly placed the bundle in a small basket that fit inside my backpack. To Kosari, I think, these fragments of old things a few seconds away from crumbling into dust and nothingness were of ambiguous worth. Pottery, tile, metal, he understood their value. Actually, I don't really know what he thought. Perhaps it was just a job to him. He had stopped talking to me, and a little later led us back out of the city as if nothing had happened. It was already growing dark.

A few meters from the entrance Darya had set up her surveying equipment, and Petakhov was taking her picture. They said Bruno hadn't felt well so he'd ridden back to Zahedan. Did Petakhov's grin only increase in size as he motioned down the rocky alley, the only way in or out of the site? Darya looked fierce, a nasty you-broke-the-rules kind of face, though what had I done, and what business was it of hers? She often looked this way, like someone in a crowded train was pinching her, and Petakhov's standard mug was that icy parody of a grin. In the growing twilight perhaps I only imagined their expressions, these Soviet imps dancing around a bonfire, pitchforks in the air. The only concrete thing they knew were the angles measured by the theodolite they set up when they surveyed a stretch of sand. I looked around for Kosari but couldn't see him; whether he had already ridden out of the site while I was talking to Petakhov or had gone back into Suolucidir, I didn't know. For a moment I was alone. Sitting on a rock some distance from the others I glanced quickly at the scroll inside my backpack. I could do little more than identify letters, the lightning *lameds*, the *tets* like rooms whose only door opens inward, and the smallest letter, *yud*, sprinkled in many places on the scroll. The first letter of the word for the exodus, *yud* represents the cosmic messenger, change the *u* to an *i* and then what? I carefully unrolled a bit more, but the scroll was so brittle, so near to splintering into a hundred fragments, I unfurled no more than a few inches. The columns of letters ended. The following section was a pattern of hands made of letters. One of the hands had been torn away. I was anxious to show Bruno the scroll that had been waiting three thousand years to be found by refugees from a land the original scribes couldn't possibly imagine or predict. He had been able to read the marginalia written on Yanek Motke's map, and would know whether the ranks of letters represented a parable, a riddle, or an interpretation of dreams. We didn't have much time. Twentieth-century oxygen was fatal, and the fragile text wrapped in a scarf was close to disintegration.

April 16, 1937
When I got back to our rooms Bruno was nowhere to be found, nor had he ever arrived. No one had seen him. Each hour of the night is more urgent than the last. I keep expecting him to walk in the door. Also disappeared is Esme's simurgh and Feigen's map.

At dawn Petakhov and Ulanovskaya knocked on my door looking for Bruno. They were the last people who had seen him. Darya said something to the effect that, yes, it would appear your husband is missing.

"My apologies, profoundly." Her eyes looked empty behind her glasses, uncertain whether to view me with suspicion or pity or to say: maybe this is all your fault — for a moment's pleasure you can lose everything, and end up in a cattle car headed to Niski Novgorod. "Maksim and I will help organize a search."

For a couple of days they divided the landscape into square areas, trackers, hunters, and guides going over each plot whether it contained only a rocky outcropping, a wadi, or a cluster of huts. Ulanovskaya and Petakhov, the fantastic orienteer who can travel without a compass from the Shoals of Disappearing Desires to the Infinite Regrets Range, got a group together of local men who knew the terrain well, and though they combed the area between Zahedan and Suolucidir, no trace of Bruno has been found.

April 18, 1937

Though their commitment to finding him was short-lived, I was astonished and convinced by their sorrow when no clue to his whereabouts surfaced. I was splashing water on my face when Petakhov knocked for the last time. The front of my dress was wet, and I wiped my hands on the skirt, then threw a shawl over my shoulders, so almost my whole body was covered before I opened the door. Petakhov rubbed one of his sunburnt ears, and it occurred to me, didn't he know by now that you shouldn't go into the desert without your head covered? He explained. They were, as they had said, the last to see Bruno, and for this they were sorry — if only they had detained him for whatever serious or light-hearted reason, and then tragedy could have been averted. But be that as it may, their work was completed, and it was time for them to return to Tehran and from there to Moscow. Here are our addresses in case you ever return to the city where your acrobat father left you with the porcelain-firing Nieumachers. They hoped, for my sake, the rest of the Franco-Soviet Friendship Dig, Antonov and Bezymensky, would arrive soon.

April 19, 1937

I wandered the city looking for Kosari and found him about half an hour
before the sun would have gone down completely. Lamps were being lit, and
in their hurry to pack up, a merchant's assistant spilled a bag of rice, which
made a sound like a waterfall as grains hit flagstones. Bolts of cloth from
Egypt, bars of olive-oil soap from Aleppo, bottles of dye from Kurdistan were
all packed up or locked away. Kosari stepped out from behind a coppersmith's
stall, shallow dishes and jazvahs jangling behind him. He said it was time for
him to return to his wife in Alibad — he had worked for the Russians before,
and probably would again when they or another group returned. Kosari was
done and owed nothing to me, or to his former employers, for whom he'd
already taken great risks.

Before we married, Venyamin and I, before we became Bruno and Sido,
we met only once in a room that smelled of dried peppers, cloves and vinegar
in my aunt's house; my aunt, the arranger. Venyamin slouched in a chair
spinning a gyroscope on the edge of a table. I couldn't untangle the strings
and wind them up properly; for him it was effortless. He read comics in two
languages when he could get his hands on them, a child chess prodigy, a
champion who won local tournaments, but he wanted to go backward and
read about ancient people who lived on the Euphrates River, those who invented glyphs, pictorial writing, and ur-chess. Uncles were angry: why would
you want to do that? *Feh*, rank stupidity, *nareshkeit*. Do something useful: furs,
grain, accounting. In a blink we changed our names, our identities. In a blink
we, who'd never left this gibernia, were on a train traveling west to Berlin. I
could never have imagined becoming marooned here in a cave. If Bruno could
escape the Saint Pierre prison, he could escape from anywhere, or so I kept
telling myself.

Could I continue the Franco-Soviet Friendship Dig on my own, waiting for others who will never arrive? Maybe. Back in our rooms, I began
to pack like an automaton, not taking everything, entirely unsure where I
would go. Among Bruno's papers I found a letter from Amman. *What have
Bezymensky and Antonov done since last report? Has Bezymensky showed you the
meter? Has he spoken about it?* More information was demanded, and if a sub-
stantive report was not made within a fortnight, arrests would be made and
deportations begun. In the same folder I found a half-written account on the
movements of Petakhov and Ulanovskaya addressed to the British Governor

General in Amman. Last among the papers was a love letter from Natalya Bezymenskaya. The handwriting looked unfamiliar, unlike any I could immediately recognize. Who wrote this letter? Bruno could have forged the handwriting, or perhaps Natalya Bezymenskaya was a real person, a flesh and blood Russian beauty. I don't know where they were supposed to have met, but she was trying to make her way south to join him in Istanbul. She signed her letters, "your N." She knew about his studies in Berlin, his failed business, the scar behind his left knee. She longed to spend the cool nights with him in rooms with a view of the Bosphorus. I could hear Feigen saying to me, to Bruno, to his Oranienburgerstrasse acolytes, and desperate customers at the edge of the sea: what do you know? You know nothing! He was always right about that. Venyamin K. is like the Chelmite who falls asleep on his way to Warsaw leaving his boots pointing the way to the city. While he sleeps a blacksmith, a prankster, turns his shoes around so they face back to Chelm. Then Bruno wakes, puts on his boots and walks back in the direction of Chelm. Upon arrival at the city gates he believes he's reached Chelm II, an identical city, but not the real Chelm I where his real wife and children reside. Even the elders come to believe they preside over Chelm II, and there must be Chelms III, IV, perhaps one hundred Chelms. Why not? But each contains at least one foolish traveler. In this case: Venyamin Katzir. I left the love letter out in full view on top of the tales of Firkowitsch, the Con.

Unlike Antonov, Venyamin wasn't interested in finding treasure in Suolucidir in order to pay off creditors and thugs. Unlike Feigen he wasn't interested in fame for discovering the city of the Lost Tribes. He never wanted the spotlight on himself for any reason. Suolucidir was about forgetting, for enabling him to resume his old life in Berlin, to turn back the clock, to pick a universe parallel to the one we now seemed to occupy. On one of our first nights in the city we were walking around somewhere on the edge of the Tiergarten, not knowing where we were, sort of happily lost. A man in a black overcoat and hat had set up a telescope on a street corner and was focused on the stars, of which there were not so many. It was a cloudy night, but you could still see something marvelous, he said. His coat billowed in the breeze, making a flapping sound, otherwise the street was quiet and empty. It was to us he addressed his celestial comments. The amateur astronomer waved at us, holding his hat in his hand before replacing it on his head. Smiling broadly he asked us if we wanted to see Saturn, the planet with the rings.

A city with friendly star-gazing citizens, what a marvel, I thought, let's take a look. For a moment I was no longer homesick. He told me where to stand and what ribbed band to turn in order to bring the planet into focus. Saturn was tiny and grey, like a black-and-white photograph. The rings were vertical, as if it had tipped.

What if those men who tucked their pants into their boots hadn't ever taken power, but had been laughed at instead, scuttled into a corner? Venyamin steps onto Oranienburgerstrasse, while a woman shakes a carpet from a balcony, and all that will ever fall on him is twentieth-century dust. He studies Mesopotamia and the ancient culture of the Euphrates, and never has to produce fake books, or identity cards, or anything else that isn't true. Suolucidir means Bruno can put his hands over his ears and shut his eyes. Suolucidir is one big what if.

The Soviets who knew so much, did they know Bruno was spying on them, but not really spying, making up stories? To those who tell jokes about Stalin and penguins eating ice cream on hot days, it doesn't really matter. They could have had him spirited back to Moscow, to Lubyanka or Lefortovo prisons: neither one of these can one leave as easily as the leaky St. Pierre. Bezymenskaya with her luminous bituminous coal-black eyes and her broken nose like a macaw's beak would be waiting for him: cellmate or escaped and lingering on a Turkish barque, what do I know? I know nothing.

April 26, 1937

A knock on the door in the middle of the night. It was the Soviet surveyors, Darya Vasilisa and Maksim, who had returned, or perhaps never left. I began to greet them, what's happened at this hour that they should pound so, but they pulled pistols out from their jackets. Against whom? What revolution had snapped into place at half past midnight in the middle of nowhere? I looked around for enemies of the state, but there was no one else here. Darya had a face like a heel of stale bread and was just as silent. Maksim told me only that I wasn't going anywhere. Am I a prisoner, I asked him? He gave a funny shrug, like, isn't it obvious, then bolted my door from the outer hall with what must have been newly installed hardware.

Not only the door, but the shutters to my windows have been sealed, and it feels as if everyone has evacuated Zahedan. I can't see the streets, and can't hear the sound of merchants unrolling carpets in the morning, so I imagine the city empty and silent. My room feels as if it's been turned into a submarine floating in limbo without bearings or radar. The person who brings me meals will not speak to me.

Two days later Petakhov unlocked the door and this time entered unarmed to tell me I'm under house arrest. Eliana Katzir, he pointed at me as if I had any doubts as to my identity, will soon be deported. Whether he has the authority to keep me locked in this room I don't know, but no one from the hotel or the city seems to be standing in his way. When I asked if this is arrest or kidnapping, he said, the state has long arms, you see. Then Darya joined him, shifted her gun to her left hand and snapped open an empty suitcase, which she handed to Maksim. While Petakhov proceeded to search my room, confiscating a variety of papers and objects, Darya Vasilisa kept the gun aimed at my head. When he finished Petakhov informed me of their intentions.

They are preparing to dynamite Suolucidir, so no trace of it will remain. The entrance has already been sealed. Reason? It lies over an oil field, and if no city ever existed on this spot, no city will need to be preserved. Oil drilling can begin as soon as the smoke from the explosions dissipates. However, the erasure must be total, and any evidence of Suolucidir that exists above the earth's surface must also be destroyed. Relics removed from the city were so far very few, most had remained at the site. He knows about the scroll. Darya saw it. I have three days to hand it over or disclose its location.

Three days came and went, but I'm still here. If I'm executed, he'll never find the parchment, so it's in his interest to keep me breathing. I'm kept alive as long as I'm of use to him, but there are limits to how long I can keep Scheherazade animated. Petakhov, anxious to begin the drilling process, explained something called the Zagros fold belt in the western part of the country. These folds contain enormous reserves of petroleum, and he believes there is just as much below the surface here, directly under what he calls my ridiculous city, a pit of nothingness. All I can do in the face of the oil bursting from under my feet is to buy a little time in the hope of preserving one message in a bottle, one document that will prove Suolucidir existed. Even if he doesn't succeed in finding the scroll, he'll blow up the city anyway. No one here will notice or care about an explosion somewhere in their desert. He is quite certain of this because all will benefit from the oil field. No one, he assures me, cares about your city.

"The British Legation in Tehran is a secret power, like the Vatican. Nobody knows what they're really up to," Maksim says. He holds up papers from a file, and I recognize the letters Bruno wrote to the Englishmen who held us up on our way here. He'd had his eye on us for quite some time. Intercepting communications was all part of surveying and surveillance.

"The Imperial Bank of Persia," Petakhov continues, "is actually a British company. The English get their way here by economic maneuverings so complicated no one knows they've been hit on the head until they're carried out feet first. Their skullduggery, so deft at de-stabilizing a viable if shaky economy, is a marvel, but they underestimate," he taps his fingers on the table as if lecturing a daydreaming student, "the military force Stalin can command just over the border. You can only slap the bear so many times before he hits back. The capitalist corporate hydra isn't the only entity capable of unseating archaic civil governments."

This is a new Stalinische Maksim P., adept at mixing zoological and mythical references, very different from the sentimental cartographer who fooled us so completely. But maybe underneath the hard-as-nails apparatchik is a less confident orienteer feeling for the lichen-covered side of the tree to point the way north.

Petakhov drunk is much more frightening and unpredictable than when he's sober. He can be very careful about his clothing and hair, but now he smells, his clothes are stained, and his cuffs are streaked with dirt. His glasses slip to the end of his nose, and looking over the tops of the frames with half-lidded eyes, he doesn't bother to push them back up. He reads files with raised eyebrows; to a microbe the ridges on his forehead become the Himalayas. In a haze of vodka or anise-flavored arak, he describes the smell of singed muscle when the soles of the feet are burned, torn joints, stretched limbs, memories from his days in Lefortovo prison. Geographically, he's on the thin edge of what was familiar to him, but these tales meant to scare are exercises in nostalgia, I think, though what isn't nostalgia to a drunk, it's hard to say. A drunk, a *shiker*, a word used to describe an embarrassment at a wedding, a word that for me, is its own pill of nostalgia.

Maksim believes I know where Bruno is hiding: Marseilles, a city full of Pinzas and Feigens, where new St. Pierres with less beneficent-sounding names will begin to pop up at every turn. He would slip away without telling me, it was very like him, I tell Petakhov, if he planned to find some safe place, Palestine or the United States, somewhere he could send for me later. Or was he meeting this Bezymenskaya who remembers scar tissue, the names of his lost sisters, and the name of the street in Grodno, not Moscow where the Katzirs, not the Nieumachers, were poor nobodies who could barely spell porcelain, much less have fired plates and bowls for Katherine the Great.

Perhaps Maksim wants to keep one or two things for himself. They're worth a fortune, and with them in his possession he could find safe haven in Bern or Monte Carlo should the Stalinist bear, the one he's so fond of, decide he merits a good and permanent *zetz*, a smackdown. He talks about the relationship between visualizing maps and visualizing the course of pain through the body, traveling from limbs to brain, for example. The topography of waves of pain, relief will come in small shallow moments, but remember, these won't last long before the next wave arrives. Imagine another map: plateaus of respite, underwater banks of unconsciousness before shoals of throbbing and stinging. Pain occurs over time, while as a geographer, really, he's more concerned with space; the analogy he says, adopting his whispery, almost gentle voice, is not a perfect one. It's possible some part of Petakhov believes me when I tell him I don't know where the relics are. Who would endure torture for the sake of a little evidence that may or may not prove a city exists?

The worst is when he strokes my hair with long dry fingers and talks about what a good shot Darya is. How he and Darya Vasilisa, he claims, were ambushed by Pashtun tribesmen, but she is such an excellent markswoman, many were killed. They need to return to those hills, but how can they do so with this history of shoot first, ask identities later? Here's a solution, Petakhov proposes, answering his own questions and moving his hands from my hair to the place where my jawbone meets my neck. He presses hard. I could be given to the Pashtun in exchange for safe passage. This way everyone gets something. Pretty girl can stop wandering from place to place looking for a city where she can finally hang her hat. He's been reading a confiscated book by the British Kipling. He sees himself as a king of the Khyber Pass; the natives worship him as a god, at least for a while. How will Petakhov travel to that gap in the mountains? The torture artist is so drunk, he can barely stagger in and out of my cell.

Yesterday he pulled a table from the side of the room and motioned for me to sit a few feet away. From his case he retrieved not pincers and clamps, but Bruno's report on Antonov and Bezymensky. In the first dispatch Bruno had written an adventure story about how the other half of the Franco-Soviet Friendship Dig had been followed from Moscow through the Caucasus. In the second posting he described the papers and books they read on particular trains and what they bought in markets along the way: flashlight batteries, aerogramme paper, a kilo of apples, cardamom tea with milk and sugar. Antonov grew ill, and to pass the time retreated to his pornographic reverie, which frustrated Bezymensky in what he saw as a lack of seriousness. Antonov fed Bezymensky's suspicions about the wife he left behind whom Bezymensky could never reach by phone. The two men argued between one another. They didn't trust the Nieumachers, and referred to a man in Marseilles with particular distaste and suspicion, a rare book dealer who, though erudite, had been reduced to survival by treachery, his only goal was to save himself. What seemed like a great opportunity to expand international scholarship and co-operation had a dark underside, and Bezymensky believed they had to be vigilant so as not to be taken as dupes. Antonov accused him of being overly cautious. So little attention is paid to this part of the world, the people who live here don't appear in films, radio, are rarely photographed. They assured one another: you can do whatever you want, no one is looking, express doubts, walk around naked. The pair sounded as if they had something to hide. Maksim had swallowed all of it.

Did I know who the man in Marseilles might be? Any idea? Petakhov asked several times. A man who got rich from the suffering of others? You know this person? I shook my head. Feigen who used to trace around the bottom of inkbottles with a pen, then filled in the space with drawings of a half-naked woman as if sitting on a crescent moon, who believed in a phantom from his childhood no more solid than a ratty shadow, a former self-declared skeptic who would hang by his fingernails from a ledge, then suddenly pray like crazy before he dropped to the ground, who might never run back into a burning building to save anyone else, and well can you blame him after all, you might ask?

"Gennady Pavolich Antonov and Ivan Sergeevich Bezymensky have arrived in Zahedan, too late for the dig, unfortunately. They've been detained and are being held in cells in another part of the city. Sidonie, I have run out of patience with you," he sighed. "Unless you hand over the scroll, not only you, but they will be executed. You have twenty-four hours."

You can't kill people who don't exist, but then Petakhov pulled out a wad of cloth. He unwrapped it to reveal a severed finger. It couldn't have belonged to any Soviet member of the Friendship Dig, so whose was it?

When he's gone, lessons in the art of forgery in the accidental classroom, a Berlin apartment, turn out to be useful. Among our trunks is a case of parchment pieces Bruno bought in the market as incidental souvenirs, not that old, but the average person wouldn't know they're not worth much at all. Also, I'm figuring Petakhov can't tell the difference between ancient ink made from cuttlefish or lampblack or carbon and a bottle lifted from the desk of an Englishman in Amman. I'll finally hand over this invention, then he can finish his job. Thinking it's the original, he'll bury the copy in the city's entrance before it's completely sealed off and blown to bits.

I imagine riding out to Suolucidir, but the entrance has been sealed, and I can hire no one to help me open it again. I pull at the stones myself. A boy wanders by with his sheep, and he asks me who I am, what am I doing at bottom of the ravine sitting on a pile of rocks? Eliana Katzir, I tell him, a citizen of Suolucidir. I'm not going anywhere.

Bruno is in the city waiting for me, knapsack packed with the mythological creature, half-lion, half-bird, scarves against the windstorms, pistachios, a map from an old man's childhood.

POLICE REPORT
Department of Alien Affairs
Motahhari Boulevard
Zahedan, Iran
Date: April 20, 1936
MISSING PERSON: BRUNO NIEUMACHER AKA VENYAMIN KATZIR
DESCRIPTION: Approximately 5' 10" Brown hair, brown eyes, thin, moustache, beard. Approximately thirty years of age.
LAST SEEN

Interview with suspect Ramin Kosari, an employee of the Franco-Soviet Friendship Dig, conducted by Nurallah Sahim

NS: Tell us about your last conversation with Bruno Nieumacher.

RK: He was very anxious and wanted to return to Europe as soon as possible, even though his work in Zahedan wasn't yet complete.

NS: Why did he confide in you?

RK: I'm not sure. You work for someone long enough, and they tell you things.

NS: This is not a typical experience with the French or the Soviets, not here, not really. How did you come to work for Nieumacher?

RK: Through Russian geographers who were already working in the region.

NS: Are you referring to Maksim Petakhov and Darya Vasilisa Ulanovskaya?

RK: Yes. They had arranged for me to work for the Franco-Soviet organization.

NS: So let's talk, for a moment, about your other employer, Petakhov. He claimed to be a geographer, a guest of the Shah's Royal Ministry of Cartography. Is this an accurate representation, in short, of his reason for being in this part of the country?

RK: No, not at all, though I didn't learn the true

198

reason for his residency here until Nieumacher did. I, too, believed they were geographers commissioned by the Shah, nothing more. I had no reason not to believe them. Russians and Germans were often hired for surveying and engineering.

NS: How did you first come to be in the employ of Petakhov?

RK: I met them when they came to the region last year. They would leave for periods of time, then return for a while. While residents of Zahedan, they paid extremely well. Also, they spoke some Farsi. When the Nieumachers arrived, Petakhov set me up to work for the Franco-Soviets, but at the same time I was to keep an eye on them, and my pay was doubled. In fact, the Friendship Dig probably would have been harmless, like so many others, but they found an archaeological site in a place that Petakhov believed to be the source of large oil reserves. The site needed to be destroyed, not excavated, to get to that oil. This was his concern.

NS: Was Nieumacher aware of this?

RK: He became very much aware of it.

NS: So how did Nieumacher learn about Petakhov's intentions to blow up Suolucidir?

RK: Nieumacher liked to go to teahouses in the evening, scrounging around for foreign newspapers. He was hungry for information about the cities he'd left behind. One night he saw Petakhov and Darya Vasilisa, which by itself would not have been unusual, except they were supposed to have left the city for a few days. They didn't see him coming out of the teahouse. Why? It was not physically possible for them to have done so because the two of them were down an alley wrapped around one another, you might say. It was high-risk behavior, but they would do this from time to time. Nieumacher later explained to me they probably got pleasure from putting their hands all over one another in a town where the penalties, if caught, would be severe. Even knowing that people did this in other cities of Nieumacher's experience, their behavior in Zahedan did surprise him, so he said.

NS: What was the relationship between the two Russians?

RK: Neither Nieumacher nor myself ever knew. They weren't married.

NS: So you were saying, Nieumacher evidently watched them and began to tail them.

RK: Yes. This is what he told me. They stopped kissing and made their way to the southern quarter of town. Still unseen, he followed them as they unlocked an iron gate, barely sustained by its hinges, and ducked into the abandoned house that lay behind it. Nieumacher waited a few minutes, pushed the gate open, made his way through an overgrown yard, found a ground floor window of the small house, and it was here he positioned himself. The room was dark, then Petakhov appeared holding a flashlight. He let go of Darya Vasilisa's hand. Once inside, they got no pleasure from each other and reverted to their ordinary businesslike selves. Nieumacher remained so still, peeking through gaps in a shuttered window; a whip snake slithered across his foot, pausing to wind around his ankle, and began to go up his leg, yet he made no noise nor did he move, so he told me. Lucky for him, the snake changed its mind, uncoiled, and moved on. The two Russians looked over some papers, then turned their attention to boxes stacked against a wall. Petakhov's flashlight played across a partition-like barricade of crates labeled "Mineral Water" in Russian. Nieumacher told me he could even make out a Moscow address. Who in Zahedan imports mineral water from Moscow? Nieumacher was naturally curious about these boxes, and fortunately for his curiosity, Petakhov and Ulanovskaya didn't linger in the house. As if magically conjured to come and go quickly, they finished their accounting and departed for the desires of the street. As soon as they were out of sight, he broke into the house and promptly discovered what was really in those boxes: dynamite.

NS: How did Nieumacher determine in what way the explosives were to be used?

RS: Petakhov was, by turns, overly careful, constantly looking over his shoulder, and at the same time he could be very careless. Not locking the gate behind him, for example. He believed Russian was his secret tongue that few understood, occasionally forgetting this was not the case. Perhaps eager to resume their exhibitionist tendencies, they had left a roughly drawn map of Suolucidir labeled in his native language on the floor, with the spots where explosives were to be lodged clearly marked.

NS: But he kept this information to himself, no?

RK: Unfortunately, he did not. That evening I was present in Petakhov's rooms when he broke in. Bruno confronted Petakhov. He was convinced that Suolucidir was his, and the Russians had no right to blow it up or to drill for oil. Nieumacher was the taller of the two, but as thin as an alef, not a fighter. He pushed Petakhov hard. Petakhov grabbed a bottle, smashed it, then seized Nieumacher by the front of his shirt and pressed the broken glass neck up to his jaw. Though taller, as I said, Nieumacher's feet seemed to dangle, inches from the ground. The fight was not a pretty sight. Petakhov went for his face and his stomach. Nieumacher didn't have a chance.

NS: How did the fight end?

RK: Well, you've seen Petakhov. He's built like a steel jerrican of gasoline, solid, not designed to be knocked over, and just as potentially flammable. Petakhov shook his opponent who, unarmed, couldn't offer much resistance. I will tell you this only one time, Petkahov said, if you stand in my way, you and Sidonie will be sealed in Suolucidir till the sun collides with Mongolia.

NS: Are you saying Petakhov was responsible for Nieumacher's disappearance?

RK: All I'm saying is threats were made.

NS: What did you do when you learned about the dynamite?

RK: I tried to disappear, but Darya found me at my cousin's madrassah. It didn't matter this was the last place she should be; she barged in shouting in Russian. Pushing boys aside, as if they were rabbits, she grabbed me by the shirt, leaned down, and whispered to me that if I informed, there would be consequences. She could be more frightening than Petakhov. For a woman to burst in like that, you can imagine, no one does that ever. She could have been beaten, thrown out, but everyone froze. She left as quickly as she broke in.

NS: So when Nieumacher disappeared, what was Petakhov's reaction?

RK: He went berserk. It was important to Petakhov that nothing, no object, no photograph leave the so-called Suolucidir site, and he was very anxious about Bruno's whereabouts, because with him went not just a few artifacts, but also the knowledge that the site did, in fact, exist.

NS: You were in a unique position to know the desires and co-ordinates of both men.

RK: For a time, you could say so. Petakhov didn't threaten idly. He meant business. Nieumacher was not a coward, but a realist, you might say. He took a few valuable things and made plans to leave the country. In truth, he never wanted to engage in the Friendship Dig, the desert was to him the end of the earth, and he just wanted to return to Berlin or wherever he was from.

NS: And is it fair to say that Nieumacher became the man who knew too much? The man who knew too much about

Suolucidir? Too much about his wife? What was your relationship with Sidonie Nieumacher?

NS: Kosari, please answer. It's really in your interest to respond to our inquiries. No? Okay, let me
tell you, Mr. Kosari, we already know the answer to that
question. Did the discovery of your relationship with
Madame Nieumacher by her husband have anything to do
with Nieumacher's departure?

RK: It's possible.

NS: So once again, I'd like you to tell me in
your own words, what was your relationship with Sidonie
Nieumacher?

RK: I don't know how to answer that question. We
didn't speak the same language. I couldn't tell you what
she wanted.

NS: But you enjoyed her company.

RK: I enjoyed myself. You could say that.

NS: How did he learn about you and his wife?

RK: I was never sure. The other Russian, Darya
Vasilisa, and Sidonie didn't like one another, you could
tell. At first they barely spoke to one another, as if
each viewed the other as an untouchable, you know, a
leper of some kind. If they'd met in their country of
origin, they probably would have openly disliked each
other. It was easy for Sidonie to avoid Darya Vasilisa.
She was always drawing in her notebooks, behaving as
if she were possessed, you might say, as if the spirit
of the mason who designed the labyrinth or a ceramist
laying tiles inhabited her. Darya spoke to her only
in clipped, bullet-like sentences, as if she were the
object of both pity and contempt. Sidonie referred to
her as a dumb babushka. However, Darya, brutish though
she was, was not stupid. It was when Sidonie was most
possessed by Suolucidiri demons, talking to herself
and removed from the site only with difficulty, that
Darya found an opening to insinuate herself. In this

203

state Sidonie may have told the other woman things she wouldn't have if she had been herself. So, gradually Darya learned one or two things, and ultimately everything was repeated to Maksim. He was the one who coated the kite strings with ground glass.

NS: Are you implying Darya told Nieumacher about you and Sidonie?

RK: Yes. I think it's possible she spoke to Bruno late at night. In the morning, while we were preparing to leave for the site, he was distant. I assumed he was provoked because Petakhov was coming with us. He couldn't stop the Russians, and wasn't happy they trailed after us, knowing what their plans for the lost city ultimately were. Madame Nieumacher had gone ahead. She was not yet aware of any of these revelations. Just as we entered the chasm leading up to Suolucidir, Ulanovskaya caught up to me, leaned over and said in her distinctively audible whisper, he knows about you. Watch your back.

NS: Your boss wanted Nieumacher dead. Was Petakhov provoking a personal situation between you and Bruno so it would escalate? Though since he'd already been in a fight with Nieumacher, he's easily a suspect in the disappearance.

RK: You're making a lot of assumptions that have no basis in proof. My impression of the Franco-Soviets was they did not engage in petty jealousies and just wanted to get on with their work, which for Nieumacher meant, at that point, saving the city or evidence of it.

NS: Are you sure? No answer. Okay, you know that after Bruno disappeared Petakhov was keeping Sidonie in her room at the hotel. Her husband had disappeared, and he could do whatever he wanted with her.

NS: Kosari?

RK: Sidonie was only held for a short time, maybe one week, I'm not exactly sure.

NS: Why did they release her?

RK: Petakhov thought she would lead them to Bruno, and in this he was correct. In fact, he had not disappeared, but he was in hiding. After the fight with Petakhov Bruno decided the best way to save the site was for him to get to Tehran and announce what he had found there, taking some things from the site as proof. Sidonie was to pretend he was missing, to provide a distraction, to delay blowing up the site, if possible.

NS: What made you want to collaborate with them? It seems to me you had many reasons not to: money, Sidonie herself.

RK: You misunderstand.

NS: Explain to me.

RK: Who does drilling for oil benefit? The resources don't linger and pool here, do they? The pipeline seems to end up in Moscow, London, Berlin. If all we get is a tin can's worth of drippings from a faulty joint weld, why help them out?

NS: The Shah has great admiration for Berlin at the moment.

RK: The Nieumachers thought differently, but we didn't discuss Europe much, to tell you the truth.

NS: Despite what you say, you have in your possession Nieumacher's identity papers, passport, exit visas, and documents relating to the Franco-Soviet organization. Were you planning a visit to Paris? To London?

RK: I gave Bruno my identity papers and some clothes. He was to travel to Tehran as Ramin Kosari. We thought it would be safer.

NS: But Bruno Nieumacher never made it out of Zahedan, did he?

NS: Kosari? Tell me about the last time you saw Nieumacher alive?

RK: Petakhov's handlers were not patient men. They didn't care about what they were blasting, or what the

world would think about what they destroyed. The wolf
was at their door, too, they needed the oil, and about
this one might say, possibly, who can blame them? But
their fight isn't my fight. The site was by now timed and
wired to blow up. All those crates of so-called mineral water had been trucked to the site. We knew this.
Sidonie had been released in the hope that she would
lead the Russians to Nieumacher. She somehow managed to
evade them, however, and as soon as night fell the three
of us met at the site. There was a waning moon, we had
some light, and maybe four hours to move whatever we
could to a part of the city that was deeper underground,
just out of reach of the explosion due to go off at
midnight. Bruno had a watch, and he called out the time
every thirty minutes. Let me describe.

    NS: Please.

    RK: 7:30 baskets of pottery moved

    8:00 armloads of weapons taken to a far chamber

    8:30 Bruno fell down a ravine and sprained his an-
kle. We spend one hour finding and rescuing him, trying
to bandage or brace his ankle so he can walk, but he
limps and uses some kind of spear as a cane. We split
up, though we are all still within earshot to hear Bruno
call out the time. The city is labyrinthine and full of
echo chambers, so because you can hear someone doesn't
necessarily mean they're close by. They could be behind
a wall, but your passage and his might not meet for half
a mile or more. To separate is risky, but we are racing
against time.

    10:00 panels of mosaics

    10:30 cooking implements

    11:00 clay figures

    11:30 We have to find our way out in thirty minutes.
I locate Sidonie, but we can't find Bruno. We call his
name, and we hear his voice, but we can't find him.
Twenty minutes. Fifteen. He's shouting that he's in a

cul de sac but all ways out lead to other dead ends.
His torch has gone out. He's feeling his way along
walls, but this is taking time we don't have. Sidonie
is weeping. She doesn't want to leave Bruno, but the
explosives will go off in a matter of minutes. He yells
through the wall, his voice rasping, but audible, we
should make a run for it. There is no more time, but
Sidonie will not leave. I grab her hand, and we flee.
Just before the entrance, the explosion blows us off
our feet. Rocks tumble down all around us. We don't
lose consciousness but are able to crawl out. It's the
middle of the night.

NS: We found you, but we have not found Sidonie.

RK: She was hysterical, beyond distraught.

NS: So the scroll is buried in the city.

RK: No, it is not.

NS: That was the most valuable find, the object Bruno
would have wanted to take to Tehran.

RK: That was the intention, but she had confused the
two cases. Bruno should have had the original but he had
the copy. When Sidonie looked in her rucksack, and saw
she had given Petakhov the original, that made things
so much worse. Not only was Bruno dead, but it was the
copy he died to save. All that for nothing.

NS: We'll recover it.

RK: Not if Petakhov and Darya escape.

NS: They won't be a problem. We arrested them shortly after we found you.

RK: How long will you hold them?

NS: They're no longer with us. Kosari?

RK: Yes?

NS: They did away with themselves in their cells.
You look surprised? These things happen. Kosari?

RK: Yes?

NS: But Sidonie Nieumacher, we haven't been able to
locate.

RK: I must have lost consciousness from the shock of the explosion. When I woke she was gone.

NS: A madwoman walking through the desert doesn't have good survival odds. She will turn up somewhere.

RK: When she does she'll deny all of this.

NS: That will not be our problem.

THE POLICE RECOVERED THE SCROLL from Petakhov's room. The theft of an antiquity was only one of his crimes, the evidence of which lay the groundwork for the spies' assisted suicides, I'm guessing. The real scroll, the one I was never able to access, languished in Tehran. But the oil drilling languished also. I'd seen no trace of it: no toppled derricks, no rusted pipes, no hardhats scattered in clusters. Only sheep. Perhaps those veins turned out not to be viable. If they had been, Jahanshah, and possibly his father, would have reaped the benefits of such a well or series of wells. Or maybe they knew and kept the location to themselves. I like to imagine rivers of oil so far below the waterways of the lost city that they remain just out of reach, no matter how deeply the desert is drilled. For Suolucidir, oil didn't float on water.

Kosari's interrogators never found Sidonie Nieumacher, but I found Eliana Katzir, and she did deny everything. There were countries sealed behind the Iron Curtain, so my search was limited to the borders that were open. I was lucky.

When the letter arrived, Alyssa the psychic laid her hands on the manila envelope, shut her eyes, and said the object had a murky aura, but then Alyssa had admitted she made things up out of the random bits and pieces on the conveyor belt of reality flotsam that passed her way. Once in a while she turned out to be right. Maybe more than once in a while, or so her fan mail told her. She offered a joint to share as a way of easing into whatever the envelope would reveal, but I waved her out the door. Maybe later.

March 1986
Dear Mr. Bokser,

I sincerely believe you have the wrong person. My name is Eliana Katzir, and I was married very briefly, but my husband was neither a scholar nor a con man. The similarities in our married names can only be coincidental. If you're looking for Nieumachers, then look for Nieumachers. Frankly, they sound like first class suckers. I've never heard of Suolucidir. Have you looked on a map?

As a retired art teacher who lives alone in a senior center I don't ordinarily get inquiries about my state of health or my thoughts prior to the last few days. Journal writing is something I've never undertaken. Until recently, I'm speaking about my life before I was moved to this facility, I didn't even own a refrigerator. However, if you send me this woman's journal or a copy of it, I'd be curious to take a look at the pages written by this Sidonie N. We appear to have been born in the same city in the same year. Like the Nieumachers, I left at university age but unlike them, traveled east to study painting in Moscow.

I didn't leave altogether willingly. I was supposed to have an arranged marriage. My beloved aunt had organized several meetings already for which I was meant to be very grateful, and in a way I was. Each candidate was like a voice crying out from an old newspaper or book, you know how paper feels before it crumbles into nothing, half a story is left, you can only guess how it might have ended. None of the candidates were my cousins or cross-eyed or proposed that I should cut off my hair and wear a headscarf or a wig, but I just couldn't see myself married to anyone and surrendering to a cycle of holidays and children, year after year, if you know what I mean. Maybe this is difficult for a person such as yourself to imagine, living, as you do, in twentieth-century New York, a city where I've heard food comes out of machines you feed coins into. Now I'm not so sure. Perhaps I made a mistake, though had I stayed I'd be worm food several times over. Nonetheless, I have to say it wasn't an entirely easy choice. The possibility of staying and marrying had pulled at me. Could I do it, maybe, would it be so bad? Finally, no, I decided to leave.

Most of the family looked at me as if I was a dispensable oddball, so fine, send her to Moscow, what does it mean to paint pictures? They had no idea. Moscow, a city of underground trains and ice sculptures like blue houses, was not an easy city for me, coming from a smaller metropolis, and at first I missed my family terribly, considered returning, but never did. Moscow, of seemingly infinite electric lights and a tangle of streets too complex to be accurately mapped, all this became a heady delight. I felt like I'd gone through a tunnel and come out an entirely different person, but I made a lot of mistakes. No one had told me how much money it would take to live as a student, even a poor one, but I made friends quickly. Who were these people who came from all parts of the Soviet empire? Ukrainians with their geometrically painted eggs, Georgians with their all-night parties, Tatars hiding their Korans. I felt very small beside them, my past a secret tucked away in a pocket, never to be openly discussed. The drawings I did as a child of the people and things around me seemed to have no connection to my classes, where everyone believed fanatically in Dada or was devoted to constructivism as if they were warring sects of competing religions. Groups formed, this person stopped speaking to that person. You'd think they were building monuments, not arguing over ephemera.

I constructed drawings embedded with photographs cut from newspapers, black and red floating shapes, puns lifted from Chagall, El Lissitzky, Malevich, and Altman, printed in block letters. These pictures were full of secrets that some of the students deciphered while others shrugged and moved on. I soon abandoned painting with its endless debates about planes and abstraction for something more practical: design. Then my money really did run out. One of my teachers recommended me for a job at the Soviet Yiddish Theater (SYT). At first I thought he mumbled something about *emet* or *emes*, truth, the letter on the Golem's forehead, but no he was talking about only a small troupe, insignificant, a dry bone tossed to a starving dog. I could tell he was thinking 'this is good enough for her, and then she's out of my class,' but little did he know it was, for me a very exciting place to be. How did he know about this theater in the first place? He would never have told me. By the way, remove the first letter from *emes* and you get *meis* or death. Erase this letter from the Golem's forehead, and that's the end of him.

My first day I walked to a part of the city I'd never seen before; no trains or buses could take me all the way to the doors of this theater, located in a drafty wooden building that smelled like it must have housed, somewhere in its many floors, archives of moldering paper, genizahs of old plays, lists of actors, drafts of set designs, forgotten props and costumes. The director shook my hand, asked my name, and without much reflection, instructed me to join a fellow named Lapshov, a set designer who rarely left his basement workshop.

Down a narrow iron spiral stairway I found Lapshov, a giant paint-stained man, small eyes behind round black glasses. He nodded and pointed, gave clipped instructions. Lapshov seldom spoke to his apprentices, whether we were beneath discussion, or his preoccupations were elsewhere, I couldn't say at the time. Working for him was a very different process from the art school I'd been immersed in only a few days before. The link between drawing or plan and three-dimensional execution had to be as direct and as feasible as a blueprint for a bridge or an airplane. The things had to work, to swing open, fly through the air, snap shut. Yet the moment when ink soaked into a page was mesmerizing, pure color, and the resulting drawing less static than the work I'd done in classes. Then, one way or another, the flat thing developed angles, levers, gears. A notebook of sketches wasn't a static thing: a market square shifted into a series of alleyways or the interior of a house. A costume designer's journal was full of people transformed into demons, beggars, a fish, a sorceress. Flip the pages, and it's like an animated cartoon.

Actors were always coming and going through the swinging

doors, from the stars (luminaries within a very small universe, it might be better to call them people with big parts) to extras and a fairly large number of crew workers. Often I needed to watch rehearsals, and during these study breaks, feet on the chair in front of me, I found myself drawn to one actor in particular. He wasn't a romantic lead, but a comic actor who contorted his features into all kinds of hysterics. Itzik, it must also be said, had a mean streak, his comedy had an edge of sarcasm. Yet he was very charismatic, and so people tended to overlook the fact that his mimicry was deadly, especially if they felt included in the joke rather than the object of it. He had long straight hair that swung out fan-like when he moved his head, and Asiatic eyes, like an Uzbek. He made faces behind Lapshov's broad back, pushing his nose up with one finger, pulling his cheeks down with the other hand, for example, but paid no attention to me whatsoever, and how I wanted to be included in the jibe, even if it meant making fun of Lapshov, who had never thrown acid at my often inadequate efforts. Or anyone else's for that matter. Now that I look back, many of Itzik's targets were harmless schmucks. Itzik slouched in seats with his legs slung over the legs of a golden-haired actress or a confident fellow actor waiting for make up, gesturing into the air. How were these people blessed by his attention when they didn't even know how lucky, how singled out they were, while I waited outside in the cold? How to participate in the circle of his knowing humor without incurring the risk of becoming the object of it? (You might ask why did I want this? Why embrace this engine of pranks and cruelty? Sometimes one is infatuated one night, and by the following morning, afternoon at the latest, you see the ass's head where a human head was, realize your mistake, and look for the exit signs.) I began to take great care in how I dressed before I arrived at the theater, even if my work involved painting, sawing, gluing, I wore what nice clothes I had. Sooner or later maybe he would notice me, I hoped, thinking we had all the time in the world.

After about six months working with Lapshov we were

painting sets for *The Travels of Venyamin the Third*, a play based on Don Quixote. Venyamin III, from the small town of Tuneiadovka (Droneville), dreams he's married to a daughter of a tsar. It was a fantastic set in which actors dressed as bottles of wine and roast chickens had to pop out of trap doors and fly through the air. I painted all morning, but Lapshov never showed up for work. This was unusual; the workshop was his whole life, as far as I could tell. Maybe he's sick, I said to the director. He shrugged. For a week Lapshov didn't appear. In the middle of the day, instead of taking lunch and trying to eavesdrop on Itzik, I made my way to Lapshov's apartment building on Pavlovskaya Street and stood for a moment at the big double doors, entrance to the courtyard. I knew little about him, really, what was I getting myself into? I didn't have much time to make a decision, lunch break was finite, and so finally summoned the courage to inquire at his neighbors if he was ill. He lived alone, this would be the right thing to do. I told myself Lapshov would have done the same for me, though why I believed this as a kind of false fuel to go forward, I don't know. Maybe he would have. Maybe the answer is a resounding no. There was no answer at his door, so I tried some of his neighbors in the hopes they would have some idea where he might be. No one behind any of the doors I knocked on knew who Lapshov was. If the doors opened at all, I was met with only blank faces. A man dangling a bottle by its neck as if to either spill its contents or swing at me, told me to get lost. I trudged back to the theater. Later I showed the address, scrawled on a piece of paper, to the director and he said, yes, it was the correct address. Lapshov would never be seen again in this life or any other, he said, and I should take over his job. I was too young and truly had little actual experience, but there was no one else. Lapshov, wherever he was, left no forwarding address. Lapshov died, do you think? There's no funeral, no memorial service, nothing, I asked? The director shook his head. No shiva? The director told me to get back to work, please, don't even speak about this anymore. Okay, sorry, I said, but truly I was very bewildered.

Over the next few months others in the troupe disappeared, and without anyone offering direct explanations finally I understood why this was so. The arrests were made in the middle of the night. Poof. The next day maybe Aronovsky, Boris, Rabinovitch, Yulya, Rosenberg, don't show up. Bit by bit we were being eaten away. Replacements came and went. The core, who for unknown reasons were not yet arrested, became more nervous and suspicious of one another.

We called a meeting in secret, not all the troupe, just the few who had been there from nearly the beginning, and discussed what should we do. Dialogue went like this: Was Ginzberg an informant? He has parties. He invites everyone. Yes, but he's the kind of person who serves you a wonderful fragrant cup of coffee, and just as you bring it to your lips, you realize there are sharp tacks sticking out from the brim. What about Leonid? He's always taking notes. He's a production manager. That's his job. What's to inform? We performed plays where Jewish landlords looked really bad, and rich merchants act from self-interest only, ruining their families and everyone else. Naïf! Moron! Someone shouted. Informants make up stories. It doesn't have to be what really happened in any known city, on any known planet in the solar system. We talked about disbanding, but then what? Still, they would find us. It wasn't so easy to dissolve into the chaos of movement that characterized the city. Anatoly, the carpenter, made a suggestion no one had voiced before: we should leave for Birobidzhan, the autonomous region advertised as a Jewish homeland as far east as you could go before you got your feet wet. He had seen *Seekers of Happiness*, starring Benjamin Zuskin as Pinya Kopman, shot in the exact province, a beautiful place. Itzik said no, this is a worthless plan. The oblast that was promoted as a treasure box waiting to explode with arable land, fruit trees, and rivers of gold was a swampy capital dominated by mosquitoes the size of bulldogs half the year and an arctic wasteland the other half. We would find it populated by the only Yids stupid enough to believe the teardrop-shaped province lying on top of China was a paradise. Or maybe they had come from someplace worse, if it was possible. He, Itzik, wasn't going anywhere. Everyone argued back and forth. The Moscow State Jewish Theater was already installed at the Kaganovich Theater in Birobidzhan. This was a well-known fact. There was no room for a little nothing group like us. We would only get their crumbs. But at least we'd be alive. We'll have our own theater eventually. Fat chance. You'll have your own bug spray, that's what you'll get. Finally it was decided the troupe would apply to travel to Birobidzhan as a theatrical entity, anyone who wanted to stay in Moscow was welcome to. The disappearances had made everyone so nervous that debate petered out, and the truth was, most were in favor of leaving as soon as possible. By the time the meeting ended you'd think bags were already packed.

Applications made at the KOMZET (Committee for the Settlement of Jewish Toilers on the Land) were accepted, the process of packing up sets, costumes, props, and winding up our own lives in Moscow was begun. On a late spring day we were at the crowded Yaroslavksy train station, ready to board. I saw Itzik, who had changed his mind, in the crowd, and then in an instant, he was gone. His gray hat had been toppled from his head, his arms grabbed by two unknown men, his suitcase trampled underfoot, and he was hustled out of the station. The snapping up of the acidic satirist was more painful, more pathetic than the disappearance of our youngest, sad-eyed set painter just the week before. Itzik had always seemed like the kind of person who could do a back flip at the last minute and escape down a fire pole, so when he appeared vulnerable, paralyzed and mute as he was dragged away and disarmed, towed away like a rag doll, it flipped all certainties into chaos. As I looked into the crowd others began to disappear in the sea of bodies. Ordinarily I'm very short, but in heels, standing on tiptoe I made out someone who was only a seamstress, pulled into a van, Belkin who wrote melodramas, his eyes bugged out as if he were being strangled, Zapir, the carpenter, a rigger of mechanical genius who could make actors fly through the air was pushed to the ground and dragged away. Gone before my eyes were Zeisser who played Lear and the diva, Malvina, who played the bride in *The Dybbuk*. Pulling a scarf over my head, I melted into the mass of bodies pushing toward the rails. Police boarded the trains and some of the passengers held back, a reflexive movement like a giant jellyfish recoiling from a poke with a stick—if that's where the police are going, you may not want to move in that direction. Then I slipped off those high heels, and in stocking feet, the pavement cold under my heels, lowered so my head and shoulders, an instant hunchback disappeared beneath the surface of the crowd. I pushed my way to the end of platform where the passenger cars gave way to the freight cars. The doors to these cars were still wide open. I passed cars laden with boxes, crates, bundles of clothing, barking dogs. Finally I found the last car, which contained, among other things, our trunks and sets. I hid between angular flats, phantasmagoria that looked like the inside of a giant watch. Stairs, platforms, sharply painted shadows used in the brothel scene from *God of Vengeance*, the town square for the village of fools in *The Travels of Venyamin the Third*, reconfigured again for the marketplace in *The Sorceress*, the graveyard, scene of possession in *The Dybbuk*. The sound of boots and a clicking noise I imagined had something to do with guns could be heard just outside the open doors. Two officers began to speak perhaps only a few feet away. Did they whisper the names of those yet to be rounded up? Did I hear them say Eliana Zoyakovno, that one, over and over? Maybe, maybe not. Between cracks in the flats I could make out elbows leaning against the metal run where the doors would be slid shut. What was holding up this train? Shut the doors, let's move already. The two police leaned and smoked, waiting for what, I can't say. One threw a stub of a smoked-down cigarette into the car, and I put it out with the heel of my shoe, still held in my hand. Finally their voices diminished, and I assumed they had left. The day wore on, it grew hotter, then the chill of the evening took over, and still the train didn't move. Other men, inspectors of some kind and other police, came round and looked in each car before

217

the doors were slid shut and locked. I could hear them speaking in loud voices. When they climbed to have a look around I shrank against a plywood gravestone.

"What's this?"

"Building materials. Nothing."

They unlatched a trunk.

"Old clothes."

They didn't even know what it was they were looking at. These inspectors must have been newly hired from some backwater who only wanted to be done with the Yaroslavsky station and go out for the night. They jumped down and locked the doors behind them. Still the train didn't move. I fell asleep.

When I woke up the car was moving. Light came through in slivers here and there. I stretched and tried to find a crack in the wood wide enough to afford a view of the passing countryside as we sped east. What can I tell you about it now? I couldn't see very much: plains, farmland, mountains, more mountains, some desert-like landscape that I took for outer Mongolia. What did I know, and what did it matter? I didn't have a map and had lost any sense of time, but I had escaped and would soon be safe. The train stopped in a few towns here and there, but with my limited vision from my hiding place, no signage could be seen. As far as I knew I was the last of the group, and when I arrived in Birobidzhan I would make my way to the Kaganovich Theater and find work, easily. The smell of paint was still viable enough to be inhaled if my cheek was close enough to a flat. Climbing into a trunk, I nestled into a well of costumes that had been sweat in and not washed very well. It was comforting. I'd brought food with me for the trip across the Soviet Union. The journey on the Trans-Siberian was supposed to take many days, but after I don't remember how long, the train came to its final stop. I'd packed quite a bit of food to take for the journey, and had maybe half left, but I wasn't eating so much. So as I said, the train came to a stop, the doors to my car were unlocked and slid wide open.

I hadn't expected to arrive in Birobidzhan so quickly, but

there I was. The bright sun shown in my eyes, even as I peered around the edge of the door. My first impression was that the town looked nothing like the photographs we'd been shown. The buildings appeared quite old and in the middle of a desert ringed by mountains. Dazzling sunlight poured into the car, light that should never have shone on angular expressionist flats meant to represent the landscapes where dead souls possess brides and deluded tradesmen look for the lost tribes in a city of fools that turns out to be just down the road. Unlike the Yaroslavsky station bustling with people and anxiety, this station was nearly empty. Men who watched me jump from the train car wore long shirts, baggy trousers, ridged caps of felt shaped like pillboxes. There were daggers in their belts, but a few carried guns as well. Perhaps I'd landed in the Crimea, and these armed men were Krimchaks. When I spoke to one in slow Russian, thinking it wasn't his native language, I was right, it wasn't, and he answered me in a language I'd never heard before. Guttural sounds slid, then seemed to end upward before coming to a stop. The language was not the Sibero-Korean dialect Itzik had imitated as he told us what to expect from natives in Birobidzhan. It was Farsi. The train had been traveling south, not east, and this was its last stop: Zahedan, Iran.

You know this city, so I don't need to describe to you what it was like to find myself in a country where I didn't know the language, had the wrong kind of currency, and knew no one. In those first hours I felt I'd landed on the other side of the moon, and groping in the dark with dwindling supplies of oxygen, could no longer see the earth. Where was I? Thousands of miles lay between my point of origin and where found myself standing. There were few women on the streets, and since my coat only fell a few inches below my knees I was stared at continuously, unable to speak to anyone, unable to pay for food with worthless paper rubles. A man offered me a pomegranate, but I'd never seen one before and didn't know how to eat it. He split it open with a knife and handed me a cluster of seeds encased in red juice, their skins burst between my teeth.

How I found rooms in a sort of hotel where there were a few other Russians I can't begin to explain. One person guided me here, another who knew a few words of Russian, guided me there. At the hotel I was befriended by two chemical engineers, Maksim and Darya Vasilisa, who worked for Petro-oil, a state petrol company located in Rostov. Though this part of the country was under British control, Maksim believed there were rich deposits here, right under everyone's noses, these hidden reserves only had to be sniffed out and claimed. At first it seemed so lucky to have found these two, even if Darya was stiff, remote, and formal, while Maksim laughed too hard at his own imitations of what he took to be obsequious Persians. We were in my room, talking as if we were old friends. Darya's shawl slipped, revealing a bare but reddish arm. She stood so close to Maksim, a proprietary proximity, only a few atoms could have slipped between his pumping elbow and her bare arm. As he guffawed, he moved away slightly. The gap of molecules became the length of a small child, and Darya shifted to close it again.

At this point you're probably thinking that there is far too much coincidence here. How can I have met the same Russians that Sidonie Nieumacher encountered? I have no answers for you, Mr. Bokser. Your notebooks are fairytales, penned by someone who lifted my name, which, in some parts of the world, is not such an uncommon one. Someone who knew pieces of it, but not the whole. Why they did this? Who knows. In the name of controlling land, squeezing oil out of rocks, stranger things have happened. You figure it out. Someone wants to throw you off a scent, how should I know? I insist my story is the true one.

Slowly they earned my trust, especially because they were the only Russians, as far as I knew, for hundreds of miles around. They promised to help me find my way to Birobidzhan, assuring me it wasn't all that far. They were so enthusiastic about the kingdom to the east where I needed to travel. Petakhov envisioned Birobidzhan, a completely modern city with automobiles that could take flight and also navigate estuaries. The cities have moving sidewalks, the weather as balmy as he has heard California to be. A place where you can give yourself a new name and completely re-invent yourself. He would become Maksim Gorky or Maksim Ispovednik, the Confessor, or Maksim H. Houdini. Lucky Jews. Yes, even here in this far flung corner beyond the empire, they had heard about Birobidzhan, and how wonderful it sounded. A utopian paradise, an empty landscape waiting to be built upon. A bursting gold seam begging to be mined. If only they could claim some Hebraic ancestor they would both be on the next train. They would help me. It would be a pleasure to do so. And some day maybe I would return the favor. Petakhov described how I could take a train to Rostov then switch to another Trans-Siberian line, never having to return to Moscow where I would surely face arrest. He offered me glass after glass of arak, and when I shook my head, he passed the glass to Darya who swallowed its contents in one gulp. When he asked about who or what I'd left behind, at first I was very careful about what I told him, naming only Lapshov who was probably long dead anyway. But now, I think even stories of the dead are dangerous. The fact that I knew this man, went to his apartment out of concern, these were little seeds that planted themselves in Petakhov's brain.

Maksim asked about who else could have been disappeared like this? He claimed he'd heard rumors, but never knew anyone personally who had their rooms searched and were taken off in the middle of the night. He sounded so naïve, so innocent, like he'd spent his adult life studying bridge spans in barely populated areas, and knew nothing about lists, and doctors' plots, and the assassination of theater directors made to look like car accidents. Though I didn't drink with him, bit by bit I found myself believing he was, indeed, this know-nothing nudnik, and slowly the names of those who disappeared from the theater slipped from my tongue.

Petakhovsky spoke like a newly minted Chelmite visiting from that City of Fools. Did he know Birobidzhan was a wasteland of an ethnic homeland, impossible to strike it rich within its borders? Sometimes it's easier to agree with relative strangers on whom you depend, to a certain extent, than to shout, you know nothing at all! In trying to be amenable, to show him I was sympathetic to his ideas, I mentioned others arrested at the train station. Believing dead people could no longer be harmed, might even be vindicated in some way, I might as well have been drunk and liberating all my thoughts. Would it be possible to find out what happened to Itzik and the others? Maksim always listened so attentively, then spoke with such misguided authority, and Darya Vasilisa backed up every word. Maksim nodded. Darya nodded, too. Though he spent a great deal of time in the provinces: Tbilisi, Baku, Samarkand, Azerbaijan, he knew people, he was proud to say, yes he had some connections here and there. Anything was possible. Maybe he could get some of them out, maybe Itzik. People bartered knowledge for money, why not for people? Darya assured me, this could be done. He wrote down the names of the entire group who had disappeared. Darya made a copy. Is this complete? Can you sign it?

Sign it? Why?

Pause. No one spoke.

Just say to me: sure, Maksim, why not?

The next morning when I tried the door to my room, it wouldn't budge. I banged on the door. What was going on? Someone made a mistake. Why should I be locked in a room? Silence. It was as if I were barricaded in my cabin on a sinking ship, and everyone else had long since forgotten me as they sped away on lifeboats, at least that's how I felt. Such silence you can't imagine. This makes no sense, you might think. Why didn't anyone hear me? Perhaps now I think servants, other guests, whoever, had been paid off to ignore sounds coming from my room. Later that day I heard a key turn in the lock. There was a pause for a few minutes, then the key turned back the other way, as if checking the door to be certain it was locked. Petakhov whispered at the wood panels: you, Eliana are a Zionist spy. You should be sent back to Moscow. You haven't fooled anyone. What was he talking about? I laughed nervously and pounded at the door as the sound of his footsteps receded.

The shutters to my windows were hooked closed from the outside. How they managed to do this I can't say. I could no longer see the streets, nor hear the sound of merchants unrolling carpets in the morning, so I imagined the city empty and silent, a ghost town. My room felt as if it had been turned into a submarine floating in limbo without bearings or radar. The person who brought me meals was mute, illiterate, and resistant to sign language.

Looking back now, I don't think Petakhov and Ulanovskaya had been sent out to look for enemies of the state in isolated places in order to turn them in, no that wasn't their job. I believe they were who they said they were, but they acted as if they had something hidden in their pockets, something they knew all too well and turned over and over in their hands, kept far from everyone else. It wasn't enough that they'd chosen to be sent to this remote place, but the two wanted to be exactly here in Zahedan, a place where they could share a room and never come under suspicion as far as what went on in it. They were nervous, drunk, had been accused of something. It could have been anything. Perhaps Petakhov had once traveled to America, had met with Charlie Chaplin or Diego Rivera, had contact with a renegade group of trade unionists in New York or Chicago. Others had been purged for less, but this couldn't have been Petakhov's story. He'd never been across an ocean. I'm sure of it. Further possible crimes: Darya Vasilisa had fallen in love with a visiting British student, envoy, mineralogist, some profession or other, and for a few weeks he fell in love with her turned-up nose, the broad expanse of her face, almost oriental, but white, white, white. Maybe the man promised to take her to London, but left her waiting at the train station, bag in hand, only to be arrested, never to see home again. Or she had unwittingly taken sensitive papers from French embassy trash that just happened to be lying on top of some really interesting garbage, discarded clothing from Paris, so she wrapped the papers around the dress to disguise her theft, because she couldn't believe a dress so stunning would have been tossed out. She didn't know what the documents were, she couldn't even read French, but they were military secrets transferred by an Esterhazy in the house of Stalin. Petakhov witnessed the assassination of a Trotskyite. It was supposed to look like a car accident, but the man had been shot in the head, and bullet wounds never looks like wounds produced by a shattered windshield. He knows their secrets, what the hired assassins botched. Whatever the reason, Maksim and Darya were in trouble and needed to throw a Christian to the lions. I just happened to come along at the right time on my way to Birobidzhan and managed to fill the bill. They were nobodies looking for a lifeline to pull them out of exile in the desert, a prize to hold up and say: she's a far greater criminal than we are. See, we're not so bad, look how we prove our loyalty even from exile in the desert. Even now, these are my assumptions.

On the third night someone I'd never seen before unlocked my door holding a large bundle of laundry. It was after midnight. Though the man was dressed like a Zahedani servant, he whispered in Russian and told me I should collect my things quickly. At first I assumed he was working with the two engineers, summoning me on their behalf, to my deportation or execution. I looked closely at my jailer, though in the dim light, it was hard to see his face. The man looked somewhat Persian, but spoke Russian like a native, this Leonid of Arabia who dropped an armload of blankets on the floor then looked at the bottom of his shoe as if afraid he'd stepped in something. He rubbed the side of his head and his right ear, which was very red, as if he'd just been socked, and told me his name was Venyamin Katzir. I had little more than the clothes on my back, and where I was headed, a hole in the ground outside Lefertova prison, I wouldn't need much. I asked him if he was working with Petakhov. He shook his head; we should leave quickly before the fellow who'd locked me up should return. He was nervous. There was almost nothing left of my Moscow life; I was wearing traditional Zahedani dress, but underneath was the skirt from the bride's costume in *The Dybbuk*, all that remained from the theater that had once been the center of my life. He tilted his head toward the door, and we were gone. What other choice was there?

How had he found me? Entirely by accident. He told me nothing until we reached the street.

Earlier in the week he had visited a teahouse where he had become a regular, and he overheard two men having a heated conversation in Russian. Russians, or Ivans as he called them, came and went from time to time, and apparently their presence wasn't all that unusual in this city, so far from what I still thought of as 'my' or 'our' borders. Not only were they speaking with Moscow accents, but one of them, face partly obscured by some kind of thin wool scarf, had a high voice and on closer examination looked like a woman dressed as a man, but let me assure you, that, in its own way, wasn't so unusual. Women weren't allowed in the teahouses, so a Russian or European couple might resort to a temporary costume in order to go out as they had been accustomed to. Unnoticed, Venyamin leaned in a bit closer. The woman's face contorted, a walnut of frustration, and she smelled of garlic and salt. Assuming no one within earshot could understand what they were saying, the pair talked at length about a second Russian woman locked in a room. This hostage was a pawn, a great find who would solve many of their problems.

When the pair got up to leave Katzir quickly swallowed the dregs of his bittersweet coffee and followed the Russians out onto the street. They were so caught up in their argument that they were oblivious to him, and he was able to maintain a fairly close distance. He was a skilled tail, and when Darya paused to make a point clear to Maksim, Venyamin paused too, and pretended to look at a display of narguiles or sacks of dried lemons and tamarind sold on the street. Though they snapped at one another, he also observed them ducking into dusty corners: the alley between the teahouse and an attar maker smelling of jasmine, rose, and olive flowers, then again, 20 minutes later, in an elbow-shaped space at the back of a dyers' works. Thinking no one could see them, they did things standing up, pressed against a wall, that I'm too old and embarrassed to describe, and allowing I didn't see first hand, am reluctant to write exactly what they did when they thought no one could possibly witness their sweaty moments of groping. On the other hand, Zahedan was not a city where men and women touched in public, and perhaps that was part of the excitement for them. Darya, the good markswoman, gave the impression she had left interest in men behind her, as if it were an island she'd once visited but now barely remembered, and upon reminder found its culture both baffling and tedious in its isolation and self-absorption. But apparently my first impressions were mistaken, however deeply biased. The way she handled a Mauser, her confidence and expertise — perhaps this was part of her seduction. Who knows what goes on with such people behind closed (or not so closed) doors? After, I don't know, 15 or 20 more minutes, Katzir got tired of waiting for them to finish up already, and he left, guessing he'd never see those two again.

Three days later he observed Maksim and Darya Vasilisa once again arguing loudly in the teahouse. Maksim wanted to go somewhere, to a site of some kind, and Darya was lagging, holding him up, complaining of sore feet crammed into boots that were too small, yet she would go because he required her company. He was overly concerned with details, recording the amount of money spent on every cup of tea in a small notebook, measuring the sticks that pierced every camel's nose. Venyamin pegged Maksim as a dumb Moscow galoot, but this was a mistake. Darya Vasilisa gave the impression of a woman who followed this man to what she considered the ends of the earth, who would endure some deprivations, but not all, and now too much was being asked of her. Their bickering grew more heated. Katzir observed bruises on Darya's face. Perhaps she no longer found Maksim amusing, was no longer sure why she ever had, but now was attached despite her occasional change of heart, as their furtive clutching and pawing revealed. Katzir followed them along the streets unnoticed, until they reached a building, a hotel of sorts. He heard more snippets of their arguments.

Maksim was growing tired of her complaints about Zahedan. She didn't want to be in this dusty backwater, it was an exile, a place to shrivel up under the heat and wind and become a shell of your former self.

As they entered the arcaded doors of the hotel she was still yammering, and so they still didn't notice Katzir. Maksim waved her away as if she were a mosquito, and he stormed up a flight of stairs, while she remained below, fuming, arms crossed, tapping her fingers against the points of her elbows in acute frustration. Still undetected, Venyamin took a back stairway, and from a position at the top of the stairs was able to watch from the hall. After maybe 15 minutes Maksim emerged from their room pocketing a small pistol. He walked down the corridor, stopped at door down the hall, barked a few sentences in Russian, before finally departing. This was the prison room. They had led him right to it.

As soon as Maksim was out of sight, his footsteps receding into the distance, Venyamin examined the door. He had been an apprentice to a locksmith and was skilled at gaining entry to places that were meant to be secure. "This particular lock was so simple," he said, and I remember he made a kind of stabbing gesture, "Houdini could have liberated you in his sleep." As a boy he had studied how locks are made and how they're disassembled: metal puzzles of latches, spring bolts, and pin tumbler chambers that will defeat you if you fail to conquer them. You can spend countless hours trying to open a particular difficult lock, before you finally triumph. There are no half measures, he explained, you're either in or left out in the cold. The lock on my cell was an easy business, and in a few minutes, I was freed.

We left the building, and traveled via a series of back streets. As we rounded a corner near one of the markets, I could make out the silhouettes of Petakhov and Ulanovskaya, the very people for whom I needed to be invisible, behind some kind of gauzy muslin curtain, all over one another. Yes, they were just as Venyamin described, it could have been no one else. They argued and fought, then slammed back together again.

How did I recognize them so quickly? No woman in Zahedan had Darya Vasilisa's waved blonde hair. Even in silhouette, no one had that hair. How strange and desperate, this long sticky kiss, and the volatility of their mutual attraction and repulsion. Maksim, though obsessed with how engineering problems were solved (a concrete dam, a railway tunnel through mountains), had appeared to me as someone profoundly uncomfortable in his own body. His shoulders were permanently hunched, and he had a stiff, self-conscious walk as if some of his bones were fused. His body conveyed him from swamp to desert to city; he didn't need to know how it worked or what it desired beyond fuel to keep going. There they were, shadows glued together, and I stared. Maybe they were drunk, which was one thing if you were in a room, out of sight, but a dangerous state to be in while walking the streets.

Venyamin quickly pushed me into an archway. The kiss between the two, even between two people who didn't seem very fond of one another, had a strange effect of eroticizing the street corner: the curved rinds amassed under a window, the sound of someone close by whispering, the resonance of an oud coming from a courtyard, it was as if these dissonant bits and pieces put a spell on you. But we only stopped for a moment to decide which direction our detour would need to take in order to avoid Ulanovskaya and Petakhov, hidden, easily missed, but if you looked closely they were entwined like a couple of Soviet jellyfish. While Katzir was trying to figure out which way to turn to find the train station, the curtain blew aside, Darya opened her eyes, and saw me. She tried to push Maksim off her, but it wasn't a good moment for him to disengage, if you know what I mean. She pointed and squawked while he dawdled.

We ran to the station with as much lead as it took Petakov to pull up his pants. At this point I had no idea Katzir intended to accompany me. I was hoping to get on a train, any train traveling in any direction away from a city where I had no business, and as far as possible from the kidnappers who thought I was their ticket to a big apartment in Moscow or a new life altogether. Zahedan was small, but it was still a city. There was a station, there would always be trains going somewhere, but when we arrived, the station was shuttered. No one was about; there would be no trains that day. Tracks had been blown up in the Zagros Mountains, or there had been a derailment on the edge of the Caspian, I no longer remember the reason, but I had a sinking feeling there was no exit here.

We walked quickly further and further from the center of town. Making our way through narrow dirt streets to a group of outbuildings at the edge of Zahedan, where I saw a caravan was getting ready to depart the city. Katzir grabbed my arm, and we ran to catch up to them. As we ran I felt as if I was in the last frame of a movie. I would get to the plane and fly off just as soldiers, hunters, predators were nipping at my heels. The group was traveling west to Susa, but Venyamin insisted we should make our way to a city that had a railroad station, and Susa was isolated in the west of the country. This made no sense to me. Petakhov and Ulanovskaya would round the corner any minute. Trains weren't running, and this outpost was a logical place they would look for me, just as you would search in a bus or train station for someone anxious to leave town. This edge of the city where caravans departed was actually very dangerous. They need me alive, I told him, you're the one who's going to be shot. To not leave immediately was like waiting for the right color car while your house was on fire. I considered leaving alone, but not able to speak any language that was usable within hundreds of miles, I was also afraid to be completely on my own.

So we waited for another caravan. We waited all day, all the while watching for Petakhov and Darya. At night Zahedan is completely still. No person can be seen on any street; even alley cats and feral dogs are huddled somewhere out of sight. Venyamin didn't seem all that worried but did keep asking around about when the next group would be departing. I listened closely to his voice. His accent sounded as if he came from a town similar to the one I left behind in Russia, but this was mostly at the end of the day, after night fell, when he was tired and less guarded.

We sat on the ground, our backs against the walls of a burnt brick house. I was bundled in so many layers of cloth, I felt invisible. We bought tea from a man across the road, and as we drank, Venyamin smoked the last of his cigarettes, and told me something about how he found himself in Zahedan.

There was a locksmith he apprenticed to, a tyrant over six feet tall with fists like boulders. To work for him was to be a slave. The boys he indentured were forced to work long hours every day of the week, given minuscule amounts of food: cold boiled cabbage and a little fried onion, the burnt bread a baker threw away. They hunched over workbenches in a cavernous basement where you either turned to ice or roasted. In the winter the metal numbed your already frostbitten fingers. It would take a long time to finish a piece, and the master would all but urinate on the slow boys. In the summer the same molten substance burned your fingerprints off from an arm's length away. Their tasks were repetitive, assembling locking systems that would insure an infinite number of filing cabinets, trunks, and boxes would be extremely difficult to open unless you knew exactly the trick the master had invented to keep them sealed shut. Before and after the revolution, the business had no shortage of clients, as rows of indentured little pishers, and some not so little any more, fashioned boxes for state secrets, files that held informants' names, and other valuables, whether paper or mineral. The intense boredom was relieved at odd moments when the master descended into the cellar and boasted of the time, years ago, when he had seen Houdini just before he was locked up in a Siberian Transport van. Launched from Moscow, the key to the van lay thousands of miles away in Siberia, but Houdini walked out in only 18 minutes. 18, remember, a number of enormous kabalistic significance. The boss had even gotten fairly close to Houdini, the Prince of the Air, and yes, he had a broad forehead, his face shaped like an upside-down pyramid. He'd always remember that face. The story changed a bit each time. Strolling past a café he'd stopped to ogle Houdini eating herring, drinking vodka, chewing a sprig of dill. The famous escape artist had repeatedly and without question swirled his tongue in his mouth where some claimed between cheeks and gums he kept an assortment of small tools for picking locks.

As Venyamin grew older, he became a trusted head apprentice. He was relied upon to make deliveries, and little did the master know that Katzir was pocketing money customers paid him on the side. He soon found other ways to steal from the company, and at the same time planned his own escape. One day after delivering a set of locks to a factory that specialized in high-powered drills, he got back on his bicycle, rode to the Moscow train station, and bought a one-way ticket to Odessa. As the train, which ran through the night, rocked him back and forth, he slept for what seemed like the first time in his life. In Odessa Katzir set up his own small shop, but he'd stolen quite a sum of money over the years, and the man who shut his eyes in deep concentration when he described Houdini's face understood, in the immediate aftermath of Venyamin's sudden absence, that he was, in fact, a spectacularly skilled thief.

One morning Katzir arrived to find his shop a wreck. Very little was salvageable, and left on a counter was one of the old Soviet lock boxes that had always defeated him. Who had robbed him? All his neighbors were suddenly blind and deaf. No one had seen anything, yet the signature of the crime was clear. He had been found. Thugs, who could have been sent by no one else, had appeared out of nowhere and destroyed his shop in the middle of the night. Property vandalized today, proprietor tomorrow, so Katzir decided the time had come to leave the country once and for all. There was no life for him in Russia. Abandoning what was left of his business, with only a few tools in a bag, he crossed the Black Sea, and made his way south until he eventually reached Zahedan.

In this part of Persia, he believed or had been told, he would find veins of titanium ore, a valuable metal used for submarines, artificial limbs and the most unconquerable locks. Let others waste their time drilling for pockets of oil. He would become rich in no time. He searched the surrounding foothills, but hadn't found any titanium yet or anything remotely resembling this miraculous mineral. Grabbing my arm again as he spoke, he insisted that titanium lay hidden in the hills, he was sure of it. What he did find were the ruins of what might have been a city, but there was practically nothing left of it, and he considered the site worthless, little more than a pile of carefully arranged rocks. (You can call it Suolucidir, if you like, but it was an empty nothing, completely forgettable.) No magnificent temples, plazas, hanging gardens, not even a fragment of a wing showing above the ground. There were only a few scattered ashlars carved with intertwined symbols: eagle, olive branch, goat to show any humans had ever inhabited the place.

When he got to this part of his story he handed me a piece of shale with a trilobite etched in it. I didn't know it at the time, but since then I've learned he'd found the leavings of Cambrian-era creatures: some looked like pincushions with legs, some like coiled spirals with eyes on the ends of antenna. I have the piece of rock still. The whole region was once under water, you see. Katzir found no titanium mines, but he did find flinty bits of these records of earliest life, amazing in their own way, though they meant little to Katzir. Imagine these rocky records as fossil filing cabinets. Eventually most life imparts no trace whatsoever: footprints, red blood cells, writing on clay, celluloid film, monuments to King Tut and Stalin all eventually disappear, but what Katzir found in the lost city was like a hand signaling above the ground. Trilobitic tenacity, even if we had known the word back then, was not what either of us were looking for. I turned the stone over and over in my hand as we waited. The evening approached, and it grew cooler. I worried that we would have to find a place to sleep on the outskirts of a city far from any home we had ever known. Finally a camel driver told us of a group that was leaving in a few hours for Shiraz. We joined them.

If the story of Katzir, the locksmith, sounds like I'm telling you about a man who remains calm even when being chased by Soviet police, Moscow gangsters, and extreme poverty, then

I have given you entirely the wrong impression. Katzir was always alert and nervous, always ready to sprint away, a good survival trait when you think about it. Even Houdini was said to have gotten panicky and claustrophobic when he was buried alive and had to dig his way six feet to the surface. Imagine someone who has the potential to be an escape artist, and sometimes is such a person, but most of the time is as nervous as the Prince of the Air was that moment when he realized he had five and a half more feet to dig. Short and solid, spine permanently curved from years hunching over a workbench, some part of his body was always motorized, always moving, a foot jiggling, fingers tapping. When he removed his jimidani, his receding hairline was a severe W shape, but as if to compensate, he grew a beard, which allowed him to blend in more with the local people. I, too, traded in my old clothes for veils, a skirt worn over trousers, an embroidered jacket, and tragacanth gum, a substance used to straighten hair.

Traveling together was awkward. Caravanserai, if they noticed at all, assumed we were married, and I didn't mind so much, to tell you the truth. We were both completely alone in a strange country, but soon we would reach a border where we would need documents that proved we were married. In Shiraz we found a small Mizrahi community living in a mahellah, a warren of lightning-shaped alleys. The cul de sacs were important, in case of mob invasion, the better-off families lived at the end, the most difficult part of the mahellah to gain access to. We had the ceremony in a place where few asked us questions about our families or what we were doing in Iran. Venjamin bought me a yasmahi, a chain of gold coins and small fish that's meant to encircle the bride's face. Our wedding was sort of like what you have in Las Vegas in your country. We had barely known one another a week, but I tried on the idea of being married to this ex-locksmith, and allowed myself to enjoy the warm bath for as long as it lasted. It was quite a while since I'd had any contact with my family, and the news, such as it was, from that part of the world seemed entirely invented. If it was true, and as you know, it did turn out to be so, I had no family left. So in this place of white stone buildings, and the ruins of Persepolis, I became Eliana Katzir. I never truly knew how he felt about me. A market arcade near where we were married was beautifully lit at night and filled with shoppers. Men carried large trays on their heads, selling all kinds of things from them. Women and children had yellow dots made of turmeric and water on their foreheads to ward off evil, though many of these people were later killed in a Farhud. I know this because I saw a photograph of a foot covered with dust sticking out from rubble. The caption said it had taken place at this market, but I would not have recognized the place from the image itself without the words underneath.

The Shah was an admirer of Hitler, and the country was filling up with Germans, from civilians to abwehr agents who had been in the country since at least 1936. Some were easy to identify, if only by the way they held their cigarettes and peered through glasses. Tangled up with their appearance were tales of the Shah and his family. His first wife, a beauty named Fawzia, was said to take baths in milk while her subjects starved. However the shah's twin sister, not loved by the people either, was said to have mixed caustic acid into the milk, purely out of personal spite. I heard these stories and wanted to leave the country as soon as possible. From Shiraz we were able to take a train to Esfahan and from there another train for Tehran. At some juncture we switched to the Hejaz railway, and made our way to Amman where two British officers stopped us, jug ears translucent red as the sun set behind them. I had a Soviet passport, but Venyamin had no papers whatsoever. The Englishmen were ready to let him wander the desert completely stateless, but he was not allowed to stay in Amman. They assumed I would go with him, but by then it had become my plan to get into British Palestine, though this had hardly been my destination at the start. I had no intention of wandering in the desert with him or anybody else. Our last conversation, with the reddish-haired English officers watching, was awkward. We behaved like strangers who had met by accident on a train and now had to go separate ways. He assured me that after he found his titanium mines he would look for me in Jerusalem. I didn't believe him, and if it were possible to hand back a coat that said 'Eliana Katzir,' this I would have done, but some coats you can't take off, and I stuck with the name all these years.

I arrived in Jerusalem to find that the British military had set up a brothel called the Sodom and Gomorrah Golf Club by the Sea. As you might imagine, it was on the Dead Sea. You couldn't get away from them, everywhere you turned there they were, jug eared and sunburnt. Once I followed an English officer traveling from a Russian neighborhood, my neighborhood, in fact. What was he doing here? After he'd walked a couple of blocks, just before he got into a car, he handed his homburg to his assistant, who handed him a tarboosh hat, which he put on his head, and they drove off in the direction of east Jerusalem. Though we, too, now went to plays and concerts in work clothes, shedding hats. Some of my fellow Russian immigrants began to prefer narguiles to cigarettes, and thimble-sized glasses of thick coffee to tea with jam.

Did Venyamin make it all the way back to the site of what you believe was Suolucidir and was he the body in the ruins? This, I can't tell you. He could easily have come by the papers of your Kosari person and, as I've already written, passed for a number of identities, and few would be the wiser. It's a common enough name. There are surely many of them about. In 1964 I had a student from Haifa who got into a car accident with a man who claimed he had left a mine and a fortune behind in Iran. He promised to pay the fellow a large sum, however my student was never compensated for any damages or injuries. Was this Katzir? Who knows? Needless to say, I never saw Venyamin again.

You had your fragments of clay, your bits and pieces. I have a piece of shale, a kind of geological daguerreotype, an accidental death mask of early life forms. This piece of rock reminds me that we are nothing more than a microscopic intersection of two rays that extend out into infinity, behind and ahead of you. They cross, then bleep! That's it! You're done!

So now I'm in Ashdod, a city on the edge of the Mediterranean, as you probably know. From a café on Ha Tayelet Street, a chess teacher tells a boy about the Sicilian Defense. From here, if you had a very strong telescope perhaps you could see Sicily or even Marseilles, and watch someone there drinking Turkish coffee and playing chess. In the evening, the elderly residents sit outside and watch everyone else who might be more ambulatory. I call them, my fellow gossipy residents, the Knesset. They watch, make judgments, issue useless edicts. A one-armed mechanic who claims to have been a pilot during the 1967 war describes flying to Cyprus in the middle of the night, a woman talks to her to her cat in Yevanic, a Yemeni travel agent who rarely leaves his room joins once in a while, a record producer who recorded something called Yiddishe Mambo and Ladino marching bands for weddings. He hums and sings constantly as if he's still in business, and dispenses advice, such as, if you drive just a little in the middle of the road, you avoid certain kinds of accidents.

When I was 18, I had a choice to go west or east. If I'd taken his advice, I might have stayed put. Either direction, provided one survived, would, I thought, lead to very different outcomes, but now I'm not sure it didn't really matter which way I went, I might still have landed exactly where I now sit.

I'm sorry I can't be of any further assistance.

Eliana Katzir

THE TWO ELIANAS WERE OPPOSITE ends of the same barbell who would never meet, or perhaps in a feat of pumping iron, ore and alloy amalgam had been bent, and they passed each other while walking through the corridors of a nonexistent train. Though I'd found the site of Suolucidir, propelled by Sidonie's account, it's still possible she didn't write those pages at all, and my father, in his translation, made the whole thing up. There are days when the fact that I have nothing genuine remaining from the lost city, makes me wonder what it was I did find.

In Berlin, or even Marseilles, in 1936, Mar Eldad's story about a principality somewhere in the east where "Hebrew, Persian, and Tatar" are spoken, and "all are at peace" and you live openly with your own king, for Feigen, what could be better? He sends the Nieumachers (Russian Katzirs trying to pass as Alsatians) east with little more than tape measures and string, and waits for a postcard from Suolucidir. I arrive about 40 years later with trigometric tables, mason lines, clipboards, diamond-shaped Marshalltown trowels made in Ohio and a Theodolite, which measures angles, especially useful on rough terrain. It's manufactured in Russia and looks particularly cool. Maybe the Nieumachers used a Landrover jeep. We used a Toyota landcruiser. After the Revolution, some of us pack our bags and look for these lost, wandering souls. The worse things get, the more attractive the search appears. Trying to catch the Lost is like trying to pin down your shadow or the memory of a particular shadow. It looks like you, but can't ever be captured or questioned or embraced. Feigen believed if the lost tribes would suddenly return, all human suffering would end. I finally found Sidonie Nicumacher, only for her to pull another hood over her head and deny everything, or almost everything, but I think I'm going with Feigen. The story of the lost tribes extends a hand to those who might want to re-invent themselves. Travelers and emissaries in search of the lost tribes are called *shelihim*, a word he surely knew and used with pleasure.

At the end of her field notes Sidonie Nieumacher revealed her real name was Eliana Katzir, and Bruno's real name was Venyamin. They took on new names in Berlin. Will the real Katzirs please stand up? The other contestants shuffle in their chairs, rise slightly, knees bent, they sit again. If I had to choose, if the television cameras pan to me, who do I chose? Or perhaps — and yes I know the audience will gasp as two people stand to acknowledge their legitimacy — they're really one and the same person.

But what about the second Eliana's version, which undermines the Nieumachers, Feigen, the Berlin-to-Marseilles trip, substituting an eastward trajectory through Moscow? It's full of holes. A direct train from Moscow to Zahedan? There weren't any. There still aren't. Titanium mines? Never existed. How could Eliana reference the murder of Solomon Mikoels whose assassination, clumsily made to look like a car accident, wouldn't happen until 1948? Also, the alleged doctor's plot against Stalin had yet to form in the dictator's head. Perhaps there was no actual arrest, but she was trapped by sheer geography, unable to leave. Somehow she escaped from the house. She has her reasons for laying a false trail, for a partial invention of what might have been, and believing in it. It's too late to pull her back from the edge. For whatever reasons, she doesn't want the lost city to be found again. Now sitting in a café on Ha Tayelet Street, the umbrella has shifted, she's getting too much sun and perhaps becoming a little delusional, turning the rock with the markings of a trilobite's exoskeleton over and over in her hand, not knowing where it came from or how she got it. From here, her letter, too, turns into an adventure tale. Katzir keeps some part of herself locked away, hidden so securely, only she has access.

There were no broken bones in Bruno's body when I found him. Eliana left him to die, leaving her identity as Sidonie to be buried along with him. There was no one left in the city of her childhood. It would have been impossible to return to it. Sidonie Nieumacher served her purpose. Her story had gotten her out of Grodno, Berlin, Marseilles, and Zahedan. Now, once again, she was only Eliana K., as if that was all she had ever been. The sojourn in Moscow was all conjecture. What if she'd gone east instead of west? Could she still have ended up in the same place? She tried to put herself in Suolucidir, in ur-Chelm, a city that attracts fools, via a railroad that hadn't ever been built.

There remained untouched one part of the documents that Jahanshah had sent. The papers of Alicia Congreaves-Sutcliffe. I had shelved them, thinking who cares about Kipling-era plunderers? Now there was nothing left of Suolucidir to unearth but these.

HILLIARD AND CONGREAVES

Alicia Congreaves-Sutcliffe

His First Attraction

The Crystal Palace was not known to be a dangerous place, but it wasn't without risks. Besides the pickpockets who harvested tourists and preyed on daydreaming citizens, freakish accidents grabbed headlines away from the death of Edward VII, the Dr. Crippen poisoning, the exploration of Antarctica by Scott's Terra Nova Expedition. A man had died in a hot air balloon accident. There were no photographs, but detailed descriptions of two people tumbling through the glass, fragments of burning balloon landing in trees, were provided by those who happened to be in the park. On a second occasion a man was trampled to death by an elephant that had escaped from its pen in one of the exhibition spaces. Deprived of space to roam and removed from their hierarchical clan relationships, elephants will become disoriented and unpredictable.

Ryder Congreaves, who had grown up in Rhodesia, could not imagine a beast contained in the filigreed cage allotted to it within the Palace. Any keeper who stepped inside its confines to feed or groom the animal would risk his life, but was this known to those responsible for housing the animals? His experience in England made him guess that it wasn't, and he was curious to see this phenomenon, animals on display. The explosive crash of the hot air balloon, though not likely to be repeated, was also something he would have paid money to see.

Ryder had come to England to study and was at Oxford, working with a protégé of the great Persianist Henry Rawlinson, famous for deciphering the Behistun inscription, a panel engraved on a rock of the same name, which was a kind of Rosetta Stone for ancient Persian. Born to civil servants stationed in Rhodesia, England was a country he knew mainly through children's stories, and so it appeared to him to be fantastic and dreary at the same time. No sooner had he arrived than he was impatient to leave, to go on his own excavation party, to discover ancient directories of gods and laws, as if all the attention that needed to be paid to the Rawlinson protégé and the world of cold rooms and warmed-over tea was a quick nod, then you could be on your way again. In photographs Ryder was a tall man with a long neck whose pants were always too short, whose jackets pulled at the shoulder seams, a man who found the need to stoop increasingly irritating, putting the blame on lesser beings: men, women, tables, shelving, flowering shrubs, who all failed for not rising to meet him. He was dogged by lack of funds. When he lost a hat he couldn't afford to replace, either his colleagues thought him hatless, and therefore rude, or they didn't understand the cheapness of those who must go without. At Oxford, Ryder, with a big smile on his face, was repeatedly high-hatted and cold-shouldered, and more than once overheard the word common attached to his name. No one would introduce him to anyone. His clothes were unpressed, his hair uncombed as if he was always in a hurry, and words tumbled out in an excited cataract. He needed to slow down, he was seen as an upstart, too enthusiastic when more reserve was called for, and so he wasn't entirely trusted. An embarrassment, better to get him out of sight. He'd heard of England all his life, but it was a house he couldn't get into, and he was left peering in through grimy windows. The furniture within looked comforting and about to fall apart, layered with dust; he could rub the panes, but towers of moth-eaten upholstery receded out of reach.

About a year after his arrival in England, on one of his infrequent trips down to London, he decided to view the Crystal Palace, which had by then been moved to Sydenham. He told none of his acquaintances, who would have looked at the Palace as a venue for cheap thrills, five-pence beers, and low-lifes who spoke in rhyming slang.

After paying for his ticket, he wandered from one hall to the next, finally joining a tour led by a guide who was exceptionally animated, ushering the crowds from the dinosaur park to the model of the sphinx with great enthusiasm. Sunlight glinted off her frazzled auburn hair, making a red halo. The Crystal Palace behind her looked like a Hall of Diamonds. Looking up at the iron fretwork, Ryder felt as if he were in a huge stringed instrument. It felt good to get away from lectures about ancient Persia. At Oxford he was often made to feel like a gormless colonial, educated by his mother; betrayed by his accent, a man who fussed over bills and lost things.

"Here," the woman said, "in the year 1911 the coronation of King George is to take place. To your left you will see a three-quarter-size model of the Australian parliament building, part of the Festival of the Empire."

The young woman who navigated the model parliaments of the British Empire with such knowledge and ease represented a different empire altogether. Ryder, who was lonely and missed the suburbs of Bulawayo, was entranced. When they arrived at a hall of stereoscopes, as others peered through magnifying lenses at illusions of three-dimensional Eiffel Towers, birds in flight, a marksman in a costume of the American West, he stayed close to her, trying to think of a conversation he could begin. She looked through a stereoscope at an image of an Egyptian Sphinx.

"Here, look at this," she said, and her hand guided his to the sides of the walnut box. She pushed his head down to the lenses. The brilliantine he'd slapped on earlier in the day left sticky patches on her fingers. "Isn't that amazing?" She made him look.

When the tour ended, he lingered. He asked her out for coffee, which she didn't drink, but she went with him anyway. There was a café on the grounds of the Crystal Palace, and the guide, when she was allowed to go on a break, led him there. The sound of a gramophone from the bar did little to overpower the sound of nearby conversations, but she liked the loudness, the sense of business, and other people's urgencies. She shouted that her name was Edna. A waiter swept crumbs from the table in a desultory fashion as if to communicate that they were hardly worth bothering with, slopped tea, looked into the distance. Ryder wanted to go somewhere else. Despite the waiter's rudeness, Edna wasn't sure she wanted to be in a secluded place with this Ryder who had trouble coughing out a sentence and couldn't look straight at her. Edna's mates at work, Simon, Nigel, even the fallen-on-hard-times Carrington, were nothing if not smooth talkers. That was their job, flooding the acreage with explanation and did you know. They knew all kinds of astounding facts: world records, the fastest human, a girl who looked like a monkey, and famous people (Wilde, the fellow who wrote Peter Pan, Disraeli's ghost), seen out for stroll right here in this very place. Edna fidgeted and tried to turn her head to look at the clock in a way that wouldn't appear obvious. It was impossible.

"I do like my job," she gestured with her arms to include the whole of the palace grounds. He looked startled. It hadn't occurred to him this was a job you could like.

"From the time I was about seven or eight I'd come here and pretend to be the Empress of the Crystal Palace. The problem was my subjects. The wax figures in the foreign exhibitions—Japan, Romania, Brazil—would threaten one another with continual war and annihilation. I mean, they couldn't help themselves, could they? In order to insure peaceful co-existence I figured they had to live in entirely separate municipalities, all within my domain but with distinct boundaries, currency, traffic laws. Even the model dinosaurs would have to be entirely fenced in." Her sleeves slipped and Ryder noticed she had sinewy arms like a junior lady weight lifter, and she had a laugh that came up from somewhere down her throat as if it had been trapped there for quite a while. He watched her mouth as she said the word *megalosaur.*

"So when I applied for this job I already knew every square inch of the place, every fountain, every amusement, every parliament."

"Are you a despot, ruling all these tribes?" He tried to sound cynical and smart, but was afraid his words came out forced and parrot-like, like the people he knew at school; it was a tone he disliked, but now he found himself speaking just like them. Ryder mistook the queen of costumed dummies, plaster elephants and model parliaments no bigger than the desk of an assistant bank manager for a ferocious imaginary sovereign, posing in high-heeled boots, one foot balanced atop the head of her prey. That wasn't exactly Edna. She was fine on her own, ironing her own uniform, but she didn't really want to be a custodian to anyone else.

"What do you mean?" She wasn't sure of the word despot, how he used it, and what he meant to imply, but didn't want to let on this was so.

"Are you a benevolent dictator or a tyrant?" He leaned forward. He sensed Edna's confusion, and he was still timid enough to censor himself, but it was too late. He tipped his head to one side, as if he could make all the conclusions he jumped to slide into bunkers on the right side of his brain and lie there in secret forever. He also tilted his head to one side because he was slightly deaf in one ear.

She could see threads straining through his shoulder seams, sleeves about to separate, fall to the floor, make a hasty getaway. Behind the friendly puppy eyes was the flicker of a pitiless Darwinist, intrigued by carnivores who aimed for more than just successful subsistence. Ryder believed if you weren't coded or hadn't mutated to survive, off you went down the extinction chute with no questions asked. In Edna he saw a girl buccaneer ready to cross swords. Once again he misfired, and she still looked confused. Tyrant? How much longer until her break was over? What was she meant to say to him? She twisted her napkin into a topographical map and laughed again, nervously. Finally able to catch a glimpse at the clock, she saw that in fifteen minutes her break would be over, and she could run back to her post. Another tour needed to be led at four.

American girls at the next table complained about the cheapness of their hotel and the smallness of their allowances. To Edna and Ryder they were complete aliens who happened to speak in a language they understood as they figured conversions from dollars to pounds aloud. Their voices filled the silence when Ryder should have said something. He looked at his hands. "Walking through the dinosaur park made me homesick."

This, too, baffled Edna. How could monster lizards made of brick, tile, stones, and cement make anyone miss their home? Where was this fellow from? How soon could she dump him and get back to her job?

He pushed his chair back over the tile, finished with Edna who understood so little of what he hoped was clear, but tried one more time to explain himself before he would leave her to her kingdom. The dinosaurs reminded him of the pods of hippopotami he used to see along the shores of the Zambezi River. If you could put them end to end, he imagined, you could span the river, and by walking on their backs you could reach the other side. One of their servants had died from a hippo bite, but still, for him this was one of the images of the home he left behind.

"Really?" Edna tilted forward in her seat. She didn't want to appear too interested, but now Ryder's strange ideas, these awkward outbursts had a history, now the guy had his reasons. She began to be sucked in. She imagined he'd grown up in a jungle outpost with no other children; his only companions were clans of chattering chimpanzees and servants' children whose language he learned when his parents were away.

"Well, they have very blunt snouts. They may look round and slow and jolly, so you may not realize their mouths are huge. You have no idea how lethal their teeth really are."

The American girls laughed into their hands.

"Were you yourself ever bitten?" The Sultana of the Crystal Palace ignored the Anglophones, crass and ruffle-edged.

"Not by a hippo, no, but by a boomslang snake once, yes." He crossed one leg over the other, rolled his trousers up over his knee and showed Edna the pink-white scars — tiny fang marks, twin jagged trails. Edna ran a finger over the raised skin several times as if they were braille characters she needed a bit of time to decipher.

"The boomslang isn't fatal, but its bite stings for days, like someone stuck a knife in your shin, and you have to walk around with it poking out of you for quite a while. You can't ever entirely pull the blade out. That's how it feels, but the 'slang's not like the puff adder or gaboon viper or black mamba." He drew snakes in the air. "Once that venom hits your system, it's curtains, I assure you."

She gradually became spellbound when he described sleeping out in the veldt, hunting knife clutched in his hand, and she knocked over a glass of tea as he reenacted the time he found an altar to Ndebele ancestor gods under the stairs in his parents' house. When he spoke about his future, returning to Africa or traveling further east, Edna nodded, transfixed. He rolled down his trouser leg, but she traced the map of the snake bite on the tabletop. She wouldn't have minded looking at those tracings on his leg one more time, but worried that he would get the impression she would like to see him again. When he spoke about how he planned to follow spice caravans and look for the Babylonian hanging gardens, she thought he meant traveling among the wax figures of palace. It was what she did every day, no holiday in that, she said.

After two years of finding no one who would listen to him, Ryder thought he had discovered the girl who would chuck everything and take on the difficult life he projected for himself once he was able to leave England. He'd never seen a woman lecture large crowds of tourists before, and if she was capable of handling the Berliners har-rumphing in skepticism when she referred to the future King George, she could, he thought at that moment, handle the demands of life in far-flung parts of the Empire. She invited him to try the flying ma-chine with her, with its cranky music and gravity-defying cars attached to a very high pole by mere filaments. The vertiginousness made him think the day was full of hope and promise as London spun into a cyclone of tilting buildings, and he flew higher and higher into the air holding Edna's hand.

Ideas of Home

Ryder and Edna married and quickly had two children. Alicia and Ry-der II needed too many things and made too much noise. They tipped over bowls of soup and pulled down books, picture frames fell into teacups and the soggy mess crashed to the floor. Though pouty and fat-cheeked, cute as daguerreotypes of baby fairies, the pair of them kept him up all night with squalls and illnesses that required all kinds of costly attention. It does him no credit to say at this point Ryder was less and less at home.

By marrying Ryder, Edna had been looking upwards. She thought her husband possessed African coffee plantations and platoons of ser-vants, but during the brief time they were together she learned wicker chairs set out on a long porch with a view of the savannah was as much a part of Ryder's inheritance as her glassy fiefdom in Sydenham. If his parents sent letters asking for English tea, tins of biscuits, bolts of cloth, then Edna passed the employment ads, suggestions circled, to Ryder over breakfast. He passed them back to her. Edna grew uneasy. She already felt the pull of the greengrocer's, of Wallingford's, long before she even knew of the shop's existence, as if some voice was say-ing: if you stay in London you walk on these flagstones, and this is as far as you'll ever go, so make the most of it.

Ryder joined a club, which didn't, to Edna, seem so very un-usual. The club was called the Possum Club, not after the animal, but from the Latin word for *able*. The members of the Possum Club believed they were able to go anywhere on earth, to triumph over adversity, hence their motto: *potestas triumphalis supero adversus*, ability triumphs over adversity. Stuffed wombats and cheetahs haunted the stairwells, studies contained bookcases supported by elephant legs and lamps with bases made from coiled cobras, wiring threaded within. The map room housed tens of thousands of maps from the charts purportedly used by Magellan to the more helpful, especially if you were headed to Antarctica, navigational charts of Admiral Perry. Globes of all sizes, not just of the earth, but of the moon as well. Their archives contained the journals and papers of great explorers. Ryder attended lectures about Central American tropics, matriarchal clans of the islands off Nigeria, how to survive in Greenland should your food supply peter out. He was supposed to feel at home with the stuffed lions and gorillas but didn't somehow. Increasingly anxious to not be in England, and feeling increasingly stuck in the fog and mud, he felt out of place everywhere he turned.

One evening Ryder fell asleep, nodding out over topographical charts of the Nile delta. He was woken by another gentleman, a fellow Possumist named Archer F. Hilliard, who needed to study the maps. He was annoyed a fellow club member had been so careless as to allow his head with its indifferently pomaded hair to fall on valuable and much needed documents. Though younger, Archer had accordion-like chins that collapsed in displeasure, and he a-hemmed into them loudly. Disheveled Ryder, kept up by two children, slumbered on, oblivious, but Archer summoned a stronger fellow and together they lifted the sleeping man and carried him to a couch. In the process, Ryder woke with a jolt. Tall, rangy, not overly powerful, he struggled with his aristocratic bearers even though he himself was only half-conscious. Ryder succeeded in knocking them to the ground, and Archer Hilliard, despite his initial irritation, was impressed. He had heard a bit about Ryder Congreaves, an oddball in a club that had its share of oddballs.

Archer Fairfax Hilliard had the cash and a passion for the Orient, but like Ryder, he was looking for a ledge from which he could stand at a height in order to peer in on the festivities he felt shut out of. He offered his hand to the colonial with some reservations. Ryder grasped it, nonetheless. Every hand, including Edna's, that had been offered to him since he arrived on these shores, had been extended with reservations made plain.

Archer slouched in a chair, long hands steepled over his chest, looking like Lytton Strachey, even down to his reddish-brown beard. He planned to leave for Egypt and needed a companion. Did Ryder speak Arabic? He did, but Ryder didn't want to go to Egypt. He had debts that were growing more urgent, and had been studying Farsi more recently. When he said this, Archer unsteepled his hands, and for a moment became more animated. A man had spoken at the club about a lost city is eastern Persia. It had gone off the map, but had once been a real city with kings, armies, gods, temples, courts, markets, coffee houses. It had streets and squares, a language, and laws. Walls you could lean against. Doors you could pass through and come out of again. The city had been protected by battlements and towers of unprecedented height from which guards could spy invaders approaching from great distances. Even if the exact location of the city had been lost, or temporarily misplaced, the man had said he would bet half his fortune it did exist, and whoever was able to find it would see with his own eyes marvels and riches that were unimaginable and indescribable.

Another man argued that this city could not ever have existed. He had traveled on camel-back throughout the region, fought in hand-to-hand combat against Baluchi marauders, of which there are many, and they are both artful and cunning in the extreme. The mountains and plains of the region compose an empty, barren place. There's no viable metropolis either above or below ground and never was, he claimed. Why? How could he be so sure? No water, no springs, rivers or effluvia, Archer ticked off one, two, three, four fingers, exist or ever have existed in amounts adequate to support the lush life the speaker hinted had once thrived there. Indeed temperatures are severe both at the hot and cold ends of the spectrum, and this has always been so. The challenger said he would state for an absolute fact that the existence of the so-called phantom city was a hoax. Any exploratory party would engage in a very risky enterprise with no guarantee of reward, a reward based only on the say-so of a man who had never set foot outside of the British Isles. The name of the city was Suolucidir. Ryder had heard the name, he thought, but he knew nothing about it. His Oxford professor, the Rawlinson protégé, had occasionally referenced places Ryder neglected to write down or think very much about.

One drizzly late afternoon Ryder saw a veiled woman in Camberwell, and he followed her for a few blocks until she abruptly turned around. She might have been Persian or Kurdish, he couldn't say for certain. Perhaps her father traded her, sold her to a merchant traveling west, and like Pocahontas in Queen Elizabeth's court, or the Taino Columbus brought to Ferdinand and Isabella, she found herself in London. He pretended to look at a post box, check his watch, turn up his collar against the rain. Only the woman's eyes were visible, yet they held him spellbound, or so he would later say. He imagined her long black dress was ever so slightly transparent, like a gauzy black fog, and he could see the shape of her body through it. A long rope-like braid fell out of the back of her veil where a knot must have come undone. Later that day he wrote to the Rawlinson protégé; he was ready to travel to the land he'd studied for so long, but first he was going to Egypt where he'd been offered a position.

Archer would never follow a woman in the street, and though the debate about Suolucidir piqued his interest, he had long planned a trip to Ghiza. They were to excavate a site he'd identified as having some potential, where there were likely to be older pyramids of marl and slate, easier to unmask than limestone structures. They were due to leave in a month. By now Archer had been paying Ryder's bills, and the relief caused Ryder to trust him more than he should have. Now he had no choice but to go. Edna had only met Archer Hilliard once. He made it clear to her that as far as he was concerned, she was no more than a turnstile Ryder had to pass through in order to move on to a more exalted life. Edna found him repulsive.

His beard, she said to Ryder, is the color of bloody shite. What woman would want to touch someone like that? The answer, Ryder knew, was none, but he ignored her. He put off telling Edna he was leaving for Egypt until a few days before they were to sail.

"I have a job," he said pushing the employment pages back towards her. "I'll send for you as soon as possible, as soon as we set up camp."

Edna wiped banana mush from Ryder II's mouth while her husband described the easiness of life in Cairo.

"You'll have plenty of servants. Our Alicia can go to a *lycée*, have her own personal maid, live like a princess." He looked at a spot on the wall where the paper was bubbling slightly. A man in silhouette tipped his top hat to a woman in a flouncy dress, but the tiny tears in the peeling paper severed some of their limbs. The bowing couple were repeated hundreds of times around the room, but Ryder couldn't take his eyes off the amputees. "You need only pack summer clothes, though the nights, I'm told, can be chilly."

Edna nodded, expecting she should plan to vacate their flat in two months' time. She still believed him completely. His parents could just as well be sent their tea from Egypt.

By attaching himself to Hilliard, Ryder gained entry into places where Edna couldn't quite follow. She would have been the one to find firewood in Sasketoon, water in the outback of New South Wales, fix the boat in the Falklands, and never complain about the tedium or hardships of the journey, but those weren't the kinds of places that interested Ryder. He was convinced Edna wouldn't know what to wear, what to say, couldn't remember names, would botch pronunciation of any syllable not native to the English language. He began to side with Archer. Achieving social distance from Edna was even easier when corroborated by actual distance. By the time they reached Genoa, though he wrote, she was no longer in his thoughts much at all.

Ghiza

They took rooms at *Le Pharaon Royale*. Ryder knocked on Hilliard's door as planned for their first outing, a trip to a souk. When the door opened Hilliard stood before him clothed in long robes, his skin dyed brown from walnut juice in the manner of Sir Richard Burton. Ryder lost his breath in a loud *paaugh* sound, cigarette jettisoned from mouth in a spray of spit. After an initial bug-eyed second, he decided the best course was to ignore the costume and say nothing. Archer's pale blue eyes stood out against his dyed skin. He expected some kind of response, but Ryder only looked away. Archer interpreted the silence as respect and awe in the face of a benefactor's radical choice, embracing the culture of their hosts. They left the hotel like potentate and interpreter, or so Hilliard believed. Hilliard had only a smattering of Farsi and Arabic phrases, his speech roughly the equivalent of a memorized Edwardian guidebook, but from the moment he set foot in Alexandria, and for remainder of his life, Hilliard wore a Sikh turban and a Saudi dishdasha.

Keeping his lips tightly pressed together Ryder guided his wealthy colleague through wide boulevards, and ever narrowing streets to a series of alleyways. Stalls tumbled one after the next selling oranges, branches of yellow dates, rosewater, jasmine oil, incense, olives, carpets, silver lanterns, and low tables made of inlaid wood. Jews, Greeks, Turks, and Armenians were all alike to both of them. Ryder didn't know how to translate Hilliard's giddiness in front of men in red aprons selling sherbet who held out all kinds of brightly colored sweets. When they argued about buying a green turban, a sign the wearer had been to Mecca, Ryder pushed further ahead, deeper into the souk. It was like shopping with a child. You haven't been to Mecca, you can't wear it. Why not? No one will ever know. Archer watched the top of Ryder's cane tapping his shoulder, bobbling above the kefiyas and fezzes that surrounded him, and he struggled to keep up with him, though he wasn't finished with looking around. Should Archer lose sight of his friend he very well might never be seen again. He remembered they were in a part of the city that was unmapped and unmappable, but he felt buoyant and at home. Archer believed traders looked at him with welcoming expressions. Phrases intended to induce him to buy this knife or that basket of amber he read as a series of signs between brothers. He nodded and smiled at them in a way he would never have smiled at merchants in London, especially those hawking wares on the street.

"You see, they think I'm one of them." Hilliard grinned from ear to ear as he caught up with his interpreter and escort.

Ryder felt sweat roll down the backs of his ears, and he wiped it away with a handkerchief embroidered, *E.C.*

"Did you hear me?" Hilliard put a concerned hand on Ryder's shoulder, which only exasperated Ryder more. He was the one who'd lived in Africa. He could stand the heat and dust. He shrugged the hand away.

"They," Ryder jabbed his cane in the general direction of any and all men in the souk, "see you and think they've got a Wally gone native. They'll cheat you out of your shirt."

"I'm not wearing a shirt."

Ryder squinted into the distance as if he'd never seen Archer before.

"I know what you're thinking, but it's you who look ridiculous. Do you see anyone else in a helmet and riding pants?" Hilliard had begun to speak English with an Arabic accent.

Ryder was reminded of the inky newsprint pages Edna pushed at him across the table and how much he needed this job. Ryder transferred the moneybag from the folds of Archer's dishdasha and made him hang it around his neck. Hilliard felt Ryder's brusque hands searching his body, and stood very still, convinced that though he felt slightly humiliated in a way he couldn't quite swallow, it was really Ryder who suffered more humiliation.

Ryder recalled a lesson from school about orchids whose petals and scent mimicked that of female wasps. Male wasps were duped into believing they courted females of their own kind, when in fact all they were buzzing around was an orchid. In frustration at their betrayal, they will fly to another "wasp" orchid, thinking it's a real female, only to be duped once again. This is a fantastic trick for the flower. It gets pollinated. The subterfuge is a disaster in the long run, you would think, for the future of the wasp population, and ultimately bad for the orchids, too. If the wasps die out from continually mistaking an orchid for a female insect, soon there will be no more neatly evolved wasp-parroting orchids either, yet both seem to thrive. It was a mystery, and Ryder had a feeling he and Hilliard had a similar symbiotic relationship, Hilliard dressing up, masquerading, and Congreaves taking his cues, going along with it because of his debts.

Hilliard didn't like the idea of money around his neck like a belled cat, but said nothing. A cluster of Bedouins at first eyed them with suspicion, then turned their backs on the pair. The women's faces were tattooed with indigo, and their lips were completely blue.

"I don't see any other Europeans here," Archer breathed deeply. "I'm really in my element. I feel as if I've lived here all my life."

Hilliard pointed at a pair of Ethiopians in striped robes, gold necklaces around their necks, thick bracelets spanned their arms. He asked Ryder if they were slaves. In a letter to Edna written that first night Ryder wondered if his patron felt he was reliving scenes found in *Tales from the Arabian Nights* and *The Blue Fairy Book* all rolled into one.

Ryder's life in Cairo and Ghiza was very regimented. He was scrupulous in his work and at first wrote regularly to Edna. Dressed in white he would ride out from his house in Cairo, cross the Nile, and carry on to the excavation site six miles away in Ghiza. Unlike Hilliard, Ryder made a point of preferring horses to camels. In the evening he would return to socialize with other Britons who, for whatever reasons, found themselves in Cairo before the outbreak of the Great War. He watched crocodiles swim alongside his *dahabeeyah* as he floated down the Nile and warned Hilliard when a hand dangled over the edge. Once again he saw the animals of his childhood, but he wrote with contempt about the Ghizan and Cairene workers he employed.

Archer didn't often spend time at the site, but one afternoon he arranged for a driver to take him out to Ghiza where Ryder was already at work. At first Congreaves spoke of ordinary things: the heat and dust, the price of shipping winches, gears, pulleys, and quality of local rope. He didn't feel comfortable with Archer on the site. Hilliard squatted under a palm drawing a map in the sand with a stick. The hired diggers had been working in silence, even the sounds of picks, shovels, brushes, and camel bells were muted in the desert. Hilliard erased the topographical sand map with his foot.

Just as the map was being erased they heard the hollow sound of axe shattering dried clay, and Ryder turned to find a digger had unearthed, then accidentally cracked open a canopic jar. Mummified intestines or other three-thousand-year-old organs were instantly exposed to the heat of desert air. It was the most amazing object he had found to date, and now it was shattered. Ryder went berserk. Desiccated strips of tissue, not even recognizable as much more than ancient shed snake skin, were pulverized. Plumb lines and pick axes went flying. At first the man cowered, but he could tell others weren't cowering at all, and then something shifted, and in a ripple of attention, everyone turned to look at Ryder. Their gaze wasn't a display of passive voyeuristm, watching someone get angry in a spectacle of out-of-control rage, and Hilliard standing a few feet away from Ryder, became very aware there were only two of them, and all the Egyptians held objects that could inflict quite a bit of damage. Hilliard ordered the scattered equipment collected. Speaking in Arabic, Ryder hurled a final insult at the man, who shuffled off.

Hilliard tried to appease Congreaves, to calm him down and, not for the first time, block his explosions, though his patience with his translator was growing thin. Ryder felt chastised and humiliated, but he relied on Archer. Without him he would be bankrupt, adrift, and he knew it.

When he wrote to Edna about the event, he complained about Archer's presence: he was a distraction, he made the men anxious. He used the word detestable. Edna couldn't imagine the connection between the use of the word detestable and the fellow so taken in by the Crystal Palace, one who stood so timidly at the threshold, hat in hand.

In their relationship to their own history, the letter went on, Egyptians were like lizards who ate their own tails. Ryder envisioned finding the tomb of an unknown king or queen, not just full of untold treasures, but containing unfamiliar writing or ancient mechanical devices that only he could reanimate. His unhatched schemes grew increasingly grandiose, as if a crown floated just over his scalp, and if he tilted his head a certain way and reached up fast he could grab it. Then he, too, would be knighted and treated everywhere and by everyone, from his London landlord to the Cairo embassy, as someone who should be listened to. People would stop in their tracks to hear him describe how just under that outcropping of rock or hill of sand, round the next bend in the Nile he followed a trail of amber fragments to the temple of the child queen who ruled before Amenhotep, before Ramses or Tutankhamen.

Then his letters became few and far between. Edna thought Archer had finally poisoned Ryder against her. In response, she wrote back to him constantly, filling page after page, detailing the lives of their children down to the most insignificant minutiae about them, making almost daily trips to the post office, as if she could flood him with the brass tacks of their everyday life to bring him back to it. Letters back were short and colorless.

Esme

Esme Canonbury, fine-boned and aggressive, turned heads with her clipped accent, sarcastic tone that made you feel included in the gibe, looking down at troglodytes below, bobbed brown hair, and a taste for what was taken to be harem clothes, but were really filmy trousers and long silk vests of her own devising. She was married to the cultural chargé d'affaires at the Consulate. Esme and Ryder met at an embassy event Hilliard had persuaded him to attend, telling him to leave off your charts and maps; it will be great fun, really. In a sea of swirling white dresses, men in uniform, and Egyptian bearers serving sherbet, lime tea with ginger, soda and gin, Ryder's height and discomfort stood out. Despite his stoop, leaving London had transformed him.

"Your Archie is worth a *fortune*, but he's going to end up in an Alexandrian jail if he doesn't watch out, honestly." No one had ever spoken so directly about Ryder's colleague and patron. No one had ever said Archer would end up dead in an alley. Once, Ryder had found Hilliard holding a tortoise-shell cigarette case, not his own, staring at the panorama of Cairo visible from his hotel balcony. Hilliard's eyes were red-rimmed, he was oblivious to Congreaves' entrance, and so he quickly left the room before Archer turned around. Ryder preferred not to embarrass, and he preferred not to know. It wasn't his place. He himself rarely spoke about Edna, folded her letters into pockets, never read them in front of Hilliard. Esme put one hand on his shoulder for balance as she bent over to fix a strap on her shoe.

While her husband sat with his back to the dance floor, Esme whisked Ryder in circles out onto the balcony where all of Cairo seemed to lay at his feet, a present she'd given to him. The small metal shapes, mirrors and bells, sewn into her costume clanging, she kissed him hard on the mouth. Esme smelled of ginger, gardenias, Indonesian clove cigarettes, and Ryder felt like the deluded wasp trying to screw an orchid. A few minutes later Esme began to introduce him to someone and turned to him as if she couldn't remember his name exactly, what was it again? Ryder felt nothing he could see or touch was familiar, yet everything he needed was in his control.

By the next morning the memory of Edna was like one of those paintings of eighteenth-century naval battles, left in a forgotten, rarely visited museum annex. It was once very exciting, a true action painting, but now no one remembers or cares who was fighting whom, and no one gives a damn. Later Hilliard, himself a grand vizier of delusion, would say of Esme, what a mirage, what a first-class hallucination, but Ryder would dismiss him, as if the monkish Archer didn't know what on earth he was talking about. Esme floated into a room wearing what to Ryder were wisps of Sirius clouds. He thought about her all the time, and she didn't disappoint him.

Mrs. Canonbury fell in love with Ryder and his tales of hidden treasures buried somewhere in the far reaches of the Persian empire, a city full of treasure, the remains of counting houses, tea houses, scimitars and skeletons. His partnership with Archer only increased his capital. They began to meet whenever Esme could get away, but always referred to each other in private as well as in public, as Mr. Congreaves and Mrs. Canonbury. Hilliard saw them in a café in the French zone and again at Esme's jeweler's leaving a watch to be repaired. They were careful to appear as if nothing more than formal acquaintances, but Hilliard could see they stood very close to one another and that Mr. C would hold Mrs. C's elbow a little longer than necessary. He'd bought a present for Ryder, prayer beads made of aventurine and gold. Taking them from his pocket, he handed the paper-wrapped loop to the first beggar he encountered.

Bribery

An issue arose over some survey permits, which required them to meet a local official, and Ryder protested the hour of the appointment and the way in which the whole process was a waste of his time. On their way to the domed and filigreed ministry, sitting in the back of a hot cab, he referred to the fellow as a little Walid. Hilliard didn't know if the remark was meant as some kind of slur or that really was his name, but the man had the power to issue or withhold documents. Their initial permit had expired, and they wanted to expand the acreage under their purview.

The pair sat in a waiting room for over nearly an hour. Ryder was supposed to meet Esme at the hotel. He studied the pattern the shadows a wooden grille fit over the windows made on the floor, and imagined the languid Walid cooling his heels, smoking a nargillah in a back room while Esme looked at the clock in the tearoom of *Le Pharaon Royale*, finally swallowing the dregs of her drink, picking up her bag and making for the door in order to return to her house in time for a fitting with her dressmaker. Ryder pushed himself out of his chair, heading to the door, but Archer insisted he was needed for the appointment. Finally they were called in. Hilliard swept ahead of him, hand extended, all smiles. He had told Ryder the meeting was an hour earlier than it had actually been scheduled for.

The official sat behind a desk cluttered by paper and pieces of stone used as weights. Fan spinning overhead as Turkish coffee was poured, Ryder translated, turning increasingly red as the man made it clear that he would grant their permit based on certain contingencies that would primarily benefit himself, and as far as Ryder could see, himself only. Ryder refused to give in. Neither did his Egyptian opponent, who saw nothing amiss in his demands. It was the way business was done. Now it was Hilliard's turn to grow impatient.

"Let's just get on with it. Pay the man."

"You can't give in to the Walids. We'll be emptying piastres from our pockets to theirs, from now to eternity."

"That's an awfully long time." Sometimes Hilliard pretended to be stupid, especially when he knew he was about to be manipulated into doing things he was completely opposed to.

The Egyptian told them he was busy, and if they needed more time they should return another day. He made a gesture as if to point out the door. Without warning or consulting with Ryder, Hilliard stood up from his chair, reached into his robes, and handed the man a bundle of notes. The official nodded without smiling and put the notes in a drawer.

Ryder exploded, saying in effect, the Egyptian was an oriental despot and Hilliard was a first class moron.

The "Walid," who, unbeknownst to them understood English fairly well, replied, "And we will be minding our sphinxes and our desert long after you're returned to your island, which I've heard is swampy and covered in fog."

If Ryder believed this was the last time they would have dealings with the functionary who had humiliated him, he was mistaken. They would need to have future meetings with this man, and they would all be conducted by Hilliard in English. Ryder was overlooked as if not even in the room. When he raised objections, Hilliard paid no attention to him. Standing by in mute irritation as Hilliard voluntarily increased payments, Ryder imagined a bag of gold coins being poured out a window. He wrote to Edna that he felt like a dog whose nose is rubbed in its own crap. Ryder's comments weren't forgotten in a hurry, nor were angry ridges of offended pride entirely smoothed over by extensive transfer of piastres. Hilliard intuited protocol and tried to get the older and more experienced Congreaves to step aside as gracefully as possible, but Ryder insisted on being present even if the oriental ignored him.

The Effect Of Gravity On Earth

Hilliard wasn't at the site when it happened. Ryder was occupied with his horse a few yards from the pit when he heard a loud crash and screams. Hurrying to the edge, clumps of sand giving way under his feet, he could make out the head and upper body of one of the diggers. The lower half of the man's body was caught under a large block of stone that had toppled from some height. The lower half of his torso and his legs were trapped and probably destroyed under the weight.

Blood pooled under the boulder. He yelled to the other men at the site. There were only six, but even all of them together couldn't budge the rock. One offered to ride for help and began to run toward a horse, but Ryder stopped him. It was too late, even if he took the fastest one, which was Ryder's own. They were too far for help to come on time, he was sure of it.

The anguish of the man's screams was unbearable. He was not losing consciousness yet, though he was dying. Another digger began to pour water on his head. Ryder pulled his arm away. The digger hadn't much time left, and they needed the water they had. As luck would have it, that day there wasn't much to spare. He argued with the foreman, an Alexandrian Greek. Blood coagulated in the sand under the trapped man. His screams were unbearable. Ryder took out his gun and shot him in the head, then ordered them all back to work.

Assassin's Creed

The letter was delivered to Hilliard scribbled in Arabic. Unwilling to make an effort at reading the page, which he assumed was a tradesman's bill, he passed it over to Ryder, who crumpled the paper and shoved it in a pocket.

"Letter from Mrs. Canonbury?" Hilliard asked. He was joking. Esme wouldn't have written in Arabic and never, ever would have addressed a letter to Hilliard, who was fairly open about his dislike of her. He found her archness tedious. When something obvious was narrated, whether a government failing to protect the water supply or late arrival explained by a cab that had broken down, Esme liked to say, *is that not so?* An early twentieth-century way of saying *you're kidding me?* But said too many times with sarcasm it annoyed Archer no end. Conversation and gestures Ryder found charming Hilliard found false and parvenu. What his friend and partner saw in the woman with jangly clothing was a mystery to him. Hoping the affair was drawing to a close, he envisioned Esme writing a tear-stained letter on embassy stationery. Archer imagined Mr. Canonbury had his embassy toadies who informed him of hotel assignations, but he probably didn't need to be informed. Ryder thought no one knew, but everyone did.

Perhaps Canonbury didn't care, he was tolerant and glad to have a bit of relief from Esme, then, because of appearances, put his foot down. A woman of ellipsis and multiple exclamatory and interrogative punctuation marks and never one to shirk before an underscore, she would write: *Farewell, I'll always think about you when* . . . Or maybe it would be an angry final communiqué: *you've shamed me in front of servants for the last time!!!* Hilliard imagined all these scenes as he rolled a fragment of flat bread into a cylinder and popped it into his mouth.

"No, no, not at all." Ryder tapped his fork against his plate making repetitive taps to the tune of *A Little of What You Fancy Does You Good,* a music hall song made popular by the chanteuse Marie Lloyd. Ryder's humming was meant to signal, it's nothing, don't bother me, but that particular tune was also meant to annoy Archer with a song that was a form of low entertainment. Hilliard could tell he didn't want to talk about the letter, but this only made him more curious about its contents.

"What is it, then?"

"Nothing like that."

Everyone carried a knife here. Blade pulled from a belt made no noise. It would be so easy. An oriental, as Congreaves himself would say, could disappear into a warren of streets or the desert itself. No one would find him, ever. Archer would then have to return to England. He couldn't really survive without Ryder, and going back to London was not something he wanted to do, not yet.

Ryder picked an ant off the table and rolled it between his thumb and forefinger so it quickly became a bristle of broken ant legs, head, and thorax. When he frowned his eyebrows looked like question marks lying on their sides. He flicked the ant ball off his palm. Then he slammed his fork against table, and egg went flying. He and Esme were staying in Egypt. He flung the wad of paper to the floor and stormed out of the room.

Tucking up his dishdasha, Hilliard padded to the shadow on the tile floor, picked up the ball, proceeded to smooth it out on the table. The scalloped curves of Arabic were illegible to him, but he dressed hurriedly and called a driver.

He found the "Walid" in his office, gold spectacles pushed onto his head, reading documents, smoking. He didn't look up when Hilliard entered the room. A highly placed functionary, if it weren't for funds that would shortly change hands, the Egyptian would have been too busy to see Hilliard.

"*Salaam Ali,*" Hilliard paused, "*Kuum,*" he added. This much Arabic he knew. He touched his fingers to his forehead and bowed slightly, "*Masa'a AlKair, Sayyid*" — he had learned to say 'good afternoon, sir' — "please, I need some discreet help." Archer passed the page across the man's desk. "I would be so very grateful if you could translate this for me." Apart from Ryder there was no other person he could call on for such services, a measure of how isolated Hilliard felt, even after several months. Despite his costume, Archer was often paralyzed when it came to acting on his desires in the city where he claimed he felt so at home. Archer would stare too long at camel drivers, café musicians, and sometimes they returned his gaze.

The Egyptian picked up the wrinkled paper, read the few lines.

"This note you should take very seriously," he said, picking up a cigarette as if he had all the time in the world. "The message is clear. Remain in Egypt and both of you are dead."

"You're certain?"

"Come, my friend, let us not joke. I make money from your presence. I wouldn't advise you to depart otherwise, would I? Do I have rivals? Yes, of course. Would they kill to make my life more difficult?" He shrugged as if to say, maybe, maybe not, who can tell? He stood from his chair and poured tea holding his arm high so the stream of tea fell several feet into gold-rimmed glasses little bigger than chicken eggs. He handed a glass to Hilliard.

"We could make a payment, I suppose, if you think it really necessary." The glass was hot. Hilliard shifted it from hand to hand before clearing a bit of space from the desk and putting it down. The man shook his head and looked at the glasses, but offered him no milk or sugar.

"Whoever wrote this note pens beautiful calligraphy. Someone educated who knows what he's doing. Perhaps he was only hired by someone else."

He was offered more tea, but shook his head, no; his first glass sat cooling, precipitously close to the edge of the desk. His host frowned, picked up Hilliard's glass, nestled it back on the tray with the teapot, and motioned with his head that the interview was finished.

Archer pushed the fretwork iron gate, left over from the French, looked back at the dome behind him and ventured into the street. Unaccompanied by Congreaves he had to pretend he was deaf when beggars followed him and tugged at his robes. He pushed them away, wishing he remembered what Ryder had said when the unwashed masses approached to get them to leave him alone. Hilliard was no wiser than he had been a few hours earlier, apart from the knowledge the threat was genuine. It wasn't that he didn't feel brave, although he wasn't particularly. The local constabulary, he believed, might be less than helpful regarding a threat to an Englishman who was known to refer to them as incompetent poobahs, administered mercy killings, then got back to work. He imagined Ryder stabbed to death in the street and himself lost, wandering the desert unable to be understood by anyone within hundreds of miles. Though he knew this was a silent film hardly grounded in actual facts, the idea haunted him.

Hilliard and Congreaves left Egypt in the middle of the night.

The two men packed their tents, collapsible canvas bath, folding canvas chairs, mosquito netting, pots, pans, tea service, and silver, made their travel arrangements and procured whatever documents they needed by cabling the India Office in London. The province they meant to explore was located in the part of Persia that had been parceled out to the British, as opposed to the oil-rich province of Khuzistan that had been grabbed by the Russians. They intended to set up base camp in Duzdab, now known as Zahedan, a small town where they could launch themselves from the comfort of what they considered likely to be habitable dwellings, situated so their forays into desert and mountains would be easy outings, or so they thought. They would be looking for the city that had once flourished in the mountains of Sistan va Baluchistan.

Debt

While Ryder disappeared into the land of pomegranate and sand, his family moved to even cheaper lodgings in Spitalfields, where they shared two rooms with another woman and her children. Maybe Edna didn't have Esme Canonbury's slightly horsy elegance, and at embassy parties she probably would have felt like a rubber oven mitt thrust in a drawer of silk opera gloves, but Edna never curtsied to anyone. She got her children food and shelter while the hard-edged yet ethereal Esme, in the same situation, might have turned to opium or morphine or scotch and soda and left the planet earlier than expected to more applause than expected.

Back in London, the younger Ryder was four years old, and his sister, Alicia, was six. Money was running out. In desperation Edna wrote to her in-laws in Rhodesia. My dear, their letter replied post haste, we simply haven't got the funds ourselves. To celebrate our anniversary we had a modest tea party on the veranda. Love to the children. She wrote again. Lucky you to have tea and a veranda. We're lining our shoes with dust bunnies against the cold. Her desperation was interpreted as cheekiness and was met with silence. Edna had, by now, long doubted the veracity of the stories he had told her about hunting elephant for ivory and skinning leopards alone in the savannah that stretched for miles around him. It's unlikely he or his family had ever actually done such things. With two small children there was no returning to the Crystal Palace or any similar line of work. The Crystal Palace job was a moment on stage Edna thought would last forever, but then her identity as a guide vanished without a trace. Even her best clothing was worn and stained. No one would grant her an interview. Doors were shut in her face. She hadn't the necessary training or certificate to teach in a school and had no one to care for the children while she furthered her own education.

The landlady pounded on the door, threatening eviction. Edna's children were taught how to be still as mice, as if their lives depended on it. She put her hands over the children's mouths, whispered they should make no sound until the knocking passed. Ryder II whimpered, he was frightened, while Alicia made a silent counting game out of the predicament: how long would the landlady knock? (This was the beginning of Alicia's lifelong interest in odds, betting, and a gambling habit.) They made a practice of dodging the landlady, not only going in and out of the small building where they rented rooms, but also on the street. Edna would listen, ear to the space where door meets jamb, to hear her footsteps down the hall as she prepared to leave the house, and only when she heard the key turn in the front door lock did she herself venture out. The family's comings and goings were measured and calculated, distance and time, in relationship to the known habits of their landlady. They knew she did her shopping right after breakfast and was out all morning so this was the optimal time for venturing forth, but Edna figured they had to be back before the woman returned. Despite all her reckoning, mistakes were made. Once when rounding a corner backwards Edna knocked right into the landlady's bony butt as she bent over a basket of eggs in front of a grocer's. She straightened up with difficulty as if she'd been knocked over by a wrecking ball. In an instant she wiped the egg from her face and went off right in the street in front of shopkeepers and customers, sounding like a human abacus clacking what amount was in arrears and what fees had gone unpaid. Edna and the children were always hungry. Utter destitution was visited upon the Congreaves family. At one point Edna trained the children to nick food. She was ashamed, but did so anyway. At first their attempts at pinching a loaf of bread or an apple were met with humiliating failure. Shopkeepers vented anger at small children and constables offered cute warnings about special gaols, but hunger can be a shrewd teacher in this regard. They got better at it.

Persia

Arriving in Duzdab on May 17, 1914, Hilliard took a villa with a garden bordered by mango and apricot trees. He plunged into the bazaar and came back loaded with kilims and hookahs of all sizes. Meanwhile Congreaves bargained over the price of camels, wheelbarrows, makeshift sieves, buckets, and rope. Ryder wrote that on warm nights people slept on carpets on their rooftops. He was enchanted by this scene, a patchwork of colored carpets spread out before him, but the vista only served to make his partner silent and depressed. In a photograph of Hilliard from this period, he temporarily abandoned his Egyptian costume and adopted the sartorial agenda of an upper-class Tehrani: a long collarless shirt, high narrow trousers held in place by a cashmere sash, a long V-neck coat slit at the sides.

They toured the Sassanid ruins in the Kahjeh mountains and had their picture taken sitting on the crumbling ridge of a wall. They studied topographic maps looking at likely spots close to sources of water. Congreaves interviewed local shepherds, hired guides and diggers, and began looking for clues in the area several kilometers due east of Duzdab. No one could tell him anything about the lost city. He began to have doubts, it was possible the whole thing was a hoax. Its kings, battles, and ingenious irrigation systems were no more concrete than a toll bridge in Atlantis. At the same time, he was anxious to get to work one way or another, arguing with Archer, kicking the rolls of carpets Hilliard had collected, but Ryder, too, had his distractions. He was often waylaid, intrigued by the ruckus of cockfights set up in dusty alleys or narrow courtyards.

One night, the fight hadn't gone well for Ryder. He'd lost a little money, not much, but had to ask Hilliard for more, and this always made him feel humiliated and irritated. Dawn was at hand, it was time to leave, but as he elbowed his way to the edge of the crowd a man with a caprine face and a long split beard holding a dead rooster by its feet bumped into him. It's unlikely this was really an accident. Word had spread around the city that two Englishmen were poking around looking for ancient sites. The man followed Ryder, talking about the fight, the different birds and their owners, trying to strike up a conversation. Swinging the rooster as he walked, he smiled and bobbed his head, not put off by Ryder's coldness. Egyptians and other Africans had known to keep a physical distance from the Englishman. The man's obliviousness to custom, his lack of respect would have ordinarily infuriated Ryder, but he was so distracted by his losses, he ignored the man until he described something he had seen while hunting a gazelle in the foothills. Congreaves stopped short and turned to listen more attentively, as the man holding the dead rooster knew he would. He described trailing the wounded animal to a cave he'd never seen before. The gazelle was an easy quarry, so once he got to the cave he looked around. Though dark he could make out the shapes of large urns and piles of pottery, some metal, too, glinted in the depths. Fearing the encroaching night, robbers, djinns, British or Russian mercenaries or who knows what, he finished off the gazelle, slung the animal over his shoulder and quickly returned home.

Telling the man to leave the dead rooster by the side of the road, Ryder led the way to Hilliard's villa.

First Signs

Archer received them in the main room, lying on floor pillows, smoking, playing with the untucked tail of a sky blue turban. Taking stock of the expensive carpets from Tabriz and Esfahan and strings of camel bells used for decoration, the loss of his prize rooster earlier in the night was forgotten. Ryder had the hunter repeat his story, which he, translated for Hilliard. In the second narration the descriptions of what lay in the cave grew increasingly ornate. Archer looked surprisingly impassive, perhaps he had finally learned the art of bargaining. Gesturing with his hands to indicate the size of the urns and the shape of some of the pottery he had managed to see, the hunter raised his voice, feeling he was beginning to lose ground. Ryder, too, turned skeptical and feared that the man had smoked too much kif. Still, it was a tantalizing clue, and they had no others.

Finally the hunter showed signs of giving up. Arguing with the white man in a turban was going nowhere. He let Ryder know he had wasted too much time with them already when he had the lost investment of the rooster to deal with. The hunter turned to go, taking his leave like a supplicant with a secret axe to grind. As he began to make his way to the door, Hilliard stood up abruptly, but in doing so his whole turban fell apart and landed in a mass of cloth at his feet. Strips of longish red-brown hair fell around his ears, though he had very little on top. Ryder believed all was now lost. The ridiculous are not in a position to make deals to their own advantage. Headgear down around his ankles, Hilliard rasped at the native to wait. At first the hunter smiled like someone who, after an unforeseen struggle, suddenly lands a big fish.

Then his expression changed again. Examining the drying rooster blood on his sleeve, looking as if greatly pained, the man spoke.

"The route out beyond the edge of the city is deeply rutted and fraught with dangers: bandits, wild animals." The hunter crossed his arms, appearing stern and concerned for their safety. "Perhaps it isn't worth the trouble to take such risks. Maybe I've been too rash. Yes, I too, am decided against the venture. I can't insure your safety, and I'll lose a day's work in the process."

Hilliard doubled the amount they'd agreed to pay him. After stroking his beard in stagey contemplation, the Duzdabi relented. For that amount, plus the cost of food he himself would provide, he would show the Englishmen the cave of the wounded gazelle.

They engaged him, giving him a bag of krans, flattened balls of silver and alloy that passed as coinage, and the next morning the hunter appeared at Hilliard's door. Hilliard noted the man was wrapped in a shawl, long white shirt, white trousers, a round hat made of grey sheep's hair perched on his head, and he carried a gun.

As they made their way through the market on their way out of Duzdab, Ryder stopped to speak to a Bakhtiari woman in a long scarf with tiny mirrors and coins sewn into it. Her eyes were outlined with kajul, ornaments sewn into her headscarf dangled over her forehead and glinted in the sun. Neither their guide nor Hilliard were amused, and they walked ahead of the laggard. Over the course of the night, recovering from his humiliation and loss at the cockfight, Ryder had begun to have doubts about the hunter's story, but they'd made an agreement. If they reneged there were ways a local could make life difficult for them. At least Ryder now realized this. No longer in a place where there were many other Europeans, Ryder packed a knife in his belt, as usual, but this time he was afraid that once in the desert the man with the dead rooster whose tale, by the light of the next day, seemed much less credible, could slit their throats and rob them. It is a marker of how much of a dead end Congreaves believed the hunter to be, that he stopped to flirt with a woman, endangering all of them, rather than get on with the exploration they'd traveled so far to undertake.

The hunter led them out of the city into the hills. They were nearly a day's hike from Duzdab, and during the trek he took a few wrong turns, causing the small party to backtrack and lose valuable daylight hours. Ryder suspected they would have to set up camp in the mountains, unable to return to the city by nightfall, and this made him uneasy. The hunter spoke to their porters in a dialect Ryder didn't fully understand, though he strained to hear every syllable. Finally in a small rock-strewn ravine the hunter led them to the entrance of the site where he had followed the wounded gazelle. Walking several kilometers into the dark cave they couldn't see anything but veined rock face. Impatient and still far from convinced they had found anything but another dead-end they'd paid dearly for, Ryder went ahead of the others. Cursing and stumbling, deaf to the sound of water dripping somewhere ahead of him, he stopped when the passage forked, and then his torch lit on something he'd never seen before: a long notched blade leaning against a tall clay vessel, as if the warrior who guarded the thing had only stepped out for a moment's cigarette break. The edge was still sharp. The blade was curved and serrated, designed to inflict maximum damage. He held his torch higher. More objects lay in the crumbling channels further on, and he shouted for his companion as he'd never in his life shouted before.

They spent hours marveling over the cache of scrolls and other objects, then against their guide's warnings, Ryder took a torch and walked further into the cave. The passage dipped and bent, the ceiling dropped so he had to stoop, but just as he was about to return, convinced they'd found all there was to unearth, his torch light glanced upon the bones of a female skeleton lying near a series of plates. Her shredded clothing was splattered with clay slip and flecks of paint. Her skull was some distance away, but there was no evidence looters had found the site. Apart from headlessness, the woman was so complete, other victims might be nearby, executed by the same sword. Though he moved rocks, dislodged clumps of wet clay from the cave bottom, no other skeletal remains were located, only a second notched blade with an inlaid handle stuck point down in the dirt near the skeleton's foot, as if dropped in a hurry. He tried to measure the chamber, but he was so excited the tape kept getting caught on his rifle stock, though it was slung over his shoulder.

Hilliard and Congreaves had found, if not the city itself, then evidence of it hidden in and around the caves. The cuneiform and other markings were distinctly different from other Seulucid city-states that Rawlinson or anyone else had ever documented. They claimed the newly discovered relics could only have come from Suolucidir. Local people were quickly hired as diggers and porters, and the excavation process began. Each and every item Ryder and Archer inventoried, packed up, and dispatched.

Suolucidir, Found and Lost

The plates found near the skeleton were sent separately to London, and these found their way to the storage vaults of the British Museum. Perhaps Ryder and Archer considered these to be the least valuable, if the not the most curious, of the relics they plundered, and so made a token donation out of all their takings. Though Ryder wasn't ordinarily a superstitious man, the plates' proximity to the beheaded skeleton made him leery of keeping them in his possession. Hilliard and Congreaves ultimately took everything they could lay their hands on, leaving not so much as a bent coin or bronze tool behind. Thin-ankled camels staggered under the weight of the loot, their bells ringing plaintively as they carried the treasure from the hills of Duzdab to the Persian coast where the sum total of the surviving relics of Suolucidir were loaded on a ship bound for Deptford, England.

Their ship, *HMS Dorchester*, sank on the 14th of July 1915, torpedoed by a German sub in the Straits of Hormuz. Apart from the plates sent to the British Museum, whatever else that had been culled from their excavations, including valuable maps of the area locating the sites where they dug, all now lay at the bottom of the Gulf of Oman, along with the remains of Archer Hilliard and Ryder Congreaves.

Edna, What Remains

In England, from Oxford to London, many of those who had sneered at Ryder now filled trenches in France and Belgium. As they and others shipped out, bound for mustard gas and battlefields, jobs were left behind, waiting to be filled.

"You're looking for a place? Well, I don't know for certain, but it seems to me they're a bit short-handed down the road. Tell them Jackie sent you."

A casual conversation with a neighbor led Edna to a position behind the till at Wallingford's, a greengrocer's a short bus ride away. The Wallingford sons were fighting in Flanders, and Edna soon proved she was quick with sums. The sons never returned, and Edna found her calling: weighing pineapples, wrapping fruit in brown paper, chatting up, and making change. Edna had no other family and was very much on her own. The Crystal Palace job had been all about talking and conversing with other guides when the opportunity presented itself, but with no real companions at Wallingford's, the loneliness of the long hours while her two children rolled oranges and cabbage heads around a back room, was often acute.

She saw so many return from the foreign adventure of the Great War missing not just limbs and bits of their sanity but parts of their faces: eyes, noses, chins. A young man in a metal mask would patronize Wallingford's from time to time. Most of his face had been blown off in a trench, or more likely, as he emerged from one. One of his eyes was a blue marble, but the other one could see the piles of peaches and radishes and Edna herself licking her forefinger as she counted pound notes. Did he, too, want to ask her out for a coffee she didn't drink? He noticed when Edna gave him too much change and corrected her with as much annoyance as if she'd shortchanged him. He didn't want her charity, and so when he came in she drew on what reserves of small talk she could drum up. The weather? Off limits pretty much. You ought not, she felt, suggest a man in a metal mask should especially stay indoors in case of rain. As seasons slipped by quickly, strawberries and asparagus giving way to tomatoes and squash, then sliding to apples and root vegetables, Edna wasn't sure she could comment, ah well, we're all getting older, aren't we, to a man whose face never aged. Though bus conductors looked into the distance, and his landlady stared at objects to the left of his face, Edna looked directly at him. She searched the surface of the mask the way someone would search any face, remembering the tilt of the eyes, the arch of the nose, a constellation of freckles, the kinds of things that become imprinted when one falls for someone, and can't get their face with its ballet of reactions out of one's head. The metal man's face offered none of these signs or anchors and couldn't reflect even a glimmer of affection. His desires couldn't be telegraphed through the watchmakers' screws, invisible hinges, joints, and rivets. They were dammed up behind it. Edna wondered how could she or anyone kiss him? If you bite into a peach, it's a living thing, you taste the juice, and so on, but the man in the mask stumped Edna, and made her uncomfortable. She felt sorry for him, and he knew it. Eventually he stopped coming in to the shop. Edna resolved to always keep her children close to home.

In due course she became the shop's manager, performing so well at the job and so efficiently, Wallingford's was able to expand to the shopfront next door. She and the children were also able to move to a bigger flat closer to the store, and if Edna learned to be certain of her place in the world, at the same time she was never altogether happy with the limited horizons allotted to her. She wasn't sure how and exactly when the boot heel came down. Perhaps conversation with a certain class of customer swerved toward the familiar, the personal. Yes, my husband, too, ran off with a woman from the embassy in Cairo, was not something you were supposed say to the red-eyed woman who asked for a pound of nectarines, assuming she, and not her cook was doing the shopping. Edna tried to make conversation from time to time, but Wallingford's lay very close to an expensive neighborhood, and for these customers, the gap between grocers and residents was very wide. The door slammed shut in her face again.

The business thrived, hired more employees. Now, when Edna spoke of Ryder at all, she only used his name as a synonym for a slack-off. Telling shop girls who worked under her to stop rydering around, for example, or scolding a non-family-related child not to be a little ryder. They intuited the meaning without ever guessing the true root of the word.

Young Ryder grew up, but university was out of the question, and for Edna, that was one more black mark against his father, about whom by now neither she nor anyone else could remember much. Ryder II married a postman's daughter who found unpacking crates of orange pippins and making sure the Estremoz plums from Portugal didn't slip out of their tissue paper wrappers to be entirely beneath her.

Photographs of Edna from this period show a woman with a small mouth aswim in a large chin with a halo of tightly curled hair, like the kind you see on statues of Roman Empresses. But that tough customer look was deceiving. The former Crystal Palace guide who had lectured to crowds of visitors about the promises of the future, who had learned to make do, to survive, even to survive well, and not cause too much trouble to anyone, was seething inside. Television, when it came along, made Edna angry. The images on the screen said: here's a taste of the world. It reminded her of what might have been.

Tilda Congreaves-Sutcliffe
30 Regent's Crescent
Hackney, London

April 1986

Dear Mr. Bokser,

It was a shock and a pleasure to get your letter, and I am sorry you went through so much trouble trying to find me. You were correct in your assumption. I'm the last of the Congreaves branch that migrated from what is now Zimbabwe to England. Ryder Dunleavey Congreaves, the archaeologist, was my great-grandfather. My grandmother was Alicia Congreaves-Sutcliffe, whose papers you have acquired. Alicia never really knew her father, but in 1959 she traveled to Cairo and Iran in order to learn what had happened to him, and to write of his explorations that had been forgotten by the rest of the world. It was her desire to learn something of the man her mother rarely spoke of, so her trip was of a personal nature, as well.

I do have letters from Ryder to Edna, pictures, some bits of ephemera (trunk labels, receipts for Channel crossing tickets, train to Marseilles, boat to Alexandria) and have enclosed photocopies because I'm using the originals in a huge installation piece under construction for one of my classes at Royal Art College. The project, I firmly believe, is the best use for this material that comments not only on my own family, but on Britain's colonial ambitions and shortcomings in our post-colonial marketplace. It's entitled: A Brief History of the Congreaves, a Double Self-Destructing Panorama. My installations are formed of all kinds of cultural detritus: a fan of postcards, bottles arranged on a fir-like bottle rack (borrowed from Duchamp), stuffed animals, old books, programs from plays, dolls, discarded toys of all kinds, a grill made of cigarettes, gum wrappers twisted into stamens of fruit wrapper flowers. I find material in anything biodegradable. My soon to be unveiled personal Congreaves Family Pyre is the least doctored, least transformed of all my works. I've pasted everything on a portable wall, then next Tuesday, in a week's time, will light a flame while a friend films the whole disintegrating shooting match.

I can tell you the pictures of Ryder sent back from Cairo reveal a different person, less browbeaten and more in charge of things. Though it may have been downhill from there in the looks department for generations of Congreaves, RC I looked like a blond Errol Flynn, and I think he knew it, even if he'd never seen Errol Flynn — no one yet had — but you get the idea.

Apart from my grandmother, Alicia, no Congreaves has left the country since the doomed 1914 expedition. Edna, who didn't believe in luck or fate or astrology, only hard work, joked about the Curse of Suolucidir, that obsession that caused Ryder's early demise and now dogged all his descendants. (Well, let's say they haven't left in any serious long-term way. My father visited Spain once, and I did a holiday in Amsterdam, if that counts.) We Congreaves stay close to home fearing the curse of Suolucidir is still with us, that you'll wander so far, returning is impossible, and you'll end up dashed to pieces, falling head over heels for some siren's song. Suolucidir passes A levels in mirage manufacture if you ask me.

My grandfather went into the printing business, and my father later joined him, forming Sutcliffe & Sons, Ltd. The printing works made money for a while. My grandfather died of a blood disease, induced, one theory goes, by exposure to chemicals in the inks he worked with. Every night he and my father came home covered with the stuff before it was known or even suspected that adequate ventilation was necessary. I still remember the smell of ink, how it would be present even when we were walking blocks from the works, so you always knew you were getting closer to it. My father had that smell about him all during the week, and he met a similar fate. Odd, we take it as a matter of course, chemicals = precaution, an old science teacher of mine used to write on the chalkboard, but back in the early days of Queen Elizabeth II, I guess they didn't. Perhaps this could be construed as yet another black mark against RC I, rakerottercad, who ran off to the ends of the earth chasing skirts and djinn so his children couldn't better themselves, Edna would say, and as a consequence, his descendants suffered early deaths due to the inhalation of plumes of benzene or whatever chemical lodged in their bloodstreams, mutating, blocking, doing monstrous things.

I was very small when Alicia left, so I don't remember her very well. Coral beads, a serious smoker, her hands were stained with cherry juice, handling soft unsold fruit when she helped Edna out, but she did not get along with her mother at all, as you can see by the way she wrote about her at the end. Alicia was difficult, like her father, she wanted to be somewhere else, I've been told. She had no interest in the printing company, only insofar as the money it earned launched her on her trip to the east. Her writing came back to us, these few pages, but she never did, not even a body was found. How she died in Iran is unknown. The consulate learned that she ventured into the Black Mountains, where people often vanished — even with experienced guides it was considered a lawless borderland. My grandfather made inquiries through the embassy, but was left empty-handed, saying only that nobody wanted to cause an international incident. My grandfather clung to a number of conspiracy theories: what she learned cost Alicia her life. These ideas were fueled by a reporter who interviewed him, but never published his story. Maybe my grandfather was right to believe in the man's ideas about secret arms deals, but at this point in time, I say it was the Great War, who cares anymore? My grandfather was a homebody who liked his life's geography to remain in what was a known and familiar city. His wife wanted to be a citizen of a larger world, and she dumped him. Say it was the curse of Suolucidir and be done with it. At any rate, Alicia wrote in the third person, to keep herself out of the story, as if she herself already no longer existed.

The printing works I remember as a child are long gone. I've pictures of the company at its height, a blocky red brick building, blackened windows never opened. Its demise came with my father's death. Congreaves & Sons was shuttered, and until the building was sold it was a shopping mall for rats and feral cats, who may have developed blood diseases, too. After the building was sold, the quaint brick shell was converted into luxury condominiums. My installation includes photographs of the business from thriving industry with humming presses and busy loading docks to vacant husk to deluxe accommodations complete with doorman and atrium.

Wallingford's, the greengrocers where Edna worked, is still there, in case you're wondering. A Pakistani family now owns it. Who knows, perhaps their ancestors traded with your Suolucidiris a millennium ago. I photographed the shop for my installation on a day of pouring rain. In black-and-white it looks much like it did seventy years ago, I expect. See enclosed.

I've included miscellaneous photographs taken in Cairo of a cook holding a skinned sheep, an unveiled Egyptian woman in a harem, urchins collecting camel dung for fires. It's a sort of August Sander-like collection. I don't know who took these pictures, or how Ryder acquired them. Also, and this is really interesting, a copy of a newspaper clipping regarding the sinking of the *HMS Dorchester*. It was, as you can imagine, in all the papers the day after the disaster, but Edna didn't know her husband had been aboard until she received a telegram from the company that owned the ship. His name and Hilliard's were on the manifest. Bodies were never recovered, nor was any cargo, that I know of, ever raised from the ship itself. Divers, treasure seekers, have made a few failed attempts over the years, but the *Dorchester* wasn't a splashy ship like the *Titanic*, nor was it known to be carrying anything extravagant or particularly valuable like the *Atocha*, although it certainly was. Sometimes I wonder if RC I and Hilliard were ever actually on board. Perhaps it was a ruse, and they re-invented themselves in Tahiti or Auckland or Johannesburg. Somewhere, with slight variation, there's another Tilda Congreaves looking out at the Pacific or Indian Ocean, putting together her own self-destructing history.

Before I leave off, your letter inspired me to take a closer look at what might well be considered my property stored in the basement of the British Museum. It wasn't easy to track down the few surviving relics of the Hilliard-Congreaves loot, those shards that, for whatever reason, weren't on the *Dorchester* but were sent back, donated to the museum. The antiquities department is vast, so I first tried ringing a Pamela Nargezian, listed as curator of the Persepolis Division. She referred me to a Mr. Caterva, archivist. A few more calls were made, and just as I was about to give up on this chain of referrals, I finally reached a Mr. Vaismin in charge of storage, the man who knows where everything is.

"Just show up anytime, no appointment necessary," his annoyed, croaky voice gave the impression I was interrupting something of critical importance.

On a day when I had no classes I made my way to Great Russell Street. A young man directed me to the south stairs, which would eventually take me to Vaismin's. He gave me directions as if knowing he was sending me into a downward spiral toward an elephant graveyard ruled by an angry despot who, despite near blindness, knew with extraordinary acuity when some adventurer with black market connections thought he could take advantage of the haphazard storage system and make off with an Incan mask or a handful of Roman coins. The office was located on one of the lower floors of the museum where many paintings, objects, and documents are stored right out in the hallways, lying in stacks against the walls. At the end of the corridor was a pebbled-glass door, the entrance to Mr. V's office. Opening the door, my eyes reddened immediately from dust and a distinctly vinegary smell. The narrow octagonal room had a very high ceiling, with bookcases whose upper shelves bowed under the weight of masses of papers, books and catalogues accessible via wheeled ladders. Vaismin himself, small and buzzing like a fly, was leaning against a ladder, leafing through a catalogue. He stood on small spatulate feet, and his black jacket, shiny at the elbows, sported a lapel pin of a sphinx and a button that read: How may I be of service to you? Rings of keys jangled from his belt, so I guessed I was in the right place.

I have to say the archivist was so white and crumbly looking, perhaps he lived in his office with no one ever checking on him. He might do, eating in the cafeteria, bathing in the bathroom after hours. Honestly, I couldn't imagine him outdoors, wrenched from his octagon and walking down an actual street.

Storage, it turned out, was helter skelter, all over the place, there is no system, objects are mainly catalogued in Mr. Vaismin's head. He's ancient and irritated at everything and everyone, so if the stuff is all to be moved to new storage facilities and registered in a computer, the board of directors better get a move on. My guess is Mr. Vaismin is closer to one hundred than to eighty. No hello. Just a "What do you want?" He pushed up his shirt and jacket sleeves in a way that's fashionable with people a fraction of his age to reveal long arms, perhaps lengthened from a working life spent reaching for things. I caught a glimpse of a blue-ish black number, written or tattooed, I couldn't tell before he quickly rolled his sleeves down again, picked up links lying on his desk, put them through his cuffs.

"Persian," he muttered. "We've objects in this category that haven't been touched since landing in this domicile." He slid sleeve protectors over his jacket sleeves, motioned for me to follow him down a hall, and opened a hatch door. Really, a hatch door, like the kind you might find on a submarine, I kid you not. Then we descended a metal ladder. I worried about Vaismin's frangible old bones, but he scrambled like a howler monkey. His long, curved hands opened cabinet after cabinet, unwrapping clay bits and pieces, he would then hold a cup or bowl up for my inspection, but none looked like plates. Air rushed out through his nose. "This, you should be aware, is taking up a fair amount of my time, escorting you from A to B. I have many places to be instead of spending time shifting boxes. You sure you want Persian?"

"No, I'm not sure at all. Perhaps Suolucidiri."

"Make up your mind what it is. If you want Suolucidiri, that's only a small quantity of material. No one has asked to look at these things since I've been at this post. Invisible cities sometimes leave no trace of themselves. Who knows what cities lay under out feet? We could evaporate violently, leaving burnt shadows on walls if we're lucky, and become just as traceless, but here we have just three objects to hint at a metropolis no one has ever seen. Follow me."

Back up the metal ladder, down a series of corridors to the main lobby of the museum. He unlocked a door under a flight of stairs. This door was so hidden you wouldn't notice if you didn't know it was there.

Mr. Vaismin flipped a light switch, and the rhomboid-shaped space was illuminated. Boxes were scattered all over the place, but Vaismin knew exactly where to step, what to lift, and what to pry apart. Raising a dented and damp cardboard box, he pulled off the lid, and the surviving relics of the Hilliard-Congreaves expedition were before me. At some point, a person living in the twentieth century had Krazy-glued the shards back together again, and so three large plates or circular platters were assembled. Figures painted in sequential "frames" ringed the borders in much the spirit, if not the style, of Edward Muy-bridge's photographs.

"Dated by testing thermoluminescence and radioactivity, but never been on display." He might have been saying, "Always a bridesmaid, never a bride." Vaismin pulled a pair of white gloves sheathed in a plastic wrapper from a pocket and handed them to me.

"Always wear these, whether handling museum property or performing surgery."

I obediently slipped on the gloves and lifted the plates from their beds of wood shavings. For the first time I held them in my hands, and tried to imagine my great-grandfather's hands had been in exactly the same place mine were. I ran my fingers over the web of lightning cracks.

"I've no time to sit with you. Keep the gloves. Just shut the door behind you when you leave. It will lock by itself."

When Mr. Vaismin left, I shut the door, sat on the floor and spun the plates as if they were tops. These figures, painted on ceramic, might be the first examples of animation ever discovered, and yes, they did look like filmstrips.

Plate 1. A man walks to table, lifts a cup, puts it down, backs away. Process begins again.

Plate 2. Two men fight with daggers and swords. One is an apparent fatality, but after one revolution, he's reborn and the fight begins anew.

Plate 3. Man and woman — erotic, cycling endlessly with no rest.

I sat under the stairs for quite a while, surrounded by the heaps of stuff from god knows where, all left forgotten in storage purgatory. Three stories: drinking, fighting, fucking. If the plates weren't so large I could easily have smuggled them out, but then Mr. V would, if he ever checked, know the identity of the thief, more or less, that is to say if he remembered me at all. So, what little evidence there is of Suolucidir may not be very impressive, insofar as it's not grand-scale stuff, and one can't help wondering why would anyone bother? But then four thousand years from now, who will concern themselves with my art installations? I wrapped the plates with great care, shut the door behind me and made my way back to the surface of the earth. On my way out of the museum I bought a postcard of a winged creature with a human head, a Persian symbol so old, the back of the card said, it had witnessed the destruction of the world over and over again.

The copy you sent me of my grandmother's writings on our family matches the copy I own. How your copy came to be in the possession of a fellow in Tehran I don't know, except that Alicia did spend time in that city, and could have mislaid or given a copy to a researcher or translator who assisted her. There is only one difference between your papers and mine. Alicia added a postscript in which she says that she had discovered Esme Canonbury was a patient at the Kierling Sanatorium in Austria, and it is there where she, Esme, died.

I hope this answers your questions. It's the best I can really do, given there's just me left, but your letter came at the right time. The family pictures and documents I've been collecting for my Experimental Studios class are quite a pile. The project is taking the form of a giant installation, which, as I said, I plan to burn when the exhibition comes down. It will be a kind of ekphrasis moment. Once my art piece eats itself I expect I'll feel free from the shadow of Suolucidir, and all the bitterness the expedition cast over generations of Congreaves. Perhaps the curse will be lifted, and yours truly can then swim the Channel if she feels like it. I'm off now to Brixton to see Three Mustaphas Three, Orchestra Jazzira and Frank Chickens, an all-girl band from Japan. They come out screaming: *We are Frank Chickens!* What a great bill. One more thing. I just saw *Quartermass and the Pit*, a movie about a man who digs under the London Underground and finds an unexploded German bomb left over from World War II. My advice is: be careful what you dig for — just when you think you've found Queen Isabella's emeralds, you've got your hands on one of Saddam Hussein's gas canisters circa 1980, and suddenly the fog is impenetrable.

Please don't hesitate to write again if should you have any further questions.

Yours truly,
Tilda Congreaves-Sutcliffe

THE KIERLING SANATORIUM NO LONGER exists to claim or disclaim records of Esme Canonbury, but the sanatorium had some famous patients, Kafka among them, so there was a chance those records were kept somewhere, in a university or medical facility with a wide-ranging library. That somewhere turned out to be the Zwieg Institute, an Austrian foundation located in a five-story townhouse around the corner from the Morgan Library. The New York location was due to an American donor and, like the Friendship Dig, presented itself as a fortuitous union of two cultures. As I stood outside for a minute rehearsing a set of bogus reasons for my interest in the Kierling Sanatorium, tourists wandered by on their way to Fifth Avenue: a little girl in a *Lady and the Tramp* tee shirt seemed to be saying something about the building I was about to enter.

The man at the front desk told me the archives were housed in the library on the top two floors and directed me to a glass and wrought iron elevator just behind him. Though the interior of the Institute was Bauhaus-like in its austerity, the elevator appeared to have been imported from an era of telegrams and carrier pigeons. It was a vertical box that had space for myself and the operator, an Austrian teenager happy to have a summer job here in the States, who cranked the metal wheel, moving the handle from notch to notch, announcing the offices that occupied each floor with gusto until we reached the fourth. There, a woman with short, spiky blonde hair was typing with a thoughtful, preoccupied air. Seeing us, she quickly hid a cup of coffee that was probably not allowed in the library and came out to ask me how she could be of service. It was not the kind of library you could wander around the stacks, and I got the impression she could sit typing for a long time before anyone disturbed her, a good job for a writer or a student.

No one, she told me, not even Kafka scholars, had ever looked at the Kierling records, but she never asked me why I wanted them. She would be happy to show them to me, and discussed the matter in accented English, relying on the subjunctive tense, as German speakers tend to do. The files were in the basement, but she would allow me access, and so we, all three of us, squashed back into the elevator, this time descending to a pristine, well-ordered cellar, rows of boxes, books, and files stretching back perhaps an entire city block. The donor had wanted to preserve these records: data, all kinds of documents related to citizens of her country in the years surrounding the last war. The librarian pointed out the Kierling section, two rows of shelving organized by year. I was guessing I needed 1939. She handed me white gloves, I pulled down the acid-free archival box, and she showed me to a desk, complete with adjustable overhead lighting.

Each year was further organized into alphabetical files according to the last name of the patient. Esme's papers were under C, and the librarian, peering over my shoulder, offered to make a copy of them for me, gratis. She couldn't leave me alone in the basement, and she had things to do upstairs.

No one had looked at the Canonbury papers in almost 50 years — the 1939 box had been coated with dust. The Canonbury papers were about one obscure patient among many obscure patients, and it was entirely possible no one would ever look in that box, or the others, again. As the librarian herself said, "Who would care? Who would be left?"

Esme Canonbury
Kierling Sanatorium
Austria, 1938

A nurse's aide brought me a bowl of coffee with a gingerbread man nestled in the overhang where curve meets saucer. His collar, cuffs, and buttons outlined in icing, no visible zipps; even anatomically correct cookie people have no troublesome private parts. I put him into the cup, arms resting on the brim, as if he were soaking in a warm bath, oblivious to his imminent mortality, an event transacted when I put the lower half of his body in my mouth and let his gingery coffee-flavor dissolve on my tongue. The nurse herself came round pushing a trolley clinking with blue, red, and brown glass bottles labeled with the name of each patient, harbinger of vileness to come. When she reached my post near a window, she selected a blue vessel labeled "Esme Canonbury." Christalmighty, the stuff tastes and has the consistency of liquid toad.

How did I get here? With income from the sale of the last of my treasures, including the creature Ryder had sent to me from Suolucidir, sold to a man named Feigen, I boarded a train, and crossed the Alps to find rest and recovery. This sanatorium is world famous, and my companions are those for whom money is never a concern. They can't tell the difference between the sound of a pine bough brushing against a window and a rat scratching between walls or in layers between ceiling and roof. I have a private room between Lydea Diamantopoulos, daughter of a Greek banker, and Emily Topper, daughter of a Manchester industrialist. My third English-speaking companion is Casper Wakefield, who claims to be the unrecognized son of a duke or earl, someone, and a young woman who had been in the employ of same. Wakefield's true story is unknown. I'm the oldest one here. The ailments from which many visit Kierling in order to convalesce, still snatch them away as soon as the opportunity presents itself. In truth, for many, this is only a brief respite, a stopping off point; for a small number only, it's a cure. We all hope to be among the latter, chosen few.

After I swallowed my medicine, took a final gulp of coffee and the remains of the gingerbread man, I looked for my companions. Emily is in love with Casper. Wherever they are, I'm sure they want to be alone. I feel left out and try to interject myself into the solitude they seek. Mr. Wakefield was shunted around Europe by both his failing health and a father who desires only that he be kept out of sight; he wants nothing so much as to swim the Bosphorus, cross the Indian subcontinent in a hot air balloon, and map the bottom of the Sargasso in a bathysphere. In this regard, though unsteady of gait and with a face lined by the desert (prematurely, please!), I can out-Scheherazade young Emily Topper, whose life beyond the woolen mills of Manchester (even if viewed from the top), is limited indeed. It's what I do. It's what I've always done. Saturnine Emily with her tartan skirts and cherry beret; she's hardly the first, nor will she be the last I can top. Nor is Casper the first or last fellow whose family wanted him as offshore as he could possibly be.

I made my way down the hall, paused to listen outside the pebbled glass door of the first-floor clinic. No discernible voice could I identify as belonging to Casper or Emily. A sitting room populated by patients made drowsy by potions, syrupy suspensions, inhalants propelled into their nostrils by a unique atomizing device designed by one of the institution's founders — none of my companions were here. I stepped over a copy of a magazine, a photograph of Leni Riefenstahl looking though a camera on the cover. She was in Hollywood to promote her film about the Berlin Olympics. It was odd to imagine Olympians soaring off diving boards, running in vast circles, spinning around parallel bars while surrounded by those whose lungs, and consequently their bodies, were at the opposite end of the physical capability spectrum. I turned back, picked the magazine off the floor and put it in the trash, papers covering the evidence.

At the library Lydea Diamantopoulos waved from an alcove seat and slowly made her way to the door. *Tales of Hoffman* under her arm, Lydea was bored and wanted to gossip about the other patients. Should I trust her enough to ask if she'd seen Casper or Emily? Lydea was shrewd and might guess, somehow, why I wanted to find the two lovebirds.

Esme, she put her downy hand on my arm, have you had tea yet? A small square-cut emerald glittered on one of her fingers. She withdrew a flask of rum from a pocket, just to show me, then quickly slipped it back. Yes, I'd had tea, as for the rum additive, thanks but no thanks at the moment.

Lydea's honey blond hair seemed to have a life of its own, not like Medusa's snakes, but I often felt if I spent too much time in her company, I'd become immovable. She never married, though there had been suitors and wild parties on boats sailing from Crete to Istanbul. Now she fretted about her stepmother and stepsisters tying up all her father's money while she was stuck in Kierling. While others gasped for breath, she couldn't stop talking. Tales about these junkets and her anxieties about dwindling resources were frankly depressing. While smothered in lap rugs, plied with tonics, coaxed with warm liquids, there was, if you gave into it, a terrible sense that gay, mad parties were going on somewhere else in the world, and you would never be invited or missed. The sound of two people laughing in the middle of the night, a perfume shop window, anything could kindle memories that rarely failed to remind you that your exclusion was fierce and definitive. Lydea, more than anyone else, added to this particular cloud of loss. Some felt their lives saved by Kierling, and those who'd had enough of trenches or of doors shut in their faces were content in a state of reclusitation. Sometimes I was one of them, happy to curl up in a soft, clean blanket, but not consistently, so I told Lydea the post had just arrived, and she left quickly for the front of the building where mail was sorted. Lydea was always frantic about the post, always hoping for letters that never seemed to arrive. Her sailing companions went on without her. With no letters, was it as if she'd never set foot on those boats? Was she so forgotten? But then one could always hope for the next day's post, so like someone who always assures you his next cigarette will be his last, Lydea turned her disappointment into optimism, unmatched by anyone I knew at Kierling.

With the first floor thoroughly searched I began on the second. Like many patients here, Casper can walk and do stairs, just occasionally needs the chair, mostly when he's outdoors. On each floor, whether you're capable of stairs or have taken the tiny glass lift, you will find a number of wheelchairs, should you need one. The second floor echoed with a hacking cough, but none of my companions could be found there. The third floor housed the even more marginal cases, those whose residency in Kierling depended upon charity, and these guests were late stage tubercular, highly contagious, generating airborne death, and more or less hidden away. There was a fear on my and Lydea's part, that if funds dried up, we would be removed to the third floor in less time than it would take to fill a syringe with fluid. I didn't expect Emily or Casper to linger in the vicinity of the charity ward, but there was no place else to look. I doubted they'd gone back outside in the snow. On the north side, a solitary wheelchair was parked near a paneled door. Most patients' doors had windows, but this one didn't. I pushed the chair aside; the door opened to a narrow spiral staircase. It could only have led to the attic and the uppermost gabled windows you could see from the street. Whispers and pauses, the sounds of kissing, and if I listened closely, the noise of a scratchy wool skirt being pushed aside. Casper may have been sitting on something squeaky. Not wanting to surprise them, I was thankful the stairs creaked underfoot. Yes, I was right, Mr. Wakefield was sitting on a wicker chair. Miss Topper jumped off his lap when she heard me coming. Casper did look genuinely pleased to see me. Emily did not.

Mrs. Canonbury, he smiled, translucent skin sweating slightly.

Esme, please. Just thought I'd let you know the mail's come. I sounded chipper, as if I this were my daily routine, making marginally useful announcements.

I never get any letters, Emily said to the ceiling. She twirled her beret on the tip of a finger. Standing behind Casper, other hand on his shoulder, she glared at me. In wet, stockinged feet, they must have dumped their coats and boots in the hall, then gone directly to the space under the eaves to smooch. That's not true about her letters. Emily gets all kinds of post from concerned family and friends; she gets what Lydea misses.

I think you got a package today.

Well, it can wait, can't it? I mean it's not as if paper and cardboard have legs, do they?

I tried not to show how that scorched. The attic was full of stuff left by deceased patients, trunks never picked up, broken medical equipment, old calipers, lancets, and clysters, textbooks on the pulmonary system that looked as if they dated from the time of Copernicus.

No, seriously, Emily, I think you got something special delivery from London. I do hope they've sent you Kipling Cakes. It was so kind of you to share them last time.

I could hear Emily thinking, the old dingbat, what's she doing here? Why doesn't she buzz off already?

Know what this is for? I picked up a clyster but didn't wait for an answer. Treating syphilis, before penicillin was found to be cure. One could insert this into a penis, you see.

Mrs. Canonbury, I don't think we need the details. The package couldn't have been for me. My parents are in Egypt, doing a tour of the Pyramids.

Cairo! How lovely! Where are they staying? When my late husband was stationed in Cairo, I lived there for a few years, then traveled further east, alone. Such an adventurous time! (I gushed like a silly goose who lived in a teacup, but still I had my opening, and began to tell my story. Thanks to Emily, it was a start.)

Really? Casper pricked up his ears. So far I'd told them very little about myself. When I first arrived, I was a wreck and stayed in my room. It was only until I felt well enough to walk down a hall unassisted, clean, and wearing new clothes, that I began to meet my fellow guests. I told no one, not even the doctors, about where I'd been for the last thirty or so years, and in this self-contained shelter of maladies, where most are entirely and perhaps justifiably, concerned with only themselves, no one asked.

Tell us about Egypt. I'm dying to go.

I described diplomatic life in Cairo, meeting aristocratic women who lived in harems, shopping in Qasr al-Nil or Jazira, a European quarter some distance from the center of the city, boating up the Nile to Rosetta and on to Alexandria. Wakefield was all ears.

This was before the Great War?

Yes.

The Great War is old news. Emily was annoyed. She opened a dustbin full of old newspapers and poked around until we all started coughing.

Oh, leave that alone, Emily, will you?

I kept talking as best I could.

Even in Cairo, we knew war was imminent. Churchill had converted the royal battleships from coal to oil, so they could travel at far greater speeds, refuel at sea, cover greater distances, and require less manpower. This seemed like a good idea, but the problem is, as you know: there are no oil wells anywhere on our island, while in other parts of the world it exists in great subterranean plenitude. My husband, Aidan, had consulted for Anglo-Persian Oil Company, now known as British Petroleum, so this was something we discussed quite often. Churchill signed an agreement with Anglo-Persian Oil regarding the oil wells in southern Persia, but there were no guarantees in that chaotic, unstable country, that such an arrangement would be carried out seamlessly. Many other players had set up camp in the region. The Nobel brothers had built derricks to the north in Baku. We coveted a piece of this gooey pie, and more than a question of random desire, we needed reserves very badly. Another headache: Russia, as vast as it was, had no open seaports in winter, and not only wanted waterways desperately, but had the secret support of Germany for its Asian incursions. It was essential Britain keep its foothold and control that area which, it was predicted, could well fall prey to a German or Russian attack. It was absolutely imperative our resources not fall to the Kaiser or the Tsar.

The Tsar, Emily said. Hardly. What did he care? He was about to lose his head.

Not yet, Emily, a bit later. Casper gave her a do-shut-up-numbskull look I haven't seen in a very long time.

Archduke Ferdinand was still a long way from Sarajevo, the Lateiner Bridge had, as yet, no significance for Gavrilo Princip, and the diplomatic corp in Egypt had the most fantastic parties. At a Saint George's Day celebration I met two tall bumbling Englishmen, Ryder Congreaves and Archer Fairfax Hilliard, my own personal two shots that changed the world. Ryder was the awkward one. Archer was effusive and in his element, a man who clearly loved parties, and seemed to already know many of the guests by reputation, if not in actual fact. He beamed, pinkish, raffish, slicked-back blond hair clotted into ribbons, he shook hands with twice as many as were offered. However, when I was introduced to the pair, Archer became nervous, looked at other clusters of people, as if he needed to get away from me. The scent of attar wafted past, and he detached himself to tap the elbow of a young rajah strolling around the edge of the crowd. Ryder followed as if on a leash. I watched the two disappear in the crowd, then promptly forgot all about them until the next day at breakfast, at which time Aidan told me the story about the one called Archer.

The newcomers were supposedly on some kind of dig, but Ghiza was just a place to stop for refueling, to assess the landscape, and for Archer to get his bearings and briefing, so to speak. His real mission lay in Iran, where he was charged with the task of finding out what the Germans and Russians were up to in Persia. Unknown to Congreaves, Hilliard had contacted my husband immediately upon his arrival in Egypt. The Great War would distract Europe from Asia, but hadn't done so yet. Germany and England were already rattling swords, building their fleet of dreadnoughts. Archer Hilliard fervently believed he could be of service, while Ryder was only dimly aware of current events. His days were filled with taking measurements, sketching Sphinx heads weathered in such a way it looked like a comb had been dragged across them, writing long letters home. Head literally buried in the sand, whether dreaming of riches or screaming at Ghizan coolies, he remained steadily oblivious.

Hilliard, Emily said, I know that name. She stopped spinning her hat.

The Hilliards were arms merchants, from swords to bayonets to pistols to whatever martial innovation could keep them ahead of all others. Hilliard Armaments had made a fortune in the past, but toward the end of the century, the company had fallen far behind its main competitors. They tried, but someone else always seemed to get to the patents on machine guns, rockets, and artillery tripods first. Though Archer was somewhat estranged from his family and rarely spoke to his father, even when he lived in England, he still wanted to prove himself to these people who generously paid his bills. Nonetheless, his family wanted him out of the country in no uncertain terms.

Why? Casper leaned forward in his chair.

He had proclivities. Everyone in Cairo knew.

Casper leaned back.

Archer's motivations, which seemed all about defending his Majesty, more or less, weren't unalloyed, and Aidan, whom you might have called his handler, had some misgivings. While charged to protect England's interests, Archer was also driven by the desire for his family to take him seriously, to redeem him from exile. In order to do this, he dreamed of saving the family fortune with such inventions as repeating artillery, submarines coated with ice-resistant titanium, equipped with periscopes and fabulous enlarging lenses, sulfur for poisonous gases and gunpowder, not to mention large amounts of cheap labor. Persia, he believed, was rich in all these things. An interesting idea, it was thought, but a distraction from the matter at hand. Hilliard could be seduced and distracted by a trail of smoke, a taste of fresh bread dipped in olive oil, the outward swaying motion of a loose sleeve — or so it was believed. Perhaps unfairly so, because actually he was superb at dissimulation, pretending he was one thing, when he was something quite different. There were women in Cairo who were taken with him, and he allowed, even reveled in the circulation of rumors.

If you could keep an eye on him whilst he's in Egypt. . . . It was not an unusual request. The British Foreign Office often used observers in those days. In this capacity Gertrude Bell was reporting on Turkish Arabia and Iraq. If you were accustomed to staying in the background, as I was, you were well suited for the job. I'd kept an eye on people before, and because of what were called his tendencies, it was perfectly safe for a married woman to spend time with Archer Hilliard.

It's an odd business, was all Emily would say on the subject of proclivities.

Though I continued to encounter the pair at parties and formal events, Hilliard remained elusive. I invited him to go boating, on outings to historic sites, and a tour of the souks, but he politely refused each time. Not only did Hilliard intend to travel into regions that were unmapped in more ways than one, but he needed to get his partner to continue to accompany him without suspecting his true mission. Congreaves, earnest dupe, was his cover. Ryder, who had only a patchwork of social graces, was incapable of hiding either his contempt or his excitement. He slightly lowered his head to his food and focused on his rice or meat as if it were possible that each might grow legs and escape his fork. It was difficult to sit opposite him in restaurants, formal dinners, or even cafes where he held his tea or even tiny coffee cups with two hands. Here was a dog, Aidan chuckled, who would guard a shredded, dry, rotten old bone with his last remaining teeth, yet would still bite your hand off even if you offered to give him a better one. Ryder barked at waiters with his mouth full, but shut his eyes as if in some kind of blissful trance when he first laid a hand on a pyramid.

It wasn't until I bumped into Ryder at the shops in Jazira, about a month into their sojourn, that I found myself alone with half the pair, the patsy half, I would say. This was the first time we spoke without a lot of people we knew looking our way, and as we walked down narrow streets whose overhead enclosed balconies almost touched, I ventured into the treacherous waters of the subject of Archer Hilliard.

Your friend doesn't seem to like me very much.

He likes to be the center of attention, Mrs. Canonbury. People who know more than he does, put him ill at ease. He leaned in closer. You may not be aware of the effect you have on men, he said in a stern voice, as if repeating lines from a melodrama seen through a stereoscope, then he laughed and offered me a cigarette.

I turned to Emily: this is the kind of scene that will be repeated thousands of times over, in movies, plays, and in actual experiences of countless women. It can be read as comic, corny, or sincere, it's up to you.

I don't smoke, Emily replied.

What can you do with such a person? I returned my focus to her companion.

At this point in time I was getting bored with chasing Archer Hilliard, and had I not run into Ryder that afternoon, things might have turned out very differently. Hilliard was always a few steps ahead of me, just out of reach. I kept returning to my husband empty-handed, and I did have other things to do. During my time in Egypt I'd been photographing portraits of people in the diplomatic corp, their families, visiting princes, and petty potentates. At first it was only a pastime, something to keep me occupied, but also I wanted to keep a record of the men and women who had been my friends. Just as I became close to someone, they were posted on to India, or Singapore, or returned back home. Then I began to take pictures of other kinds of people: tea bearers, local merchants playing chess on the street, children employed by an olive presser, women in harems when I could get permission to do so. This was tricky, but not impossible. I was looking for archetypes, as if I could construct a vast catalogue of every kind of person from governor to dung collector, a record which, if found two thousand years from now, would tell the unearther everything they would need to reconstruct a long-dead society from the ground up.

Where are your pictures now? Casper asked.

I have a few, but most were lost when I left Egypt. Let me tell you about what I was looking for that afternoon. For a while I'd wanted to take pictures in the desert, to travel beyond a day's distance from the city. To do this I needed quite a bit of special equipment. When I looked up for an instant and saw Ryder, I was absorbed with the task of searching for a kind of black material that would be impervious to light. Why? I needed to have a small tent made. Panchromatic film had just become available, and it had to be developed in total darkness. Today one could easily find plastic or rubberized sheeting, but then it was almost impossible.

What were you going to do with this stuff?

There was a man who studied the Maya, a Frenchman, Le Plongeon, who invented a portable darkroom. Out in the jungle, he and his wife took hundreds of pictures of ruins, buildings, small artifacts, architectural details, but had no place to develop their plates, and so constructed a darkroom they could take on their travels. One shake of your hand, and the whole apparatus fell into place. In order to take the pictures I wanted to, and be away for some time, I needed such a darkroom.

Ryder listened to me attentively, and though he had his own list of equipment he was meant to procure that afternoon, he spent the rest of the day with me. I had no idea exactly how Le Plongeon made his structure, but Ryder, drawing in a notebook, came up with a workable plan. We searched for wood and metal rods to construct a lightweight frame, bargained over hinges, metal drills, and coils of rope. I was utterly charmed by his Arabic. Toward evening, when we approached the gate to my house, he invited me to spend a day with him at Ghiza, and I accepted. Don't necessarily expect Archer to be present; he disappears for hours at a time, only to resurface with no explanation. He laughed again in a strained sort of way. Ryder assumed he was the main attraction, not Archer Fairfax Hilliard.

Over the next couple of weeks, Archer became a neglected chore, as I began to look forward to outings with Ryder. In the morning I would pack up my tripod, a 4 x 4 Kodak camera with detachable telephoto lens, and wait with increasing anticipation for his driver who would take me to join the crew. Some photographs I anticipated taking and would plan them the night before with an imaginary Ryder looking over my shoulder. I wanted to impress him with my artistry, ingenuity, and willingness to take risks other women might not, at least I wanted to present myself as that person. There were days we were the only white people on the site, far from civilization. If a rifle shot was heard close by, I trained myself not to flinch. Also, the photographs added another layer to the justification I gave Aidan for these excursions. I did some of my best work in Ghiza: camels drinking at a pool, so clear their reflections looked like upside-down exact doubles, a cistern filled with rain, the killing of a sheep, and its subsequent roasting over a camel dung fire. If I had them with me now, you would be as transported as I was. Yet sometimes it was as if Ryder stepped in front of the camera. His face was all I could see.

You were supposed to be using Congreaves to get to the impenetrable Archer, but what your husband didn't count on, what nobody could have predicted, you would fall in love with Ryder. Emily now hung on my every word. It had begun to snow again. The attic was not well heated or insulated. I would have to speed things up.

Though some photographs seemed to fall into composition with a kind of crystalline clarity, there were instances when I couldn't snap the shutter, and my hand just scratched my head instead. The further I entered into some kind of a relationship with Ryder, the less able I was to photograph the people around me, as if I was questioning all dealings of any kind. I kept asking myself, what is my relation to my subjects that gets into the picture, my decisions about light, expression, background? None of it was arbitrary or random (the snapshot had not yet been invented). All I had thought was incontrovertible, was re-examined as testimony by an unconscious liar — possibly. The wife of one of my husband's Cairene associates who lived in a harem could be photographed huddled in a dark corner, or at her door in a yashmak, a Turkish traveling veil, ready to go out into the street. You wouldn't necessarily even think it was the same woman, if you saw the two photographs. This seems obvious now, but at the time it was a novel idea. People were more inclined to believe the camera and be seduced by what was presented as a series of absolute accuracies. The train arriving on the cinema screen is actually crashing through the wall, people screaming — the kind of response that seems laughable and naïve — it wasn't so uncommon or strange thirty years ago.

So what happened between you and Congreaves? Casper grinned a bit from his perch.

How would Lydea tell this part of the story? Everyone on the boat was so drunk. I woke up and didn't know where I was or whose bed I had fallen into. Even if she was exaggerating, that's how she would choose to remember, not wanting to appear calculating, but spontaneous and lighthearted, no big effort involved. I have no memories of making plastered, blotto decisions, and suspect I was always completely conscious and sober. I leaned in close to Casper, smelling the medicine on his breath, and explained.

A German magician was once hired for a children's party at the consulate. He made an elephant disappear, he escaped from chains, emerged from within a sealed box, and did a few card tricks that were really extraordinary. Later when I was alone with him, he showed me how they were done. Fascinated, I practiced the cards over and over. Sex is sort of the same set of card tricks. You have to do everything in order, more or less, and hope that your audience, new to your ploys and sleight of hand, is blown away. It's all about control, setting up the impossible, putting up more roadblocks, more impediments that logic and gravity can't remove, until you get to the completion, the final surprise.

Casper smirked, though I would have guessed, what did he know about what people hide in their pants? Emily in her languid way looked quite interested, like a student who stops doodling in a book at the sound of the word poke, and wonders what she might have missed that sounded so suggestive; though maybe I should have used 'how you develop a photograph' as an analogy. I had a cigarette hidden in a jacket pocket. You weren't supposed to smoke, but I kept a few, like worry beads, I stroked them or held a tip close to my nose and inhaled, but never lit one. For obvious reasons cigarettes were forbidden in the sanatorium, but I always find, as a rule, it's a nice gesture to keep a forbidden substance somewhere on your person. You never know when it might come in handy. I offered one to Casper. He shuddered, as if I'd offered him strychnine, and shook his head.

Can I give you some advice?

It's not a good idea to sleep with someone while pretending to be someone else? There's a price for all our actions? There was more to Emily Topper than I would have thought. I decided against imparting advice for the moment.

We all want something for nothing, sweetie, was all I said.

Only on one afternoon did Archer put in an appearance at Ghiza while I was present. Entering the camp dressed as a desert Arab, but walking like a man reviewing cadets at Sandhurst, he never looked at me, but only addressed himself to Ryder. He claimed he had gone swimming in the Nile, an obvious falsehood. No one we knew swam in the Nile. Upstream from the crocodiles, I hope, was all I said.

Meanwhile Aidan knew Archer was laying the groundwork for the next leg of their journey. He wanted some substantiation of clandestine trysts, screw-ups. I want reports of street contacts, glances that led to meeting under a grove of palms in Midan Ataba or in the shadow of a Heliopolis tomb. I know these things happen, and he will one day say the wrong thing to the wrong man. What did he want me to do? Hide myself in a hotel lobby men's room? I was not invisible. Didn't he know I was trying as best I could, though Hilliard avoided me? I began to be afraid someone was watching me. Had Aidan guessed what had become my real reason for going to Ghiza and was therefore asking the impossible with increasing insistence?

One day, though I wanted very much to go to Ghiza as had become customary, I claimed illness, and stayed behind in Cairo. I made my way to the street near El Gamia Bridge where Ryder was lodged and bribed the concierge to let me into his rooms. I looked through his things, hoping for some clue about Archer, as my husband had advised. In truth, I was very reluctant to undertake this kind of snooping, but growing impatient, he insisted, handing me a wad of cash for payoffs. What did I find? Displayed in frames were pictures of a family, his family back in England, and in a drawer a stash of pornographic postcards was wedged between socks and underwear. At the sound of footsteps, I froze, pocketing one of the cards. I have it still. The footsteps paused, then continued. When it was quiet again, I departed, but as I opened the door, it slammed into a woman in a Tyrolean hat making her way down the narrow corridor. She snapped at me in German, which I didn't understand, so I shut and locked the door as if nothing were irregular and she didn't exist. Would she remember me if she saw me again? Yes, I think so, but what could I do?

Next I made my way to Archer's quarters. His concierge looked up from sipping tea in her little wrought iron booth, extended a hand to accept a bundle of piastres, and passed me the key, as if this sort of thing happened every day. Archer's rooms were quite beautiful with a balcony and view of the Nile. I found books about Persia and Farsi grammar coated with a thin layer of dust, and letters to his father which, unless they were copies, had never been sent. In them he made great claims about the future of poisonous gas and described a delightful evening spent with a niece of some duke I never heard of and probably had never been born, any of them. In another letter he described the failure of his design for a repeating rifle, and the loneliness of his walks along the Nile: I feel like someone who was forced to attend a dance, but couldn't hear the music, and was barred from stepping onto the floor. In a third letter he wrote that Ghiza was just a dress rehearsal for their imminent trip to Persia. I sat down on his bed in a heap, because of course, that meant Ryder would be leaving soon as well. I forced myself to read on.

Esme Canonbury is an abomination. Her clothes, her way of speaking, all irritate no end. I would like nothing better than to knock her all the way to Queer Street. She is married to my handler, but her insistence on seducing Ryder endangers all of us. The two of them may think they're secretive, but everyone knows about their so-called outings to Ghiza. Anyone can see the way they look at one another. I've asked Ryder to consider what the repercussions of his actions will be over a woman who's so clearly not worth the risk. Pick anyone, anyone else, I've pleaded. He either ignores me, or shrugs off my concerns as the hypocrisy of a prude. What he doesn't realize is that as we are about to go into the desert, she's burning all our bridges. There will be no shelter coming from the outposts of Albion, should we get in too deep. I would cut Congreaves loose, if I could, but I need him to accompany me as we go forth. I've told him about a lost city to the east — we would be the first to find it — instead of stagnating here, following in the tired footsteps of Napoleon's army, but he is resistant to this enticement and doesn't want to leave his Esme.

Archer's pillow smelled of attar. I looked around the room at his collection of souvenirs: small clay and bronze sphinxes, pyramids, tiles arranged on his shelves, rugs laid out in studied disarray. His hoard of knickknacks were suffocating. On my way to the door I pocketed a chipped Isis with onyx eyes. He thought Ryder provided a cover, a pretence, for the real reason behind his trip, but in fact the truth was the reverse. Archer had, unwittingly, provided a cover for me. Now the three of us were at risk of losing everything. Points on a map, A leads to B leads to C, but C is the end of the route, and it's impossible to back up or go anyplace else. Archer: a cream puff laced with cyanide. Does Aidan really know? He may have been trying to put Archer off the scent, so he wouldn't suspect what I was actually up to, and also try to save face for himself. Or was I being set up? Does the photograph show a woman living in seclusion or one about to go out, able to go anywhere she pleases? Which is true, if either? Archer could tap out a complicated rhythm on any dance floor, spin, and then lob a dagger into an unsuspecting spectator just for the hell of it. I was sure of it.

In the days that followed my incursions into the hotel rooms, I stopped going to Ghiza. Though I tried to see less of Ryder, we met at an embassy dinner at which we were seated side by side. If everyone knew, as Archer had written, I wondered if the seating arrangements were some kind of cruel act of connivance on the part of the hostess. I felt awkward and spilled a glass of whiskey. Ryder was withdrawn and tense, bent over his food with even more intensity than usual. He barely looked at me, and I'm sure the gossips noticed. Had the Tyrolean woman said something to him? I would never know. Cardamom rosewater sweets were passed around, and we were careful that even our fingers didn't touch. Still without turning in my direction, he invited me out to Ghiza, and I believed the invitation was sincere, so two days later I went out with him one last time.

He left me alone, and I pretended to be overly concerned fiddling with my cameras and equipment, as if the plated scissoring rods that allowed the lens to move in and out were not working properly. When he circled back from overseeing the diggers to where I fumbled, he told me about a lost city further east that Archer wanted to have a go at. Hilliard wanted to leave Egypt as soon as possible, abandoning Ghiza, which no longer interested him. Ryder relied on Hilliard's money, he had none of his own, so he would have to go, and he was a Persianist, after all. I couldn't tell him the lost city was nothing more than a front, because I couldn't let him begin to suspect how I knew what I knew.

So he dumped you. Emily was very blunt.

It wasn't that simple. In fact, Ryder didn't want to go, didn't want to leave me, though I no longer knew why. We found a place in an abandoned structure near the pyramids where we could talk in private, but we didn't talk.

I didn't know exactly how to proceed with my story, and so paused for a moment.

Sand in the underwear, I'm guessing, Emily said in a Manchester accent that had no doubt irritated her governesses, but she was right.

We could hardly stand one another's company, but we were stuck to each other like an old married couple who make their partner depressed and irritable, but still in some corner of their hearts, can't live without one another. That sounds very sentimental, and it is, but I wanted them to believe it.

I arrived back home that day without the energy or desire to even tell a servant where to put my tripod. Aidan emerged from his study with a fantastically cheerful expression on his face. His smile turned momentarily to concern, and he handed me a cool glass of gin, mint floating on an ice cube. Don't worry, dear, I've just the thing. He had planned a short trip to Alexandria, a vacation that would do us both good. We would stroll along the Corniche, and play at the casinos, a welcome break, no? I had no choice, downed my glass, and nodded. Though being away from Ryder made me nervous, being with him was a source of anxiety as well.

The urbane European crowds of Alexandria who, in the evening, multiplied like hydra, were always a respite from the more formal, careful life of Cairo. I was left alone most of the time while Aidan continued to receive telegrams and all kinds of messages from his office that I was not privy to. I walked along the beach near the merloned walls of the Qaitbay Citadel, observed sand erosion, and tossed Archer's Isis into the sea. Some day, when the sea has dried up, some archaeologist will find it and may not realize he's only laid his hands on a cheap Edwardian imitation. I played at the casinos, won a bit, lost more, drank too much.

We returned to Cairo, and Aidan seemed energized, eager to get back to work Monday morning. About an hour after he left, I went round to Ryder's apartment. The concierge, a Greek woman who spoke some English, told me no one by that name lived there anymore. If I hadn't just been at her courtyard a few weeks earlier I would have thought one of us was hallucinating. I insisted. She shrugged and told me to go look for myself which, not wanting to appear mad or desperate, I declined to do. At Archer's residence I was told exactly the same thing, but more. There had been a murder in Archer's rooms. A boy had been found dead. Mr. Hilliard had disappeared. They'd left with no warning or goodbyes. A murderer in this building, the concierge raised his eyebrows. Mr. Hilliard had always seemed like a gentleman. He paused, and I realized if I handed him a bundle of piastres, I would hear more, but I'd none to give.

I rushed back to tell Aidan that his spy had gone, but he already knew about Hilliard's departure.

A dead Egyptian boy, I've been informed. And not just any anonymous boy, the son of a minister. It happened while we were away. Of course, Hilliard claimed he had no knowledge of the boy or how he got into his rooms. He just woke up and the corpse was there.

Don't you believe him?

No, not really.

What if he's telling the truth?

It doesn't particularly matter, because no one else believes he's telling the truth. Khedive Abbas wants a quick trial followed by a swift execution, and we don't give him much, but we have to give him that. Hilliard had no choice but to flee the country, and with so much unfinished business on his part, it was very inconvenient timing. More's the pity he'll never be able to return, but he's left an awful mess for me to clean up. Look here, Esme. He held out a newspaper. The largest luxury ship ever built has just left Southampton for New York. It was supposed to be unsinkable. Hardly any lifeboats at all.

Do you know where they went?

I told you, the ship is bound for New York.

No, Hilliard and Congreaves.

How should I know? Suolucidir, I believe, was the name of a city Hilliard mentioned.

I left that night, taking my cameras and a large box that contained my attempts at constructing a portable darkroom.

In order to get permission to travel east, I had first to go to Smyrna, where I met with Consul General Henry Lamb. He had advised Gertrude Bell before she trekked toward Baghdad, and he was not keen on letting ladies travel further east. There were railway lines from Kirman to Bandar Abbas, then what? The camel, I told him, has been invented. He laughed at me as if I'd arrived at his map room intending to navigate the desert with astrolabe and orrery. "Was the game worth the candle?" he asked, incredulous. I can tell when people think I'm an idiot, whether it's Archie Hilliard or that Jew in Marseilles. The problem is, even knowing this, I don't know how to get the better of them, really I don't.

Lamb had embassy parties, similar to those we'd had in Cairo, though conversations were turning more to the possibility of war at our doorstep. Some said it would never happen, there would be no all-engulfing war to end all wars, others said, just you wait and see, and get your family to some remote safe place. Lamb introduced me to W. Morgan Shuster, an American economist who had been posted to Tehran, on his way back to Washington. Shuster had a very clear, direct gaze, and he spoke with despair about Persia, as if it were a delinquent child whose behavior was due more to his living conditions than acts of his own will. I had trouble following the tangled history, and though I frowned in concentration, I remained rooted to the spot, listening. Like the General Consul, he advised me to go no further.

Expect a cast of European characters shoving the Persian government toward bankruptcy while enriching themselves. Russia panders to the vices of the Shah, like one who gives rum to a drunkard. Watch out for a Monsieur Monsard, Belgian Customs official, a Russian tool. The War Department is a brilliant galaxy of uniformed loafers and scoundrels.

I plan to photograph Suolucidir.

Never heard of the place.

Vita Sackville-West, while visiting Iran in 1936 for the coronation of the new shah, wrote that her hosts saw to it she was up to her elbows in pearls and emeralds trying to find what to wear, Emily piped up. I didn't know who she was talking about. We were getting cold in the attic and would have to return downstairs soon.

Tell us about how you got to Iran from Smyrna.

I never went to Iran. I ran out of money, sold my camera, then a package and letter arrived from Ryder. They had found the lost city, and had made plans to return to England. Just as no one could have predicted I would fall in love with Ryder, the lost city, when it was found, was as much a surprise to Hilliard as it was for Congreaves. Hilliard looked on the artifacts of Suolucidir like a peach pie bought at the side of the road, a nice thing found by accident. What happened to his titanium mines and Baluchi slaves, his reports about German treachery and Russian double cross? Dropped in the face of Suolucidiri riches? No one knows. Archer wanted to dance on my grave, but look who's left, eh?

I wrote to Ryder that my heart was in his hands. I would meet him in England. A few weeks later their ship was sunk in the Gulf of Oman. From Turkey I returned to Europe, slowly making my way, dodging the bombardments of the Dardanelles, embattled Sarajevo, and so on. Snow was clinging to the fenestrations. The attic was no longer habitable, and we would have to leave. Were the things Ryder sent me really from a place called Suolucidir? Impossible to identify, though some thought so. Impossible to know for certain. We mine and extract and define ourselves accordingly: eyes as green as emeralds, black as coal, red as rubies, etc., but eventually the supply runs out, or the waters wash over us, the sun explodes, and we eventually become rocks ourselves.

We made our way downstairs. They wanted to look at my photographs: Shuster posing with his wife, the Jerusalem gate, a Cairene cook dressed in white holding a skinned lamb, an arched corridor in the Qaitbey citadel, gamblers posing with hands held behind their backs, top-hatted German magician with the tools of his trade, what a smile he had, a little girl named Rigg whose father worked under my husband, stockings down around her ankles holding a tennis racket that's too big for her. Assistant attaché, a young man named Blanckenship holding up headlines about the *Titanic*. No pictures of Ryder or Archie? Emily asked, growing familiar. I shook my head.

The following day when the sun was bright and high we got permission to go on another walk in town. A midnight snowfall had settled over Kierling. The name glides off as your tongue, dances from K to G. Outside the sanatorium, scalloped wrought iron fences turned into a series of toothy smiles. I brushed snow from pine cone–shaped finials while Emily Topper struggled valiantly to propel Casper Wakefield in his wheelchair down the walkways. We listened to children practicing the violin, cello, clarinet maybe, as we strolled.

Around one corner we glimpsed a man pulling down a red and black poster, shreds stuck to his hands, and he ran when he saw the three of us plodding along, though surely he must have guessed we were only foreign guests from the sanatorium. Kierling is sleepy, peaceful, and incredibly quiet. Very little news of the outside world has penetrated the town. Beyond the city limits there is only snow, trees, mountains, and it's easy to imagine the forest populated by reclusive souls who have never heard of Kurt von Schuschnigg or Kurt Schwitters. I take pleasure in the idea that Kierling is the whole world.

Despite the storm the night before, the snow was beginning to melt, it was so warm, and we felt as if we were witnessing the first hints of spring. Wakefield, sitting in a wheelchair, with a rug over his lap, pale yellow hair plastered to the sides of his head not covered by his homburg, was in high spirits. Since Emily had had a good night's sleep, she was up to challenging everything she'd heard the previous evening. It's all a story and therefore not real, she said as if she'd suddenly discovered something, part of a long complicated, branching narrative that reduces each constituent part as time moves on. I parried: as layers accrete, the bottom gets compressed, turns into coal, oil, diamonds. At the end it doesn't matter which version is true, though they all fit together. I took over pushing Casper, who craned his neck, inhaling as deeply as he was able. The town was its usual sleepy self, but as we rounded a corner from Klosterneuberger onto Medekstrasse we saw a very frightening sight. Four or five larger children were beating up a small one, well perhaps not so much smaller, but certainly outnumbered. There was blood on the snow. We shouted for them to stop in our limited, badly accented German, but really we were powerless. Emily put her hands over her eyes while Casper torqued his body around in the chair in order to see more clearly. I told the others, whatever's going on, it's not our affair, after all, let's press on. And so we did.

THE LIBRARIAN TAPPED ME ON the shoulder. The Institute was closing, she took the box of sanatorium records from me. Did I want to make an appointment to come back another day? No. I was done. This small sliver of Esme Canonbury was all I needed to look at, and with that she was returned to deep storage, perhaps never to be seen again. Who would find her and haul her out into twenty-first century air?

Outside it had begun to storm, and hailstones the size of robin's eggs fell from the sky. They tore through papers, skidded off umbrellas and awnings, collecting in growing mounds as if the city were preparing to be packed and shipped to another planet. With no hat, helmet, or even papers to hold over my head, I ran to the subway. Underground felt crowded and safe. If Esme could be summoned and ferried from one underground, presumably Austrian location, to another, here to New York as the F train hurtled under the East River towards Coney Island, only to burst into the sun as it emerged from the tunnel, what would she have chosen to photograph?

The river of kids just out of high school at 3:30, flooding the subway, shouting over their walkmen, rehashing the days' fights and rifts and pranks, suddenly quiet, grabbing seats when a policeman is sighted? Their music silenced, or at least turned way down. Would she also photograph the policeman, a young guy with tattooed arms? Take the shots quickly before the train plunges back underground, because with the kind of old camera she has, you have to use available light. Esme stumbles. She's just one more artifact.

Just when you think the city is sealed, and it's vanished along with much evidence of its existence: pornographic plates, spineless Weimar-era notebooks, passports assembled in basements, votives made from gaskets and wing nuts, all of it rises to life like the broom splinters in the Sorcerer's Apprentice, fully formed, ready to carry water until the palace, if not the whole city itself, is flooded.

The Zwieg Institute of the Future will marshal all our bits and pieces in oxygen-free containers. But if there is no degrading air in the room, neither can humans spend much time within unless they have special equipment. The bits and pieces travel from the unlivable to the livable and back again.

What drives people to explore inhospitable parts of the planet where oxygen thins, water pressure is deadly, light can't penetrate, extremes of heat and cold are unbearable? So you make it to these remote extremes, and return to the surface, to sea level, holding your trophy, your evidence of early life, of rare minerals, but still a part of your audience will ask, so what? Why bother? What's it good for?

JEWELED RICE MADE WITH ORANGE peel, saffron, and dried cherries, fessenjan perfumed with pomegranate, walnuts, and cardamom — impossible to taste again. In place of desert air I inhaled truck exhaust from the construction pit outside my window. I looked at the cranes and backhoes parked in the pit, site of a future tower, as if I'd just landed from Mars and had no obvious way of returning home. No Americans were going back the way I'd come. The construction pit, at first, was a parody of the work I'd done in Suolucidir. As backhoes and shovels went deeper, below the initial layers of bottle caps and empty stolen wallets stripped of cash and credit cards, there lay olive oil tins, trunks with false bottoms used on the underground railroad, and cornhusk figures made by the Lenape people who greeted Henry Hudson. All ended up tossed into a garbage barge on the Gowanus Canal. I found maps of Suolucidir in the layers of peeling paint on girders on subway platforms. Seven layers, each a different color, made topographical patterns, ridges: here were the teeth of a coastline and further up somewhere in the ridges of paint lay the caves, here a wadi, there was where cold air blasted out of the buried city. I sat opposite a man reading a book on the double R train, his place marked by a crumpled blue aerogramme, humming *Da Ya Think I'm Sexy?* That song was everywhere. Behind his head subway mosaics flashed by at stop after stop: Chinese lettering at Canal Street, a beaver at Astor Place, while halfway around the world other underground mosaics were probably being looted, carried off bit by bit in the middle of the night. Winged lions, scorpions, a bull balancing the earth on his horns his hoofs treading on fish scales, all of it ending up embedded in a lucite table in a Tokyo, Paris, or Milanese living room. I set a row of limes on a radiator and let them dry until they turned brown and hollow. When they seemed ready, I smashed them with a hammer, swept the pieces into a pot of boiling water, strained the sour, bitter liquid, then added sugar in an attempt to replicate the tea I used to drink in cafés in Zahedan. Around this time I learned that the archive in Tehran that had housed the Suolucidir scroll had burned in a riot, though I have no way of knowing if the scroll had been returned, or if it had been stored or hidden elsewhere. You hear of cases like that, antiquities disappear in times of chaos only to reappear safe and sound, protected in another city. I could only hope that the scroll, if it existed at all, had met the latter fate.

There's a group in Italy who are building some of Da Vinci's inventions, based on what they found in his notebooks. They began with his hang gliders. Leonardo watched birds for hours, studied how they fly, and based his drawings on what he observed. The group built a replica of Da Vinci's hang glider using systems of pulleys and levers, but the bird model turned out to be unstable. They added a tail, and then it did fly, though it wasn't exactly true to his original design. I've written to express my interest in joining them, and in my letter I made a reference to Da Vinci's *Citta l'Ideale*, a multi-layered city he designed with houses situated above roads and navigable canals that would connect the metropolis to the sea. Reconstructing cities is something I have some experience in.

One or two things I know about Suolucidir: the lost city is the object that always recedes just out of reach, and at the same time mirrors its excavators whether they recognize their reflections in its pools and canals or, momentarily blinded, catch sight of only unfamiliar phantoms beckoning with riches, escape hatches, trunks full of anything you think you desire.